W9-BIK-597

TOR BOOKS BY GAIL DAYTON

New Blood
Heart's Blood

HEART'S BLOOD

GAIL DAYTON

TOR®

paranormal romance

A TOM DOHERTY ASSOCIATES BOOK
NEW YORK

This is a work of fiction. All of the characters, organizations, and events portrayed in this novel are either products of the author's imagination or are used fictitiously.

HEART'S BLOOD

Copyright © 2009 by Gail Dayton

All rights reserved.

A Tor Book
Published by Tom Doherty Associates, LLC
175 Fifth Avenue
New York, NY 10010

www.tor-forge.com

Tor® is a registered trademark of Tom Doherty Associates, LLC.

ISBN 978-0-7653-6251-3

First Edition: January 2010

Printed in the United States of America

0 9 8 7 6 5 4 3 2 1

To Steve, Cathy, and Laura—don't remember y'all ever not being in my life. Growing up was more fun with you around, and the world's a better place because you're in it.

To Carla, Lewis, and Allen—because you put up with this crazy family. Love you all.

I owe a *huge* debt of gratitude to Ian White, the Brit Across the Desk. Thanks for all your help with London streets and slang and for answering all my questions about your hometown, whether they were dumb or not. Glad you decided to hang out on the island for a while.

HEART'S BLOOD

1

GREY CARTERET woke in a foul mood.

One generally did when one woke lying face-down in a gutter reeking of things best left unmentioned, with no idea of how one arrived in said gutter. Particularly when one also woke feeling as if all the angels in heaven and the demons of hell had spent the entire previous night fighting across each of the 206 bones in one's body. Even more particularly when such rude awakenings had been occurring with increasing frequency.

He groaned, which made the pain in his head crescendo with unfortunate familiarity, and he rolled over, which was worse. Every one of his battlefield of bones shattered.

Or they felt like it. Grey supposed they must still remain fastened together, since he could, after a fashion—the fashion of an ancient crone—move. He brought a hand to his face and wiped away the worst of the stinking muck, so that he dared open his eyes.

Nothing seemed to offer imminent catastrophe, given what his blurred vision could tell him. Little, save that he was in a dark, narrow, and more important, *empty* alleyway. So he shut them again.

He thought he ought to pause for a moment and count his blessings, since he apparently wasn't in danger of dying in the next few moments. Not that he could stop it—death—in his current condition. Which led him back around to blessings and the counting thereof.

One, he was alive. Two, he was still reasonably well clothed, as it seemed he had retained his frock coat, which was a true blessing in the damp chill of a London October. Three, his bones were not actually—he didn't think—broken, though his head *felt* decidedly shattered. The odd thing was, he didn't remember drinking. Not last night.

Grey had decided, after too many recent mornings waking up like this, that he wouldn't have any alcohol to drink. Not even a single "off to bed" brandy. He wouldn't go out. He wouldn't toddle around to any of his clubs. He would stay at home and work in his workroom. Had he changed his mind?

He would reason all that through later. The time had arrived to assemble himself and get the hell out of wherever he'd landed this time.

He crawled up the rather slimy brick wall beside him to a more-or-less sitting position, cracking an eye open again. He hoped the state of his vision was due to the lack of light in the alley, and not the state of his eyes. "I've lost another damned hat," he muttered.

"No, you ain't."

Grey winced at the piercing voice right next to his aching ears, and turned to see his hat hovering a scant few inches beyond the end of his nose. Good thing he hadn't opened both eyes. They'd have crossed.

He took the hat and settled it gingerly on his head. It hurt even his hair, but perhaps it would keep all the pieces of his head contained in a single whole.

"I got your stick, too," the same agonizing voice shrieked. "I watched 'em for ya, wouldn't let no one pinch 'em, nor your coat neither. An' I wouldn't let 'em cosh ya nor shiv ya. I been watchin' out for ya, guvnor."

Grey cracked open his other eye to acquire an accurate view of his walking stick. It took a moment for the two images to swim their way together and become one, so that he could know which stick to reach for.

The stick was attached to a surprisingly clean hand that sprouted from a wrist positively black with dirt.

Grey squinted, trying to see the person beyond the hand and wrist. There was a checked cloth cap with a blurred face beneath. "Who the bloody hell are you? And where did you come from? You weren't there before. I looked."

The silver-headed stick vanished, pulled back beyond Grey's admittedly meager reach. "Wot kind o' gratitude is that? After all I done for ya?"

The lad had a point. Grey assumed the creature was a lad, given the high-pitched voice and the trousers.

"Sorry," he said, since a gentleman never failed to offer apology when one was due—though everyone agreed Grey wasn't much of a gentleman. "Foul mood. Bad head. Makes one a trifle cranky and forgetful of good manners." He took a deep breath so he could go on. "Thank you very much for watching over my person and my belongings."

"Weren't nuffink."

"Now, give me my bloody stick and tell me who in blazes you are!" Grey couldn't roar as he'd have liked to, given his head and the rest of his aching bones, but he did his best. It wasn't as if he really wanted to know the boy's name, except it seemed as if he ought to know who had done him such a favor.

"Cor, you ain't got 'alf a temper." The boy eased a fraction closer and held the stick out, tip first, as if afraid to get any closer. Smart lad. Even if Grey wasn't quite up to snuff at the moment.

"Foul mood. Remember?" He used the stick to haul himself to his feet. "Your name, young sir."

"Parkin."

"Ah. Parkin. Yes, thank you." Grey's eyes were beginning to focus more effectively. The lad was tall for eleven, or maybe twelve. He had delicate features beneath the grime coating his face. Poor lad.

Grey had suffered the same affliction at the same age, though he'd finally grown out of it. Mostly. These days, women called him beautiful.

Men gave him a wide berth. Partly because he'd long ago taught himself to fight viciously with any weapon at hand, and to hell with so-called "rules of honor." Primarily, though, they left him alone because as magister of the conjurer's guild, he was the most powerful conjurer in all of England.

Who couldn't keep from waking in odd places with no memory of how he arrived there. At least this time he'd acquired a protector.

Grey searched his pockets, but they were empty of coin, as well as wallet or watch. He sighed. "I suppose it was too much to expect that you might have guarded my pockets as well as my person."

"If your pockets're empty, they was emptied 'fore I found ya."

"Ah." Grey frowned. Parkin did deserve a reward for his faithful service. More than just a coin or two, if the lad was willing. "Whereas after I arrived and fell, literally, under your care, I lost nothing. Perhaps I should hire you to escort me back to my home."

"P'raps you should." Parkin swaggered a little. "But it ain't coin I want. Wot I want is for you to make me your apprentice so I can learn magic."

"I don't take apprentices." The instinctive response was out before Grey recalled that just this past summer in Paris, he had considered breaking his longstanding rule against apprentices. But that had been in special circumstances.

He turned to start hobbling down the dark, narrow alley, unable to stride away as he wished, due to his crumbled-up bones. "Go to the council hall. Take the test. If you pass it, they'll admit you to the school."

The boy followed, offered support on the side opposite Grey's cane. "No, they won't," Parkin said. "Even though I have enough magic to have kept you hidden and safe half the night, they won't let me in."

Grey gave the lad a sharp look. What had happened

to his speech? "Of course they will. You'll be admitted straightaway. That's quite a good talent."

"I've been hiding myself for years now. It was simple to hide you as well. And they won't admit me because—" Parkin tugged Grey to a halt—an easy task—and looked around. A broad-backed laborer stomped past the end of the alley. Otherwise the street was empty.

Parkin leaned in, stretched on his toes. Grey reluctantly bent his head to listen. He truly did not want to hear Parkin's pitiful secrets.

"I can't go to magician's school," he whispered into Grey's ear, "because I am female."

Astonishment shivered through Grey as he straightened to stare at the boy—the girl— No, she was a young woman.

He could see it now, the feminine nature of the delicate face. Her small frame didn't boast many curves, but she was past childhood. He couldn't see the color of her hair beneath the flat cap, but eyes of amber rayed over a blue outer rim gazed back at him beneath dark brown brows. She might be almost pretty if she weren't so thin, and so dirty. Her true age was impossible to discern, but children aged early on the streets.

He wondered whether he ought to be offended that she'd lied to him, and decided against it. Offense would be expected, and he invariably did whatever was not expected, or he tried to. Though he supposed that could become expected. Besides, she hadn't actually lied. She'd merely allowed him to assume.

Grey shook off the wandering thought and indulged his curiosity, another thing he did whenever possible. "If you're not Parkin, who are you? Were you using magic just now to hide the fact of your gender?"

He walked on down the alley, able to do so a bit more efficiently now, though the pain refused to leave him. He hurt in every joint, every tiniest part of his body. If he wished to reach home sometime before the day's end, and he did, he would have to find a cab. "Parkin" followed him, of course. She wanted something from him.

"Parkin is my family name. My Christian name is Pearl." She whispered the last, looking about her again for eavesdroppers.

They'd emerged from the alley into a slightly wider street, one a carriage might actually be able to pass along. They were near the Thames. Grey could tell by the reek of mud and rot and wet, and by the speech of the people clustering thicker on the street. Speech Miss Pearl Parkin had echoed until recently.

It was early, dawn barely beginning to lighten the sky. Grey usually saw dawn because he'd been up the whole of the night before, rather than waking to greet it. *Had* he gone drinking last night? What could he have imbibed that would leave him in such a state? He'd never had a hangover like this one.

A knot of people—idlers and children, the sort who slept in doorways—had gathered around one of the doorways off to the right, toward what appeared to be an even larger street. Grey paused, watching them because they were there, trying to get his bearings. Until he knew *where* near the river he was, he wouldn't know which direction to take for home, or where to find a cab.

Miss Parkin planted herself in front of him. "I use magic to disguise myself, yes," she said. "When I'm not hiding myself altogether. If I were a boy, I'd go to that school. But I'm not, and I can't, and now that my father has died, I need a way out of this place where he's left me. But the only thing I can do is magic, and that will earn me nothing here but a short drop."

Grey firmed his lips to hide the effect her desperation had on his unruly heart. It was too soft by far, usually in what his family deemed inappropriate circumstances. He, and they, would prefer it remain cold and hard at all times, but he could not prevent it from reacting to the oddest things. Like Pearl Parkin's plight.

He watched the gathering crowd, augmented now by people heading off to work with their baskets and carts and tools, who tried to pass and got caught up in whatever was happening.

Pearl clutched at his coat, trying to pull his attention back in her direction. She'd never lost it. His eyes might be turned toward the growing crowd, but all his attention—what he could squeeze past the regiment of drummers beating on his head—was focused on the dainty creature beside him.

"My hiding magic would be perfect for thieves," she whispered, her fingers digging into his forearm. "There's some as 'ave—who have asked me to do it for them. I've put them off. I've hidden from them, but I can't hide all the time. I have to earn my supper, don't I? I can't do that if I'm hidden, if I want to do it honestly, which I do. And if I give in to Nosey, I don't know how long it'll be till he finds out I'm a girl and—"

She shuddered, and Grey's heart twisted. Or maybe the twist was lower, in his gut. He knew someone who had suffered that sort of insult at far too young an age. She'd recovered admirably, but the attack had left deep scars. He wanted to help this girl. But to take her as apprentice?

"Magicians can take female apprentices," she said. "I read the papers. I know about the lady Mr. Tomlinson took as his apprentice, even though he's alchemist and she's wizard. If he can take a girl apprentice, so can you. And if he can climb out of Seven Dials on the back of his magic talent, then *so can I*."

Grey wanted to help her. He did. But not that way. He didn't take apprentices. He didn't want to be in authority over anyone, hemming them about with rules. He paid no attention to rules himself, except for those immutable ones like gravity and inertia and conservation of magic. How could he be expected to impose rules on others?

"What are they doing there?" He indicated the murmuring crowd, and edged around Miss Parkin to hobble in that direction. Hangovers didn't make you ache so much all over, did they? By the time he reached them, Pearl Parkin at his elbow, he could walk almost normally, or appear so. It still hurt.

"Toby's gone to fetch the bobby," someone said in a confident tone.

Immediately, a good quarter of the crowd melted away, no doubt due to a disinclination for an encounter with London's police representative, and Grey was able to move closer. Though not to shake off Miss Parkin.

"'Oo are *you*?" One of the locals turned a suspicious eye on him. "'Oo's the gent?" she asked the general vicinity.

"'E's Magister Carteret," Miss Parkin said in her husky, pretend-boy's voice. She pronounced Grey's surname "Carterette," rather than the correct "Carteray." Oh, the woes of Norman French ancestry.

"Magister? Wot's that? Some kind of fancy magistrate?" asked someone else.

"It means I'm head of the conjurer's guild," Grey said, trying to infuse a soupçon of authority into his voice. "And one of the Briganti, the magicians' police. What's happened here?"

And how did Miss Parkin know who he was? That question should have occurred to him much earlier. He would have to ask it later, in the unfortunate event that there was a later with Miss Parkin.

The crowd parted like the Red Sea, exposing a sea of red.

No, not a sea. Not even a pool. Blood covered the murdered man's naked, mangled body, but it had not flowed onto the stones of the street below him. He'd been tossed after his death into the doorway where he lay, like a broken doll.

Grey opened his senses—sight, smell, hearing,

touch—and that other sense with many names. The sense that registered the presence of magic. He was a conjurer, attuned to the magical range of spirits, but he was able to sense the deep tones of the alchemist's earth-and-elements magic. He could sometimes pick up the lighter range of a wizard's herbal magic, though it was a strain. In the past few weeks, he'd learned to faintly hear, or feel, or—or *taste* the thick, coppery cry of the blood magic of sorcery.

He could taste it now. The faraway cry of innocent blood for justice. But overlaying everything else, over the soft booming of the stones beneath their feet, over the faint scent of herbs and talismans worn against illness, over the taste of blood that settled in the back of his throat, Grey could hear the loud, off-key, echoing blare of conjury twisted awry.

Rage surged up in a towering wave, sweeping away his aches, clearing out the lingering fog from his mind. Someone had used this man, his agony as his bones were broken one by one, and then his slow death as he choked on his own blood after the bones of his face were broken—used it in an attempt to call a demon. Spirits were not powerful enough, that this murderer thought he required a demon to do his bidding?

Grey's hands hurt. He realized he'd closed them into fists so tight they began to cramp, the pain worsened by last night's unremembered abuse. He wanted to find the murderer, this stinking smear under society's rock, and inflict the same torture upon him.

"Who is he? Does anyone know? Can you tell?" Grey found his handkerchief miraculously still in his pocket and bent to collect a bit of the dead man's blood. Perhaps the sorceress could do something with it.

There was only one sorceress. In the world, not just in England. Amanusa Greyson was currently in Scotland, taking stock of her sorcerous inheritance as well as enjoying a belated honeymoon with her new husband.

"I fink 'e's Angus Galloway. By the red 'air." Someone pointed a grubby finger, and sure enough, the man did have red hair. Curly. Almost the same color as the blood beginning to dry on his obliterated face.

"Has anyone seen Angus Galloway this morning?" Grey stood to ask.

"I smell magic—" An old woman's voice wavered in a raven's croak over the crowd.

They parted again and she came through. Withered, gnarled, bent so far over that her head came no higher than Grey's waist, she was led by the hand toward the murdered man. She sniffed, turning her blind eyes this way and that. They'd brought out their local witch.

Grey eased back, unnerved by the way those milky eyes seemed to see things not there. He knew better, but she unnerved him nonetheless. She might have some magic ability, but it was untrained. Most likely, she used confidence tricks and the ignorance of the masses to bolster her reputation, until her abilities were more rumor than magic. Still, those eyes disturbed him.

"Dark magic," she croaked. "Black as the depths of hell." She got that much right.

"I smell magic, too." Pearl's whisper startled him, though it shouldn't have. He hadn't been able to shake her yet. "But it doesn't smell dark. It smells . . . like blood."

"Gather it up," Grey murmured.

"How?" She scowled up at him.

"That sense you have that can smell it—reach out and touch the magic with it."

"All right."

Grey watched her, but he couldn't see, or sense, anything. "Have you done it? Can you touch it?"

"I think so." Pearl's forehead creased in adorable effort, just between her eyes. Damn it.

"Grab hold of it." He held up a finger to forestall her

speaking, whether question or complaint. "Works differently for different people. Some wrap around it like arms and scoop it in. Some suck it up like a liquid. Some sink their fingers in it like a wad of raw wool and drag it in. Experiment. See what works best for you."

Her hands twitched, but she didn't actually move them as her frown deepened. "Scooping," she said finally. "But it's rather like trying to fill a water bucket with my bare hands."

"Improvement comes with practice." Grey watched the old woman.

She moved around the pitiful twisted body from one side of the door where he lay discarded, to the other, sniffing and peering and finally tasting. She reached out with a shockingly long arm to touch a sticky droplet of blood on the poor man's face and touched it to her tongue.

"Conjury," she cried. "Great and powerful conjury was worked here! Magic from the depths of hell." Didn't the woman have any other metaphors?

All eyes snapped to Grey. Eyes filled with rage.

He drew himself up straight, refusing to cower. He did hope Toby arrived quite soon with that policeman. "You might want to scarper," he said to Pearl from the corner of his mouth.

"I'll stick." She backed off a step. "But from here. You might need someone on the outside." And her features blurred. She became unnoticeable, unimportant.

A man's rough shout rose over the rising angry mutter. "*Demons* come from 'ell. Conjurers kill to summon demons!"

"Conjury cannot summon demons." Grey spoke loudly and precisely, hoping the locals' ingrained deference toward their "betters" would outweigh their native resentment of those born to privilege, at least temporarily. "Only God has power over hell's demons. God and their master, Satan, who works according to his own whims and not those of petty mortals. Satan may have been present during this abomination." He let his rage and horror into his voice. "But Satan's presence was *not* due to conjury."

"'Ere! Wot's all this, then?" The policeman—and Toby, presumably—had arrived at last.

Grey took advantage of the distraction to slip his bloody handkerchief to Pearl and watched it vanish into her blur. He expected to be taken up for questioning at the very least, and wanted to be sure the handkerchief with its innocent blood got to Amanusa. Who knew what would happen to it, or to him, if the police found it in his pocket?

The people in the crowd all spoke at once, allowing the uniformed man through to see the body. Grey could pick out the words "murder" and "conjury" and "hell" from the cacophony. He saw fingers point at him, felt hands grab and hold him, felt the little jabs and vicious pinches where the bobby couldn't see.

He couldn't see Pearl's blur anymore. He hoped she got away. He hoped he didn't see her little elfin face again. Not unless he was there when she delivered the handkerchief to Amanusa's justice. He didn't need an apprentice. Especially not a tempting little morsel like this one.

The policeman blew his whistle. Other officers arrived. Higher-ups were sent for, and a detective to begin inquiries into the murder. The hands holding Grey were exchanged for policeman's hands, and then for manacles. Eventually he was put into a wagon and transported to the nearest police station, where he was locked up and left to rot.

Or to contemplate his dire situation. Whichever came first.

While Grey felt very much as if he were already rotting, and while most would agree that he had always been spoiled rotten, he thought he ought to try contemplation first. It seemed more productive than rot.

Astonishingly enough, given his checkered past, Grey had never actually been arrested before. Not the sort of arrest where one had one's wrists pinioned by dashedly uncomfortable, heavy, cold, iron manacles and was placed in a dank, cold, stone-walled cell with an iron door that closed with a forbidding, permanent-sounding echoey clang. While still wearing the uncomfortable, hard, rough, cold manacles.

Grey considered calling out, requesting the manacles be removed, but he rather doubted anyone could hear him, and if they did, he doubted even more that they would comply with his request. He was a conjurer. Next to sorcery, conjury was the most feared of all the magics.

Since there hadn't been a sorceress in existence the past few hundred years, until Amanusa took up the mantle so recently, conjury suffered the slings and arrows of the superstitious and fearful. Likely these poor ignorant souls thought cold iron a bar to his magic, as if he were one of the fae.

The only thing that barred his magic was the willingness of the spirits to rise, and that depended on the rise of the moon and the dark of the night. Mostly.

He sighed as he slumped against the wall behind him. The cell was small, but it didn't need to be large, as it held nothing but a solid metal bunk hung from the wall with heavy chains, where he now sat, and a bucket for a chamber pot. At least the place was dry, though this near to the Thames, "dry" was a relative term. He saw no actual droplets of water trickling down the gray stone blocks of the walls.

There were ghosts, of course. He could sense them all through the building, which had been properly warded by a government conjurer to keep them at bay. He supposed he could entertain himself by counting up the ghosts, or reinforcing the local man's work. Later, maybe.

Ghosts were tetchy. One never knew what might set them off, and unlike spirits, they weren't reasonable. They'd been trapped on earth, usually by the violent circumstances of their deaths, and those circumstances sent them out of control. Or would once night fell. Ghosts were as shackled to night as—as his hands by these manacles.

He tried to be grateful that they'd shackled his hands in front rather than behind, so he could use the chamber pot when it became necessary. Which, actually, it rather was, since he'd woken not long ago and hadn't yet made his toilette.

That took up a few minutes of time, which then became instantly endless again. Grey feared he wasn't very good at this contemplation business, and even worse at rotting. He needed something to *do*.

The blasted cell had a tiny window high in the wall at the end opposite the door, nearly blocked by other buildings crowded around. It let in a pale watery shade of almost-light, and did not allow him any view of the sky when he tried looking out it. Yesterday had been a daylight moon, rising at 9:33 a.m. and setting at about 4 p.m. The days were getting shorter, but hadn't yet reached December's darkness, so he had had to deal with a strip of moonless daylight before nightfall had given back his magic.

Today would be a daylight moon as well, as would the next several. He didn't have his charts to know the exact time of moonrise, but it would be sometime between 10:30 and 10:45 a.m. He felt his waistcoat pockets again. No, he did not have his watch. Whether stolen or left behind in his night of . . . forgetfulness, he didn't have it now to know what time it was and whether the moon, or any spirits, were awake.

He had one spirit who would answer his call whatever the time. But he hated to disturb her. Surely he was not so feeble that he could not endure a few hours of isolation without having to conjure up a bit of distraction. And he didn't dare risk disturbing a ghost without a spirit to back him up, even in broad daylight. Relatively speaking. It wasn't precisely broad. More watery gray.

Grey lay down on his hard metal bunk, without the comfort of even a single thin, moth-eaten blanket, and threw an arm up over his eyes. Of course, since his hands were bound together, the other arm came, too, and he nearly brained himself with the blasted manacles. The weight of his arms dangling one from the other made the cuffs dig even deeper into his wrists. And now that he was motionless, rotting, his body reminded him that the whole of it still ached. Especially his head.

No, his face. His forehead and his cheekbones and his nose and even the hinge of his jaw throbbed and pounded as if they'd been stuffed with lint and set afire, and then placed in a linen press and the wheel turned till it crushed him.

A faint idea stirred in the depths of his brain, possibly rolling to the surface, but it sank again when a voice came whispering through the door.

"Mister Carterette?"

2

HE KNEW THAT voice, with its husky, dusky tones crawling inside him to twist up his innards. He knew that mispronunciation. He lowered his arms and sat up.

There was a little window in the door. It had been opened and a pair of eyes peeped over the bottom rim. Pearl wasn't so tall, was she? Standing on her toes, likely.

"What are you doing here?" Was that a snap in his voice? What happened to the languid, disinterested dilettante, the Grey Carteret everyone knew and . . . tolerated? "And it's 'Carteray,' not 'Carterette.' 'Carterette' sounds like I've 'et' something, and I ain't." Damn. He was letting his annoyance show. She shouldn't have followed him to this dismal place.

"I'd like to say I've come to break you out, but alas, that is beyond my capacity." She sounded more refined than he did. How had she wound up in this part of London? In those clothes?

"Why did you come, then?" He glowered at her. One of his best tricks, glowering.

"To see who you wanted me to inform that you've been tossed in clink." The slang term combined oddly with her educated speech. "If no one knows you're here, who knows when they'll let you out? Maybe never."

She had a point. Eventually, they would have to either charge him with a crime or let him go. English law was funny that way. But Grey didn't know how long that "eventually" might be, and once they charged him, he doubted they would let him go. Not for murder. Especially since he was who he was.

"All right." Grey didn't have to think. "Go to Henry Tomlinson. He's magist—"

"Magister of the alchemist's guild. I know." Pearl's tone sounded snappish, too, but her eyes had gotten big. Impressed her, had he?

"Yes. Well. He's a friend. Got a big house near mine in Albe—"

"Magician's Street. I know."

"Might you perchance allow me to finish what I'm saying before you tell me you already know it?" Grey's irritation at her interruptions outweighed his amusement at her eagerness, but not by much. She must have made a study of London's magicians, and so knew who he was.

A study from a distance, or she'd have known how to pronounce his name.

"Beg pardon," she said, almost sincerely.

"Go to Harry," Grey repeated. "If he's not at home in Albemarle Street—" He stressed the proper name of the street where they lived. "Then go to the guild house, and to the council building if he's not at the guild house. He's bound to be one of those places. Give him the handkerchief I gave you, and tell him what's happened."

"Then wot? What?" Her eyes sank below the opening, then rose again, as if she had to rest her toes a moment.

"Then go home. Back to whatever you were doing before."

Guilt suffused his every pore. His stomach soured at the knowledge of what he was sending her back to. But he simply couldn't take an apprentice. That thought curdled his insides even worse, all that responsibility. "I don't take apprentices."

"Well, you'll take this one. I'm not carrying any message for you until you promise me—promise in blood—that I am, from this very moment, your apprentice."

"You'd better nip off and deliver that hankie or you'll be found. Bobbies go up and down that way all the time." He didn't want to argue with her. He'd made up his mind.

Apparently she'd made hers up, too. "They won't see me. I'm hidden. I want your promise, or no messages."

"Then I suppose I'll just have to stay here." Grey cringed as he said it. The dank chill and the absolute lack of mental diversion already oppressed him. "I've survived the past hours. I can survive the rest."

Pearl's quiet laugh echoed around his cell. And when had he started thinking of her as Pearl, rather than as Miss Parkin?

"It's only been a quarter of an hour by the bells, between when they brought you here and when I arrived."

She sounded obnoxiously amused and beyond cheeky. "Are you sure you're up to waiting *hours*?"

Grey swore. Under his breath, since she sounded like a lady, even if she didn't look much like one. No, he wasn't at all sure he could do it. But he couldn't take an apprentice. "Look here, I am a conjurer. Even when females were working magic, conjury was a predominantly masculine guild. What makes you think you can learn conjury?"

"What makes you think I can't?"

He wanted to reach through that tiny window and shake sense into her. Or at least jostle her a bit. "Perhaps the fact that you were able to gather in magic from all that spilled blood on the pavement. That's sorcery, Miss Parkin, not conjury, and I am not a sorcerer. The new sorceress is taking apprentices. I am sure she'll take you on when she returns from Scotland. I'll give you a glowing recommendation."

"She's not here, is she? You are. Besides, Mr. Tomlinson's new apprentice isn't studying alchemy, even though Mr. Tomlinson's an alchemist. She's studying wizardry. So I can be a conjurer's apprentice and still study sorcery."

"You don't understand." Grey ground the words out through gritted teeth. *"I can't have an apprentice."*

"Then I suppose we're done here. Good-bye, Mr. Carter*ay*." The window cover squealed as she swung it closed.

Leaving him shut up alone in this tiny, empty, dank room forever. For who knew how long, which was the same thing as forever. Grey leaped to his feet, lunged halfway across the cell, crying, "Wait!"

The cover swung open so quickly, he knew she'd been waiting for his change of mind. She'd have gone if he hadn't changed it. Grey had no doubt she was that ruthless. But she'd waited first.

"What?" Those amber-shot blue eyes appeared in the

little window. He was close enough now to see individual rays of gold in the indifferent light.

"All right," he said, recalling what he'd meant to do. "You win. You can be my apprentice. *But*—" He waited until he was sure he had her full attention. "If your aptitude proves to be for sorcery, as I strongly suspect it does, when Amanusa—Mrs. Greyson, the new sorceress—returns to London, your papers can and will be transferred to her, no harm done."

Pearl narrowed those intriguing eyes at him, as if suspecting he was weaseling out of something. Clever girl. But she wouldn't lose by his weaseling.

"Agreed." She nodded, one brisk nod, then disappeared from the window.

Grey moved closer and peered through to see what she was doing.

She drew a penknife from a trouser pocket. A very sharp penknife, for it pricked her finger with the slightest of pressure. "Now you."

"Why is it women are always wanting to stab me with things?" Grey protested as a matter of form while he brought an assortment of fingers up to the window and presented them. Manacles were such inconvenient things.

"Probably because you deserve it," Pearl said without a trace of curiosity as to what he might mean by his cryptic statement.

He'd meant it to be cryptic. Probably been too cryptic. He'd have to go for less crypticity—crypticness?—in the future.

She selected one of his fingers—the left fore—and poked it so that a drop of blood welled up. She pressed her own blood-daubed finger to it. "Now say it," she said. "Swear that I'm your apprentice."

What was it Elinor's papers had said, when she'd signed them to become Harry's apprentice?

"I, Greyson George Arthur William Victor Carteret, swear that I will take to apprentice one Pearl . . ." He paused, in case she had any additional names. He was feeling peculiar. Almost dizzy.

"Pearl Elizabeth Parkin," she said quietly.

"One Pearl Elizabeth Parkin," Grey repeated, "as magician's apprentice, to teach her knowledge of magic, and hereby undertake to provide such accoutrements as are customary."

Grey had firm opinions about oaths. It was why he didn't often swear them, or make promises. Once made, the promise had to be kept. Which meant, now that he'd made this one—in blood, no less—he would be the very best magic-master he could. No regrets, no looking back. It was done, or would be when Pearl said her part.

"And I, Pearl Elizabeth Parkin, swear to follow Greyson George Arthur—"

"William Victor," he prompted in a stage whisper.

She repeated the names. "—Carteret as my master in magic." She peered past their fingers at him. "Is that it?"

"Enough for now." Grey withdrew his hands and leaned a shoulder against the door so he could look through it and she didn't have to stand on tiptoe. "There are papers to be signed, but later," he said. "We're sworn in blood."

That alone could be causing this peculiar feeling, the light-headedness that had set in moments ago. He could stomach the sight of anyone's blood but his own. "You have your promise. Now go find Harry."

"Yes, master." She tugged the front of her cap in exaggerated obsequiousness, and slipped down the dark corridor, wrapping her blur around her. Grey watched her through the window, able to do so only because he knew she was there.

She had to wait at the exit for someone to come in, so she could stay hidden while she slipped out. It wasn't a long wait. A bobby came in shoving a thickset bully boy ahead of him. Pearl flattened herself against the wall next to the flung-open door and vanished in truth as soon as the pair passed her by.

The bobby thrust his prisoner into a cell just beyond Grey's. On his way out again, he noticed the open window in Grey's cell door. "What's this doin' open?"

Grey looked blandly back at the copper. "It's been open since I was shut in here."

The officer scowled more fiercely, obviously suspecting magic.

Grey lifted his shackled hands. "Well, I certainly didn't open it. Not from inside here."

The cop snorted, disbelieving, making a sign to ward against evil. Superstitious idiot.

"It's daylight," Grey reminded him. Not that it made any difference for Grey, given a daylight moon. But if it allowed his jailers to relax a bit in his presence . . .

"Right." The policeman slammed the tiny window shut and locked it down, so tight Grey feared Pearl wouldn't be able to get it open next time.

Next time, it would be Harry visiting, not Pearl. Grey hoped. Harry could be difficult to find at times. Grey trudged back to his cold, hard metal bunk and lay down again, hoping he wouldn't have to wait too long.

PEARL GOT OUT of the police station without much trouble. It was so full of bustling bodies, no one noticed an extra jostle. When she was a safe block or two away and didn't have to hide so much, she let loose with a caper and a bit of a jig. *She was apprenticed to a magician.*

Not just any magician, neither. Either. Greyson George Arthur Something Whatsit Carter*ay* was, besides a man of many names, the best of the best. Tip of the top. He was a *magister*.

The mere word sounded impressive. And she, Pearl Elizabeth Parkin, was his apprentice. Sealed in blood so it couldn't be taken back.

Her pricked finger felt a bit peculiar. All hot and tingly. Excitement, that was. Anticipation. It made her a touch light-headed as well. Which she had to get over right quick, because she most certainly did not want him thinking she was light-headed because of him. Even if he was the most handsome of all the magicians in England. Handsome didn't matter.

So what if he had the face of an angel from a museum painting, with deep, soulful brown eyes and dark silky hair that he wore too long? So what if he possessed broad shoulders and a narrow waist and wide hands with long fingers? None of that mattered. Only that he could teach her magic and help her escape from the hell where her father had abandoned her.

In fact, Mr. Carteret's appearance was a detriment to her goals. She would simply have to ignore it, and focus on magic.

Pearl slowed her pace. She had a long way to go—clear across town. She couldn't run the whole way. Or dance, either, much as she might feel like it.

Albemarle Street was in Mayfair, but after Brown's Hotel had opened on the street, the high sticklers considered it a less desirable address. Which likely was how the first magician had been able to buy a house there. Once one magician moved in, it became easier for the next. Must be half a dozen houses occupied by magicians on the short street.

If not for that, Pearl would bet her left eyetooth that Harry Tomlinson wouldn't live here, no matter how high his rank among magicians, or how rich he might be. The man came straight out of the East End's dark, crooked streets.

He was definitely rich now, given the size and elegance of the house Pearl stared up at. She screwed up all her confidence and dug out her natural accent from beneath the Cockney veneer she'd laid on thick these past few years, and she marched up the front stairs. She might look like a grubby street urchin, but she wasn't. She was Magister Carteret's apprentice, with an urgent message for his friend and colleague, Magister Tomlinson.

There was only one way to pronounce Tomlinson, right? It couldn't be Toom-linson or Tom-line-son, could it?

Pearl shook off the stupid panic. She'd heard Mr. Carteret say it. She drew herself up to as many inches as she could possibly claim, seized the door knocker, and let fly. Moments later, the door opened and a butler stared down his nose at her.

"Beggars go around to the area door," he intoned, and prepared to shut the door again.

"I am Magister Carteret's apprentice, with an urgent message for Mr. Tomlinson," Pearl said fast as she could.

The butler hesitated, his scowl deepening. He held out his hand. "Give me the message and I will convey it to Magister Tomlinson." At least the man had a proper pride in his employer's rank.

"It isn't a written message. I have to tell the magister personally." Pearl wasn't risking leaving her master of magic stuck in jail. He couldn't teach her from jail. Her sense of urgency had nothing to do with how lost he looked in that cell.

"Who is it, Freeman?" A woman's voice floated from the depths of the house, and soon the woman herself appeared, gliding into the entry hall. Pearl leaned sideways to see around butler Freeman. Was this Tomlinson's famous female apprentice?

She was a few inches taller than Pearl and a few years older, softly rounded and serene. Her serviceable gray dress and medium brown hair smoothed into a knot at the nape of her neck only emphasized her dovelike appearance.

"A . . . person claims to have an urgent message for Magister Tomlinson from Lord Greyson." Rather than shutting the door on her, the butler opened it wider, apparently so the woman could get a better look at Pearl. "He claims it must be given directly to the magister, in person."

Wait. Mr. Carteret was a *lord*?

"Come along then, young sir." The woman smiled at Pearl and extended her hand, as if to lead her by it.

"Ma'am." Pearl bobbed her head and stepped through the doorway, setting aside for the moment her master's rank in society until she had time to think. "I am Magister Carteret's new apprentice, Pearl Parkin."

The woman's eyes widened as she stared. A moment later, a brilliant smile rose on her face, transforming her sedate attractiveness into a dazzling—not beauty, but something deeper. More real and alive. "Of course you are. I am Elinor Tavis."

With the hand she'd already extended, Miss Tavis took possession of Pearl's hand and squeezed. "It is a true pleasure to meet you, Miss Parkin. Pearl," she amended, her eyes gleaming. "For of course we are certain to be friends and be Elinor and Pearl together."

Pearl felt grubbier than ever, but she managed a return smile. "I should like that. Very much."

"Then it's settled." Elinor used her grip on Pearl's hand to draw her with her, deeper into the house. "It's a good thing Grey sent you so early, while Mr. Tomlinson is still at his breakfast. Once he's gone into his laboratory, he's nigh impossible to rouse from his concentration. I adore your clothes. They seem so practical. You shall have to tell me where you acquired them."

The flow of words set Pearl at ease. It had been too long since she'd been in such surroundings. She feared bumping into something and smearing it with her dirt, or breaking it beyond repair. Elinor's conversation wore down the worst of her nerves.

"I didn't know Grey had taken an apprentice," Elinor was saying. "When did this happen?"

Oh dear. She expected an answer.

Pearl scrambled for one. "Ah—about an hour ago, I'd say." She felt the edges of a blush creep round her ears. She hadn't had a friend—a real friend—in years, but she knew one didn't lie to friends. "I more or less blackmailed him into it."

"Did you?" Elinor's face was alight with laughter. "Good for you. I'm sure he needed blackmailing." She opened a door. "Here we are."

Sitting at his breakfast table, Mr. Harry Tomlinson didn't seem quite such a formidable creature as he did when striding around the halls of power, in and out of the Magician's Council Hall, or Whitehall, or Parliament. His light brown hair stuck up all directions and he had a crumb of toast on his chin. He wiped it away with a napkin and stood the instant he realized they were there, which was a bit of a while after they entered, as he'd been engrossed in the morning newspaper.

"Harry, this is Grey's new apprentice, Miss Pearl Parkin."

Pearl didn't know whether to curtsey as was proper for her sex, or offer her hand to match the clothing she wore. Mr. Tomlinson solved the quandary by offering his, and they solemnly shook hands while Elinor kept talking.

"Pearl has become Grey's apprentice just this morning by more-or-less blackmailing him into it, and she has brought you an urgent message from him."

"Like that's anyfing new. Grey has to be threatened into everything." Tomlinson gestured Pearl into a chair. "Pleasure to meet you, Miss Parkin. What's this message, then?"

Pearl squeezed herself into a chair without pulling it out. Her ears burned again. Blackmail was definitely not proper, much less legal, no matter the reaction she'd received here.

"It's why I could blackmail him, sir. He's been arrested, and I wouldn't deliver his message unless he swore to apprentice me." She was ashamed of it now, of putting such pressure on him when he was in such a defenseless position.

Tomlinson laughed out loud and slapped the table. "Time somebody got the better of Grey. So, what's he been arrested for? Simultaneously flipping up the skirts of all the ladies at Lord Hartington's soiree?"

"No, sir." Pearl eyed the food laid out on the sideboard. The aromas were making her dizzy. She'd eaten well last night, a whole pie to herself from money she'd earned honestly with protection spells. But that was the first time in a while. "Mr. Carteret's been arrested for murder."

"Murder!" Elinor cried.

Mr. Tomlinson choked on his toast and turned red with coughing.

"He didn't do it," Pearl said quickly. "At least, I think he didn't. I'm reasonably certain he didn't do it. But the man *was* killed by conjury, and Mr. Carteret *was* near where the man's body was found."

She realized something and sat up straighter. "No, I know he didn't do it, because the body wasn't there when we passed the night before, and he didn't stir from the place where he fell till he woke this morning, so he couldn't have done it."

Tomlinson nodded and ate one last rasher of bacon before he stood. "I'd best be seeing what I can do to get him out of this mess, then. Elinor, get some food inside Grey's new apprentice and do whatever else you need to do to make her presentable. Not that she ain't perfectly presentable now, but presentable to the stuffy folk with sticks up their ars—their backsides who make the decisions as to who gets out of jail and who doesn't."

The man spoke with an odd mixture of accents and grammar, the Cockney seeming to float in and out of his speech at whim. Its own whim, not Mr. Tomlinson's.

"I'll take care of it." Elinor smiled serenely at the alchemist, who nodded brusquely, cleared his throat, tossed his napkin on his plate, and departed.

Pearl looked from the door where Mr. Tomlinson had left, back at Elinor, wondering. Had she felt undercurrents in that conversation? Undercurrents of what?

"Let's begin with some breakfast, shall we?" Elinor glided to the sideboard. "What would you like?" She held a plate in her hand, looking expectantly at Pearl.

She shouldn't. But she had to. "Everything."

Elinor laughed and proceeded to heap the plate with little dabs of fluffy eggs and strips of bacon and slices of ham and one scone and half a muffin and . . . bliss.

MR. TOMLINSON RETURNED to the house about an hour later, just as Pearl was emerging from her second bath. It had taken two to rid her of all the dirt, and she felt as if she were nearing heaven itself. She hated the filth, but hadn't had the luxury of a real bath, a whole bath where she could sink herself into hot water and let the dirt soak off, since they'd had to move out of their lovely, elegant house in Portsmouth.

Elinor came into the bathing room after the maid had wrapped Pearl in a soft dressing gown and was busy toweling her hair dry.

"Complications," Elinor said. "The magistrate's proving recalcitrant. He won't release Grey to Harry's custody as magister, because Harry has neither warrant nor authority in his individual person to transfer the investigation to the Briganti, despite the fact that the crime apparently reeks of magic.

"Nor will he release Grey on Harry's word that we have a witness to his innocence. You are Grey's apprentice, and could well be colluding in the crime. However, he will forbear arresting you for now. So, we are going to the jail, to give aid and succor to Grey, while Harry goes to build a fire under the Briganti to get the machinery moving to take over this magic-reeking murder from the regular constabulary."

She narrowed her eyes at Pearl. "Though where we'll

find a dress to fit you, I don't know. I'm not surprised to find someone more slender than me, but I am utterly astonished that you are shorter. Are you even five feet?"

Pearl shrugged. "I don't know. I haven't been measured. My lack of height did make it easy to maintain my boy's disguise."

Elinor pressed her lips together. "We will have to make do." She gave Pearl a sharp look. "But don't think that you will escape telling me all about why you felt a disguise necessary and—and everything."

She laughed at Pearl's wary expression. "I suffer from insatiable curiosity. An excellent quality in a magician, but perhaps not so excellent in a friend. I'm afraid Harry's rubbed off on me, and I no longer have the manners to keep from asking. If you don't want to answer, just tell me it's none of my business and I'll leave you be. I seem to respond best to bluntness these days. I've lost my talent for subtlety."

Elinor had quite a talent for sweeping people along, however, for a short time later, Pearl found herself clothed in a dress borrowed from the youngest maid, with her hair twisted up and pinned to her skull and her boy's boots hidden beneath her new skirts. No one had feet small enough to loan her shoes.

Elinor escorted Pearl back to the police station with only the company of a large, rather sinister-looking footman. Pearl had trouble staying awake on the journey. She'd had a long night, watching over Mr. Carteret. Lord Greyson. Greyson was his given name, but was it also his title? Or was it the courtesy title for a younger son? Whose son was he? She didn't remember reading anything about it.

She must have dozed after all, for she startled awake when the carriage stopped. The very large footman handed the ladies out and passed a large basket to Elinor, who led the way inside.

Pearl didn't like this building. It was dark and dank,

with narrow corridors and cramped rooms and tiny windows that kept out what little light there was. And it . . . felt bad.

There was magic here. Angry magic. Old magic that pulled at her, wanted things from her. Things she didn't know how to give. It frightened her.

"Are you all right?" Elinor whispered, holding tight to Pearl's arm.

"I don't like this place. It makes my skin crawl," Pearl whispered back.

"I don't like it, either. It feels dead."

"It doesn't feel dead to me. It feels much too alive."

3

THE POLICE LET both the ladies enter the cell after searching the basket for weapons or tools. When the door clanged shut behind them, Pearl couldn't deny the frisson of horror that shivered down her back.

She wasn't trapped, she reminded herself. The nice, sullen policeman would come back and let them out. Surely.

Mr. Carteret stood, looking hollow-eyed and bedraggled. Had he winced at the clang? Was his head still hurting? He looked dreadful. And too beautiful for any human male. Drat him.

Elinor gave a little cry and rushed forward to envelop him in her embrace. "How are you bearing up?" she asked when she released him. Did she have feelings for the handsome conjurer?

Pearl would be safer if Elinor did, for Pearl did not poach. It was another of her rules, made up just now.

"Terribly. It's positively hideous in here." His shackles rattled as he invited them to sit on the only seat possible, the bare metal bunk. "I don't know how they think I could work magic with a blanket, but they didn't give me one, so they must. What did you bring me?"

He swept the basket from Elinor's hands and began poking through it. "Raisin cakes! I think I'm in love." He batted his eyes at her, speaking around the cake as he stuffed it in his mouth. "I'm *starving*."

The manacles rattled as he tucked the basket under his arm and rummaged for another cake. "So what's the word?"

"Harry couldn't get you out." Elinor settled herself on the bunk. "Even though Pearl is a witness that you didn't place the corpse where it was found. The magistrate still denied bail."

He frowned, but didn't look surprised. He pulled a bottle of ale from the basket and almost dropped it all. The manacles made him clumsy.

With a roll of her eyes, Pearl stepped forward and took the basket from him. She set it on the bench, took the ale away, ignoring his protest, opened it, and handed it back to him. Then she picked up the basket and held it within his easy reach.

Mr. Carteret stared at her a moment, the astonishment on that brooding poet's face fading into thoughtfulness as he took a two-handed swallow of ale. "Perhaps it won't be so bad, having an apprentice."

"It will, if you can't get out of jail," Pearl retorted.

He only grinned at her, merriment dancing so brightly in those dark eyes, it made her want to smack him. But one only smacked siblings, not one's magic-master. Alas.

"Where's Harry?" He pinned Pearl with a sudden scowl. "I sent you to fetch Harry, if I recall. Obviously, you've *been,* given your clean, clothed, and breakfasted state. And given the presence of Elinor. But where is Harry?"

"He's been and gone again," Elinor said. "Just now,

he's off to the council house to see about getting this murder transferred to the Briganti."

Carteret grimaced. "Curse it. Simmons will be a perfect as—I mean, a perfect donkey's backside about it all, if it's transferred before I'm sprung. He'll take advantage. You know he will. Start lording it over I-Branch. His bully boys will be tramping their massive feet all over positively everything."

"Who's Simmons?" Pearl put in when the complaints slowed.

"Head of the Briganti," Elinor said.

"Head of *Enforcement,*" Mr. Carteret corrected. "Colonel Simmons is not in charge of the Investigations Branch. Investigations reports directly to the council head and the guild masters. Enforcement steps up only after I-Branch has finished its part."

He frowned at Pearl again. Even his frowns were beautiful. Blast it. "Why don't you know that already? Who Simmons is? You know everyone else."

She hefted the basket a little higher. It was heavy. "Simmons isn't a magister. Who is head of Investigations, then?"

"Me." He tipped up his bottle and took a long swallow of ale, his throat moving as he swallowed.

"Oh." Pearl made herself stop watching his throat, and slid her pieces of knowledge around until they slotted into place. "So if the case gets transferred, then you'll be released?"

"Not likely." His face tightened to grim. "Simmons isn't any more likely to believe my innocence than the magistrate here is. Less so, given that I've been a thorn in his side for years. Ever since the Investigations Branch of the Briganti was created."

Carteret tucked in his chin, thrust out his lower lip, and spoke in a blustery tone. "Change? It's pernicious. No need for investigation. Obvious what's happened.

Just let my boys at 'em. We'll get these rogue magickers sorted in no time."

He made a disgusted noise and handed the ale bottle to Pearl. "Still, transfer is better than the alternative."

"I can understand how you wouldn't want to stay here." Pearl shivered, looking around the cell. It wasn't any worse than some of the places she'd stayed the last several years, except for that barred iron door. That made all the difference.

He paused on the verge of plunging back into the basket. "That, too. But mostly, no ordinary will ever believe that no guild conjurer committed that crime."

Pearl frowned, holding tight to the basket while he rummaged. "But . . . I thought you agreed with that old woman, that conjury was worked in the murder."

"It was. But no sane member of the conjurer's guild would have worked it." He emerged triumphant with the last raisin cake and continued his explanation. His willingness to do so without complaint surprised her a little. For a man who didn't want an apprentice, he was awfully patient with her questions.

"Guild members know conjury can't call demons. We have it hammered through our heads. There are still rooms in the guild hall that haven't been touched—that can't be touched—since the debacle that resulted from the last experimental attempt to summon a demon. Students of conjury are taken by the rooms. Journeymen are taken inside, so we can *know* the horror."

His eyes saw something other than the cell where they stood, the half-eaten cake forgotten in his hand. "The blood is still fresh in those rooms, do you know? Fresh after four hundred years. Can't be cleaned up. Can't be touched. Old Bizzault still looks surprised. And quite, quite dead, since his head's been separated from his body that same four hundred years. But the worst isn't the blood or the gore. It's the evil.

"You can sense it. Feel it, taste it, smell it— Evil

seeps in through your pores and screams in your ears and—"

"Grey." Elinor jolted both of them back to the present, for Pearl had been as caught up in her master's words as he in memory.

Elinor held onto Mr. Carteret's elbow another moment, staring into his eyes until she found whatever she searched for. She patted his shoulder and returned to her seat on the bunk.

"Murder conjures nothing," he said, staring at the cake in his hand as if he'd never seen one before. "Murder spills innocent blood, and innocent blood cries out for justice, and that's sorcery. But it will take conjury to find the murderer."

"Isn't Colonel Simmons a conjurer?" Elinor asked. "Doesn't he know all that, that no conjurer would try such a thing?"

A bitter smile flickered across his face, there and gone again. "Ah, but remember. I said no *sane* conjurer. The good colonel isn't any too sure of my sanity. He'll be happy to accuse me of this crime, because anything else might require him to actually think. And of course, it will get me conveniently out of the way. No more diluting of the power."

"But, didn't you just say innocent blood was sorcery?" Pearl's talent leaned toward sorcery. He'd said that, too. Perhaps she could be of some real assistance.

"Sorcery would help," he admitted. He seemed to recognize the raisin cake, and bit into it finally. This time, he swallowed before speaking again. "But I'm not wiring Amanusa and Jax to summon them from their belated wedding trip. They'll come back to London when they're ready. Hopefully before the weather becomes so utterly abominable that they can't travel. No, I'll just have to get out of lockup and look into this myself. Somehow."

As Pearl watched, his fallen-angel's face hardened, became fierce, angry, darker than grim. He cursed, under his breath, but Pearl stood close enough to hear the filthy word. She wasn't shocked. She'd heard worse on London's streets.

"What is it? What's wrong?" She swung the basket to the floor, but stopped herself reaching out to him. "Have you remembered something from last night?"

He gave her a sharp look. "No, nothing like that. Only—I am forced to do something I swore I would never do. *Ever*."

"What?" What could have him this agitated? Pearl didn't know what to do, how to help.

"Call on my father for aid."

"Oh." Elinor's response meant something, but Pearl didn't know what it was.

"Who is your father? How can he help?" She'd read every newspaper she could get her hands on, but they'd been sporadic and often smeared, and she didn't remember any of them mentioning Mr. Carteret's parentage.

"The Duke of Brandon," Elinor said, when Mr. Carteret merely continued looking fierce.

Oh. A duke would certainly have enough influence to spring his son from jail. But why the anger and the cursing? It wasn't as if his father could lose everything he owned and drink himself into a stupor every night. Well, perhaps the stupor, but not the rest of it. Not with entail.

He reached for the ale bottle she discovered she still held, and his look met with her confusion.

He laughed, a bitter sound that edged along her skin. "Never mind. With any luck, you'll never meet him."

Mr. Carteret quickly drank down the remaining ale and handed the bottle to Elinor. "Did I feel paper in this basket?" He bent and Pearl hastily picked the basket up from the floor. She was closer and got there quicker.

"Yes," Elinor said. "I thought you might need to write a letter to someone. Instructions for your solicitor. Introductions for your apprentice."

"Pleas to my paternal parent?" He raised an eyebrow, then winked at Pearl, and her heart went thumpety. He should not be so handsome.

He drew out a few sheets of paper and appropriated the bunk, displacing Elinor so he could use half for his chair and half for his writing desk. He dipped his pen into the inkwell Pearl opened for him and began to write in a slashing, left-handed scrawl. He wrote a letter to his father informing him of the situation; a letter to his household introducing Pearl; a note to Harry regarding apprenticeship papers. There may have been another letter. Pearl wasn't sure.

All this decisive, purposeful activity left Pearl feeling spun around in circles all over again, as Mr. Carteret displayed yet another side to his multifaceted personality. Would she ever get a grasp on who he was?

He rose to his feet, as if realizing the women were standing, therefore he should as well, since his business was conducted. He blew on his last letter and handed it to Pearl to fold, then took it back to write the direction on the outside, bending over the bunk to do so. His frock coat stretched across his shoulders and rode up on his back. Pearl gazed down at the basket by her feet. It wasn't proper to ogle one's employer.

The policeman came to usher them out again just as Mr. Carteret turned to give her the letters.

"There's sandwiches for your lunch," Elinor said quickly, pausing near the door.

"I *am* in love." He pressed a closed hand to his heart, that lush mouth curved in a tiny smile. Men shouldn't have lips like that. And Mr. Carteret shouldn't say things like that, not even teasing. Not even to someone else.

Pearl took her turn to linger at the door and look back at him, her master of magic, her teacher. Her beau ideal. *Drat.*

"Go," he said, as the policeman began making hurry-along noises. "I can survive a night in this place."

"I hope you don't have to."

"So do I," he said as she slid through the closing door.

The clang of metal on metal echoed through the stone-walled corridor as the officer shut and locked the door.

PEARL TALKED ELINOR into hand-delivering the note to Mr. Tomlinson. So, after a pause to post the other letters, they drove straight to the Magician's Council Hall, reasoning that he couldn't have finished the necessary paperwork in so little time. He hadn't.

"I swear, I think Simmons is throwin' up barricades just so Grey stays longer in th' straight box," Tomlinson growled as he paced furiously outside the room filled with clerks and copyists, his accent thick with annoyance. "I knew Brigantis wasn't all sunshine and roses, but Grey never let on it was this bad."

"I doubt it was," Elinor said. "Not while Grey operated from a position of power. This situation has weakened him."

"I never said anything about Grey being arrested. 'Ow does 'e know?" He scowled at the frosted glass in the upper half of the door at the shapes of the people beyond.

"You know how quickly rumor spreads."

"So how will we get Mr. Carteret out of jail?" Pearl asked, feeling even more anxious.

"We have to get this mess in the hands of somebody who knows how conjury works," Tomlinson said. "That's the first thing."

"But I thought—" Pearl shook her head, trying to shake out the confusion. "Will transferring it to the Briganti get him out? He said it wouldn't, but— I don't understand."

Tomlinson banged his walking stick hard on the tiled floor, starting up his pacing again. "That's the tricky part. Simmons can claim, rightly, that Grey's men will be loyal

to him. Simmons'll want his own men investigating."
Tomlinson fell silent, scowling at the door again.

"Do they know anything about investigations?" Pearl
asked. "Simmons's men?"

"No." Tomlinson banged his stick a few more times.
"And they'll be as biased against Grey as Grey's men
are in his favor. Simmons types, every one of 'em."

"What about Mr. Archaios?" Elinor spoke up. "He's
done investigations for the Conclave."

"Who's Mr. Archaios?" Pearl asked. "Besides an investigator for the Conclave. And what's the Conclave?"

"Magician's Council is where all the guilds get together and discuss things as affect all magicians in England, right?" Tomlinson paced down the corridor the
other way, Pearl and Elinor swiveling to watch him.
"The Conclave is where all the Magician's Councils from
all the countries—England, France, Hungary, Greece,
and so on—get together to work out things that affect
magic at the international level.

"We got back from a Conclave in Paris about six
weeks ago. That's where we met Archaios. He's come to
London from Greece, where 'e's from, to consult about
the dead zones."

A chill ran through Pearl and out her spine at mention of the dead zones. There was one not far from the
docks, where a fire had raged, burning warehouses, blocks
of hovels, and even ships out on the river, stretching
clear through Bethnal Green. People and vermin had
flowed out in a sweeping rush of screams and ratty
scrabbling feet. The fire had smoldered for weeks at the
warehouses of the shipfitters, where it had started in
the stored barrels of pitch, canvas, caulking cotton and
other ship's fittings. The embers kept burning everywhere the hot pitch had flowed. When the fire was out
and the people began to creep back in to see what could
be salvaged, they found plump, glossy bodies of rats

that had gone in ahead of them, now lying dead in the ashes.

And they saw other things. Things that clattered and banged and lived when they shouldn't have. Things made of nails and bits of brick and wire and bone.

The people who stayed too long in the burned-out area, who weren't driven out by horror, or fear of the half-seen things clanking in the shadows, those people weakened. Their limbs failed them. They had trouble catching their breath, and they fell. Collapsed into the ash like rag dolls. It didn't happen quickly. Took longer if they came out at night, less if they bunked down in a burned-out shell of a building. Once a person fell, if they didn't have someone to pull them out, they died.

That's when the talk started. How folk had died there before the fire. Strong men, bully boys and stevedores, who dropped dead from living or working in the wrong place, not just the old and the weak.

The fire had happened not long after Pearl and her papa had gone to live on Half Moon Yard. They'd had a set of rooms well away from the fire, and had hung onto them grimly. Pearl had, at any rate. She'd gone with the other boys after, to look for salvage, but she wouldn't go in. No matter how they teased, no matter how she feared her cowardice might expose her disguise.

She'd *felt* how dead the place was, and how the death crept out from its center, faster and faster as it grew, until it was swallowing whole houses in a quarter of a year. If it kept growing at that rate, kept increasing its pace, all of London could be gone before the decade was out. Because it wasn't the only zone in the city.

"This business with Grey and the murder is going to distract everyone from the real work," Mr. Tomlinson was saying. "We've got to get it solved and behind us so we can focus on the dead zones."

"Then we need to send a message to Mr. Archaios," Elinor said decisively. "Straightaway."

Pearl had a new question. "What do the dead zones have to do with magic?"

"They're caused by magic." Tomlinson stopped pacing, spinning his walking stick almost like a weapon there in the narrow corridor. Pearl backed up to give him room as he spoke.

"Or by the absence of magic. The magic is dying, already has died, in those zones, in the earth and the stones. And without magic, everything else dies. The zones are growing because the earth is trying to pull magic back, as it always does. It's replenished by the things living on it. But there's not enough magic to fill it back up, so it keeps pulling more and more, and what it pulls—that dies, too. It can't survive in the zones. And so the zones get bigger.

"We figured out in Paris 'ow to stop 'em from doing that. It takes all four of the great magics: alchemy, conjury, wizardry, and sorcery. But since we only got the one sorceress, and she's the first in two hundred years, it'll take a bit longer before we can wall up all the zones and stop 'em from growing.

"In the meantime, we got to figure out how to reverse it, make the zones shrink. That's why Archaios is 'ere. He's got experience working with other magic. Got perfect pitch, you might say, only for magic instead o' music."

He tossed his stick in the air and caught it again. "Right, then. Elinor, your hand's better'n mine, so you write the note to Archaios. I'm off to call on Sir Billy, to see if 'e'll call in the Greek on council authority, send 'im over to get Grey out o' clink."

Sir William Stanwyck was the head of the Magician's Council of England, knighted for his service to the crown, and for his abilities as master wizard. Pearl knew that from her newspaper reading. Hearing Mr. Tomlinson refer to him as "Sir Billy" shocked her.

"Pearl, you'd better head over to Grey's house and

take charge. They'll 'ave got the letter 'e wrote by now, so they'll be expecting you."

"What about my apprenticeship papers?" Pearl blurted out, without quite intending to.

"Oh, right." He reached inside his gray pinstriped jacket and pulled out a sheaf of printed papers. "I figured you'd be needing 'em, so I already hunted 'em up. Most lads come through the school nowadays, but as Elinor's my apprentice, I knew where to look. This 'ere's the standard lot."

He turned and spread the papers out against the wall, beckoning Pearl over. Only two sheets, she saw, now that he'd gotten them unfolded; extralong legal pages.

"Your name goes here, and Grey's over here, and there's other bits and pieces to be filled in—support and any wages and like that." Tomlinson pointed to the various blanks. Then he folded the papers back up and handed them to her. "You'll want to read them over 'fore you sign 'em."

She didn't, actually. She wanted them *signed*. And sealed and recorded and whatever else was necessary to make them official. So she took them.

"A'right." Mr. Tomlinson offered Pearl his arm. "Let me order a cab for ya."

"Thank you, sir, for your kind offer." She laid her hand lightly atop his gray-clad arm and they proceeded to the door as Elinor hurried to find paper and pen to write her note.

Pearl's new life seemed off to a good start. If they could get her magic master out of jail.

4

GREY'S WAIT WAS interminable. Endless. An eternity of waiting that felt like days, *weeks,* and lasted perhaps five hours. The watery light wasn't strong enough to indicate the sun's position, so it might have been longer. Might have been less.

He catalogued the lingering aches and pains of his body. Residual now, as if they didn't actually belong to his own body, and growing less noticeable as time went on. Still it was something to do that didn't involve provoking ghosts. He ate the last sandwich Elinor had brought in her lovely basket. Would Pearl be the sort of apprentice who brought sandwiches?

She seemed more cheeky than Elinor, though Elinor was well supplied with that commodity. In Elinor's case, it seemed more an unwillingness to put up with his nonsense. How did cheek relate to sandwiches? If Pearl mocked him while bringing them, he could put up with cheek.

Pearl had looked quite different in that dress than she had in her boy's costume. Quite, *quite* different. She'd been clearly female in her trousers once she dropped the illusion magic. Small as she was, she had curves enough to fill those trousers nicely. But in that dress—

It wasn't even a pretty dress. Obviously borrowed from a young servant not grown into her adult size and shape, the dress was made of a coarse brown twill, faded slightly with wear. It sagged at Pearl's waist and strained across her bosom and, ugly as it was, made her look utterly feminine. Even the scraped-back knot of her hair—a rich dark brown that had been invisible under her boy's cap—emphasized her newly displayed womanhood.

And Grey had no business whatsoever thinking of her that way. She was his *apprentice*.

Grey had almost convinced himself that he could indeed fall asleep on his bare metal bunk when keys rattled in the lock and the door to his cell squealed open. He'd imagined it so often, he only cracked an eyelid to see if this time it might be true.

"Get up, you murderin' scurf." The bobby poking him with his club felt all too real. "The magistrate wants you."

Grey sat up, surprised that his fragile bones and aching muscles didn't protest more than they did. He stood and obeyed the policeman's prodding. Another bobby waited in the corridor. They escorted him fore and aft through the warren of the police station to the front room with its high desk.

"Hullo, Archaios." Grey greeted the magician waiting there, a tall, dark brooding sort of chap with silver just beginning to streak his temples. Sometimes Grey wanted streaky temples like that. He rather thought it might make him look distinguished. But most of the time, he was pleased that his hair showed no signs of wear. "Come to get me out?"

"I am here solely for my magical expertise," the alchemist said with a little bow. "*He* has come to get you out."

Grey looked at the other man waiting in the room, and his stomach knotted up. "Hullo, Wright. Been a long time."

"Indeed it has, Lord Greyson. I had thought you long ago moved past such misadventures." The man's hair had gone white and—away—in the fifteen or so years since he'd seen him last. Otherwise, Wright looked much the same as when he had dragged Grey out of his various youthful . . . "misadventures" was a good word for the things he'd fallen into then.

"I would say this was something more in the nature

of a calamity." Grey's attempted smile came out a lop-sided grimace, but he tried. "Or I'd never have bothered asking the sire to drag you away from your business."

"I am quite aware of that, milord." The solicitor's smile was far more genuine than Grey's, and seemed actually to have a bit of fondness beneath it. "And I have appreciated the lack of interruption. But I must admit, life has been a great deal more boring these last several years."

Grey grinned at the old gentleman. "I always knew I liked you, Wright. I shall have to make it a point to pay you a visit from time to time, just to liven up your life."

He did like the man. Always had. But Wright had been a reminder of too many things Grey had not liked at all, which was why he'd avoided him.

"As long as it is merely a visit, milord." Wright tipped his head in a tiny bow. "And might I suggest—? If you have reason to need my services again in future, contact me directly, without going through His Grace."

Grey felt the flush of embarrassment and thanked his Gallic ancestors for skin that refused to show it. "I shall. I suppose it's simply that I haven't been in this sort of difficulty in so long—"

"For which I am sure His Grace is grateful." Wright smiled. "As am I."

"When do we see the magistrate?" Grey was anxious to get the manacles off. Though he didn't know if going before the court would do it.

"We don't." Wright turned as a uniformed policeman with rank insignia on his sleeve climbed up to the desk.

"We don't?" When would he get out of this blasted place, then? He truly did not wish to stay the night here, even with the warding and the assistance of his spirits. Conjurers interested ghosts. They tended to come calling, and their lack of control and dangerous moods made them uncomfortable guests.

Wright handed a paper to the sergeant at his lofty

height. "That is the release ticket for Greyson Carteret, the gentleman here." He indicated Grey in his manacles.

The sergeant studied the ticket, leaned forward to peer over his parapet at Grey, who tried to look as innocent as possible, then looked at the ticket again.

"Really?" Grey spoke in a stage whisper. "You're getting me out without me having to go before the magistrate? How much was the bail? I'll have my bank forward the funds—"

"That was Mr. Archaios's doing," Wright said. "I have merely expedited paperwork. And there is no bail. You have been cleared of all charges, thanks to Mr. Archaios."

Grey raised an eyebrow at Archaios, who returned an enigmatic smile.

"Don't leave me in suspense, man," Grey protested. "I don't want to have to thrash you. How did you do it?"

"I should like to see you try," Archaios said with a significant look at the manacles. "I simply convinced the magistrate that you had nothing to do with the murder."

Grey blinked. In his experience, convincing any magistrate of anything had nothing to do with simplicity. And anything to do with magic only made it worse. "Yes, but *how*?"

Archaios tapped his nose. "My credentials are impeccable. And the magic surrounding the murder did not smell like yours."

"You smell magic?"

"Among other things." Archaios inclined his head in his own miniature bow. He frowned then. "This magic was not conjury. It was unlike any magic I have seen."

"Yes." Grey nodded. "And—?" He knew what he sensed, and if Archaios could sense more, he wanted the details.

"This was—" The Greek shook his head, frowning. "Twisted. Corrupted. Perhaps by the death. There was conjury at its base, I believe, with some wizardry and perhaps an attempt at sorcery, but a failed attempt, if so. There may even have been some mangled hint of alchemy in it. But it wasn't your magic. Yours is bright and clear, almost like bells ringing but—"

"But not." Grey nodded. He knew the impossibility of describing magic with ordinary words.

"Exactly. The magic used in the murder of Angus Galloway was nothing like. I've never encountered anything similar, or anyone who might have worked it." Archaios's scowl deepened. "I do not care to ever encounter it again."

"Then we'd best get me out of here so I can catch the fellow." Grey lifted his manacles, hopeful of release.

The sergeant ignored him. "Says here to wait for an order from the magistrate."

"Oh. Yes." Wright nodded. "An order transferring an investigation to the Briganti. It has nothing to do with the order of release."

The sergeant folded his hands. "We'll wait, all the same."

Grey supposed he did not want free-roaming magicians in his police station. Fortunately, the wait was not long. A clerk hurried in with a paper and handed it to the sergeant, who read it, matched it to his release ticket, and handed it over to Wright, who handed it to Grey, who read it.

The court officially found that as magic was determined to be worked in the causing of the death of Angus Galloway, the matter and the results of all investigations heretofore conducted in it were to be forthwith turned over to the Briganti of the Magician's Council of Great Britain. It had stamps and seals and signatures bristling from the bottom, giving it an official enough look. Like all the other transfers Grey had seen.

He handed it to Archaios as the sergeant rose ponderously from his seat and climbed down the steps from his perch, rattling a massive set of keys. Grey held out his hands and finally, finally, the manacles were unlocked and removed.

The sergeant gave him a long, stern look of warning before turning to climb back up to his place of authority. There, he stamped the release ticket and wrote something in his book. Another factotum appeared with Grey's hat and walking stick, produced a book to sign that the belongings had been returned, and it was done. Grey was a free man.

Wright picked up a battered briefcase from the floor and retreated with the others toward the door. "What will you do now?"

Grey placed his hat carefully on his head. The ache was much improved but not entirely gone. He opened the police station door and went through it first—he had to get shut of this place—then held it, inviting the others through with a flourish. "The Briganti will begin the ferreting out of truth straightaway. As soon as all the reports've been sent over."

Archaios gave a little bow, which was more a tip of the head as he came out the door. "Any further assistance I might provide, please do not hesitate to ask."

"Believe me, I shall not." Grey grinned and winked. "But first—" He released the door as Wright reached the street. "First, I have a new apprentice to see to."

PEARL PACED THE front parlor in Magister Carteret's townhouse, from the claw-foot red velvet sofa to the massive carved walnut mantelpiece to the layered, bobble-trimmed crimson brocade drapes, and back again. Whoever had decorated his parlor had been enamored of drama and dark colors and more. More of *everything*.

The rows of bobble fringe hanging from the drapes were only the beginning. Everything was tasseled, beaded, and bedecked within an inch of its life. Past that. It was trimmed to death.

But her magic-master's failures as an interior decorator—whether he'd chosen everything himself, or simply failed to restrain whoever had—did not have Pearl pacing and muttering to herself. The decor distracted her from her frustrations.

The butler had received Mr. Carteret's letter naming her his apprentice and secretary. He had accepted Magister Tomlinson's introduction of her as Pearl Parkin, the person named in the letter. And then the butler, McGregor, had proceeded to ignore her.

Oh, not entirely. He installed her in a parlor and had tea brought. He answered her summons. He intercepted her if she attempted to penetrate farther into the house, escorting her politely but firmly back into the parlor. And he refused every other request, demand, order, or hysterical rant from her with the bland "when Magister Carteret returns."

There was, however, one thing she could do without McGregor's interference. It didn't take her above an hour or two to realize it, either. The parlor possessed a writing desk, one with every kind of writing implement in existence, and ink in a myriad of colors. Pearl could have filled in the blanks in her apprenticeship papers with names that looked as if they were written in blood, whether they actually were or not.

She confined herself to sensible black, carefully writing her own name in the "hereinafter referred to as APPRENTICE" blank, and as many of Mr. Carteret's names as she could remember in the "MASTER" blank. Then she filled in the rest of the blanks as best she could, stopping to do arithmetic when necessary.

When the ink was dry, she folded the papers, sealed them with a bit of wax she found in a pigeonhole, and sat down in the dainty, fringe-trimmed desk chair to think. She had tried already to escape the house, frustrated by her situation, determined to win out over any man who thought he had her beat. She hadn't succeeded in getting out the front door when she tried, even leaving behind her coat. The butler had thrown himself bodily across the exit, like some sacrificial virgin. Not that she knew if he was or not. But there was more than one way out, and she was determined to get Mr. Carteret's signature on those papers *today*.

The front windows overlooked the street, but Pearl no longer cared about exposure. Her magic could hide her. She hoped. One way or another, she was leaving this house.

She was halfway out the window when the door to the parlor opened again and Magister Carteret strolled in, handing his hat and his walking stick to the stiff rump of a butler.

The magister looked . . . good. Disheveled. Rumpled. Unshaven, by the dark shadow on his cheeks and chin. It only brought out the "fallen" aspect of his appearance without altering the "angel" side in the least. Pearl couldn't breathe.

Though part of that might be due to the fact that she lay on her stomach over the windowsill with her legs dangling outside.

He turned and saw her there draped half in and half out the window. His gaze captured her and held her motionless, unable to move in either direction. "So eager to abandon me, Miss Parkin?" he inquired, one eyebrow rising, a perfect wing preparing to take flight.

She couldn't have him thinking the wrong thing, but it was a struggle to escape the breathless web of his gaze. "So eager to reach you, Magister Carteret." She croaked the words out on her last remnant of breath, which somehow overbalanced her and she toppled the rest of the way out the window into the street.

A shout carried through the window as the sidewalk smacked her hard. She collapsed in a heap, sharp pains stabbing her ankle and hip and the palms of her hands. Her elbow hurt, too.

Pearl sat up, whimpering a little with self-pity and embarrassment. Scandalized passers-by pretended she wasn't there, or they stared in open shock and appalled fascination. She'd forgotten her disguising magic when Mr. Carteret and his too-handsome face had come in the room.

She inspected her stinging elbow. The fabric had torn and the skin was scraped away. Drat. Now she would have to mend the borrowed dress, or replace it. She hoped Mr. Carteret didn't reduce the amount of her support, so she could pay for the dress and still have some to save.

"Miss Parkin—"

She looked up to see Mr. Carteret's head poking out the window, as the front door opened and McGregor and a footman hustled down the steps.

"Are you all right?" Carteret asked.

"Nothing seems to be permanently damaged." She tried very hard to behave as if falling out of windows while climbing out of them was something young ladies did every day of the week.

"Ah. Excellent." He disappeared just as the two servants reached her.

Pearl jerked away from McGregor's hands as he bent to help her up. It was his fault she was in this situation. She accepted the footman's hand and pulled herself upright. When she took a step, the pain in her ankle stabbed sharper and she almost fell. McGregor caught her arm, but he let go when she glared at him.

Mr. Carteret came clattering down the front steps in a billow of frock coat. "You *have* damaged yourself," he accused.

"Not permanently."

But she was ignored, or her words and wishes were, as he swept her up in his arms to carry her into his house.

Oh, this was not good. She was held in steel-banded arms, nestled into a broad, firmly muscled chest, close enough to that Byronesque visage that she could see the last of the light glinting off the individual whiskers of his unshaved cheeks. And he smelled good.

Surprising, since he'd spent a quarter of the previous night lying in a gutter, and the remainder of the day in a jail cell. But then, Pearl's nose had been reeducated over the past several years. It had gone numb perhaps, or learned to ignore the East End effluvia, though since the sewers had been mostly finished, the Thames did smell a great deal better these days. Still, Mr. Carteret simply smelled like himself.

Holding her close in those lovely strong arms, Mr. Carteret clattered up the steps and into the house as if she weighed nothing at all. And while Pearl realized that she didn't weigh much, she also knew that she weighed considerably more than nothing. This demonstration of masculine strength made her heart want to go pitter-pat.

Since it had already gone thumpety, pitter-pat was absolutely not to be tolerated. Mr. Carteret was her master of magic. Her teacher and employer. The fact that he was also the most beautiful man she'd ever seen in the whole of her pitiful life was beside any point anyone might care to make.

She perhaps should have waited for the new sorceress to return to London, and made polite application to become her apprentice. But the opportunity had dropped quite literally at her feet. Pearl had learned through painful experience to jump at any opportunity that presented itself. Opportunities never came around again. Ever.

"Why were you climbing out the window?" Mr. Carteret thumped her down on the settee and threw her skirts up.

Pearl pushed them back down again with a little screech, all too aware of the butler and footman. She pinned her skirts in place against Mr. Carteret's determination to fling them aside again, though she could only reach as far as her knees. Her ankles and bony shins were exposed to the world. Or the world inside the bobble-decked parlor.

McGregor sent the footman away. For clean water and a maid, Pearl hoped, rather than a doctor. Then he retreated with a clearing of his throat to the doorway. Mr. Carteret glanced up, then stopped trying to shove her skirts higher in the ridiculous tug-of-war. Push-of-war. Instead, he unbuttoned her boy's boot and removed it.

Pearl flipped her skirts over her shins, leaving the ankle exposed. Mr. Carteret already had her stocking foot in his hands, manipulating it this way and that.

"Do you actually know what you're doing?" she asked.

"Enough to know that if you'd broken anything, you'd be screaming." He twisted it in a new direction, and Pearl yelped.

She didn't intend to. But it hurt, and she didn't expect it. She yanked her foot from his grasp and hid it beneath her, tucking her skirts all around to keep them out of his clutches. "Brute."

"Very probably." He sprang to his feet and propped his hands on his hips, glowering down at her. The effect was quite different from when Mr. Tomlinson did it. "But I'm fairly certain you've only bruised your foot, rather than breaking or spraining the ankle. Now, if you would be so kind as to tell me why you felt it incumbent upon you to climb out the front window of my house like some schoolboy bent on mischief—though a schoolboy would have sense enough to climb out a *back* window."

Pearl blinked at him. "Are you angry?"

"Yes, damn it, I am. I don't like being angry. This is why I didn't want an apprentice. Because I have to get angry when they do stupid, boneheaded things like climbing out of windows six feet off the ground for no discernable reason at all." His voice had begun with a mild snap to it, but built in power and volume until he was almost, but not quite, shouting.

He seemed to hear the sound as it echoed around the red-on-red parlor, cocking his head to listen. The tension slid out of his body. "Bloody hell," he said gently.

Bewildered, Pearl put her feet on the floor and sat up to watch him stroll to the hallway door and bellow for McGregor.

"Yes, sir?" The butler stepped from his place of invisibility near the door inside the room.

"Tea." Mr. Carteret flourished a hand. "Go. Bring tea. Oceans of it. And scones. Or crumpets or cakes or whatever Cook's got at hand."

McGregor bowed and absented himself.

Mr. Carteret spun on his heel to face Pearl, an eyebrow rising in question. "Well?"

Oh. The window. Pearl rummaged in her pocket and pulled out the sadly crumpled apprenticeship papers. "I was going to bring you these at the jail, get them signed. Make things official."

Mr. Carteret held up his left hand, raised the forefinger, and waggled it up and down at her. "It's been sealed in blood. Don't see how much more official it can be."

"Well, I can." She limped toward him, papers out. "Signed, sealed, and registered with the council is *official.* This—" She waggled her own previously punctured finger at him. "Is *real.*"

"But why were you climbing out the window?" He sounded more bewildered than angry now. "There is a front door. For that matter, I have footmen. Any one of them could have delivered papers to the jail."

"Your blasted butler wouldn't let me out. Nor would he send a footman to deliver the papers. I was a prisoner in this room." She tried very hard to keep her voice matter-of-fact and free of emotion. She thought she did for the most part. "So I decided to climb out the window."

Another thing she'd learned in the past several years.

Her size meant that tackling obstacles head-on usually resulted in failure, but there was always a way around.

"Yes, but you knew I was on my way home."

Pearl goggled at him. "No, I didn't. How would I know? Mr. Tomlinson didn't think he could get you out before tomorrow. I was beginning to worry I might have to sleep in this dreadful parlor. How *did* you get out?"

"My father's solicitor came to obtain my release. I have been completely exonerated—"

"What? How?" She could scarcely believe it.

"Free as a bird. Cleared of all accusations by virtue of Mr. Archaios and his sensitive nose. Which you should know." He scowled at her, then spun on his heel and shouted for McGregor again.

"Yes, sir?" The butler stepped through the door, bearing an enormous, fully laden tea tray.

The cheerful rose-painted teapot that had served her earlier was retired in favor of imposing silver. Platters were piled high with fluffy scones and thick sandwiches and cakes and biscuits and so much food that it was clear Mr. Carteret's cook believed he'd been in jail for a week, starving, rather than most of the day, with sandwiches.

Pearl's mouth watered. Had she eaten lunch? She couldn't recall it, so she must not have. She seated herself, tucking her precious papers on her lap for safety, and began to pour. She'd learned how to play "mother" before . . . everything. She scarcely paid attention as Mr. Carteret began his inquisition of his butler concerning said butler's behavior. Apparently the stuffed-shirt had overstepped his bounds.

"That was not well done of you, McGregor," Mr. Carteret was saying.

"No, sir." The butler bowed again. "My utmost apologies, sir."

"It's not me you owe the apology, man. Miss Parkin is the injured party here. Apologize to her."

Both men looked at her, startling Pearl from her

domestic duties. She was holding a plate filled with teatime treats, she realized, and thrust it toward Mr. Carteret. He took it and sat on the sofa beside her.

McGregor bowed, deeper this time. "Apologies, Miss Parkin. It will not happen again."

"I should say not," Mr. Carteret grumbled.

It was not the most gracious, nor the most specific apology, but it was at least the words. Pearl did not want to make the man any more of an enemy than he already was. The reprimand in her presence had to smart. "Apology accepted, Mr. McGregor," she said. "And I hope that you will accept my apology for . . . being such a difficult guest."

"Of course." Another bow. McGregor's back had to be aching from all the bowing.

Mr. Carteret waved a languid hand at McGregor, dismissing him, and took an overlarge bite of scone. Pearl handed him a cup of tea, which he set on the serving table beside his plate, then she filled a cup and plate for herself. The sandwiches looked heavenly, and they were.

They chewed in companionable contentment for a time. Then Mr. Carteret plucked the apprenticeship contract from her lap. "Let's have a look, shall we?"

5

PEARL WATCHED HIM read, trying to guess by his expression where he was on the page, and occasionally glancing at the words to remind herself what they said. He read silently, without much expression other than the occasional frown.

His frown deepened. "That doesn't seem right."

She stretched her neck a bit further to see what he

was reading, but he stood in one of his lightning-flash moves and was across the room, using the pen she'd left out. Nervous, she followed.

He signed his name. She could tell because the pen scratched furiously across the page, like something he'd done thousands of times before. He turned then, and was brought up short when he almost stepped on her. Pearl scrambled back to a safe distance, but he beckoned her forward again.

"Come take a look." He spread the two sheets of the contract on the desk and urged her closer. Till her sleeve brushed against the open front of his coat.

"You forgot Victor." He pointed to where he'd added the name above the line with an arrow to indicate where it went. "And you forgot to pay yourself any wages."

"If you're providing room and board, I don't need wages."

"Blasphemy!" His exaggerated expression of horror made her laugh.

"The workman is worthy of his wages," Mr. Carteret intoned. "If you are paid nothing, people will assume you are worth nothing. As an apprentice magician, potentially an apprentice *sorcerer,* you, my dear, are worth a great deal. You will be able to work spells very few others can. You should be paid accordingly."

"Is that how you got so rich?"

"Absolutely." He winked at her, to devastating effect at such close range. "I am, after all, magister of the conjurer's guild." His expression lost its levity. "I can work spells many master conjurers are incapable of achieving, and I am paid quite well for the work that I do. Quite, quite well. Especially in matters of estate and entail."

Pearl had to look away. This much closeness became overwhelming in too short a time. She eased a step away, hoping for a more comfortable distance. He closed it.

"However," he said, "since I am after all supporting

you, as well as paying your wages until such time as you complete your apprenticeship and begin to cast your journeyman spells, I am only going to pay two pounds a week."

She choked and coughed to clear her throat. She'd sometimes lived on less than a shilling a week, and supported her father on it.

"And the amount you've written in for support is entirely inadequate, even if you share rooms with Elinor. This is Mayfair, not Whitechapel. You'll need at least double that." He showed her where he'd scratched out her number and written in another.

"Sir, you are too generous," she stammered.

"No, I'm not. I'm selfish and dissolute and disreputable, and I'd be ruining your reputation if you had one."

"Thank goodness I don't." Pearl took a step back. He was her magic-master.

"Thank goodness," he echoed, and took his own step back.

The contract was sent to Mr. Tomlinson with a note requesting he sign as witness and send it on to be registered with the council.

Pearl remained to finish her tea with Mr. Carteret. They were both yawning by the time the teapot went cold, so he sent her to Elinor's rooms with a footman as escort, with instructions to report back in the morning by nine o'clock to begin her first day as a magician's apprentice.

ELINOR WASN'T IN the flat when Pearl arrived, but the maid had apparently been prepared for her appearance. She helped Pearl wash her scrapes, then helped her into a too-large nightgown and into the high, soft bed. Pearl didn't wake until morning, when Elinor stirred beside her.

"How was your first day as a conjurer's apprentice?" Elinor asked sleepily.

"That's today. Yesterday doesn't count." Pearl sat up to rub the sleep from her eyes.

"I suppose it wouldn't." Elinor curled deeper into the blankets.

"Thank you for sharing your bed. And your flat. And your maid." Pearl slid out of bed, landing with a thump on the floor. It was a very high bed. She would need a stepstool.

"Happy to share." Elinor rolled over to peer at her. "You're not one of those dreadful persons who is bright and cheery first thing in the morning, are you?"

"No. I'm one of those who must get out of bed straightaway—though I don't want to—or I'll be worthless the rest of the day. I'm not particularly cheery about it. Or bright."

Elinor pulled the covers over her head against the dim light seeping through the windows as the maid brought in hot water. Pearl washed gingerly around her scraped elbows and knees, then picked up the borrowed dress and grimaced.

It didn't fit, and now it was torn at the elbow and down near the hem. But she had nothing else to wear, so she put it on atop the borrowed feminine undergarments. She needed to obtain some clothing of her own. Would Mr. Carteret give her the time, and advance her the funds to do so?

McGregor ushered her into the breakfast room where Mr. Carteret himself served her breakfast, piling her plate high with a bit of everything. She blushed to realize he'd noticed her voracious appetite.

"I don't suppose you'll actually grow if I feed you up," he mused, lounging in his chair again, watching her eat. "But a little feeding up ought to at least keep you from blowing away in a stiff wind. I'd have to lead you about on a string. Reel you in like a kite."

"That would be interesting," she said. "Flying like a kite."

"We'll have to attempt it sometime." He propped his chin on a pair of steepled fingertips. "If you survive it, then perhaps I could try."

She managed not to roll her eyes.

"I have a list," Mr. Carteret said when her plate was empty, drawing a sheet of folded paper from his coat pocket. "Of everything a young lady needs to be properly clothed. It seems a bit excessive to me—and probably is, since I requested it of my sister, the one who still speaks to me. But I believe if we cut it back by, say, a third, it ought to suffice. So when you are finished with your breakfast, we will begin."

We? Pearl cut her eyes at her magic-master. Did he intend to participate in the shopping? Men didn't do that. At least, her father and brothers never had. But she already had ample evidence that Mr. Carteret was nothing like them. He was unlike any man she'd met in her entire not-so-very-long life. Which, now that she considered it, was likely the source of her difficulty in thinking of him as she would any other man. He *wasn't*.

MR. CARTERET DID ACCOMPANY Pearl to the shops. Ordinary, middle-class shops, she insisted. His sister might be the daughter of a duke, but Pearl was not. She suspected, however, that Mr. Carteret directed his coachman to the upper crust of the middle-class shops.

His presence had the shopkeepers bowing and scraping, erasing the sneers Pearl could feel under their obsequious surfaces. He introduced her as his apprentice, but Pearl could see the shop girls roll their eyes and snicker among themselves when they took her to the back to measure her. The owner of the dress shop stopped their whispering, at least while they were in the same room, and sent them off to collect the correct sizes of undergarments from Mr. Carteret's sister's list.

Pearl's size was a problem, for few women were as

small as she. Ready-mades could be altered. New things could be made to measure, but Pearl needed something to wear *now*.

Even the simple hemming up of a skirt to the proper length was troublesome, because the voluminous skirts took forever to get all the way around. And stays were impossible, because her midriff was also short. Eventually the seamstress put together a bodice and skirt outfit from clothing meant for younger girls, removing the childish decoration. She found a capelet for warmth, to avoid the problems of fitting a jacket. Nothing matched, nor was it in the least bit fashionable, and the fit was "more or less," but Pearl was properly clothed.

More dresses were promised for the next day. The few garments that did fit—stockings and chemises, mostly—were bundled into the carriage, which followed in the street as Mr. Carteret walked Pearl to the milliner and the glover and the bootmaker. Pearl found herself captured between guilt and delight. She had once owned a wardrobe as extensive and rather more exquisite. But she had learned since that she didn't *need* silk stockings, and that delicate muslin was impractical for anyone who had work to do. When she pointed that out to her employer, he promptly added a dozen sturdy aprons to his purchases, which did not help the guilt aspect at all.

It felt utterly wrong for Mr. Carteret to be spending money on her with such abandon when she had blackmailed him into taking her as his apprentice. She would vow to pay him back from her wages, but he was paying those as well, wasn't he?

By the time Mr. Carteret declared the shopping expedition completed, Pearl was squirming in a perfect agony of self-reproach. She *would* pay him back, somehow.

He sent the carriage back to Elinor's flat with instructions to unload everything, hailed a cab, and handed her in. Pearl arranged her skirts and tugged her capelet a little closer about her. The day was cloudy, and chill from the damp, but at least the morning's drizzle had stopped.

The cab took them to the Magician's Council Hall, which took up an entire block at the edge of the ancient City, not far from Temple Bar. Pearl held her breath as he opened the door, a small one along the side facing Wych Street.

Nothing happened. No burst of smoke, or portentous disembodied voices came forth to bar her from the premises. It was simply an open door into a dark, narrow entry.

"Doesn't look like much, does it?" Mr. Carteret chuckled as he ushered her inside. "This is the working side of the council house, where the school and library are housed, and the Briganti and the council offices. The meeting hall faces St. Clement's."

Pearl opened her eyes wide to take in the tiniest detail. It probably didn't change her vision any, but it felt as if it could, so she did it, stretching and craning her neck to see in as many directions possible.

The building was old. *Ancient*. And cramped. A stairway rose to the right, only a few steps beyond the door, barely wide enough to get her petticoats through, she discovered when she followed Mr. Carteret up it. She didn't know how she would manage hoops when they came. Perhaps there was another, wider stair elsewhere in the building.

At the top, the stair let out onto a somewhat wider landing before turning to rise to the third floor. The carpet runner beneath their feet was faded purple and threadbare, though it was clean enough, given all the feet that walked upon it. The dark paneled walls, lit by a narrow window at either end, seemed oppressive to Pearl. But perhaps that was only her nervousness.

Mr. Carteret led her past the few scattered straight-backed chairs and an empty umbrella stand beyond the staircase leading upward, to a door that he flung open without ceremony. Like the gentleman he pretended not to be, he waited for her to enter.

Pearl looked out over a vast sea of male faces occupying the spacious room and swallowed hard. This was what she wanted, what she'd fought so hard for. To be able to walk into this room and do what they did. She would not fly the white flag now.

She drew herself to her full height and sailed through the door. Then she moved to the side to wait for Mr. Carteret. She didn't know where they were going, after all. Now that she looked for true, she could see the faces didn't quite make up a sea. Maybe twenty of them—maybe not that many. But it felt like a sea, and all of them staring gobsmacked at her.

The shock was beginning to leave them now, and the scowls to appear. Though not all of them scowled. Big, toothy grins spread across the faces of some of the young ones. Boys, considerably younger than her. Students relishing the potential for fireworks, most likely. The older men looked as if they'd been chewing lemons, their faces all screwed up and sour.

The room stretched deep into the building, with a fireplace at the inside end. Square, leather-upholstered armchairs, most of them occupied, sat in cozy groups around low tables scattered with books and magazines. Near the windows fronting Wych Street stood several long tables where students scratched away at their lessons. Though now, they all seemed to be staring at her.

As Pearl traversed the space on Mr. Carteret's arm, she had to look down to hide the smug smile rising on her face. It wasn't polite to rub it in, how pleased she was at her victory. Her skirt swished near one of the scowlers in the comfy chairs and he jerked his feet back as if afraid of contamination. She fought off a chuckle. They couldn't keep her out. She didn't have to go to their silly school. She was an apprentice, with a contract signed not just by a master magician, but by the magister of the conjurer's guild himself.

"How dare you?" The challenge came growling out of the chest of the very tall, thin man who stood to block their way.

Pearl assumed Mr. Carteret had been leading her to the door opposite the one through which they'd entered, for he stopped now that this other gentleman stood in front of it.

"Oh dear." Mr. Carteret turned up his feet to look at the soles of his shoes. "Have I tracked in muck again?"

"Don't be stupid, Carteret." The man's hands were curled tight into fists and anger shimmered off him in waves that Pearl could almost reach out and touch. "Though with you that's a difficult task, I realize. You know what I mean. How dare you bring that—that—"

"This?" Mr. Carteret made a graceful turn to peer down at Pearl, as if he'd never seen her before. "*This* is my apprentice. Pearl Parkin. Come to wander through the library, you know." His languid air of unconcern seemed to make the tall man more rabid.

"*That* is a female," he snarled. "Not an apprentice."

Mr. Carteret stepped back, folding one arm across his chest and raising the other to tap his pursed lips with a forefinger, as his gaze took another of those disconcerting trips up and down Pearl's form.

"You're right, Cranshaw," Mr. Carteret said. "She is most definitely female. Astute of you to notice, old chap. Most observant. But as for the other—she is also most definitely my apprentice. Signed in ink, filed with the registry, and—" He waggled his left forefinger at the man. "Sealed in blood."

Cranshaw went pale and staggered back a step. Was he one of those made ill at the sight, the *thought* of blood?

Mr. Carteret put out his arm again and Pearl looped her hand through it. "Come along, Parkin." He led the way around the Cranshaw person. To the right, which put him between Pearl and Cranshaw. Deliberately?

Through the door, with it safely shut behind them, Pearl found herself in the library Mr. Carteret had mentioned. It stretched two stories high and the depth of the building. Light sifted through windows set in the upper half of the walls on both sides. Ladders on wheels gave access to the bookcases between the windows, running past sturdy tables encircling the room. The center of the vast space was a maze of shelves, many of them bowed with the weight of the books resting there.

"And every single book is about magic." Mr. Carteret smiled down at her, as if it were perfectly natural to be reading her mind. "It still awes me," he said. "The amount of knowledge to be had in this room."

"Why are we here?" Pearl whispered. It didn't seem right to speak aloud in such a place.

"Ah." He took her hand and led her down the left-hand aisle, past the rows of tables with their sporadic clusters of readers and students, leaving a wave of whispers in their wake.

He turned into the central maze and strode briskly down a cross aisle to what Pearl calculated to be the absolute center of the library. Beneath a high skylight stood a square table, and on it lay four massive books, each facing one of the four sides of the table.

Leather bound, with elaborate latches locking them shut, the books looked and *felt* older than old. As if time itself had been young when these books were written. The book nearest Pearl showed a waterfall pouring over rock on its cover, the windblown spray seeming real enough to get her wet. Lightning slashed across one corner to ignite a little flame.

"Alchemy?" She tilted her head to indicate the book, afraid to point in this hallowed location.

Mr. Carteret nodded. "Take a closer look. At all of the books. Get a feel for them."

Pearl edged forward. "What is this place?"

"The library."

She smacked him with a scowl. "Not this place—" She gestured widely at the entire enormous room. "*This* place." She flipped her hand at the small space where they stood, at the table and the books.

"Ah. These . . ." Mr. Carteret waved his hand at the books. "These are the first books written in England concerning the four great magics. They're in old 'whan that Aprylle' Chaucerian English, so they're useless for studying, but they've been translated into modern English, and printed and reprinted, so that doesn't matter so much.

"What does matter is the magic. They're so old and so saturated with magic that they essentially *are* magic. Each its own variety. Only a magician with a talent for that type of magic can unlock a book. I can unlock the alchemy book, for instance, but it's a tremendous strain and it takes me forever and why would I want to, when it's so easy for me to open the volume on conjury?"

Even Mr. Carteret felt the weight of the age and magic in this small space, Pearl thought, since he spoke in the same quiet tones she'd used. "Why did you bring me here?"

"To determine where your talent lies. I am fairly certain already, but it has become tradition over the past century or so—perhaps since the last sorceress died—to bring each student here in the second year of study to test the locks. It could well have begun with a search for someone who could open the book of sorcery. At any rate, it's tradition now. And who am I to break with tradition?"

"The very one, I imagine," Pearl murmured.

"True." He shrugged. "Do it anyway. Because I want to know, and this is supposed to be the best way to be sure. Besides, we are flaunting tradition so mightily by making you an apprentice, it's likely best we follow as many of the other traditions as we can, to make your apprenticeship that much more traditional—and acceptable—to the old grumpuses in there." He tipped his head toward the other room.

Pearl had no real objection to doing what Mr. Carteret asked. His request and the reasoning behind it made sense. But the magic, the books themselves made her nervous.

Still, she hadn't come this far to back away in cowardice. She *did* have magic talent, and she *would* learn how to use it. No matter how many huge, frowning, weighty magical books she had to unlock.

"What do I do?" she asked. Not a delaying tactic at all.

"Walk around the table," Mr. Carteret instructed. "It might help if you moved a trifle closer to it. Look at the books. Listen to them. Pay attention to how they make you feel. And if there's one you want to try to open, then do so."

She took a step toward the table, then looked back over her shoulder at her magic-master. "What will you be doing?"

"Waiting." He leaned against the nearest bookcase and folded his arms. "Right here."

That was all right, then. She wouldn't have to go wandering through the bookcase maze to find him afterward. It wasn't at all because her stomach went tight and squeezy at the thought of being all alone with these books. Or only a little.

Pearl took two more steps toward the table and looked down at the alchemy book. She could just barely feel it booming somewhere off deep and far away. Remote and uninteresting.

She moved around the table to her right. The cover of the next book was blank. It was a deep unfaded black and had nothing at all on it. Or did it? Pearl leaned to the side to look down at it from an angle and saw shadows, texture. Her hand rose as if to touch it, and she looked up at Mr. Carteret, who had crossed his ankles now, as well as his arms. "Should I?"

His expression didn't change, remained as pleasantly, annoyingly blank as before. "Do you want to?"

Sort of. But sort of not. She brushed her fingertips across the cover and a shivery whisper slithered through her. She could feel symbols impressed into the leather, could feel the magic they held, but it was . . . thin. Wispy. Not quite real. Not quite right.

The next book had a naked woman on the front cover, staring out at the world. She stood with her feet balanced under her, arms down, palms facing forward, her hair falling straight down her back. A man stood behind her and to one side, his image indistinct but unmistakable.

Pearl realized she was tracing the images with her fingertips. The magic felt warm, safe—like home. Like home before everything had happened.

She wanted to open this book, but she also wanted to see the other one, so she walked around the table to the fourth side to the book of wizardry.

The cover of this one was a riot of flowers and trees and foliage. Pearl spied a little bird perched in one of the trees, and the face of a fox almost hidden beneath the foxgloves, but it was the flowers that dominated. Here, the magic felt warm and friendly. Inviting. But not *right*. Not like the book with the woman on it, the book of sorcery.

She went back to it, licking her thumb as she did. The latch might be stiff if it hadn't been opened in a century or so. But it flipped right open when she pushed this toggle and pulled at that one.

"Brava!" Mr. Carteret kept his shout quiet, but it was a shout nonetheless, echoing into the upper reaches of the library. He bounded around the table, captured both her hands in his, and kissed them, which left Pearl feeling all fluttery. "Apprentice sorcerer you are so proclaimed."

He tucked her arm through his and led her down the cross aisle in a new direction, so quickly she had to scurry to keep up with him. "We need sorcery desperately, you know." He sounded gleeful, triumphant. "And now I have found one more. Or rather, you have found me, if we wish to be truthful. And we can get at the sorcery books in the library, or you can get at them."

Mr. Carteret turned to the left again, toward the side of the room opposite where they'd come in. When they reached the corner, where the wall with windows met the wall without, he stopped and looked up at the portrait hanging there on the windowless wall. "That was our last sorceress."

6

THE PAINTING WAS enormous, the figures in it life-size. They looked as if they might step out of the painting at any moment. Pearl hoped they didn't. The woman, for all her dainty, caramel-and-cream curvaceous beauty, did not look like someone pleasant to know. Her expression exuded power. "She looks rather frightening."

"So she does. All that power, I think." Grey was staring thoughtfully up at the portrait when Pearl cast a sideways glance in his direction. "Amanusa—the new sorceress—is nothing like that one. Amanusa's quite tall and fair. Utterly different sort of beauty. She's got power as well, but hers is more 'Do not dare to harm the innocent,' rather than 'Do not dare to cross me.'"

He paused, his eyes on the portrait, but gazing at something far away. Pearl's heart twisted a little and she sat on it. No thumping *or* twisting allowed. Mr. Carteret's thoughts and feelings were none of her nevermind.

"Her power is so very fierce," he mused, startling Pearl out of her own musing. "She wouldn't harm you unless you needed it, but, well . . . Fierce, very fierce." He sounded as if he admired such power, and the woman who wielded it.

Pearl didn't want to think about it anymore. "Who is the man in the painting? He's so deep in the shadows, you can scarcely see him."

"Oh, that's Jax. Amanusa's husband." Mr. Carteret took a step closer and peered with her into the painted shadows. "He looks exactly like that. Different clothes, of course."

The pair in the painting wore the high, pleated ruffs and elaborate clothing of the wealthy in the Tudor reign. They looked terribly uncomfortable to Pearl. The man's features were clear, once you noticed him standing in the shadows behind the woman poised on the thronelike chair.

"It's the same man?" Pearl managed to shove aside her disbelief and speak. "The one in the painting and the one—the new sorceress's husband?"

"One and the same. As for how—" He gestured at the books in the library behind them. *"Magic."*

"Oh." Pearl stared at the man in the painting awhile longer.

He cleared his throat. "Books. That's what we're about. Since you are an apprentice sorcerer, and I am a conjurer who is also your magic-master, we shall begin with books, as I have no lessons to teach you, other than general magical principles."

Mr. Carteret stepped to the nearest shelf and gestured. *"Beginning Sorcery* seems a good place to begin. If you will collect your book, Miss Parkin."

"Yes, sir." She pulled the book with BEGINNING SOR-CERY printed in gold on its wide, dark brown spine, and opened it. The print inside was thick and black and—

"No time for that now. Bring it along. We've got one

more to collect." This time he strode ahead, leaving her to keep up as best she could. It was a bit better than being towed behind him, but not much.

"Here it is." Mr. Carteret plucked a book from a bottom shelf on the outside, near the entrance to the library. "*Basic Magic Theory*. Getting through these two ought to occupy your time well enough. Come along."

The library desk was directly across from the shelving where he had found the second book, along the wall that backed up to the lounge, the room they'd come through to get in here.

The librarian's fluffy white eyebrows raised nearly as high as his fluffy white hair when he saw the books Pearl hefted onto the high counter. Not because she was female, but because the book was sorcery. No one had taken a sorcery book out in ages, he informed her. He had to make up a card for it, since they hadn't used cards the last time the book had been touched.

"Onward, Parkin." Mr. Carteret gestured toward the library door when they were done. "Things to do. People to see. Spirits to conjure."

Mr. Carteret led her back through the common room, as he named it, and down the stairs. But rather than heading back out the door to Wych Street, he turned the opposite direction into the depths of the building.

Men of all shapes, sizes, and ages scurried and strode hither and yon on various types of business, and every single one of them stared at Pearl as she passed. Some stopped to stare. Some kept walking, their heads swiveling like owls as they passed, to keep her in sight. Some scowled. Some smiled and nodded. Some gaped like schoolboys. Pearl just hefted her books higher and hurried to keep up with her magic-master as they journeyed back to the hallway where she'd been with Elinor and Magister Tomlinson.

He went through a door ahead, then stuck his head back out. "Hurry up, Parkin. We've only got the day."

She slipped through the door and stopped just inside to catch her breath. Mr. Carteret was across the large room, speaking to the men clustered around him. Brawny, athletic types, most of them. They clapped him on the shoulder and laughed out loud—just to see him again, Pearl thought. These men liked him. They were glad he'd been exonerated.

Other men rose from the desks arranged in concentric arcs around the room, centered on the desk where Mr. Carteret stood at the far side of the room. Filing drawers lined the walls, and a freestanding chalkboard with cryptic notes and diagrams drawn on it blocked much of the light from the window behind that desk. Gas lamps on the walls made up for the blockage.

As her breath caught up with her, Pearl noticed awareness of her presence rippling through the room. Those nearest the door saw her first, and their staring drew the attention of those just beyond, which captured the next, all the way through the chamber, until everyone stared at her, except Mr. Carteret and the man to whom he spoke.

One of the nearest magicians, a young, freckled, curly headed fellow, cleared his throat. "Excuse me, miss, but I'm afraid you've made a wrong turn somewhere." He came around his desk and made as if to take her burden. "If you'll allow me to escort you back to—"

"Parkin!" Mr. Carteret had finally looked up from his conversation. "What are you doing, lollygagging about? Get yourself over here where you belong."

"Yes, Magister." Pearl smiled sweetly, and a little smugly, at the young man—a wizard, she thought—and hurried through the maze of furniture to her magic-master's side.

He set her books on the edge of his desk, then laid his hand on her shoulder. It made her shiver. "All right, you louts, harken here. This is my apprentice, Miss Pearl Parkin. She will be studying sorcery. If you are not already aware, I am telling you now. Sorcery plays an essential role in the investigation of crimes and in the administration of justice.

"Yes, she is female. Sorcerers generally are. So I don't want any larking about. Flirt on your own time. When we are working an investigation, all of you will maintain a professional and businesslike attitude at all times, when Miss Parkin is present, and when she is not.

"With the return of sorcery, gentlemen—the knife-edge of justice—we will be working more and more often with women. Best you begin to learn how from this moment. If you do not feel that you can, I'll gladly transfer you back to Enforcement Branch."

Mr. Carteret looked down at Pearl. She looked back, all atremble. Her dreams were coming true more fully than she had ever thought possible. "Parkin." He waved a hand toward the men in the office. "The Briganti. Investigations Branch."

"Sir—" One of the men spoke up—not Freckle Face. "Don't you agree that Investigations is a dangerous business? Shouldn't she study elsewhere?"

"I am her master of magic, Meade. How can I teach her if she is elsewhere?"

"Exactly my point, sir." Meade was a tall, earnest-looking fellow with a Midlands accent. "Investigations is too dangerous for a female, much less an apprentice."

Mr. Carteret's smile was thin. "I think you will find, Mr. Meade, that Parkin is not nearly so helpless as you might think." That thin smile twisted, conceding additional amusement. "For while, as her magic-master, it is my duty to protect my apprentice, she protected me from harm on one of the worst of London's streets, while a murder victim was disposed of a short distance away. Besides—"

His gaze and tight smile traversed the room. "Surely you do not mean to say that none of you would assist me in the defense of my apprentice?"

A rumble of denial rose, with "Of course not, sir," flying over the top from Mr. Freckles.

"Thank you, Ferguson. I'm sure Miss Parkin is grateful to know she can rely on you." His gaze raked over the group again. "On all of you. Now—to business. The murder of Angus Galloway. What do we know?"

While the Briganti scattered to collect their papers, Mr. Carteret pinned Pearl with his predator's gaze and gestured from her books to a nearby chair. Obviously he intended for her to begin reading while he conducted his investigation.

She laid the books side by side and looked up to see if Mr. Carteret had any suggestions for the order of reading. He was busy erasing the chalkboard, which, now that she looked more closely at it, had some rude drawings at the bottom. She picked up the sorcery book and settled into the chair, hiding her amusement. She'd seen worse.

The book was written in the "methinks," "doths," and "hast thous" of Shakespeare or the King James Bible. It was slow reading. Especially since the reports from Mr. Carteret's investigating Briganti were so much more interesting.

The reports were mostly information delivered from the regular police when Magistrate Bellowes signed his transfer warrant. Results of the questioning of the people present when the body was discovered: No one noticed anything out of the ordinary until they saw the corpse. Results of questioning the neighborhood residents: The same. No one saw, heard, or sensed anything at all.

Mr. Carteret fanned the sides of his frock coat, pushing them out of the way to set his hands on his hips as he frowned down at the floor. He paced a few steps. Pearl tucked her feet under her chair to get them out of his way, but he stopped before he reached her. He stood so

long there beside her chair that she looked up and found
him looking back down at her.

"You were there, Pearl," he said. "In the street. In the
alley around the corner where you found me. What—"

"I found you before that," she interrupted him. It
seemed to be important, that she be precise. "I followed
you there."

"To that alley off Green Bank? From where?"

"Whitechapel Road. Near Red Lion Street." She
closed the book. She'd only gotten three pages into it.
This was more important. "I thought at first you were
drunk, but now that I've had time to think, I'm not so
sure. I believe it was more likely strong spirits affecting
you than strong drink."

He rewarded her pun with a crooked smile. "Why do
you think that?"

She frowned. Why indeed? She picked her way
through her thoughts as she spoke them. "Because, you
staggered, but not in a drunk's— A drunkard is loose
and—" She shook her arms, all her joints and muscles
limp. "Floppy, sort of. He goes reeling and flopping and
sprawling all over the street. You didn't."

She thought some more, bringing up her memories of
that night, only two nights and an eternity ago. "You
staggered because I don't think you could see what was
there, where you were walking. You walked all peculiar,
too. Hunched over, like you were hurt. Every so often,
you would jerk and stumble, as if you'd just run into
something, but nothing was there for you to run into. You
walked down the precise middle of the road. You lost
your hat one of those times, you jerked so violently."

"Thank you for fetching it for me." He gave her a little bow, his forehead creasing in a small frown as he did
so. "Why ever did you follow me? Do you ordinarily go
about assisting well-dressed drunkards?"

"No, sir. Hardly ever. Never, in fact. Well, once. He was

very young, sir, and lost, and he'd caught Bill Savage's eye, so I hid him and made sure he got back safe to his friends. But that was only the once."

One of those black angel-wing brows of his flew upward. "And I seemed lost and defenseless to you as well?"

"Oh, hardly." A delicious shiver slithered through Pearl as she recalled how she'd felt. "Not lost, and definitely not defenseless. Not until you lost consciousness. Even hurt and staggering, you appeared quite dangerous."

The other brow joined the first and Mr. Carteret looked down at her in astonishment. "Then why did you follow me?"

"Because you're Mr. Greyson Carteret, magister of the conjurer's guild. I recognized you. I'd followed you before." She let her voice go very quiet. "But I never had the courage to approach before."

"Yes. Well. You're my apprentice now, so it's done." He seized a chair from a nearby desk, dragged it over to Pearl, and sat in it backward, folding his arms across the back and resting his chin on them as he thought. He straightened before he spoke, but didn't unfold his arms.

"We'll go out to retrace my steps later. There may be some significance in them. Ferguson—" His voice rose to carry across the chamber to the desk near the door. "You'll come with us. You've the keenest magic sense."

"Yes, sir." Ferguson was the young freckled man who'd first addressed her, Pearl recalled. He was the only Briganti who'd addressed her directly.

"Is that why he's a Briganti?" Pearl kept her voice quiet, not sure if her question might be considered an insult or not. "Even though he's a wizard?"

"Partly. He's very clever, and he can work a bit of conjury as well, so it's all to the good. Besides, I think it's useful to have all the schools of magic represented. Now—" Mr. Carteret tapped her book to focus her attention. "Now, Pearl, I want you to tell me what happened when I fell, and what you saw and heard while you waited with me in that alley. Can you remember?"

"I'd been carrying your hat for a bit," she began. "You'd lost it in Wellclose Square, when you went through there. You went all the way through to the dock and around it, right next to the wall on Pennington Street, and down between the two docks—London and East London, not St. Catherine's—toward the river, jerking and lurching and stumbling all the way."

Pearl looked away from those dark, mesmerizing eyes of his. They were too compelling. "I was astonished you were still standing, still moving. I'd never seen any drunk so unsteady on his feet who could keep walking. You stumbled all the way along Green Bank to Bird Street, by the basin, and back toward the dock, to Tench Street, and came at the alley from that end. You were—" She stopped to clear her throat. Those nearest them didn't bother to pretend they weren't listening.

"Go on," Mr. Carteret said gently. "I cannot be offended, nor can I be embarrassed."

"It's not—" Pearl broke off, then leaned forward to whisper. "It's *my* shame that silences me. I am ashamed of what I thought."

"You cannot be faulted for thinking what anyone would have. Please. Continue. Tell us what you observed, and we will draw our own conclusions."

"The last little bit—up Bird Street and around Tench and down the alley—it's mostly warehouses there, you know. And you were leaning on the buildings while you walked, sometimes with your hand, sometimes with your shoulder. And you jerked." Pearl demonstrated, flinging her head back so violently, her bonnet shifted askew. She straightened it.

"As if—" She jerked her head again as she had seen Mr. Carteret jerking that night, trying to fit things together. "It looked as if you'd been struck," she said slowly. "Like someone *hit* you each time you lurched, or jerked, or staggered. And there at the end, you made noises each time. A sort of strangled shout. But you wouldn't stop moving. You kept walking and walking, holding onto the wall. Until you gave a choking cough and toppled into the gutter."

She bit her lip, staring into his deep, dark, mysterious eyes again. Eyes that stared back at her. "I was afraid you were dead. But you weren't. So I turned your face, so you wouldn't drown, and put a 'don't-look' spell over you, and waited for you to wake up."

"What happened while you waited? What did you see? What did you hear?"

"Water dripping, mostly. There was that slow drizzly rain that night, that didn't stop till almost sunup."

"What else?"

"I'm thinking." She didn't snap at him, quite. "I didn't *see* anything. Except for rats and the cats that hunted them."

"What did you hear?"

Pearl shrank a little into herself. She didn't want to remember, didn't want to think about it. But she had to. "I tried very hard not to see or hear anything."

"But you did." His voice was all silken threat. Or was it a promise?

Miserable, she nodded. "I heard the Bow bells toll twice—too faint to count the strikes, but we'd been there just over an hour, I figure. And I heard noises. A horse over on the Green Bank. It was nervous and blowing, and the man with it kept cursing it, but quietly. I only caught a few of the words, and very rude they were, too," she said primly.

"What else?" Mr. Carteret leaned toward her, over the chair's straight back. His hand held on to one of hers. When had that happened? She appreciated the comfort, or encouragement, or whatever it was.

"The horse's hooves on the cobblestones—it was misbehaving, I'm sure, there was so much clattering. And it neighed. A . . . thud. Soft, but loud. Loudish. Like a great sack of grain dumped on the ground, maybe. More cursing, very quiet. The cursing went on a fair while—and it moved off. Horse, too." She was curled up into a tiny ball, she realized, except for the hand clutching Mr. Carteret's. She forced herself to uncurl and look at him. "I didn't know I heard so much."

"You were trying very hard not to." The silk in his voice soothed her this time, but it still gave her chills.

"I heard Angus Galloway's body being disposed of, didn't I?" she said very quietly. She wanted to curl up and make herself small again, but refused to allow it. She couldn't stop her voice from becoming small, though.

"I think it's likely, yes." Mr. Carteret rubbed his thumb over the back of her hand. Pearl didn't think he knew it. She ought to tell him, but if he knew, she would feel foolish.

"Why did he dump the body on the street?" she asked as a distraction. For herself. "The river was right there, just a few more steps away. Would have been easy as easy and the body not found for ages, if ever. On the street, it was sure to have been found—well, when it was."

"I imagine he meant to use the river," he said, distractedly, "but the horse was uncooperative. Horses don't like dead bodies. Likely it tossed the body off and our murderer decided to leave it lying there rather than try to convey it the remaining distance and risk being seen."

"D'you suppose anyone did see?" One of the Briganti spoke, an older man with a country accent, and Pearl was snatched back to awareness.

There were others in the room. Ten or twelve of them. Enough that she was not alone with Mr. Carteret, much as it might have seemed. Subtly, she hoped, she reclaimed her hand and folded it in her lap with the other.

"That is what you shall discover, Rollins." Mr. Carteret sprang up from his chair in a whirl of flying coattails. "Spread the word among your contacts. Usual terms. Sixpence for information, another shilling if it's verified. Do *not* stint their pay, Rollins. This is magic we're hunting, and even the maddest-sounding rumor can have an element of truth. The branch can stand the expenditure of a few pence in the hunt for a murderer."

"Still think we could get the same results for tuppence," Rollins muttered. He was perhaps ten years older than Mr. Carteret, Pearl thought, but deferred to him willingly. Of course, Mr. Carteret was the better conjurer of the two, so that was as it should be.

"Go on. Get started." Mr. Carteret waved a hand at the man and Rollins departed.

The other men in the room received their orders next. A good many were investigating other crimes and Mr. Carteret kept them at it. Pearl got another page of her book read.

"All right then, Parkin, Ferguson, let's be off." Mr. Carteret clapped his tall top hat on his head while Pearl scrambled from her chair and collected her other book.

Her magic-master took it from her and handed it to a passing clerk of the nonmagical sort as they left the room. "Have this delivered to my house straightaway."

"I'll carry that." Mr. Ferguson held his hand out for her sorcery book.

"Miss Parkin can carry her own book, Ferguson," Grey said.

"But thank you." Pearl flicked a smile at the young wizard as she marched after Mr. Carteret, wondering why she couldn't let him carry it for her. Still, her magic-master had spoken.

"It's quite large and bulky." Ferguson smiled earnestly at her. "Why not use the beast of burden—me—while it is available?"

She looked hopefully toward Mr. Carteret.

"She needs the book as ballast to weight her down so she doesn't blow away in those skirts." Mr. Carteret led the way into the street, a much quicker exit than she'd expected until she realized they'd come out a different door. The door they'd gone in was a good thirty yards down the street.

"The wind isn't blowing," Ferguson said, tugging his gloves on. He held his hand out for the book again.

"Leave it," Carteret snapped, his voice hard and cold. "It's a book on sorcery. Just leave it alone."

"Sir." Ferguson looked down, clasped his hands together behind his back, as if to avoid temptation.

Pearl frowned. "Why does that matter, sir?"

Carteret looked down at her, eyebrow arching high, then nodded. "Didn't tell you, did I? Beg pardon. You might notice that while I retrieved the magic theory book for you, there in the library, I had you collect your beginning sorcery book yourself.

"You see, just as those ancient books of magic in the center of the library are sealed against those who cannot practice that school of magic, so each quadrant of study is protected. Along the outer edges, protection is so minimal that virtually anyone can pick up the books on the simplest, most elementary beginnings of the practice of that particular magic."

He stepped into the street to hail a cab. "However, when Yvaine of Braedun was murdered in 1636—a date we've all had to memorize in school—and women vanished from the ranks of the Magician's Council of England, the books of sorcery—*all* of the books of sorcery, even the simplest—became inaccessible.

"Which is why I had you collect the sorcery book. I had no desire for another nasty shock. Oh yes, I've tried. All the schoolboys try at one point or another, and all of them fail. Until now. Until you."

"An electric shock?" Pearl didn't like that idea.

"Something like. But nastier. And—not so shocking. Not such a physical jolt. Less harmful, more unpleasant."

"I . . . see." It appeared she would have to continue to carry the book herself. Perhaps she could get a basket. Pearl stepped beside him as a cab pulled up. "Are we going now to retrace your steps?"

"Later. First—" He looked at the sky to gauge the height of the moon, but clouds blocked his view with a high, ruffled grayness. "I want to see if I might have a word with Mr. Galloway."

"A word—oh. You want to conjure his spirit?"

"He's likely still a ghost. Murder victims usually are." Grey turned to assist Pearl into the cab and found Ferguson already there, offering his hand, blast the man.

Of course, that was precisely why he was bringing him, to act as a buffer between Grey and his apprentice. This was why females shouldn't apprentice to male magicians. Because male magicians were such strutting beasts, they could not keep their minds on the magic and off the dainty charms of their apprentices. Except the buffer in question, young Ferguson, only made Grey more of a snorting, pawing beast, one who wanted to knock the younger stag aside and take the lady's delicate hand into his own.

Grey satisfied his beast by taking the seat beside Pearl—Miss Parkin—and forcing Ferguson to sit opposite, facing backward.

"Can conjurers call ghosts?" Pearl tipped her head so he could see her face beneath that awful bonnet. "How are ghosts different from spirits? Are they?"

Grey found himself explaining yet again. Too few members of the public were aware of—or cared about—the differences. "Ghosts are earthbound, trapped here for one reason or another. Spirits have ascended, and simply come back to visit now and again.

"Because of the violence or other conditions that trap

them, ghosts are uncontrollable, usually irrational, and often dangerous because of it. Conjurers must ward against ghosts, control when and where and how they appear. Spirits however, if they are willing, will work with a conjurer to do magic."

Usually it irritated him, having to explain about ghosts and spirits, because he had to do it so often. This time, it didn't. Because Pearl was his apprentice and it was his duty to instruct her. His lack of annoyance was emphatically not due to the fact that she had her face turned up to him and those amazing two-toned eyes fastened upon him the entire time he spoke.

"Ah." She smiled and sat back in her seat, turning her face away so all Grey could see was the top of her straw bonnet with its red ribbon trim.

She continued to smile, or so he assumed, for Ferguson suddenly acquired a smarmy grin. Did neither one of them remember Grey's admonition against flirtation?

"Have you been with the Briganti long, Mr. Ferguson?"

"Call me James, please."

Still, it was better that she flirted with James Ferguson than with Grey. Wasn't it?

"I was invited to join Investigations," Ferguson said, "while I was still at school. At Magister's College in Oxford. Because of my magic sense, you see."

Braggart. Or was it bragging if it was true? Grey couldn't remember. Slander was still slander if it was true. Bragging was likely the same.

"Why is that important?"

Flirt, flirt, flirt. Except she wasn't flirting. She was simply asking questions. It was Grey's mental state that turned ordinary conversation into flirtation.

"He can sense all the magics." The words came out of Grey's mouth without his conscious intent. "I can't sense wizardry very well, and am utterly awful at sorcery, at recognizing its presence. Ferguson can sense them all."

"So I can track the path of a spell," the man in question

said. "If the magister was bespelled that night, it's possible that I can pick up the traces." Ferguson looked entirely too smug for Grey's comfort.

"We should bring in the Greek," Grey said, just to see the other man squirm. "Nikos Archaios can determine who worked which spell simply by . . . sniffing around. Perhaps he has some tricks to teach you while he is in England, yes?"

"I would be delighted to learn whatever Mr. Archaios can teach me."

If Ferguson was off learning from Archaios, he couldn't be in the way—he couldn't chaperone—couldn't *buffer* Grey's interactions with Pearl. Maybe Elinor would. Maybe Grey would resent Elinor less than he resented Ferguson.

7

THE CAB PULLED to a halt and Grey hopped out. Ferguson descended behind him and both men turned to hand Pearl out of the carriage. She blushed when she saw them both with their outstretched hands. The blush didn't show on her face, except for right at the edge, near her ears, almost hidden by the bow tying her bonnet on. The blush tightened things inside Grey that did not need any more tightening.

"Come, come." He beckoned with his fingers and she put her hand in his, clutching that oversized volume to her with her other arm. Grey did not smile triumphantly at Ferguson, nor did he gloat. Gloating was common and not done by gentlemen. Too bad Grey hadn't been a gentleman in ages.

Ferguson didn't appear to notice the lack of gloating.

He was too busy catching hold of Pearl's elbow and keeping that blasted book from overbalancing her.

"Thank you, James." She grinned at him, at Ferguson. *James.* Did she wink? At least it wasn't a shy, blushing, flirtatious "I like you" smile. No, it was a cheeky, winking, flirtatious "I like you" smile. If she had winked. Had she?

"I daresay that book is larger than you are." Ferguson flirted back, the bounder.

"*Parkin.*" Grey did not bark her name. He was not a dog. He never barked. "Ferguson. Our corpse is not getting any fresher."

"Yes, sir." They both said it as they stopped looking at each other and looked at him.

Grey led the way inside. He never liked coming here, descending into the miasma of misery and ghosts draped along its walls. The hospital wasn't so bad, but the basement—where they brought the bodies of murder victims and suicides and all the other stray corpses that turned up every day—the basement was dreadful. Thank goodness Pearl wasn't sensitive to spirits.

In the hallway outside the stairs leading down, Ferguson caught Grey's arm and stopped him, virtually leaping around as if to block the way.

"You're not taking her down *there,* are you?" Ferguson said in a hoarse stage whisper.

Grey stopped his automatic retort. Ferguson, and Pearl as well, needed to understand. "Yes, Mr. Ferguson, I am. I must."

"Good God, sir." The wizard still spoke in his whisper, as if Pearl did not stand right there beside him, as if she should be protected from even hearing this discussion. "There are *bodies*—things too horrible— She should not see such things. They are too awful. Too much."

Grey nodded, doing his best to appear wise and thoughtful, though he was much better at dissolute and disreputable. "That is entirely possible, that it will be too awful for her to bear. But she will be a sorceress, Ferguson. Sorcery can see inside the black hearts of men and relive their worst deeds. If it is too terrible for her, we should know it now, so she can flinch away and guide her magic toward sorcery's gentler side."

Ferguson blinked, as if it had never occurred to him that sorcery might have a gentler side.

"Sorcery has its own healing arts," Grey said with a sardonic smile. "That also I have seen."

"I want to go." Pearl spoke up, startling both men.

Even though they'd been talking about her, they'd both forgotten she was there. Or rather, her presence hadn't been forgotten, but they'd treated her like some life-size figurine without a mind and a will of her own. As if their decision would determine what she did and where she went.

Which all too often was the case. Men treated women like dolls to be moved about here and there at their masculine whim. With the power of sorcery returning, that would have to change.

"I have already seen many terrible things," Pearl said. "I have seen bodies pulled from the river and—worse. I am going."

Grey lifted an eyebrow as he gave Ferguson a significant look. "Do not make the mistake of thinking that because a woman is small, she is also weak."

The admonishment was for the both of them. Grey had forgotten it several times already just today.

He flung open the door and led the way down the dark stone steps, walking sideways to help Pearl with her book-balancing problem. "Set your book there." He indicated the writing table at the foot of the stairs. "No one will disturb it."

Grey and the wizard set their top hats and gloves on the table with the book.

"Ferguson, go open the cellar doors for a little fresh air. However much might be available here." Grey indicated the slanted double doors at the back of the cavernous room.

Bodies lay on planks lined up in rows throughout the space, in various stages of death and decomposition, most of them covered with a coarse drape. Now that Pearl had deposited her book on the table, she had both her hands over her nose.

"I don't know that it's any better breathing through your mouth," Grey said quietly. "The taste lingers."

"If I might—" Ferguson drew a flask from an inside pocket and opened it. He splashed a bit of liquid on the floor in the center of the room and the stink began to dissipate, replaced with a strong smell of mint and chrysanthemums. Not exactly pleasant in itself, but better by far than the odor of death.

"Thank you, Ferguson." Grey drew his pencil box from his inner coat pocket. "That seems quite a splendid potion for a job like this one. I hate to have you spending your time brewing it up for the office. Can I assume it's easily purchased from any qualified wizard?"

"Not easy at all, sir. Not this potion. There's others, lighter scents that can clear out faint mildew and such, but this one, against something so strong as—" Ferguson waved his hand at the bodies in their rows. "It *can* be purchased, at a steep price. Or I can brew it for I-Branch."

"Can you teach it? To Tomlinson's apprentice, perhaps?"

"Miss Tavis, sir?" Ferguson seemed taken aback. "I-I suppose. Yes, sir. I'm sure I can."

"Do so, then. As soon as can be arranged."

Grey strode toward the table where Angus Galloway lay in state. It stood alone, set apart from the others perhaps because it was so obviously a magical murder. The magic, if any lingered, couldn't hurt the other corpses, but the living had to work among them, at least to carry them out again for burial. The body was covered entirely with a drape. It would become his shroud if no one claimed his body.

"No doubt it's him, is there?" Pearl said, so quiet it just missed being a whisper. "Even though we can't see him under that sheet. The magic vibrates around him in such an angry buzz."

"Is that what you sense?" Grey asked as he opened his case. He watched Pearl, curious to see her reaction.

"Yes, don't you?"

"Everyone senses magic differently, and I believe—" He looked at Ferguson. "Those who can sense more types of magic often sense each of them differently. Am I correct?"

"Yes, sir. It works that way for myself, at any rate." Ferguson drew nearer, but still hovered behind Pearl. Maybe he intended to catch her if she fainted. As if she would.

"The buzzing is rather overwhelming, sir." Ferguson shook his head and backed away a step. "I can't— If there is other magic, I cannot sense it through this—this *anger*."

Grey heard voices. Shouting and weeping and so much outrage it was difficult to think. This many ghosts in a confined, dark space could cause trouble even in daylight. Quickly he selected a bit of chalk and marked a simple symbol on the floor. *"Quiet,"* he said forcefully. "I'll let you know when it is your turn to speak."

"Y-yes, of course, sir," Ferguson stammered.

"Not you, Ferguson." Grey flung a hand toward the rows of bodies. *"Them.* They're setting up a horrific clamor. Always do in places like this, especially when there's someone who can hear them. Most of those poor souls are quite unhappy about their circumstances. Did that help eliminate the buzz?"

Ferguson tipped his head, considering. "Slightly, sir.

There is still . . ." He shook his head, as if to clear it. "This is my first murder, sir. It's— I've never sensed it so strong. Not conjury or alchemy or—" His eyes rolled back in his head and he collapsed. Fainted dead away.

Even as Grey leaped to catch him, he couldn't help thinking, *Oh, that won't impress her by half, fainting at the scent of sorcery.*

Pearl was there to lift his head, but before she could cradle it in her lap, Grey had an apron off a hook and folded to place there under the fainted wizard's head.

"Too much blood," Grey said. "Too much sorcery for one who's never encountered so much before. Do you remember when you drew it in, there in Green Bank, when our victim was found?" He took Pearl's hand and lifted her to her feet, leaving Ferguson sprawled on the brick floor. "You need to do it again here."

She nodded. "Yes, all right." Her hands twitched, fingers stretching and curling in again. She looked at Ferguson. "Shouldn't we move him?"

"Where? There's nowhere else to put him. He's comfortable enough there."

Pearl seemed dubious. "He doesn't look comfortable. Perhaps we should call someone from upstairs?"

"Calling in the magic would do him more good."

Biting her lip, she reluctantly turned her back on Ferguson. Grey wondered if he should have the man hauled off, since worry over his welfare distracted her so.

"Why is there so much?" she asked. "If it comes from innocent blood, wouldn't there be more where the blood was spilled, rather than here?"

"I don't know. Perhaps you should consult your book."

"I shall." She paused and tilted her head, then looked across the few feet of space toward the other bodies. "It's not all from him."

"No." Grey wasn't surprised. The number of shrieking ghosts hinted at it.

"Should I gather up the rest of it, the angry magic?"

"I think so, yes. If you can. Don't overstrain yourself. But if you can, Ferguson will be grateful."

"Oh. Yes, of course." She turned worried eyes on the fallen man a moment before stretching out her fingers again, while Grey cursed himself roundly for reminding her of Ferguson's existence, and then cursed again for caring. Why was he so fascinated with this one small woman?

Pearl drifted across the room, her eyes not quite focused, a hand raised as if to ward off something, or draw it in. "This one," she said, touching a table. "Murdered. And this one. And her as well."

She floated through the rows of corpses, identifying about a third as murder victims. Following along behind her, Grey chalked an *M* for murder on each plank or table she indicated. The police—regular and Briganti— would find this useful, just to know which deaths they ought to investigate.

"Now that I have all the magic, what should I do with it?" Pearl came back into the aisle between Galloway and the other bodies. "I feel all light-headed and fizzly."

She giggled, a sound he'd never before heard from her. Granted, he'd only known her a day, but it seemed out of character. It would have been delightful, had the situation not been so suddenly alarming. What *should* she do with the magic?

"Blast it all." He tried to curse under his breath, but knew the cursing was audible. "You should have waited. You should be Amanusa's apprentice, not mine. I know damn-all about sorcery." He'd said that aloud, hadn't he? Damn it.

"Forgiveness. Haven't been much around gently bred ladies." He dipped his head in apology.

Pearl giggled again. "I'm no gently bred miss. I was gently *raised* for a time, but my father was a merchant, not even a squire. Don't worry 'bout my ears. They're not so delicate that they won't survive a damn or two."

Her eyes widened as she realized what had come out of her own mouth, and she covered it with her pretty fingertips. "Whoops."

"Now I've rubbed off on you." Grey withheld the curses this time, running hands through his hair, trying to think what to do, how to rid her of the magic that had intoxicated her.

"Grey?" Her voice, weak and frightened, brought his head snapping round in sudden worry.

"*It burns, Grey.* I mean, Mr. Carteret." Her expression was as frightened as her voice. "It felt good at first, all bubbly and fizzy, but now, when the bubbles pop, they burn. It hurts. What do I do?" Her voice rose to a keening pitch.

"Easy, Parkin. No need to panic." The words were for himself as much as her. "Magic is magic. It just needs to be used, or sent back where it belongs."

Why hadn't he remembered that basic tenet of magic earlier? Too busy playing the peacock, fanning his tail?

Even knotted together, her hands trembled. Not surprising, if the magic burned. He took her hands, one in each of his, and the instant he held her securely, magic surged into him in an electrical rush.

His hair stood on end and every nerve tingled. Pearl went limp. Her knees crumpled and she sagged into him. Grey had to catch her, had to hold her against him to keep her from falling to the floor. Dear God, she wore no corset. Nothing to keep him from feeling her feminine softness.

She blinked up at him in a dazed wonderment, and it was all he could do not to steal a kiss. *Apprentice*, he reminded himself. Too bad he was utterly out of practice at listening to anyone, particularly his own conscience. It sounded too much like the duke. But she hadn't fainted. She was still conscious. He hadn't broken her. Was that not cause for celebration?

"Thank you," she said fervently.

For what? He hadn't kissed her yet. Had he?

Pearl pushed against his chest with her small hands. He opened his arms and let her step out of them. She turned her hands over, front to back, examining them. "What did you do?"

That dazed wonderment had all gone into her voice, and it slid low into his body from whence he could not drive it. He didn't try terribly hard.

"I thought sure my hands were burning into blackened claws, but look—" She held them up, pretty, pink and perfect. "They're not injured at all. No blisters. Nothing. What did you do?"

"I don't—" He didn't have a chance to finish admitting his ignorance.

"You took the magic." She shifted her shoulders, her eyes gone blank as if turned to look inside her. "I still have most of it, but you took the extra. What was burning me."

She looked up at him again, her golden-rayed eyes pinning him in place with the admiration in them. "What did you do?"

He shrugged, suddenly unwilling to diminish that admiration. But this was magic. Sorcery, which was all about truth. "I'm not sure." That was truth, wasn't it?

Grey took Pearl's elbow. If he didn't touch her bare hand, surely the magic would stay where it belonged. He guided her toward the open doors at the back of the cellar. Fresh air would doubtless be good for both of them. "You should rid yourself of as much magic as you can. So you don't overload again."

"Overload—is that what it was? I felt tipsy. Downright pizzled."

"Too much magic affects some people that way." Grey felt a trifle well-to-go himself, come to that.

"I don't feel that way now." Pearl took a deep breath and coughed. Fresh air in London wasn't exactly fresh.

"Nonetheless. You're still near your limit, I'm sure."

"How do I do it? What should I do?"

Time for theory extrapolation, assumption building, and conclusion jumping. "Basic magic theory. Magic, when gathered, requires either use or dispersion. Magic wants to be used. Not that it has a mind or will of its own, but like water behind a dam or steam in a boiler, it can build up pressure until it bursts. I can't have you bursting, Parkin. Burst apprentices simply aren't done. It would ruin my reputation with all the other magisters."

She laughed. Goal accomplished. It was more a chortle than that airy, carefree giggle, but delightful nonetheless.

"Therefore," he said, "you need to use this magic, or disperse it back to where it belongs."

"And where is that?"

Bedamned if I know. But Grey wouldn't tell her that. Not yet, anyway. Why had they allowed even the basic knowledge of how sorcery functioned to be lost? "Let's try using it first."

"How?"

"Questions, always the questions." His put-upon act was not entirely acting. "How did you work your 'don't-look' spell?"

"I—" Pearl licked her thumb, then raised it to his face and pantomimed wiping it along his jaw. "Then I say 'Don't look. Don't notice him. Pass him by.'"

He wanted her to touch him. He wanted her to lick *his* thumb. Or lick along his jaw there. That would do. Nicely.

Grey cleared his throat. "That's all?"

She nodded. He nodded with her as he began to speak. "I have seen Amanusa work spells. Not many, but a few. Powerful spells, most of them. She did say saliva could work magic, just not as powerfully as blood."

He paced as he tried to bring back every detail he

could remember. "The spells I saw her work—she drew the blood. Then she drank it, or placed it where it was needed. Like your—" He gestured at his face, where Pearl had placed her spell. "Then she spoke. In English, I believe." Grey wished he could remember Pearl's touch on his face that night.

No, he didn't. They should probably avoid any more touching, in case more magic tried to jump between them.

He hid his turmoil in pedantry. "Words are often part of a spell. Not so much because the words themselves are important, but they help focus the will, and the will focuses the magic."

"Do I have to learn Latin?"

"Why ever should you?"

"Don't you use Latin in your magic?"

"Yes, sometimes, but that's because the really old spirits, the ones with great power—Latin's their native language. In conjury, the magician must communicate with the spirits. We speak whatever language they do. Old German is the very devil of a language to learn.

"In the other magics, I'm not sure the language matters, though it's traditional for alchemists to spell in Latin and wizards to spell in one of the varieties of Celtic—Irish, or Cornish or Breton, or else in Romany, the gypsy language. But Amanusa spells in English, so I shouldn't worry about it, were I you. English obviously works."

"So how should I use it? Do I need to go collect blood from those victims and place it somewhere?" She broke off. "You're a conjurer. How would you know? I need to read *faster*."

"Yes, but I know magic. All magic has certain things in common, like the use-or-disperse rule. And I would say it is likely this innocent blood is already placed where it should be. A murderer is rarely untouched by the blood he spills."

Pearl's pink mouth made an *O* of understanding. It did

emphatically not need kissing. "So the magic will know where to go—" She climbed the ramp a few paces, until her head rose above the slanting doors into the open air of the city.

"Blood of the innocent," she intoned, then looked at Grey. "I did read three pages. It said the blood should be invoked."

He nodded, motioned for her to go on, hoping that conversational asides didn't disturb the spell casting. He'd keep his own mouth shut, in case.

"Blood of the innocent," she said again, "carry justice against those who spilled it. Find the workers of these wicked deeds and harry them without rest. From their coming in to their going out. From their rising to their lying down, be always before them, driving them toward the justice they deserve." She stretched her hands out and stood, reaching, straining for a long moment, before dropping back onto her heels.

Grey winced, exaggeratedly. "Cold justice, that."

"But deserved. They shouldn't rest. They should be haunted." She wriggled her shoulders and shook out her arms as if flinging away bothersome insects. Or perhaps settling magic.

"How much did that use up?" he asked.

"Most of it, I think." She shook her hands again and Grey took the chance of capturing one.

Magic flared again, but briefly. It didn't leap between them, simply lit up, as if recognizing itself. Was there magic actually inside him? How was that possible? Ought he to get rid of it? How? No, it was not possible. It was his imagining, his irritatingly inconvenient desire for her lithe little body. Nothing more.

"Perhaps you should try dispersing it," he suggested.

"How? *Where?*"

Good question. But he thought he might have an answer.

"This cellar is filled with ghosts. Packed to the rafters

behind the conjury wards." He pointed at the sigils painted on the basement walls meant to keep the ghosts under control. "Perhaps you could send the magic to the ghosts. It is their blood, after all."

"But how do I *do* it?" She sounded utterly frustrated.

So was he. "The same way you did the other," he assumed. "The blood is theirs, so its already placed. Speak the words. Send the magic home. I will help, if I can."

Pearl took a deep breath. "All right. If you think I can do it—if you think I really did something with that other spell."

"Good girl."

She glowered at him for that, and he laughed. He did know she was not a hound, to be praised so. "Good apprentice, rather."

"Better," she muttered. She stepped back down into the cellar, accepting his hand when she wobbled, and he knew she still held too much magic. She needed to be rid of it.

Back inside, she paused to look at Ferguson where he lay on the floor. She crouched to touch his forehead, feel his wrists. Grey's lips tightened, but he held back any other reaction. She stood again, apparently satisfied. Grey waited for her to speak, but she said nothing, simply moved a few steps away and stared at her shoes as if thinking.

She took a deep breath. "Blood of the innocents," she began. "Return to the souls where you belong. Give them peace. Give them the knowledge that justice is in hand and will be achieved. Take them home."

Grey gestured the sigil for peace and for grace and mercy, and whispered his own words of comfort. This time, he could feel the magic pour out of Pearl, for it was also somehow pulled out of him, filling the room like a faint scarlet fog. It filled up the ghosts, so much that they became almost solid. They smiled at him, glowing brightly as they slipped free of the horrors that had trapped them, and one by one, they faded away.

Pearl's hand slipped into Grey's as he watched them go. He looked down at her and smiled, elation filling him. "They're *ascending*. Becoming spirits."

"I know," she whispered, her eyes wide. "I can see them. Before, I *felt*—wait—" Her eyes somehow went even wider. "What's that?"

She tipped her head toward one of the lingering ghosts. "It seems to be . . . Is it—?" She squinted. "I can't see, exactly."

It seemed to be shrinking away from the crimson flow of magic. Grey could see more ghosts doing the same.

"Oh, now it's glowing," Pearl said happily.

It was, the ghost woman's harsh countenance softening as the magic soaked in. But only for an instant. The magic hit a barrier, or perhaps opened a cesspool of corruption, for the faint light was quickly drowned in a dark malevolence that ate the ghost from the inside out. Pearl gasped, and Grey turned her into his body, tucking her face against him so she couldn't see.

That were Mother Nan, a small voice whispered inside Grey's head. *She owned the biggest house o' child-whores in all Lunnontown, an' she were mean wif it. Kilt me just that mornin' wif a iron pot t'my brain box. An' then Basher kilt her the same night for the same reason. 'Cause she didn't give 'im the money 'e thought 'e oughter 'ave.*

8

THE LITTLE SPIRIT settled softly onto Grey's shoulders. *Wisht Basher coulda done for 'er a little quicker. But then, Rodey weren't much nicer'n Nan. I likes it 'ere 'eaps better.*

"I am happy to hear that." Grey watched the other ghosts shrivel and vanish as Mother Nan had, protecting Pearl from the sight. He didn't know what she could sense, but hoped he protected her from that as well. "I am Grey Carteret, conjurer. Who might you be?"

Pearl struggled to free herself, and since she didn't seem to be fighting to look at the still blackening ghosts, Grey released her, though he did keep a hold on her arms.

She looked up at him. "Who are you talking to?"

"A spirit. I am informed that these dark ghosts belong to the wicked, and are no doubt going to their just rewards, despite being murdered."

I knows 'oo you are, Mr. Magister, the spirit said. *I'm Davy.*

"A pleasure to meet you, good sir." Grey released his grip on Pearl. All the ghosts who were departing appeared to have done so. Fewer lingered than he would have expected. But then how long did sorcerous magic linger when innocent blood was spilled? And how long had it been since it was last cleaned up? Perhaps Ferguson's faint had good cause.

"This is my apprentice, Pearl Parkin. I'd like you to keep a particular eye on her, if you would. And on Ferguson, yonder. He is apparently quite sensitive to sorcery. However, we will be working conjury now." Grey wound the young spirit onto a sigil stick—his were pencils as well, with the sigils "come" and "stay" inscribed on the sides—and deposited him on Pearl's shoulders. Safer for both of them that way.

Ferguson seemed to be coming around, and Grey went to hoist him to his feet before Pearl did something hovery and fluttery and annoying.

"I think we've got that nasty pile of sorcery cleared out," Grey said to the young wizard as he walked him to the stairs and deposited him to sit there. "I'm going to do some conjury now, and won't be needing your particular talents, so why don't you sit here out of the way and finish your recovery, all right? There's a good lad."

"Miss Parkin—?" Ferguson managed to fumble that much out of his mouth.

"Quite well. Impressively so. Did you know sorcery could assist ghosts over the edge to spirits? Neither did I. Rest now. Right." Grey turned his back on that annoyingly fresh, youthful face and his gaze lit on Pearl. The name fit her, didn't it. Matched her skin with its—

He pried his gaze from Pearl and nailed it to the covered bier that held Angus Galloway's body. He walked toward it, looking in his pencil case for the proper tool. Not pencils. They required too much pressure to make a mark. Ink was too permanent, though the Chinese ink blocks had made it much more portable. Ordinary chalk required almost as much pressure as a pencil, but the soft artist's pastel . . . perfect.

He would have to buy a new one soon. This one was down to the size of his smallest fingertip. He'd used them smaller, though. This one was big enough to hold.

Moving around to the head of the table, Grey tucked the case away. With one hand, he smoothed out the cloth that covered Galloway and the table. With the other, he drew his summoning sigil, "Come," surrounded by the power inflections and imperatives.

It suddenly became easier to rake the dull green color across the rough cloth. Pearl held the fabric stretched taut between her hands. She followed him to the foot of the table and did the same there. Did he need more sigils? Grey considered.

"Do you think Mr. Galloway was one of the ghosts who ascended?" Pearl stood behind his left elbow, as if fastened there like a dinghy bobbing along in the wake of a man-of-war.

"I don't know," Grey admitted. "Ghosts and spirits, when they have form, tend to look as they did in the prime of life. I've only seen Galloway like this." He gestured vaguely at the head end of the shroud. "Doubt I'd recognize him. Murder victims take some time to escape from their traps—the anger, horror, and fear created in their deaths. The worse the murder, the longer it usually takes. Angus Galloway could be trapped as a ghost for years. Centuries."

"Poor man," she whispered.

Grey wished he hasn't said that last bit. "Then again," he added, "perhaps your magic reached him." He paused. "I didn't know sorcery could lay ghosts. It's a good thing to know."

"If he's a ghost, and conjurers can't call ghosts, what are you planning to do?"

"It's not that conjurers *can't* call ghosts." Grey knelt to mark a binding sigil on the stone floor at the table's side, using ordinary chalk. "We simply *don't*. Because, besides being dangerous, ghosts are essentially useless. Their strength is consumed by the thing that traps them, whether anger, fear, grief, horror—their reaction to the circumstances of their deaths. They cannot be controlled—even self-control is beyond them. Nor can a ghost speak understandably to the living. I'm hoping our young visitor will translate for us. All right, old chap?"

Stunning, Davy said from his perch atop Pearl's head. Grey could just make out a wispy presence there, scarcely more than a thought and a voice.

"Don't overtire yourself, sirrah," Grey said sternly. "I have many spirits I can call upon for aid."

But I'm the one wot's 'ere, Davy retorted.

Grey copied the binding and control sigils on the other side of the table, stood, and put away his chalk. He removed his frock coat and handed it to Pearl. The fashion was no longer for so tight a cut that a man needed assistance to insert himself into and pry himself out of his coat, but the coat and its length could interfere with movement. He didn't know what actions might be required of him. Best to be ready.

He motioned for Pearl to step back, then reconsidered. "Pearl— Miss Parkin, do you suppose your 'don't-look' spell might work on ghosts as well as it does on the living? Keep the ghosts from seeing what's there?"

She blinked at him, taking the idea and turning it over for inspection. "I don't know, sir."

"Perhaps this would be a good time to discover it. Invoke the spell, please. On yourself and Mr. Ferguson. And if you can find a way to include our new spirit friend, please do so."

"Yes, sir."

Grey folded his arms and waited, while Pearl crossed to the stair and stroked her thumb across Ferguson's *hand*. Grey couldn't help the fierce satisfaction that curved his lips. Though perhaps it was only that the cub objected to being essentially spat upon. *Good.*

She returned, coming so close that his arms unwrapped automatically, opening himself to her approach. She rose onto her tiptoes and he caught her arms to balance her, bending down to her upturned face. Only to hear what she whispered.

"Do you think if I know its name, I can more easily include this spirit in the spell?" she murmured.

"Why do you ask?" He wasn't particularly alarmed. She was his apprentice after all, and this wasn't exactly a guild secret. It wasn't something they bandied about, either. He wondered how she knew to ask.

"I can feel it. The spirit." She frowned. "I've never noticed spirits before. It feels peculiar. Being able to notice, I mean. The spirit doesn't feel peculiar. But you've never mentioned his name, or any spirit names, and I wondered if names were important."

"They are. Which is why a spirit's name is never spoken aloud. If you cannot ascertain the name on your own, I cannot give it to you."

"Oh." She frowned. "I can feel the spirit. But I can't hear it. Perhaps if I make my spell bigger, it can get inside."

Grey didn't think. He simply took her hand. She'd been able to see the ghosts ascend while holding his hand, so perhaps she could hear spirits the same way. "Try again."

I'm Davy! the little spirit shouted, and Pearl winced.

"Yes, I hear you quite clearly now," she said crisply. She looked down at her hand clasped in Grey's great paw.

He'd never thought of his hand that way, as he wasn't an overlarge man. He was perhaps a trifle above just-barely-large-enough, but with Pearl, he felt a hulking brute. A protective, possessive, roaring, hulking beast of a brute.

She looked from their clasped hands up to Grey's face and he dragged his thoughts from their primitively hulking tracks to look back at her. "It makes a difference, when we take hands," she said. "Why?"

"I don't know. Nor do we have time to puzzle it out now. Later, this evening, we can hypothesize to our hearts' content. Now, I have a ghost to conjure."

"Might I watch?" She squeezed his hand a fraction tighter, signaling how she wanted to do it.

"If I might watch your attempt to shield our young spirit."

"Yes, of course." She frowned. "How am I to—to apply the spell material?"

Grey blinked at her. "I suppose it would be difficult to lick a spirit. Where do you place it when you hide yourself?"

"I don't. It's inside me, so I don't have to place it anywhere. Only when I hide someone else." Her voice had risen from very quiet to normal, and Grey flicked his eyes toward Ferguson, who still reclined in the stairway, looking pale.

Pearl caught his glance, and softened her voice again. Grey had to lean closer to hear. He hadn't intended his look as a warning, exactly. But Amanusa had been so careful of her guild secrets, it made him nervous to hear Pearl speaking so casually.

"What if you place it somewhere on your person?" he suggested. This whole thing was by way of experiment, so why not add a bit more. "I worked a spell once with Amanusa where sorcery and conjury blended into something stronger than either by itself. That spell had the other two magics in it as well, but I believe we can blend just the two. The three magics we've had over the past two hundred years are often blended in every combination, so why not our two?"

"How?" She had the most beautiful eyes.

"Begin with a sigil. I would write it—" The thought made his throat go to desert sand in an instant, and he cleared it. Swallowed. "Upon your skin. Then you would apply your material, and work the spell."

"On my skin?" She blinked those eyes at him, thinking. She seemed to blink and think together often.

"I'd rather the spirit be stuck to you than to some random brick in this basement, if it turns out that way."

"Oh, yes, absolutely. A sweet little spirit like this one?"

Oi! I ain't sweet. I'm tough an' mean. An' I ain't so little anymores. Davy slid down from Pearl's head to her shoulder, making her wriggle, as if it tickled. *But I gots to admit, I'd rather be stuck to th' lady than to the cellar, if I gotta be stuck.*

"I agree completely." Pearl released Grey's hand, alas, and removed her capelet, draping it atop his coat, which she held over one arm. She tried to unbutton her cuff to little success. Not surprising, given how laden down she was.

"What are you doing?" Ferguson sounded queasy and scandalized from his post across the cellar.

"Rolling up our sleeves to get to work," Pearl said.

Grey scooped coat and capelet from her grasp and crossed the room in a few strides to deposit them in Ferguson's lap. "Make yourself useful."

When he returned, Pearl had her sleeve unbuttoned and rolled to her elbow, exposing a pale forearm utterly worthy of her name. And he was going to mar it with his scribbling.

"That chalk will rub off in a terrible hurry, won't it?" She stared at her arm, worry in both face and voice. "Will it even make a mark?"

"I have ink," he said. "Chinese block ink, and a brush. Works quite as well as a pen for marking sigils. Often better." When had he taken her hand? When had his thumb begun to slide across that pearlescent skin on her wrist? "It isn't half so scratchy. And—" He only now realized its greatest benefit.

Grey pulled out his case again and set the ink block in the lid on a corner of the table where Galloway lay. He was dead. They wouldn't disturb him.

"Spit," he said. "On the ink. It's how I usually wet it in the field. That way, we can apply sigil and saliva both at once, and perhaps it will also blend the magic from the beginning."

Pearl blushed. Grey understood. Spitting was not only impolite, it was utterly and completely unladylike, and Pearl had been at least raised a lady. But she did it. She spat on the ink. He rubbed it into the block with the brush, making the ink thick and dark, then he rolled the brush in the ink to make a point. If he had to mark up her skin, he would at least make it the prettiest, neatest mark he could.

He took her arm in his right hand to steady it, and poised the brush above the white skin with his other, visualizing the sigil before he drew it. The form took shape in his mind, the blocky lines to either side, the graceful swirl in the center. He filled the form with magic, with power, and then he poured it into the design he painted in the exact center between wrist and elbow, on the soft inner flesh of his apprentice's forearm.

When he lifted the brush and slid his supporting hand down to her wrist, he let go his breath. Pearl exhaled with him.

She peered at the black blemish on her skin. It wasn't large, perhaps two inches square. He could have made it smaller, but that would have meant less spittle for her spell. Still, he wished now that he'd tried.

"It's lovely," she said. "What does it mean? If you can tell me."

"It's one of the basics, available in any book of spells. It's the sigil 'Safety.' You see? The walls of protection, and the spirit curled up safe inside?"

"Yes. Beautiful." She smiled.

Grey had to stiffen his knees. Then he had to catch hold of the table, his writing brush clattering to the floor, for she—

He didn't know what she did. It felt as if she reached inside him and touched his heart. Not the pulsating piece of meat, but his emotions. As if she strummed her fingers over them, leaving him quivering as she passed. Humming.

"Are you well?" She had hold of his arm, over his shirtsleeve, so that was all right.

He still gripped her wrist. He should release it, but he didn't want to. Didn't know if he could. He shook his head to clear it.

Pearl repeated her question. "Mr. Carteret. Are you

all right?" She reached up, took his face between her hands and peered into his dazed and bedazzled eyes. *"Grey."*

She held his face between her hands, and it hummed a little, this thing between them. Gave a little buzz of happiness. But she didn't touch the very core of who he was. Not this time. She stayed locked safely outside.

"What did you do?" he whispered.

"I invoked the spell. That's all." Her voice held more than a hint of panic. He removed one of her hands from his face and patted it in reassurance.

"What is going on?" Ferguson demanded petulantly from across the cellar. "What are you doing?"

"Just a bit of spell casting," Grey said, striving for airily. "Seems I'm a bit sensitive to sorcery as well."

The wizard slumped back into the stairs from his attempt to rise, and laid his head against the wall. He muttered something. Grey couldn't hear it clearly, but was certain it had to do with no flirting, and perhaps with the drawing of corks. Grey hadn't had his cork drawn in years.

"We still have a ghost to conjure." Grey let go of Pearl's hand. He drew in some of the ambient magic left behind by the departing spirits, and opened his second vision. Davy looked far less wispy now, strong and contented, spiraled around Pearl's forearm.

Pearl stepped out of reach and Grey frowned. He didn't like her moving so far away from him. He caught her elbow and drew her back, before it occurred to him to wonder why he didn't like it. Could there be something more to this than simple lust?

It felt anything but simple. He'd never felt so protective, so possessive, so hungry for a woman, or so annoyed by how she made him feel.

Then there was that rush of magic when she'd been overloaded. Was that how sorcery worked? Was that how it was supposed to work? Had the sorcery somehow created her ability to see and hear spirits when they touched? Was magic the—the *sensation* invoked when she worked her "don't-look" spell? Though sensation was a poor word to use for being turned on his ear and shaken apart with joy and sorrow and anger and delight and everything else all at once.

"No more experiments," he said. "Not until Amanusa comes back, or you get further along in your reading. This experiment seems all right, but we can't keep fumbling in the dark without knowing what it is you're doing with these spells."

"Yes, sir. Likely we shouldn't have done this one, except—" Her face crinkled in a mélange of worry and hope. "I do think our spirit is safer. I know it's stronger, and that can't be a bad thing, can it? I'm not sorry we did it, sir."

Sir. "Call me Grey," he snapped, turning yet again to the corpse of Angus Galloway.

"I— It wouldn't be proper, sir. You are my magic-master."

"You've done it already. Called me by name. *Grey.* Twice. I heard you."

"But—"

"Elinor calls Harry, Harry. Harry calls her Elinor. You will call me Grey and I'll call you Pearl."

"That's different, Elinor and Mr. Tomlinson."

"No, it isn't. You are Pearl. I am Grey. Now stand right there, yes, at my elbow, and lay your two fingers on my wrist, there. Just so." The power surged inside him, then settled again. Would it interfere with his conjury, whatever it was?

He lifted his face and felt for the bits of anchor magic in the sigils around the body in question. But before he could send magic into them, his most familiar spirit flashed into the cellar. *What do you think you are doing, Greyson Carteret, calling ghosts without me?*

Grey grimaced. He'd hoped Mary wouldn't object for

once, since the other spirit was present. He addressed her mentally, not wanting witnesses to the discussion. *"You were so tired, dear heart, when you were last with me. You are after all, a very new spirit."*

I might have been tired then, but I'm not now. Stop coddling me, Grey. I'm not like I was before. For a moment, she solidified into the strong, womanly form she had taken after death. *And I'm not so new as all that. I've been passed on for ages longer than Davy. How long again? It's hard to keep track.*

"You don't have to," Grey replied. *"But if you must know, it's been seventeen years and three months. No time at all."*

Not here. Mary curled wispily around Grey's shoulders. *But there, where you are, it's been ages and ages. You've gotten old.*

"So have you."

She didn't forget her goal. *You know I don't like for you to call ghosts without me.*

"Yes, madam, I do know," Grey said aloud. "Forgive me." He paused. "May I call my ghost now?"

Of course, she said, all graciousness.

"You might want to take advantage of the sigil on Miss Parkin's arm, with our young friend," he suggested.

How clever of you. Mary floated over to Pearl. *Hullo, Davy. Good to see you again. Hello, Miss Parkin. I'm Mary.*

Did all spirits know all the other spirits? He often thought so.

"Pleased to meet you." Pearl bobbed a curtsey, which made the spirits drift a little.

Grey cleared his throat and everyone went still, turning their attention to him. He felt for his anchors again, then poured magic into the sigils around the murdered man's body. *Come.* "Angus Galloway, come and speak."

Nothing. Not a stir in the aether, except for a quick

in-and-out flicker of curiosity in a corner. He infused his "Come" sigils with more power, put more in his voice. "Angus Galloway, you are instructed to present yourself at your mortal remains."

The more recently dead sometimes responded better to officious-sounding language.

It was still daylight. The moon had risen while they'd been out on Pearl's shopping trip, so that was all right. But the sun did affect ghosts more than spirits, and Galloway was very, very new to the other side, whether ghost or spirit. He would have little strength for answering.

Grey would have to provide the strength. He reached into the aether for more magic, piling it up in the space between the four sigils, where the body lay. For the third time, he called. "Angus Galloway, *come*. Present yourself."

He was sweating in the chill basement. He could feel the threat of a massive headache looming, waiting to crash down on him. The hand he extended to hold the magic in place strained on the verge of trembling.

Calling the recently dead could be more of an effort than rousing the long-departed from their comfort. The new ones, ghost or spirit, had little of the power the old spirits did. Sometimes it took more strength than Grey possessed to call them.

He hoped this was not one of those times. How impressed would his new apprentice be if he fell over in a faint, like Ferguson?

But his hand never trembled. The headache never crashed. His heartbeat steadied and the strain in his muscles eased, strength sliding into his body from somewhere. He put it into his voice. "Angus Galloway, come forth!"

The sound seemed to echo through more than mere air. A guttural bellow with an overlaid scream came roaring back, rampaging through the cellar so loud and so quick, Pearl ducked. Grey shifted her two-fingered touch to his other wrist so he could put his closest arm around her for protection.

And for that instant when her skin did not touch his, his head pounded, his hands shook, and his knees buckled. The strength came from her, from Pearl, his tiny, fragile apprentice.

He jerked, meaning to shake her off, and Pearl wrapped her hand around his bare wrist.

"Don't," she said. "Don't you dare. I need to see what's happening. I have to know. The little spirit's faded, so don't make me let go." She reached up to her shoulder and clasped the hand he'd laid there before she let go his opposite wrist. "There. You've got your hand free. But don't let go. Together we're stronger than we are apart."

The cellar door slammed shut and the roaring shriek filled the room, so loud that Pearl had to shout to be heard. It wasn't audible merely to conjurers and their apprentices. Ferguson hunched on the stairs, face hidden in his knees, hands tight over his ears. But then he was a sensitive, poor chap.

Grey watched the ghost go screaming by, for there was a ghost attached to the scream. It zoomed around the room, bashing into corners and knocking over tables, spilling bodies to the floor in its ricochet attack, making Pearl cry out in horror. But apparently it did not see the other magicians or spirits in the room. Pearl's experimental spell was working.

He waited and watched. When it came streaking past, he bumped it toward one of the binding sigils, which snared it like a fish in a net.

The ghost struggled, its roar suddenly silenced, but it was well and truly caught. It was strong for a new ghost. Or maybe it was the magic he'd fed it. Grey was glad he'd chalked two binding sigils, though it was caught in just the one. He had the other in reserve.

Seconds ticked away as the ghost fought to break

free, shredding itself into wisps equally snared in the magic. Finally it stilled, apparently resigned to capture. Grey waited until the wisps coalesced and began to look something like the faint transparency of a man.

A man who bore little resemblance to the broken mess beneath the cloth, for he had a narrow, almost beaky nose, eyes deep-set beneath a high forehead, and a fine, firm jaw. Every one of those sharp-cut bones had been shattered into pudding. The only thing the same was the deep red of the hair curling in all directions.

"All right, my dear. Time to go to work."

Yes, Grey. Mary rearranged herself on Pearl's arm, doing the small-spirit equivalent of coming to attention.

"Please verify that this is the ghost of Angus Galloway."

It is. I asked him already.

The ghost howled, a silent howling this time. Grey hoped it had used up all its strength in that earlier display.

"Is he aware of his demise?"

What? Mary "blinked" in confusion.

"Does he know he's dead?"

Oh. A brief pause. *What did I tell you about using fancy-pants words?* Another pause while spirit communicated with ghost. *Yes, he knows.*

An' 'e's powerful pissed about it, too, Davy added.

Hush, I'm answering Grey's questions, Mary scolded the other spirit.

"Does he know who killed him?"

I can't get much sense out of him, Mary admitted.

'E's spittin' mad. Davy put in his contribution. *An' 'e's spittin' an' 'owlin'.*

Mary—did she pinch the boy spirit? Could spirits do that? They wouldn't tell him if he asked. Grey sighed. "I was afraid of that."

"What about the magic?" Pearl said. "My magic, I mean. If it helped those others ascend, mightn't it help Mr. Galloway?"

"I imagine a great deal of the magic you dispersed earlier was his. If it were going to help him ascend, don't you think it would have done so already?"

"But his ghost wasn't here. Maybe that makes a difference."

"Maybe. Might. Perhaps. The problem is we don't *know.*" Grey lifted an eyebrow at her. "No more experiments. Remember?"

He was haunting the place where he was murdered, Mary volunteered. *He does make that much sense. You had to call him from there.*

"Where was he murdered?" Grey asked. "Does he know?"

Near the river. Near Green Bank where he was found. He doesn't know much more than that.

Savin' that it were an empty building, Davy said. *Fallin' down, like.*

The ghost burst into a furious struggle, fighting once more to break free, shredding itself into a thousand flaring wisps. When it re-formed, it was less substantial than before.

"I have some of its magic left to me." Pearl's voice held quiet determination. "If all I do is disperse it, it's not an experiment, is it?"

Grey gave her a suspicious look.

"It's *not,*" she argued, though he hadn't said a word for her to argue against. "We know I need to disperse it. I know how to do that. The only thing we don't know is what will happen when his magic reaches him."

"And if he's black-hearted, we won't get another word out of him."

Pearl frowned. "Why not?"

"Because the wicked get no respite from hell."

9

"OH." PEARL BLINKED as she absorbed that information. "So you only call spirits and angels out of heaven?"

Grey shuddered ostentatiously. "Angels, no. Like demons, angels were never human. They do not answer a conjurer's magic. They have been known to appear from time to time and take a hand in setting things right, but I have no desire to encounter one. They are . . . *fearsome* creatures. But that does leave us a great many spirits to call upon. And frankly, wouldn't you rather deal with the denizens of heaven? I know I do."

"But what do we do—" She caught herself and corrected. "What will *you* do about Mr. Galloway? It seems cruel to leave him netted like this."

"Oh, I'll free him. He'll go straight back to the place where he died. Too bad we can't follow him, but perhaps—"

We can follow him, Grey. Mary startled Grey when she spoke. *We can follow, and I'll come right back to tell you where he went. Where it happened. And Davy can stay and watch.*

"Didn't you say you were murdered, little spirit?" Pearl asked Davy. "Not so long since?"

A week ago, yeah, the child spirit answered.

"So how is it you are spirit and no longer a ghost?"

He shifted on her arm. *Guess I didn't mind dyin', did I? I was some mad at Mother Nan for wot she done while I were livin', but she done me a favor, killin' me. 'Cause she can't 'urt me no more. A grateful ghost don't stay ghost long.*

Pearl nodded thoughtfully, then Grey watched astounded, as she gathered a morsel of her magic and fed it into the two new spirits through the sigil painted on her arm, giving them back the strength they'd expended in the conversation with the angry ghost.

Grey growled. "No more experiments."

Pearl narrowed her eyes at him. "It wasn't. Not this time. When you painted the sigil, that was an experiment, but this wasn't, because we did it before."

"You will not deplete your own strength by giving it away to others." He cared because it was his duty to care. Because she was his apprentice. No other reason.

Liar.

"It's not *my* strength I'm giving away. I have all this magic. Still. I got rid of the overload, of the vastly too much, but a great deal remains. I should use it. Correct?" She looked up at him with those gold-over-blue eyes and Grey had to struggle to recall the meaning of her words.

"Carefully," he said when he remembered. "Very, very carefully."

"So can't I—carefully—give Mr. Galloway some of his own innocent-blood magic back to him?"

Grey sighed. "How do you know it's his magic?"

"It feels like him." Pearl gave a tiny half-shoulder shrug. "I don't know how I know, I just do."

A deeper sigh oozed out of him. "Let's see if the spirits can track him back to the site of the murder, and then—" He shook his head, hands propped on his hips holding back the sides of his frock coat.

"Then what?" She bounced on her toes, all annoying eagerness.

"Then you may rid yourself of some more of this 'great deal' of magic," Grey said with less than his usual graciousness. He didn't like worrying over her. Over anyone.

"Thank you, sir."

Sir. Again. Grey lifted an eyebrow at her, trying his version of the duke's imperious expression.

Pearl blushed her almost-secret blush. "Thank you—" She cleared her throat. "Grey."

He gave a brusque nod. *Better.* "Are you ready, young friends?" he asked Mary and Davy, as he draped an arm around Pearl again and she took hold of his hand. "Got your 'don't-look' spell wrapped close around you?"

The two spirits hunkered down against the sigil on Pearl's arm and the ink paled, just as it should. *Yes.*

"Right, then," With the toe of his walking boot, Grey erased part of the sigil binding the ghost of the murder victim as he addressed it. "On your way, but return when I call again." He wiped out the rest of the sigil and the ghost exploded.

Its substance filled the entire cellar with a sudden, bitter cold, then vanished before Grey could work up a shiver. Mary and Davy vanished with it. "That's that, then."

"Now what?" Pearl ducked away from his encompassing arm.

Grey grimaced. She wanted magic from him. Knowledge. Not passion or possession. Why was that so hard to remember? "Now we go on about our business and wait for our young spirits to return with news."

"And what is our business?"

Grey glanced across the cellar and cursed to himself. "I am afraid that business shall have to wait."

Pearl turned to follow Grey's gaze. "Mr. Ferguson!"

The wizard sat slumped against the cellar wall, unconscious once more, so pale his freckles stood out like ink spots on parchment. And Pearl ran to flutter over him.

Grey bit back more curses. Ferguson was apparently more sensitive to conjury than anyone realized, as well as sorcery. Ferguson was one of Grey's Briganti. Grey had brought him into this place, where they'd loosed enough magic to stir up a hurricane. The man was Grey's responsibility, and of course he had to be seen to. Grey would have to handle the fact that Pearl was seeing to him. Or he could see to Ferguson himself.

Grey sent Pearl up the stairs, into the hospital proper,

to find a servant or someone with a water basin and cloth. And someone to pick up the mess the ghost made. He'd have to reinforce the warding, too, since he was the one who'd erased it to call the ghost.

When she returned with one of the newfangled nursing sisters in tow, Grey had loosened the young man's clothing and done his best to clear away the lingering magic. Ferguson's color looked better. The sister washing his face and wrists brought him around.

Ferguson began apologizing the minute he could speak coherently. "Useless. Worse than useless. Sorry, sir. Deepest, abject apologies. Won't happen again."

"No, it won't," Grey said when waving the apology off didn't shut the man up. "Obviously you'll need to work on your shielding a great deal more before you're let out in the field again."

"Yessir. Sorry, sir." Ferguson tried to sit up, paled, and sank back against the wall. Pearl hovered several steps above, beyond the sister. *Good.*

"How did you ever get past your qualifying examinations if conjury affected you this strongly?" Grey scowled down at his investigator. Such a weakness was a liability in a Briganti, whichever branch the man worked.

"It doesn't, sir. Or, it never has before." Ferguson was more upright now, leaning against the old stone wall. "But I think I was still wobbly from the—the sorcery. And—" He frowned. "The conjury was different. More. It had an unusual flavor to it. One I couldn't properly shield against."

Grey folded back his coat to prop his hands on his hips as he scowled at the floor. "Seems we should add a new class on shielding, now that sorcery's come back to us." He shook off the thought. The school wasn't his responsibility. I-Branch was, though, and the conjurer's guild. He'd have to set up training sessions for both. But that was for later.

Once the warding was back in place—a fairly simple

matter of putting magic back into the sigils carved into the bricks—Grey got Ferguson up the stairs, into a cab, and sent home to his lodgings to spend the rest of the day recovering. Then he hustled Pearl off to one of the new French-style cafés for luncheon when he realized the time. No wonder she looked so pale. He had no business having responsibility for an apprentice if he couldn't remember to keep her fed. He had no business with responsibility at all.

BY THE TIME Mr. Carteret finally believed that Pearl had dined to an elegant sufficiency—meaning she was stuffed to the ears—she was beginning to worry about the two spirits. They were so very young and weak, and they'd been gone quite a long time.

"Where do you suppose they are?" she asked as they exited the café, shivering a little against the October chill. "Your spirit. The ones you sent off to . . . you know."

"Ah." He seemed to come back from far away and gestured. Writing a sigil on the air? Or a mere fluttering of hands? With him it was difficult to tell. Maybe that was why he did it. "She is no conjurer, dear heart. Don't steal away her warmth."

And the chill went away. Some of it did. He was speaking to a spirit. Mary—he called her "dear heart." It was so frustrating not to be able to *see*. But she wouldn't grab at his hand, much as she might want to. Ladies didn't do that sort of thing, and she was fairly certain apprentices didn't, either.

"What? What does it say?" She couldn't stop herself asking.

He didn't seem to hear. "Indeed she is, so give her a bit more distance," he said, still not talking to Pearl, though she supposed it might seem so to others. "It's only polite."

Grey held out his ungloved hand with a distant smile and Pearl slipped hers into it, thrilled that he'd remembered her presence and thought to share the spirit's information with her. He turned and began an aimless-seeming stroll down the street, hand in hand. The girl-spirit floated wispily along between them, sort of hovering over their hands. Did she look fainter than before? More transparent?

"What did you discover, dearest?" Grey asked.

Mr. Carteret. Not Grey. It was hard to remember to think of him as Mr. Carteret when he kept insisting she call him Grey. But she had to. She had to try, any rate. It felt too dangerous to think of him any other way.

"How is your friend?" Pearl asked. "The one who went with you?"

Oh, fine. He's found a grand place to hide and watch. Mary did a little midair dance. *I saw the place where our ghost was murdered,* she said, her voice—

Pearl's first thought was that it sounded tinny, distant. But it didn't *sound.* She didn't hear it with her ears. The words didn't just appear in her mind, either. She "heard" them with the same sense she detected magic with. Which likely explained why Mary sounded so faint. She was borrowing Grey's—Mr. Carteret's—magic to hear her.

Want to see? Mary whirled with excitement, becoming even wispier around the edges.

Grey—Mister—*oh, stuff it.* She was tired of trying. It was a losing battle, anyway, her walls crumbling under the cannonade of his astonishing appearance and unexpected kindness.

Grey sighed. "No," he said. "I do not particularly wish to see. But I suppose we must."

He hailed a hackney cab from the corner ahead. When Pearl was settled and he had climbed in next to her, she indulged her curiosity about the little spirit.

Mary most resembled a fragment of fog that didn't blow away. Sometimes a sweet face formed out of the fog. Sometimes it came together in a youthful, dancing, almost invisible figure. But mostly she was a wisp of fog.

The ghosts in the cellar hadn't been like that. They'd looked like themselves. At least, she assumed that was what they'd looked like in life. Male and female, young and old, gap-toothed or wrinkled or brawny or thin. Maybe that was another difference between ghosts and spirits. Was it something she ought to know? After all, she was learning sorcery, not conjury.

"Does our friend look a bit faded to you?" Pearl asked instead. That was of concern to both of them.

Grey frowned at the drifting spirit. "She's expended a great deal of effort on our behalf, so it's likely. It requires energy to act on our plane. As soon as she shows us the location, she can rest. Time is different where she is, so she can rest a long time, and return only minutes after leaving, if we need her."

"What if I lick my thumb again? Pass it over the sigil?" Pearl had buttoned up her cuff for lunch in the café. Grey held that hand, so she wouldn't have to let go to unbutton it again. She reached across to begin.

"No need." He moved her hand away. "She has enough energy for this, and if she doesn't, *I* will share."

Pearl frowned at him.

He lifted an eyebrow. "Who is the conjurer here? And who is the magic-master?"

She sighed. "You, and you."

"Which means?" The other eyebrow went up to join the first.

"You know more about spirit magic than I do."

"I know more about *all* magic than you do. And therefore when I say you shall not work it, you will not."

"Yes, sir." She knew he was right. But she felt useless, not helping in some manner. Maybe when she finished reading her book he would allow her to do more. She was still carting it around with her, though she'd almost forgotten it in the hospital cellar.

The hackney ride back to Whitechapel and the docks was too rough to attempt to read, with all the starts and stops due to traffic. The shouting in the streets didn't help, either. Pearl didn't bother opening the book. She rode in the cab holding onto her magic-master's hand and told herself it was only to borrow his conjurer's vision.

The spell in the cellar calling the ghost had tired him. It wasn't strange that she noticed. Of course she would pay attention to her magic-master's welfare, to the dark circles beneath his eyes and the droop at the corners of his beautiful mouth.

During the conjuring of the ghost, Pearl had shared with him the magic she'd taken in from all the innocent blood in that cellar. Innocent blood, but not necessarily innocent souls. Even the blackest soul could be wrong-fully killed, she supposed. But that wasn't the point. The point was that she had used the magic to strengthen Grey. Could she do it again? Now?

It wouldn't violate his ban on experimentation. She'd done it already. He knew it just as well as she did. Now, if she could just remember how she'd done it.

There was a faint resonance echoing between them. A familiarity, as if a piece of her resided with him. And a piece of him existed inside her. They'd sworn their oath of apprenticeship in blood. That exchange must have created the resonance.

If so, it could prove useful. Pearl reached for that echo of herself inside Grey, and the magic there slid into syn-chronization with hers as easily as reaching out to take his hand. She gathered up some of the load of magic she carried, holding back what *tasted* of Angus Galloway, and let it trickle through the conduit between them.

She fed it into him slowly, alert to any sign that he noticed what she was doing. The magic eased his exhaustion—she could see it—and she didn't want him to stop her. Giving him the magic didn't take anything from her. She had more than enough. And in this part of London, she only had to reach out to gather in more. Murder and assault lurked in every alley.

His blood soaked up the magic, to a point. Before she realized the blood had taken all it could hold, the magic began to layer itself along his bones.

How did she know that? Pearl told herself she would look it up later, and pulled the extra magic back out of him.

It came easily, which eased her concerns. She considered letting it stay, but she didn't know what the magic sheathing his bones would do. Act as a reserve energy supply? Eat away at his bones from the inside? Or perhaps nothing at all. That made it experimentation, and therefore forbidden. She stored the magic back where it had come from. Her own blood, most likely.

"What are you doing?" Grey demanded, breaking his grip on her hand.

"Nothing." Pearl hoped she didn't sound as guilty as she felt. How had he noticed? She'd been careful. He'd said he wasn't sensitive to sorcery. "What makes you think I was doing anything?"

One of those expressive eyebrows winged upward, screaming his skepticism. "Perhaps because you protest so vigorously. Or perhaps because I am feeling more vigorous." He scowled at her. "What are you doing?"

"Nothing. Truly. I was . . . stirring the magic around." It could be described that way. "Moving it here and there. And touching. There's a great deal of it roundabouts here. I was—" She did it now, reached out and *touched* the waves of magic oozing from the alleyways. "It's a bit like trailing your fingers in the water, when you're rowing in a boat. I was just . . . tasting."

He scowled at her a little longer, suspicion in every angle of that handsome face. She stirred the magic a little more, hoping he could sense it. There was so much. A flood tide of blood magic just waiting to be scooped up and used, eager for justice. After a long, narrow-eyed moment, he huffed out a faint breath and sat back in his seat.

"I suppose it is logical," he said, "that if you can sense my conjury when we are holding hands, I can sense your sorcery in turn."

"Exactly." Pearl beamed happily at him, just as he sat up straight again and called out to the cabbie.

"Turn here. To the left."

She dared to touch her little finger to the back of his hand and was gratified when he clasped it again. Mary's eager little face had coalesced out of her foggy manifestation, looking straight ahead as the cab driver made the turn.

There. The face disappeared and a hand formed, down where a hand ought to be, pointing at an empty, rather derelict warehouse. The broad doors, meant for rolling in casks or backing in wagons, were fastened shut by a shiny new padlock. *That's the place our ghost came to.*

Magic, created by the spilling of a man's innocent lifeblood, foamed around the building in agitated waves, driven by the captive ghost. Pearl siphoned some of it off. It was getting easier with the practice.

Davy popped up. *It 'appened 'ere, guvnor. Can ya feel it?*

Grey nodded, distracted. The cabbie drew his restless horse to a halt and Grey helped Pearl alight, dismissing the man with an extra coin for his trouble. Horses didn't like ghosts, or so Pearl had heard. They didn't seem to mind spirits, though.

"Young friends," Grey said to the hovering spirits. "I have one last task for you. I need you to pass a message to my Briganti. Meade, primarily. I need a full investigations team here straightaway. With a set of bolt cutters."

Mary and Davy both saluted and vanished with matching cheeky grins.

Grey seized the lock and yanked at it, testing its

strength, Pearl supposed. "The river police have a station just one street over. I can go fetch them," she offered.

"You're dressed like a lady now, not a street urchin. Even with your 'don't-look' magic, you're not safe alone." Grey scowled at the warehouse. "But I don't want to leave this place unguarded."

"Why? It's broad daylight. He won't bring another victim here now." She shrugged. "It's padlocked, so whatever's inside is obviously important to the killer. He won't abandon it. Why not wait until he comes back and capture him then?" But what if—

Sweet heaven. Could someone already be suffering inside, bound or drugged, in pain? Pearl had to hold tight to Grey's hand to keep herself upright, she went so suddenly light-headed. "Can you find out? If someone is in there?"

Grey gestured, a sigil drawn in the air, muttering under his breath. Pearl sensed the arrival of a spirit, stronger, older than either Mary or Davy, but without any physical manifestation she could detect. It seemed to listen and depart.

"This spirit does not like to waste energy on appearances," Grey said. "But it is dependable. It died at Jena fighting Napoleon, so it is older and stronger than our young friends."

"What about the ghost? Is it here?" Pearl tried not to clutch at her magic-master, but it was difficult not to. The clouded sky and chill air, the damp brick and wood walls rising high on all sides, and the churning anger of magic crying out for justice combined into an ominous atmosphere. Pearl felt as if disaster hovered, waiting to crash down on them.

"It is." Grey tightened his grip on her hand. "After the summons to the hospital, it is likely waiting, gathering its energy. I doubt it has much left."

"You gave it a great deal of yours. Wouldn't that leave it less depleted?"

"It needed my energy to manifest so far from the trap that has ensnared it. It shouldn't have any left."

The spirit that had gone into the warehouse came shooting back out through the wall, a shimmer of speed trailed by that roaring shriek from the basement morgue. The spirit whirled itself around Grey, then coiled around the faint sigil still painted on Pearl's forearm in a chill bracelet, as the ghost of Angus Galloway took form in the bricks, thrashing to get out.

"It appears I was wrong." Only the tight grip of Grey's hand around Pearl's betrayed anything more than casual interest. "The ghost seems to have plenty of energy remaining." He drew a sigil on the air and Pearl felt the magic move to empower its warding.

No one else is inside, the spirit huddling around Pearl's sigil communicated. The silent voice held a faint accent and a crisp, almost military air. But then, if he died at the battle of Jena between Napoleon and the allied Germanic states, one would expect him to be a soldier of some sort. *Only the ghost.*

"You're a spirit yourself now, friend," Grey said as the ghost screamed at them. "Ghosts should not frighten you."

It is not their ghostliness, but their madness that . . . unnerves me.

"It is quite unnerving," Pearl agreed with a shiver.

She hears me? The little madchen? The spirit seemed to come to attention on her arm.

"She can share my magic. On occasion." Grey gestured, a simple wave of his hand this time, dismissing the spirit. "Stay close, in case we need you."

I am Walther, he said, becoming a thinly transparent soldier in order to bow and click his heels. *If you have need of me, you have only to call my name.*

"She's a sorcerer. Will you be able to hear it?" Grey sounded curious rather than annoyed. Pearl wondered, though, if he resented his spirits paying her so much attention.

I will be staying close, yes? I will watch as well as listen. Walther faded from view again. *She reminds me of my sister. I will watch.*

"Excellent." Grey gave a brisk, almost military nod of his own. He raked his frock coat back on one side to prop a hand on his hip as he studied the raging image in the bricks.

The ghost fought to escape, the bricks bulging outward as if shaped to his form, brick hands reaching to seize and rend, mouth open and screaming in—in fury? Anguish? Pain? All of those, Pearl decided.

"The bricks aren't really reshaping themselves like that, are they?" she whispered to the conjurer at her side.

He let go her hand. "Are they?"

The wall now appeared as flat and solid as all the walls around it. "No," she said. "But I can still hear him."

He nodded as he clasped her hand in his again and the wall went back to its writhing. "Ghosts rarely have strength to manifest to nonconjurers in daylight, even with the moon's rising. This one will need greater warding before night falls."

"Or we could lay him."

Grey took a deep breath and let it out. "True. It's obvious, now that we've found this place, that he's absolutely useless to us as he is. You might as well send the magic home. If it does free him, perhaps his spirit will be willing and able to help."

"Don't you think he will?" Pearl couldn't imagine why not. If she were murdered, she would want to help bring her killer to justice.

"They usually don't. Spirits have better things to do. A better place to be." He ignored the thrashing ghost to study Pearl. The scrutiny made her want to squirm.

"Perhaps they leave that thirst for justice behind in their blood and its magic."

"Then why would giving the magic back release them from their ghost traps? If blood is where the vengeance resides?"

"Perhaps because the sorceress who releases it also promises that justice will be found. Justice, Pearl. Not vengeance. Amanusa was always very clear on the difference."

She nodded. "So, are we ready for me to do that with this ghost? Send his magic back?"

"His blood was part of the spell you sent out to harry the murderers?" Grey asked, watching her again.

If she didn't watch him back, maybe his stare wouldn't make her feel quite so squirmish. "Yes. I used all the magic I had. It was all mixed up together. Like cake batter. It didn't separate out again until I sent it home. Back to the dead."

"So you've already used his blood to seek justice. Good. Try it then. Let's see if it works like it did with the others."

Pearl took a deep breath and hoped she remembered how she'd done this the last time. Only a few hours ago. Her hand wrapped around the sorcery book was damp from nerves, slippery against the ancient leather cover. The other hand was warmer, held in Grey's as it was, but if he didn't let go, she wouldn't. She wanted to see what happened with the magic.

She invoked the blood of Angus Galloway and repeated the words she'd said before, as best she could recall them. Then she released the magic. It soared toward the angry ghost and settled over his straining form like a mist, then sank beneath the surface. The struggles slowed. The expression on that sharp-boned face transformed from rage to astonishment.

It wasn't all her magic, though. Blood magic was

warm. Sweet and salty, with a pulse. Or maybe it breathed. It had a kind of rhythm to it. A throbbing. That was what she sent to the ghost. But there was other magic with it. Cool and crisp and clear. Not her magic . . . *Grey's*.

Conjury blended with the sorcery, spirit with blood, reason with passion, mind with body.

She couldn't sense how the magic did what it did, but she knew the things that trapped Angus Galloway snapped and crumbled and disentangled themselves from his ghostly appendages. She saw him step forward, out of the bricks. She saw his face, his entire being transformed by joy as light infused him, brightening beyond all vision, even the magical. And then he was gone, the light fading.

"It's not just sorcery," she whispered, finally. "Your magic was in it, too."

"We've done it twice. A third time will confirm the spell." He looked down at her, but this time Pearl didn't think he saw her. She didn't feel all jumbled up inside from his look.

Grey went on musing out loud. "I suppose we ought to check the spellbooks, to see if we're rediscovering old knowledge or if this is something new." He pulled out his pocket watch and checked the time. "How long can it possibly be taking Meade to assemble his team?"

Pearl shrugged. It didn't matter to her. She had no other appointments. Her time belonged to her magic-master.

A horse pulling a cart full of boxes and kegs came plodding around the corner from London Dock, heading for one of the other, more sturdy padlocked warehouse doors. A few men rode on the cart along with the driver. Good thing they hadn't come while she and Grey were working their magic. The ghost's shrieking wail would have upset the horse, at the least.

One of the men, dressed in a brown striped suit and top hat, rather than workingman's rough attire, hopped off the cart and unlocked the door. Grey motioned for Pearl to remain where she was and sauntered over to speak to the man in charge.

10

THE CLERK—FOR his clothing was not fine enough to be the owner of the goods or the warehouse— flipped over some pages on the clipboard he held and made a notation as the workmen began unloading the cart. Grey scribbled on the page, and a moment later, one of the stevedores hoisted a small keg and carried it over to deposit at Pearl's feet. With a polite nod and a tug of his cap, he went back to his work.

Grey continued to talk with the clerk another moment, until he noticed Pearl standing beside the keg. He excused himself and returned to her side.

"As I am now the proud owner of an entire keg of East Indian peppercorns," he said, "purchased for the sole purpose of providing you with a seat, I suggest you sit yourself upon it and continue your studies."

She had been wondering. As she sat, and he turned to go back to the workmen, she asked quickly, "What are you doing?"

Her curiosity would get her in trouble one day. In truth, it already had. Too many times.

"Questioning them. They might have seen something." He opened his hands like a book, and pointed at the closed volume on her lap. "Don't fret. I'll tell you everything I learn."

"Thank you." Most men wouldn't. Most men hadn't;

not the ones related to her. They'd patted her on the head and told her not to worry.

She opened her book and did as she'd been told. The more she knew, the better she could understand the magic.

Shadows crept across the cobblestones and up the walls as they waited. The cart was emptied and driven away. Other carts came to other buildings. Pearl slogged her way through some twenty-odd pages of Elizabethan prose. She was getting used to the syntax and phrasing, so the reading came a bit easier. It was the concepts that made her brain hurt.

Grey questioned all of the workers who came down the narrow street. Some of them had seen a man in a black suit and top hat opening the padlock and going inside the warehouse. They could give no description other that he was "shortish" and lean. Grey had already told Pearl the murderer was likely a well-to-do man. The working class were more straightforward in their murders, he said. If they wanted someone dead, they'd bash him in the head or stick a knife in his ribs and be done with it.

"This man's purpose was not murder," Grey said. "It was the magic. The choice of victim was random. I believe Angus Galloway was selected because he was available, and had some attribute required by the murderer for his magic."

"What?" Pearl soaked up everything he told her.

"I don't know, do I? Red hair. Or perhaps a man in the prime of life was needed. That's what the investigation is to determine. If we can learn what the killer was trying to do with this perverted spell of his, perhaps we will learn who could have committed the crime, and have someone to point Amanusa's sorcery toward."

I am a sorceress, Pearl thought, but she didn't say it aloud. She knew what his response would be: *You're an apprentice.* And he would be correct.

She frowned down at her book. "I know you don't have any facts yet, beyond the condition of Mr. Galloway's body and the residue of magic from it, but do you have any idea what the murderer was trying to do? You said at the first that he was trying to call a demon—but, why?"

Grey sighed and toed a pebble away from her keg, eyes focused on his action. "I do not know."

"Didn't you say conjury can't call demons?" Pearl was confused.

"I did. I also said there are idiots—those outside the guild, mostly—who don't believe it. Who say we're trying to keep the truth to ourselves, amongst the privileged few. Books exist—fragments of old manuscripts, or cobbled-together notations from ancient experiments. No matter how we deny the possibility or destroy the books, there's always one book or part of a book that is smuggled away. Hidden and preserved for the next idiot who wants to try to control the power of a fallen angel."

Grey sighed and leaned against the warehouse wall, folding his arms. "It's never been proven—because who would be so abysmally stupid as to attempt the test?—but I believe that the stories and whispers persist because it amuses the rulers of hell to play at obedience to the will of the fool who thinks he has summoned them. For just as long as suits them. Until the demons have wreaked as much havoc and sucked in as many victims as possible.

"Then they crush the conjurer, seize their prizes, and celebrate by wreaking more havoc. Demons are good at havoc."

"You sound rather vicarish." It surprised her. He put on such an air of decadence, depravity, and dissolution. As if he believed in nothing and cared for nothing. But she already knew that was false.

"Do I?" He sounded appalled. "I shall have to remedy that immediately."

Then his dilettante's mask fell away. "Conjurers deal with a reality other than the physical. We know a little of how that realm works. There is good and there is evil. It exists. We have seen it. How can one not believe what one has seen?"

He went silent then, as if shocked by his own vehemence. Pearl took the space to digest what he said.

As she considered, a pair of carriages came rattling around the corner, pulled up, and began to disgorge magicians. The Briganti Investigations Branch had arrived.

Pearl sat on her keg and alternated between reading and watching as the padlock was cut away and investigators began carrying items out. She couldn't go inside to watch because Grey directed the activity from the doorway beside her and he refused to let her move from her keg. She had no opportunity to slip away and do as she wished.

A box wagon with BRIGANTI painted in stark white over shiny black appeared a short while after the carriages. Before the padlock on the door of the wagon could be opened, a pair of investigators brought out a sturdy table to load, reeking of spilled blood and sorcery.

Pearl covered her nose, but the smell wasn't physical. She stood, wanting a look at the table. Was it stained to match the crimson magic?

Grey watched her as she stepped toward it, but didn't stop her. She eased a bit closer, until she saw the rust-brown stains soaked into one end of the raw wood, still thick and sticky looking. She'd seen worse, she reminded herself. She shivered, suddenly chilled in the shadows.

I didno' bleed till th' bastard broke ma nose. The whisper came from nowhere straight into her head, Glaswegian accent and all. *After he worked his way up through the rest of ma bones.*

Pearl yelped, jumped, dropped her book onto her foot, and hopped again because it hurt. Grey was there instantly, helped her to lean against her keg. He took her by the arms and drew her away, out of sight of the table, but not out of range of its stains.

"Are you all right?" He looked her over, head to toe, making her feel entirely peculiar. More than she did already. "You cried out before you dropped the book. What happened?"

"Was he Scottish?" she whispered, shaking, but just a bit. "The victim?"

Grey's eyes widened and he dropped his hands from her arms. "It's probable, given a name like Angus Galloway."

"I heard him." She whispered softer, so quietly he had to bend close to hear, his too-long hair brushing her nose. She told him what she'd heard, her lips at his ear.

Grey drew back, frowning at her. He scanned the area, obviously using his other vision. "Keep an eye out, lads," he called. "There's spirits abroad."

"How did I hear him?" Pearl was frightened down to her book-smashed toes. "We weren't—" She gestured at his hands.

"I don't know. We'll puzzle it out later."

"Will we have time? The number of things saved for later seems to be piling rather high."

"We'll find the time. Carve it from somewhere." He turned away to glance at a notebook brought to him by one of his men. He waved it on to the wagon.

"What are you doing with my wagon?" A blustery voice boomed through the narrow street, so loud that Pearl wondered if it didn't shake a few bricks loose. The voice belonged to a big, broad man with luxurious brown side-whiskers.

"Belongs to the Briganti," Grey drawled, suddenly all languid nonchalance. "Last I looked, I was still Briganti. As to what I'm doing with your precious wagon, I'm loading up the evidence of a murder to take it back to council workrooms so we can find the murderer."

"Last *I* looked, *you* were the one accused of the

crime." The man's chin was clean shaven, but his side-whiskers grew into his mustache in an elaborate design.

"Been proven innocent. By an unimpeachable source. You should know that, Simmons." Grey grinned and winked. "Not guilty of murder, at any rate. Haven't been innocent since I was in short pants."

Ah. This was the Briganti colonel who thought Grey usurped his authority. Grey probably did, every chance he got.

"What about this, sir?" Another young conjurer stood at the door, holding up a coil of rope. Rope saturated with sorcery.

That's what th' bastard bound me with. The mental murmur slid icy fingers down her spine, and Pearl couldn't stop another high-pitched yip.

Tied me to th' table with a rope across ma neck, so if I struggled too much it choked me. The voice paused. *Hard not t'struggle when your leg's bein' broke by a great hammer.*

She swallowed down another squeak and tugged at her magic-master's sleeve. He looked down at her.

"Take it," she said. "Can't you feel the magic?"

Grey's eyes unfocused for a moment, then he waved it toward the wagon.

"What's that female doing here?" Simmons demanded, chin tucked so deep into his neck that Pearl was surprised he could speak. "No place for a woman, Carteret. You should know that."

"My apprentice, Pearl Parkin. Parkin, Colonel Simmons. Can't teach her if she's not with me, can I?"

"What can you teach her here? Murder investigations?"

Grey's expression brightened. "Yes, exactly. She is an apprentice sorceress, you see, so of course a great deal of her practice will involve murder investigations. Innocent blood, and all that. No reason not to start her in right away, is there?"

"Abomination." The word came hissing out of the late-afternoon shadows, slithering from somewhere beyond the colonel. It would have frightened Pearl, coming out of the rising fog as it did, except it was a physical sound. One she heard with her ears. Or did that make it more dangerous?

"Oh, shut up, Cranshaw." Grey rolled his eyes. "We've heard it all before and we're bloody sick of it. Frankly, the only one not delighted sorcery's come back is you."

Simmons harrumphed. "Now see here—"

"Admit it, Freddie." Grey poked Simmons in his barrel chest. "If it didn't mean we had to admit these terrifying females to our ranks, you'd be dancing in the streets because sorcery's back." He stabbed a finger toward the box wagon being slowly loaded with items from the warehouse. "It's why the Briganti van has always been black and *white*. Black for conjury. White for sorcery."

"Sorcery is evil. Corrupt and vile. Spawned of Satan." Cranshaw crept out of the fog, hissing at Pearl as he spoke.

She remembered him. This was the man who'd tried to bar her from the council library.

"Oh, for—" Grey flung his hand toward the gaping maw of the warehouse door. *"That* is vile, Nigel. Murder done for no other purpose than to produce magic. Magic for who knows what vile and corrupt, *evil* spell."

Cranshaw winced. At least Pearl thought she saw it. "Sorcery," he hissed. "Blood spilled to call magic. It's evil. You said it yourself."

Grey's fists clenched. Pearl could feel him quivering, as if he barely restrained himself from leaping on the man. "You were there, in Paris," he snarled. "You know sorcery depends on blood *willingly* given, or it turns against the one who shed it."

"Lies—" Cranshaw snarled back.

"This—" Grey gestured at the warehouse again. "This was conjury. Some blind fool thinking he could control a demon."

"He?" Cranshaw pounced on the word. "Are you so sure the killer wasn't a woman? Women are sorcerers. They draw magic from blood, use their subtle wiles to pervert what is good and true."

'Tweren't a woman. That icy whisper returned to freeze her again. *'Twas a man. Cloaked and hooded, t'be sure, but only a man could ha' swung that hammer, the one that broke ma bones.*

"The spirits say otherwise," Grey declared.

Grey heard the spirit this time? Must have. It made Pearl feel better to know that she wasn't the only one to hear him.

"Are you here for a reason, Cranshaw?" Grey asked. "Or did you come to cause trouble?"

"I came to prevent trouble. To stop the corruption of the minds of—"

"Then leave. If you have no legitimate purpose here, go away."

Cranshaw drew himself upright in outraged dignity. "I am magister of the wizard's guild—"

"But you're not Briganti." Grey interrupted him again as Pearl watched, fascinated. The dilettante was gone, replaced by the—the conjurer. The commander of the Investigations Branch. "And this is Briganti business. No one may interfere, not even the head of council. Not even the queen."

He spoke through clenched teeth, hands closing into fists, alarming Pearl a little. She'd never seen him in this guise.

"Do you understand me, Cranshaw?" Grey took a step toward the wizard. "If you do not leave now, of your own accord, I will have you . . . escorted from here. As is within my authority."

"You are bewitched!" Cranshaw's pale eyes widened in horror, then narrowed again with hate. "She has bewitched you."

"No, Cranshaw. You've shaped my opinion of you all on your own. You have annoyed me. You have disturbed me. You have disgusted me with your twisted ranting and your stirring up hatred and fear of the very thing we need most simply because you are, for some ungodly reason, terrified of women."

"Not ungodly. *They* are ungodly with their sly looks and slinking walk and—" Cranshaw noticed Simmons's expression of shock and disgust, and fell silent.

"Egad, man, listen to yourself," Simmons spluttered. "Females can be a nuisance, but they're still only females."

Pearl thought about protesting. She would have, except the same exact thing could be said about males. Though males were more of a nuisance.

Grey snapped his fingers, summoning two of his larger investigators. "Briganti, please escort Magister Cranshaw away from our crime investigation site. With whatever force necessary. Just be sure he departs. If he does not—" The expression on his face made Pearl shiver, just a bit. "Escort him again. More emphatically."

The two men, both conjurers, as were most of Grey's force, grinned and advanced on the scowling wizard.

Cranshaw aimed his scowl at Pearl, so filled with hate it made her edge behind Grey. How could he hate her so? He'd only just met her.

Grey moved, stepping between them, as if blocking the malevolence of that stare. The escorts reached Cranshaw, who ignored them until they grasped his arms. He threw off their hands, spun on his heel, and marched away.

When he turned the corner at the end of the street, Pearl took a deep breath. It came easier simply because the tension had faded. Wizards couldn't stifle someone through malicious intent alone. Could they?

"That man is a boil on the arse of all civilization," Grey muttered.

Pearl's laugh burst out of her before she could stop it, and Grey wheeled about to glare down at her. Unlike Cranshaw's scowl, his glare felt almost warm. "You did not hear that," he announced.

"Hear what?" She widened her eyes and tried to look utterly innocent and ignorant. Innocent was probably too much of a stretch, but ignorant was naught but truth. She was woefully ignorant about far too many things.

Grey nodded briskly, lips twitching in a tiny smile, then turned to shout at his men. "Once you've noted its location in the warehouse, clear it all out. We're taking the lot back to the workrooms."

"I'm drawing as fast as I can," someone shouted back in a working-class accent. "Need more bloody light."

"Duncan, where's our light? What's the use of having an alchemist on the field squad if you can't give us light when we need it?" Grey stomped to the open door and glowered in as a soft golden glow flickered and rose to shine out into the street.

"Sorry, sir. Didn't notice." Duncan had a northern accent, not Yorkshire. Manchester, maybe. Pearl wasn't an expert on accents.

"Stop gawping at the drama, do your jobs, and perhaps we can get out of here before midnight." He backed away from the open door so a group of men could wrestle an oversized cabinet out of the warehouse and onto the wagon.

"If you fill up the wagon before the place is empty," Grey said to one of the men in a more moderate tone, "take it back to the council hall and unload it, then come back for the rest."

"Yes, sir." The man stopped beside Grey and mopped his forehead with a handkerchief. "It'll be late before we finish. You intend to keep your apprentice here the whole time?"

"Not that it's any of your business what my apprentice does, Investigator Meade, but yes. Parkin will stay until we're done." His words rode an edge in his voice that had Meade lifting an eyebrow.

Meade—Grey's second-in-command, wasn't he? Pearl watched him. Did he, too, think this snappishness was unusual?

Grey seemed to recognize his own out-of-character mood and rocked back on his heels, clasping his hands behind his back. When he spoke again, his voice was mild, relaxed. Pearl could sense the tension deep within him, but it was not coiled tight, ready to spring. "With Ferguson out of commission," he said, "we need someone sensitive to sorcery to go through the warehouse with us. Miss Parkin will be of assistance. Seems Ferguson is a touch *too* sensitive to sorcery. I hadn't realized he'd never attended the morgue before."

"Right, sir. Of course." Meade glanced skeptically at Pearl.

"If you're worried about my tender sensibilities, Mr. Meade," Pearl said. "Don't. I haven't got many, after living in Whitechapel the last pair of years."

"I think he's more concerned with your physical endurance, Parkin." Grey reached into his pockets and addressed Meade again. "Send one of the lads for food. We could all use it. And have him bring a carriage robe before he goes. The damp is rising off the river."

The damp was always rising off the river, but now that night was falling, it was getting colder. Pearl welcomed the heavy robe wrapped around her. Grey moved her peppercorn keg just inside the open warehouse doors, where the damp was less and the alchemist's light fell clearly. She opened her book again, but once more had trouble concentrating on the words it held. The activity around her was far more interesting.

It wasn't just the men cataloguing the things they found, sketching those things' location relative to everything else, and carrying them out to load into the wagon. Pearl could see magic.

She'd always been able to sense magic, as far back as she could remember, though she hadn't known what it was until much later. Magic was warm and coppery, a velvety brush against her skin. But she'd never *seen* it before now. The book had explained how to relax her vision and let that touch-taste-smell sense float up to her eyes.

It was so easy, she worried for a moment that she was borrowing Grey's magic again. But he was on the other side of the warehouse, inspecting a spot on the floor. Not paying any attention to her in the least, though she had no doubt that if she stirred from her keg, he would know instantly.

Perhaps it was easy because she'd done it first without realizing it, when she had taken his hand in the hospital cellar and seen all the ghosts. Then she had borrowed. Now she didn't.

Now it was all hers. Eddies of red in all shades from deep, purplish crimson to the vibrant, almost glowing scarlet of fresh blood pooled along the floor, piled up in a sort of drift in the center where she assumed the murder had been committed. It swirled and churned every time someone strode through it, or when a spirit plunged through.

She could see spirits. More as pale foggy wisps stirring the red liquid-solid-smoke of sorcery, than anything substantial. One of the wisps she thought might be Angus Galloway, because sometimes she could see the shape of a long-fingered hand in the mist, or a beaky nose.

Pearl could just make out the golden glow of magic feeding the light Grey's alchemist had made. It blended with the light, but had more . . . substance. She needed new words to talk about magic. She couldn't see any wizardry moving in the warehouse, but wondered if that might be because there were no wizards present working magic, rather than her inability to recognize it. Wizards were quite rare among the ranks of magicians. Male ones, anyway. Most wizards had been women, long ago.

When the food arrived, Pearl made Duncan, the alchemist, take his food first, though they all wanted to be polite and defer to her. Duncan had been powering that light steadily since he'd sparked it, and though he drew the power for it from the air and bricks and stones around them, it took his energy, too.

Another hour or so after the meal, the warehouse was swept clean of all physical items, including the dust from the wide plank floor. It would be tested for magical residues. Everyone had been sent back to the I-Branch offices to help log in the evidence, save for Duncan, Grey, and Pearl. They stood at the inside end of the warehouse, looking across the expanse toward the door.

"I should have sent a message to Harry," Grey said, "asking if Elinor could assist us, since Ferguson is ill. Cranshaw won't let any of the other wizards help. Threw six kinds of fit when Ferguson applied to join I-Branch."

"Whatever for?" Pearl asked.

"'Cause he's mad as a hatter," Duncan muttered from Grey's other side. The young alchemist had a broad, friendly face, its rounded-off edges making him look younger than Pearl suspected he was.

Grey's lips twitched, as if resisting a smile. "You might have noticed, Parkin. I-Branch is a trifle thick on the ground with conjurers. Until our new sorceress popped up at the end of the summer to divert Cranshaw with the wickedness of sorcery, he preached hell and damnation against conjury.

"He's one of those who believes conjury can call demons or spirits from hell. Apparently, to him, if you're dead, you're damned. Or something like that. But conjury is apparently the lesser of two evils."

"Surely the other wizards don't believe him," she said.

"Many do. Those who don't—most don't dare go against him. Cranshaw's got their bollock—got them in his grip because of his power as guild magister. Ferguson's an idealist, with a private income, so he was willing to join us. And as a Briganti, he's less vulnerable to the magister's power. But he's an exception."

"We'll just have to do our best without him, sir," Duncan said.

"Quite." Grey looked down at Pearl and she tried to look filled with energy and enthusiasm. She wanted to droop with weariness, but she also wanted to see this through. She'd never been on this side of a murder. Only on the "mourning the victim" and "hiding from killers" side. She liked this side better.

"Do you have the neckerchief, Duncan?" Grey looked out at the warehouse. "The one I told you to hold back from the wagon?"

"Yes, sir. Here it is." He drew a carefully folded, faded red cloth from an inner coat pocket.

Grey took the neck cloth and passed it to Pearl. "We should have brought the handkerchief with the blood I collected yesterday, but I foolishly did not anticipate needing it. If the stains on this cloth are Galloway's blood, as I suspect they are, it will serve."

He was correct in his surmise. Pearl could feel the blood, smell the magic rising from it. "Serve for what?"

"As we inspect this room for magic, to see what magic might have been used, we are also going to sweep it clean. It is part of our duty." He looked down at Pearl, a warmth in his expression that warmed her more than it should. "But now, I have hope that we can leave it actually clean of magic. Leave it without that whispering residue of 'murder committed here.'"

"You think so, sir?" Duncan sounded excited. "I've been to too many places that felt haunted like that, but I've always thought it was ghosts. Conjury, not sorcery."

"I did as well. But innocent blood cries out for justice, and without a sorceress to use the magic and release the ghosts . . ." Grey cleared his throat. "Parkin, when you gather the blood magic—and even I can feel it in this place—put it in the blood on this kerchief. Amanusa said that sorcery is held in blood and bone, so—"

Pearl gathered up a little of the magic swirling close and poured it into the small stain on the cloth. The bloodstain soaked up the magic as if it were the Sahara and the magic a few drops of water. "Yes." She nodded. "That will work."

11

THEY BEGAN. PEARL went first, because although the actual amount of blood spilled was minimal, the murder created the same amount of magic as if all of Angus Galloway's blood had been poured onto the ground. Much of the magic had accompanied his body, but so much remained here, where he'd been killed, that they needed her to clear it out so their search could be done.

"Do you suppose the murderer was afraid of sorcery?" Mr. Duncan asked as he waited with Grey. "Could that be why so little blood was spilled?"

Grey gave a sigh deep enough that Pearl heard it from halfway across the warehouse, where the table had been standing and the crimson and scarlet magic piled highest. "It is possible. However, I believe the reason goes back to those damnable demonic grimoires we've never been able to eliminate.

"Most of them claim something like 'the more painful the death, the more control the magician has over the demon.' Exsanguination—bleeding to death—is one of the least painful ways of dying. It's why so many suicides take that way out of their despair."

Pearl finished sweeping all the magic into the spot of blood on the neckerchief, and walked back across the warehouse to rejoin the two men. She marveled that she couldn't see the spot pulsing or glowing, given all the power she'd shoved into the small stain, but it remained a thumb-size, rust-colored splotch to ordinary vision. In her second sight, the color merely intensified to a vibrant scarlet against the faded orangey-red of the cloth.

"You have a fair sense of wizardry, don't you, Parkin?" Grey asked when she arrived. "I noticed you taking your time at the wizardry book in the library yesterday."

"Yes." She nodded, then made a face. "But it didn't feel right. Not like the sorcery book. Like home."

"Nevertheless, you will be able to recognize it."

"I didn't see any earlier, while everyone was working and I was practicing my secondary vision."

"I doubt anyone could, as much sorcery as was splashing about. We're going to be looking for the smallest traces of magic now. The faintest hints. Lead off, Duncan." Grey motioned for the alchemist to begin, then took Pearl by the shoulders to turn her about, and urged her forward.

Did he lay hands on her like that because he didn't trust her to turn on her own? Because he thought he could manhandle her at will? Or was he—as she was—so hungry for a touch of any kind that a shove would do?

They'd held hands for much of the day, but since he'd procured the peppercorn stool, before the Briganti arrived, he'd stayed close by without touching her once. Well, there was the time she'd yelped, the first time Angus Galloway had spoken to her. Grey had held her arms. Not as satisfying as the skin-to-skin touch of holding hands.

Pearl glanced over her shoulder at him and Grey scowled, gesturing at the space around them. "Open your magic sense to its widest. We don't want to miss anything."

Obviously he did not feel the way she did. He was her magic-master, and she had better get that through her thick head.

Duncan led the way along the warehouse walls, brushing his hands lightly over the brick.

"Does that help?" Pearl asked, deliberately turning her thoughts away from the man following her. "Touching the bricks like that?"

He smiled at her over his shoulder. Grey made a strange growling noise behind her, but she ignored him. Duncan went on. "Bricks and other products of the earth can hold an alchemical residue which is easier to sense if I touch it."

He dusted his hands off, frowning up at the wall. "I'm not sure what I'm getting here, however."

"Keep going," Grey snapped out. "The night ages while you loiter."

"Yes, sir." Duncan stiffened to an almost military attention, and moved on down the perimeter of the room.

Pearl gave Grey an aggrieved look. What was wrong with him? Did he want to do this fast, or properly?

On some contrary whim, she crouched down and brushed her hands along the wooden floor. Wizardry was plants. Wood was from plants, so perhaps a little residue of wizardry lingered.

Grey huffed an impatient breath. "What are you doing?"

"Looking for wizardic residue," she retorted. Stated. Calmly and with consideration. "You did want me looking for wizardry, didn't you?"

"I did not say you should crawl along the floor. Get up."

Pearl ignored him. Not for the sake of disobedience,

or proving any point, though she did wish he would moderate his tone. She ignored him because she sensed something in the wood.

She moved a few steps further in a scooting crouch and felt again, sweeping her hand over the floor. A splinter stabbed deep into the mound below her thumb causing a sharp pain, but she ignored it, too, to follow the magic. It hovered right on the edge of her secondary vision, but she couldn't bring it into focus. It felt wizardish, given what she knew of wizardry, which wasn't much. But it felt . . . green. Or maybe it *smelled* green.

Absently, she pulled the splinter from her hand and went back to her search, inching a few feet further to brush her fingertips along the floorboards there. Something . . . Something . . .

"You're bleeding," Grey whispered in her ear as he knelt beside her, surrounding her with his arms, his body. He cupped her hand and turned it upward, exposing the fat drop of blood that had welled up from the splinter's puncture.

She stared as he raised her hand and closed his mouth over the mound of her palm. He licked away the blood in a wickedly sensual kiss. She shuddered, magic flaring sweet and hot between them. She soaked it up, shared it with him as he licked her hand one more time. He shuddered in turn, his eyes falling closed as the magic surged through him.

Pearl felt as if she could touch him inside and out, open him up and see all his workings—mind and body. The thought frightened her. She pulled back inside herself, though she left the magic behind. She felt better, more energized. It should help Grey the same. She drew away physically, just in time.

Duncan must have noticed them no longer following, for he turned back from his brick inspecting. "Are you all right, Miss Parkin? Commander?"

Grey made a face. He much preferred the title of magister to the military sounding "commander" they'd foisted on him when the new I-Branch was created.

Pearl realized she hadn't backed out far enough. She tried again to distance herself magically, and thought she did better this time as she scrambled to her feet. Perhaps more physical distance helped as well.

"I got a splinter." She showed Duncan her hand, but pulled it back when he made as if to take hold and inspect it, uncomfortable with the idea of his touch. The barely heard rumble from Grey convinced her it was a bad idea. What was wrong with him? Other than Pearl somehow crawling inside his head?

Grey seemed a bit stunned still, actually sitting on the floor rather than kneeling.

Hoping to give him time to recover from whatever had happened when he kissed her hand, Pearl kept talking. "I thought I sensed wizardry."

Though if that were a mere hand-kissing, she was seven feet tall and Chinese.

Grey held up a hand and Pearl automatically took it, forgetting about the bizarre magic exchange that seemed to happen every time they touched bare-handed. He shuddered again, his eyes flying open to seize on hers. Then he used his grip on her to pull himself to his feet.

"What, exactly, did you sense?" he asked, releasing her hand in an odd combination of haste and reluctance.

"I don't think a spell was worked." She didn't know how to describe what she'd sensed, nor did she know much about wizardry or how its spells worked or how they felt when they did.

"Could have been a potion," Duncan suggested. "A potion would have made the victim malleable, easier to bring to the warehouse."

"Likely so," Grey agreed. "Make a note. Let's move on."

Duncan turned and proceeded along the wall again.

Pearl hung back, but Grey was emphatically not looking at her.

She asked him anyway, whispered, "Why did you do that? Lick up the blood?"

"Blood should always be handled carefully." His eyes slid toward the other man, as he spoke more softly than she had.

Everyone knew that. It was why, like every other woman in England, she burned the rags she used every month. The rag trade was a lucrative one. Still . . . "Yes, but why handle it like that? Why *lick* it?"

"I—" A dozen answers flickered through his eyes, all of them true. She wasn't inside his head, couldn't hear his thoughts, but she knew.

Heat rose in his eyes then, as if he had selected desire as the least dangerous among those true answers. A tremor went through Pearl in response, her body's reaction to that heated look. He captured her hand again, the magic surging forward to crash over them as the wave broke.

He lifted it to his mouth and pressed a kiss to the cup of her palm, his lips hot and soft, and damp where they parted. Pearl's tremor grew until she quivered. His tongue darted out in a swift, sleek, pointed caress, and her knees buckled. She caught herself, stiffening both knees and resolve.

"Does that answer your question?" His voice was deep and rumbly and so quiet only she could hear it.

She nodded. She feared he would offer another demonstration if she did not. She didn't need another demonstration, no matter how she wanted one. She could still see in his eyes that this was not the only answer. Not the complete answer. But she didn't think she was ready to hear the others.

They moved on through the warehouse, finding little that was not expected. The twisted, impossible conjury had indeed been the primary spell worked, though it seemed there may have been an attempt to anchor or bind it with other magics. Duncan had found a hint of alchemy lingering in the air where the sorcery had pooled, to match the wizardry traces.

When they finished, the warehouse looked just as dingy and dilapidated as before. It sported a few more stains. But it *felt* better. Almost fresh, definitely clean. Pearl took a deep breath, opening her senses as wide as they would go, and it still felt clean and fresh, even with the pervasive river aroma.

"Nice," Duncan said. "That's just grand. Nicer than any murder site I've ever been at."

"We've been without sorcery for so long, we didn't know how much we were missing." Grey smiled down at Pearl, and she just had to smile back. His smile went crooked, mischievous. "The entertainment factor alone, watching Simmons and his ilk hem and haw and bluster, is incalculable."

He had to do that, say something dismissive or mocking, to make people believe he didn't mean anything else he said. Pearl didn't know why he had to do it, but she knew it was what he did, what he somehow *had* to do. His first statement was sincere. The second wasn't, exactly.

Oh, he enjoyed watching Simmons's ilk in their shouting and blustering, no doubt about that. But entertainment was not the primary appreciation he had for sorcery. Or for Pearl. She didn't know how she felt about that, or how she ought to.

"What happens to the magic," Duncan asked when they were inside the council carriage rumbling off to Albemarle Street, "if a murder is never solved? If the innocent blood never receives its justice?"

"I don't think anyone's ever asked that question." Grey leaned against the corner of the carriage. "Magicians, for all we've been looking for someone to open the sorcery book, have mostly ignored blood magic. Hoped it would just go away."

Pearl snorted, though she tried to make it more of a ladylike *humph*. "That obviously hasn't worked."

Both men looked at her, expectant curiosity rising off them like steam.

"There's so much innocent-blood magic in these streets, I could fill a hundred handkerchiefs like this one—" She lifted the folded neckerchief with its little stain. "And I could do it just walking a single block. Not all of it's murder, mind. There's the bludgers and the bashers—"

The cant terms made her painstakingly acquired East End accent creep out, and she paused to clear out her mind and the accent. "Some of the blood comes from attacks that weren't fatal, from beatings or fights. It's still innocent blood. Still wants justice." She frowned. "But that justice may come easier. The victim is alive, and can perhaps seize it for himself."

"But it's been two hundred and thirty years since Yvaine was killed." Duncan leaned forward, earnest and eager. "What about the murderers who died before they were brought to justice?"

"I doubt my apprentice has the answer to that." Grey's voice was so dry it made Pearl thirsty. "I doubt any sorcery book in the library has the answer, since they were written before Yvaine's death."

"Surely, even then, killers died before they were caught," Pearl protested. "And there is the ultimate justice. We saw that at the morgue, with the spirits that . . . didn't ascend."

Grey nodded. "Perhaps God's justice wipes away the blood magic. We'll have to ask Amanusa when she and Jax return from Scotland."

"Do you know when that will be, sir?" Duncan asked. Pearl thought his eagerness might become exhausting if she was exposed to it overlong.

"Soon, I hope." Grey shrugged. "They are newly wed. Yvaine's tower hasn't been opened in two hundred years. I imagine they have a great deal to do before they can return. But they've been gone six weeks already."

"Then surely it will be soon."

The speculation continued until the carriage halted outside Grey's house. Pearl had no idea how late it was, but she got out there, and the carriage rattled off to take Duncan to his lodgings. Pearl went inside with Grey. He'd promised her food, and she was hungry. Two years on short rations couldn't be made up overnight. And the book said that magic should be fed. She had plenty of hungry magic to feed.

GREY MOUNTED THE stairs to his workroom at the top of the house, shouting orders to McGregor as he climbed. His household was used to the bizarre hours he kept, and McGregor had the servants working in shifts so someone was always available to provide food at any hour it might be requested. Though after midnight, the food would be a cold collation. Grey didn't know when McGregor himself slept. He always seemed to be about.

Pearl clambered up the stairs behind him, her shoes a quick clatter on the last, uncarpeted flight. Why had he invited her inside with him? At this hour of the night? Though it wasn't yet midnight, so perhaps it wasn't quite a scandal. Yet.

Not that he cared a nail paring about scandal. For himself. He didn't like to think of Pearl being hurt by it. He didn't like to think of Pearl being hurt, period. Exclamation point.

But she was an apprentice sorceress. Given the state of the world, he didn't see how she could escape scandal, simply because of the magic she practiced and the world's faulty beliefs about it. Which meant he ought to send her home now, before the risk of scandal became any greater.

At the top of the stairs, he stopped outside the black-painted door to his workroom and turned toward Pearl.

He opened his mouth to send her away, and the words wouldn't come. He couldn't push sound through his throat, couldn't shape lips and tongue to form sound into sense. He could not tell her to leave.

He didn't want her to leave. He wanted her to stay right there beside him, close enough that he could reach out and take her hand anytime he liked. And that realization terrified him so much, he turned and plunged into the workroom, invoking Harry's damned expensive spell to light all the gas lamps at once.

The rush of flame lit the cluttered space and warmed him with its familiarity. Nothing else was familiar to him, particularly not whatever was happening inside his head. Or wherever it was happening. Not his heart. Surely not.

Pearl came slowly into his workroom and he turned to watch her. He wanted to see her reaction to this place that was his. That was *him.* Even his physical appearance—his face, his expressions and attitudes—was a mask, a suit he put on to present to the world and protect who he truly was.

This room was Grey Carteret, man and conjurer, exposed to whoever might see it. Which was why Pearl was only the second person he had allowed inside it. And why he did not want to see her reaction. He did not want her to matter.

She stared about her, at the sigils painted on the walls in their brilliant colors. Blue fading into deep purple for "Come," bright spring green for "Safe," flaming orangey-red for "Obey," and all the rest. He'd chosen the colors himself, according to how the sigils felt to him. The magic charging the sigils made their colors more intense, and their permanence made the workroom a place of power.

He tried to read her expression. He could not help himself. Was that wonder he saw? Was she impressed, or simply cowed? Or did she hide her disgust at the piles of books and drifts of crumpled paper on the floor behind an impassive mask?

No, Pearl wasn't one for masks. She didn't need them with her magic. Blood spoke the truth.

"The maids aren't allowed in," he said, and cursed himself for making excuses.

Pearl turned to him with twinkling eyes. "Then I am even more impressed. There's room to walk. And look—" She pointed to a table against the east wall.

Grey looked. It was a table, no different from any of the others.

"A usable surface, without anything on it." She grinned.

Grey looked again and saw this time the expanse of bare oak tabletop. It only had two stacks of books atop it, and those only three and four books high, all the rest cleared of clutter. "So it is." He couldn't help grinning back at her, which brought forth a chortle from her and stopped his breath.

When had she become so breathtakingly beautiful? Had it happened when she put on her new, feminine clothes? She still had the same elfin face, those striking eyes, that slender form. Perhaps it has simply taken him so long to recognize the beauty in them. How long had it been? From one morning to the next.

He wanted her. That was the least confusing, least frightening of the things that had happened to him today. He'd desired women before. Frequently. With great enthusiasm. His desire for Pearl Parkin was just like that. Only not.

He'd never wanted to simply be with a woman he desired. Never wanted to spend time with her outside the bedchamber. He'd never wanted to talk with one of the women he had affairs with, to see what was going on inside her clever head. Most of them weren't clever. Which was likely more a reflection on him and his usual choice for female "companionship."

The only women he regularly conversed with were

Adela, who was his sister and thus did not count, and Amanusa. He had desired Amanusa, who was almost the physical opposite of Pearl, being tall and very fair and more handsome than beautiful. He had desired her, and had flirted "with intent," until she had made it more than clear that she did not desire him in return.

Not in the tiniest fraction. In fact, she had not even noticed his flirting, much less reacted to it.

Of course, once she married her Jax—Grey's great-great-times-something grandfather on his mother's side—he had ceased his flirting immediately. At least the "with intent" portion of it. Grey was fairly certain he was constitutionally incapable of ceasing to flirt entirely.

The dumbwaiter in the corner rattled and its bell dinged to announce its arrival. Grey went to collect the tray with its, yes, hot soup, since it was before midnight, and the crusty rolls and butter, sliced ham and fruit, and everything wanted for a cozy meal. Even a bottle of wine. And two of everything. Somehow, the paired soup plates and wineglasses and even the two spoons made the meal seem that much more intimate.

He carried the tray to the mostly clear tabletop and filled a plate for Pearl. He dragged up the big wingback chair he used for thinking, and took the wooden chair on wheels for himself. They ate in silence; Grey, because he couldn't think of anything to say that would not make him sound like an idiot, and Pearl, because she was hungry. At least he assumed so from the way she ate. Perhaps she *would* grow if he fed her.

Then again, she'd worked a great deal of magic today, for one who wasn't accustomed to it. Magic had to be fed.

It also required sleep, which he recalled the next time he looked up. Pearl was asleep in the great red velvet chair, her spoon still clutched tightly in her hand. Her soup plate was empty. He would feed her again when she woke.

Exhaustion pressed its heavy hand upon Grey as well, but he couldn't leave her crumpled up in that chair. She would have a sore neck in the morning. Carefully, he eased the spoon from her hand, piled up the dishes, and stuck them in the dumbwaiter. McGregor would be knocking on the door at some ungodly hour looking for them, if he did not, and Grey did not want anyone disturbing Pearl before she was ready to be disturbed.

He stopped before the chair and stared down a moment. Gathering his strength, he told himself. But he lied. He was quite good at it, lying. Especially to himself. He watched Pearl because he wanted to. It pleased him to see her there, asleep in his chair in his workroom. She trusted him enough to sleep. She trusted him to protect her from harm. Which he would.

As he stood over her and let his eyes travel along the swell of her breast, the dainty curve of her waist, he had to acknowledge the fact that he might himself be the greatest danger, and he was not sure in the least that he was capable of protecting her from himself. But she was here, and for now, she was his, and that was enough.

Grey scooped her into his arms and carried her to the bed at the far, shadowed end of the long room. It was a bed meant for one, but not as narrow as a child's cot, or even a servant's bed. Grey tumbled her into it and stood over her, staring again.

She looked uncomfortable. Beautiful, but restricted by her tight clothing. He should loosen her clothing. Just loosen it, nothing more. So she could sleep in a modicum of comfort.

He perched on the edge of the bed and she stirred, blinking at him. "Let's get your capelet off, shall we?" he said.

She made no objection, simply rolled this way and that as he unbuttoned the closure at her neck and unwrapped her.

"Now the shoes, I think." Grey unbuttoned the high-topped walking shoes and eased them off, unable to resist the temptation to caress her fine-boned ankles. A faint, ladylike snuffle had him laughing at himself. He was aroused almost beyond bearing, and she'd gone back to sleep.

He turned back for one more glance, one more long, thirsty look at her, before he went off to his lonely chair. He ought to unfasten her skirt so it didn't squeeze her waist. And loosen her bodice so she could breathe. At least he didn't have to bother with a corset. She hadn't worn one, and that memory, of her soft and warm in his arms in the hospital cellar, had his entire body turning bird dog, quivering on point at his target, the small, sweet, delectable body of his apprentice.

He should go. He would. He would get up and go back across the workroom and sit in the chair. He would go downstairs to his bedroom and leave her here to sleep alone. Now. He would go.

As soon as he released her slender neck from the buttons closed high and tight around it. He didn't want her to choke. He only stroked the pale, warm skin of he neck twice. Three times. All right, four. But he didn't let his fingers stray when he opened the next two buttons. Not more than once. Truly.

She opened her eyes and looked at him, freezing him motionless with his fingertips on the perfect line of her collarbone. He was lost in the rayed gold-over-blue of her incredible eyes, sinking fast into their depths.

"Grey?" She spoke.

What should he say? What should he do? "Yes, Pearl?" That didn't sound too inane, did it?

"What are you doing?"

Oh God. He was still stroking her collarbone. Only his brain had frozen, not his fingers. He drew them back. He wanted to jerk away from her, but his hands would not cooperate, would only leave her with reluctance. "Loosening your clothing so you can sleep more comfortably."

It was bad to be so good at lying. Wasn't it? He'd never thought so before, but with Pearl, it felt that way. Sorcery. Had to be. Blood never lied. There was blood between them.

Pearl smiled up at him and he thought his heart might stop. "Oh," she said. "Good."

He smiled, after a fashion. He wasn't sure how happy a smile it was. He nodded. He stood, or started to. Pearl's hand on his, on the hand pushing him up off the bed, stopped him.

"Stay," she said.

He couldn't. He shouldn't and wouldn't.

"Yes," he said. And he lay down on the narrow bed beside her and gathered her into his arms, just remembering to reverse Harry's spell and shut off all the lamps. And they slept.

Morning arrived far too early, ushered in with a pounding on his door, and shouting. Grey became aware of a number of things all at the same time.

He woke fully clothed. Again. But this time he lay in bed. His workroom bed. Snugged up against someone—a small someone—of the female persuasion. Pearl. His apprentice. Who had asked him to sleep there. And who was also fully clothed. *Thank God.*

The pounding and shouting had gotten louder. Harry. McGregor was there, too. Shouting. And for once the shouting and pounding didn't hurt Grey's head. It wasn't sore. The pounding slacked off and a woman's voice called out. Elinor.

Elinor!

12

GREY'S EYES SNAPPED open and he sprang directly to his feet from lying down on the bed. Half an instant later, Pearl stood in front of him, frantically buttoning up the . . . three buttons at the top of her shirtwaist. No more than that. He still had on his frock coat, hopelessly crumpled now, and his neck cloth. No wonder he'd felt a bit strangled.

He looked at Pearl, whose ears had turned a furious crimson, and who was determinedly looking anywhere but at him. He tipped her face up and put his finger to his lips.

"We came back to my house for food," he said, not loud enough to be heard over the pounding that had resumed. "You fell asleep in the chair. All truth. I moved you to the bed. Yet another truth. *And I slept in the chair.* One slight untruth amongst all the truths will not harm anyone. Understood?"

"We came here simply to eat?" Pearl murmured.

"And to discuss elements of the case and the magic you worked yesterday."

She nodded, accepting his dissimulations. Grey shot his cuffs, smoothed his crumpled coat, and strode the length of the room to the door to open it.

Harry and Elinor both crowded in, leaving McGregor in silent protest on the landing. Three persons had now been admitted to his private sanctum. Grey sighed. "Breakfast, McGregor. In the breakfast room, if you please."

"Yes, sir." The butler bowed and vanished. Grey was convinced the man had his own reservoir of domestic magic.

He turned back to the workroom to find that Elinor had apparently already ascertained his apprentice's well-being, for she was advancing back along the chamber aimed at him like some artillery piece primed to fire.

He looked for Harry, feeling the need for a modicum of masculine support, and found him among the magical texts, deliberately ignoring everyone else in the room. Grey didn't blame him. He braced himself for the attack.

"You!" Elinor poked him in the chest with a forefinger. Hard. It hurt.

Grey put up a hand in a dismal hope of preventing more pain. He wondered if he ought to respond, but decided against it. Better point of valor, and all that.

"How could you?" Elinor cried. "I realize you have no care for your own reputation. The blacker the better, I'm sure. But I truly thought you had some semblance of a brain in that bony box you call a cranium. Have you completely lost whatever meager amount of sense you might once have possessed? Are you a complete and utter idiot?"

Here, she paused. Was she waiting for a response? What response did she want? What would end her tirade the soonest, for it was obvious she wasn't yet done.

Grey's mouth opened, and stayed that way as he attempted to come up with the correct answer. He finally ventured, "Yes?"

"You must be. What is wrong with you? Is it too much effort to consider anyone's welfare other than your own? Did you stop to think what your stupidity might have cost Pearl?"

"I have no reputation to preserve," Pearl said. Brave and foolish girl, leaping into the cannon's mouth. "Besides, nothing happened. We fed the magic. I fell asleep in the chair. Grey carried me to the cot in the corner, and he slept in the chair. *Nothing happened.*"

Elinor rounded on her, angrier than before, impossible

as that seemed. "Do you think that matters? No one cares about the truth. You are the female apprentice of a male magician. The whole world is watching, expecting—*anticipating* a scandal. The least little spark, the tiniest appearance of something titillating, and the fire will blaze out of control.

"It will prove to the doubters that magic will corrupt any female foolish enough to attempt the practice, and the doors will slam shut again. No decent woman will take the risk, and we'll be right back where we were ten years ago. Two hundred years ago, when every female magician, sorceress *and* wizard, was burned at the stake."

Grey felt the need to divert some of that fire away from Pearl, even if it meant turning it back at himself. Madness obviously possessed him. "I don't think anyone would actually resort to *burning*," he said mildly.

"*You*—" Elinor stabbed her finger at him and he flinched. That finger was sharp as a knitting needle. His Aunt Minerva used to poke him with hers. Needles, not fingers.

"You shut up," Elinor ordered. "This is all your fault, because you never ever think about consequences. Ever. And if you do, you don't care. You don't care about anything, and I am bloody well sick of it."

Grey blinked. He'd never heard Elinor use strong language.

"That's not—" Pearl began.

"You shut up, too."

Pearl flinched when Elinor poked that pointy finger her way, making Grey feel minimally better. He was not the only one wary of that finger.

"This is all your fault," Elinor snapped. "You are fully capable of using good sense, even when he has none, being a man. But what did you do? You surrendered all sense completely."

"How can it be all my fault," Grey inserted himself

into the target zone once more, "and all her fault as well? If the blame is all mine, which it is, then none of it can be hers."

"Don't you dare use logic on this disaster," Elinor snapped. "Logic has nothing to do with gossip or scandal. Truth doesn't, either. It is all your fault, and all yours, too." She pointed at Grey and then at Pearl with short, sharp, scary stabbing motions. "And it's your fault, too, Harry Tomlinson." That scary finger turned in Harry's direction.

"Me?" He looked up, startled, from his determined distance. "I didn't 'ave nuffink to do wif this. I'm over 'ere mindin' me own business."

"That's why it's your fault. You weren't paying attention." Elinor went utterly, surprisingly still, then she sighed, deflating somehow to a smaller, safer size. "And it's completely my fault, because I knew something was wrong, but I didn't do anything. I should have come last night and made you come home. And I didn't. I was too tired."

"So was I," Pearl said. "Exhausted. That's why I fell asleep. I truly did just fall asleep. And Grey was too tired to drag me home."

She took her life in her hands by daring to approach and lay a hand on Elinor's arm. "Don't you think you're blowing this a little out of proportion, Elinor, dear?"

"No." The other woman shook her head grimly. "I am not. The Cranshaws and Simmonses of this world are waiting to pounce upon the least little indiscretion, and no matter what did or did not happen, this is not little. It is huge.

"The magister of the conjurer's guild took his female apprentice into his workroom late at night, locked the door, with just the two of them inside, and did not emerge until morning. They can do anything with that information. Portray Grey as a lascivious monster using magic to work his wiles on the innocent. Smear Pearl as a wicked seductress luring Grey into her clutches. Or blacken the both of you and your magic as altogether evil."

"So, what do we do about it?" Grey asked. "It's terrible, dreadful, awful. And horrible. What do we do?"

Elinor threw up her hands. "I don't know. That's how awful it is."

"Didn't happen," Harry said.

"It didn't?" Grey was confused. He often was, early in the morning.

"It did," Harry said, "but it *didn't*. You an' Miss Pearl came 'ome. But you weren't alone. We—me 'n' Elinor—were 'ere, too. We came in later, after your servants had gone to bed, to discuss what you found. And wot *we* found, which is truly why we came. It's early enough we can say we came earlier than we did. Who's goin' to say we didn't? I never knew a magician's servants to gossip when th' master—the magister—didn't want 'em to."

Grey squinted at the gloom outside. "How early is it?"

"Probably risin' toward six by now."

Grey groaned. No wonder yawns kept climbing up from his chest. "I'm a conjurer. My best work is done in the wee hours. Why would anyone think it acceptable to invade my household at such an hour?"

"Elinor insisted." Harry looked at her. So did everyone else.

"I did eventually accept the need to act," she defended herself. "Especially since Pearl did not come home *at all* last night, nor did she send word. I was worried."

"And she was some anxious to talk to you about what we found at th' Bethnal Green dead zone," Harry added. "As was I, so we toddled on over."

Grey's stomach took that moment to inform him, in a large, loud grumble, that it had not been fed since before midnight. "Let us finish this discussion over breakfast. My apprentice and I worked a great deal of magic yesterday, and we have not yet refilled that well."

"She's an apprentice." Harry frowned. "Wot sort o' magic did you work?"

Grey led the way out of the workroom, shutting the door firmly behind everyone. He wondered if the additional living presences would leave behind auras that might prevent some of his more skittish spirits from attending him.

Once everyone had gathered in the breakfast room, Grey filled the others in on yesterday's discovery, that sorcery and conjury working together could lay ghosts. Everyone exclaimed over the news, then they discussed the developments in the murder investigation.

"I am almost certain," Grey said, as they sat back to finish a last cup of tea, "that the murder was done in an attempt to call a demon. But to what purpose? Even the most foolish, magic-blind ordinary recognizes what a dangerous proposition that is." The answer to that question had him turning in mental circles.

"Could be anything." Harry shrugged. "Revenge comes to the top o' my list. Revenge for some great injustice."

"Greed," Pearl suggested.

"Ambition. Power." Elinor poured the last of the tea in the pot into her cup and added sugar. "I could read the leaves."

Tea leaves were a wizard's augury. Alchemists read the future with crystals of varying shapes, or sometimes bowls of calm water. Conjurers didn't have a method of seeing the future, unless a spirit deigned to pass on a message—which they sometimes did. Grey wondered if sorcery had its own method. Tossing knucklebones, perhaps?

"Later." Harry leaned forward, elbows on the table, and curved his thick hands around the delicate china of the teacup. "I 'eld off talkin' about what we came 'ere about, because I decided it would be better to show you than tell you. An' because we had other things to talk over."

"I am assuming it has to do with the dead zone in Bethnal Green." Grey had little patience with Harry's mysteriousness. "What is it you found?"

Harry wiped his mouth and tossed the napkin on the table as he stood. "Better you see it and decide what you think without me tellin' you wot to think."

Grey did not commit actual physical assault on the alchemist's person. But he wanted to. The information was further delayed by Pearl's need to slip back to her flat and change clothes, refresh her toilette, and do whatever else females needed to do of a morning. It gave him a chance to wash and shave and change his linen. His new frock coat was still conjurer's black, but his valet allowed him pale gray trousers.

Harry maintained his own carriage and horses. Grey could afford to, but found it a bother. Easier to use Harry's. He walked down and across the street to Harry's house to meet the others.

Pearl's appearance left him speechless. Nearly breathless. The dress was a plain one, in a pale silvery gray somewhat lighter than his trousers, without excessive trim or frills. But it was a woman's dress, not a child's, and it fit her. Lovingly followed every curve. She bowled him over with her beauty.

She noticed him staring and blushed. He could see it in the tips of her ears, as yet uncovered by her bonnet.

"Pale colors are so impractical," she said, smoothing her hands over her new skirt. In pleasure, Grey thought, satisfied that she liked it.

"Sorcerers wear white," Elinor said, "so the blood isn't missed if any goes astray. Amanusa said she thought pale colors would do fine for students."

Grey hadn't been thinking of that when they were shopping, but the shop clerks had insisted that pastels were de rigueur for young ladies. The carriage pulled up outside and the bonnets were tied on. Grey would miss seeing Pearl's blush.

The early start to the day put their excursion in the thick of the clerks' daily rush to their jobs in the City and elsewhere around London's commercial centers. Omnibuses were everywhere, as were the carts and wagons of the working classes who'd been on the job an hour or two already. Harry's carriage threaded its way through the fading traffic until, as they neared the dead zone, the streets cleared to echoing vacancy.

The carriage pulled to a halt a few blocks away from the edge of the zone where it stretched north and somewhat east of the burned-out sector near the docks. The horses wouldn't go closer. The gentlemen helped the ladies to the cobbles and escorted them down the narrow, silent alleyways. Grey wondered whether the rest of London might be so excessively crowded because this dead zone had pushed the residents out into the few hovels left.

"What happened to the magic?" Pearl asked. "Where did it go? Why did it die?"

"That's what I'd like to know," Harry growled.

"I think it got used up," Elinor said. "And there wasn't any to replenish it."

Pearl frowned. "I should think there would be, given how very much there is splashing about."

"Hadn't considered that before." Grey did now, voicing his thoughts as they came to him. "Perhaps it's not the right *kind* of magic. The magic of innocent blood is very powerful, but it's single-minded. And it's created by death—"

"Not all of it. Actual death isn't necessary," Pearl interrupted.

"But much of it, perhaps most. And perhaps it's simply not strong enough, for what the earth needs to replenish."

"Or perhaps it has to be used," Elinor said. "It's not

the raw magic itself we've been missing over the past few centuries, but the sorcerers."

"Never mind that," Harry said. *"Look."*

The alley didn't come to an end so much as disintegrate. The rickety ancient buildings to either side of what had been the alley were slumped in on themselves, creating piles of wreckage where things could hide. Grey wondered what Harry had brought them to see. He didn't want to have to cross the boundary. Bad things happened inside the dead zones.

"Them 'ouses is 'eld together as much by alchemy as by nails," Harry said. The environment seemed to have an effect on his speech, obliterating most of its refinements. Grey had noticed the phenomenon before.

"What are we supposed to be looking at?" Grey inquired. He still had a murder to investigate.

"The machines."

The strange, self-animated machine creatures had begun to appear only in the last few months. Cobbled together mostly from bits of refined metal, the creatures skittered about the dead zones on their own unknowable purposes, often seeming to defend their territory against incursion. Magic seemed to have as inimical an effect on the machines as lack of magic did on organic beings.

That, in conjunction with the machines' higgledy-piggledy construction, led to the conclusion that the machines had not been built by any human facility, but rather had built themselves. No one yet knew the how or why of that, and Grey suspected no one ever would. It didn't actually matter. What did matter was dealing with the dead zones the creatures inhabited.

Grey had first seen the machines in Paris, during the international Conclave of All Magic this past summer. There, the dead zone had encompassed a middle-class neighborhood, and the machines had been bright and shiny, made of silver-plate tea trays and polished brass fireplace fenders.

This dead zone had originally included one of the worst slums in London, as well as a massive refuse pit where an army of workers had picked through the city's discards for rags to be converted to paper, bones for blacking and glue, and even dog manure for the leather tanners across the river. The machines here were as dark and ugly as their discarded parts.

The overcast sky, promising a miserable, cold rain sometime in the day, had Grey peering into the gloom. "I can't see anything," he grumbled.

"What is that?" Pearl pointed. "See? Next to that brick wall that hasn't quite fallen over? The rusty-orange bit. Is that a machine?"

"Is it?" Grey squinted, trying to bring it into focus. Could he be needing spectacles? *Never say so.*

Pearl gathered up her skirts and strode into the zone before anyone could stop her.

Grey started after her, but Harry caught his arm in a tight grip. "She's a sorceress," Harry said. "You're not. You'll be 'arder to drag out o' there."

Grey waited, but not well. He fidgeted, rose upon his toes, leaned forward against Harry's hold, tapped his fingers on his thighs, furiously impatient, though Pearl only walked the few yards forward, bent and retrieved the object she'd spotted, and returned. She did stop twice on her way back to pick up something else, but she wasn't in the zone above a minute.

Grey fell upon her when she returned. "Do not ever behave so recklessly again," he gritted through clenched teeth, seizing her arm too tightly. "Ever. This place is called a dead zone for a reason. *It can kill you.*"

Pearl blinked up at him in apparent surprise. "But it didn't. I'm perfectly fine. And look, I got—"

"It could have," Grey interrupted her, the strength of his rage shocking him. Where had it come from? He was too angry to truly wonder. "You had no business traipsing off without, at the very least, discussing it with me, with other magicians more experienced than yourself, before doing something so rash.

"You cannot simply begin throwing magic around, or walking into areas where magic is affected, without knowing what will result. Or at minimum, having a fair idea of what *might* occur. Did you even think what might have happened?"

"Of course I did. There's folks that come in here every day. As long as they don't stay too long, they're fine. Jemmy Watt, he stays in half the day all the time."

Grey brought his face close to Pearl's, unable to shake his fury, wanting to shake sense into her. "And is Jemmy Watt a magician? Can he see the crimson tides of blood magic rolling through the streets?"

"No." Pearl's voice was a tiny squeak of its former self.

"Did you know that an alchemist can take only a few steps into a dead zone before collapsing and having to be carried out? Conjurers won't get much farther. Did you know that?"

"No, sir. I'm sorry, sir. I didn't think. I—" She cleared her throat, blinking rapidly. "I'm so sorry."

Damn it, he hadn't meant to make her cry. Grey cleared his throat, his rage subsiding. His scold wasn't done, however. "No, you did *not* think. I hope that this will serve as an inducement to remind you to do so in the future, though I have my doubts."

He cleared his throat again. "As it happens, sorcerers are the best equipped of all magicians to enter the dead zones, since you essentially carry your magic with you. In your own blood and bones and such. Which is why no harm was done. But you didn't know that, did you?"

"No, sir." She clutched the machinery to her, smearing rust on the pale gray of her dress.

"Next time, wait. *Ask.* Give us time to discuss what to do." Grey took a deep breath and let go the rest of the emotion gripping him. Emotion he did not want to name. "So, what is it you've brought us?"

"Look." She held out double handfuls of . . . junk.

Grey poked it with a finger. It had that same nasty, gut-clenching, head-pounding feel as the machine he'd touched in Paris, back in the summer. But it didn't look like anything but assorted junk, and he said so.

"But look." Pearl crouched down right there in the filthy street, pushing her skirts behind her, and laid her bits of rust out on the stones. "It's not just separate nails and wires and such. They're stuck together."

She looked at her hands, streaked with mud and rust, then looked about as if hunting something to wipe them on. Her pale dress was already smudged, but Grey didn't blame her for not wanting to make it worse. He offered his handkerchief.

"My hands feel dirtier than they look." She grimaced as she scrubbed them clean. "It feels nasty. Disgusting."

"Lack of magic." Harry poked the largest bit with a metal rod he'd pulled from his pocket, his alchemist's wand. This one appeared to be made of silver, but might as easily be nickel or zinc or tin, or even steel. Grey didn't really care.

"Look here," Harry went on. "This bit looks like an articulated arm, with a cog down on this end to allow for turning in all directions."

"This, too," Pearl said, using the handkerchief to pick up a slightly smaller piece in order to peer at it more closely. "It's missing the cog, though."

"So the machines are falling apart. Is that it?" Grey didn't want to get any closer to the things, but if Harry could, he could. He was a conjurer, after all, and less susceptible than the alchemist.

"They didn't *fall* apart." Harry stood and scowled into the dead zone, hands propped on his hips with the silver-colored wand pointing behind him.

Grey moved to one side so the wand didn't point at him. One never knew what a magical item might do next.

"There were more of them yesterday," Elinor said. "Dozens. Maybe scores. Pieces of machines scattered everywhere. Piled up against the walls."

"Guess the other machines scavenged parts," Harry said.

"Or maybe they retrieved the bodies for burial," Elinor countered.

"They're *machines*," Grey interjected. "Not human beings. Not even animals, which—remember—are known to eat their young."

"They were torn apart," Pearl said from where she still crouched, investigating her finds.

Grey bent to see what she had discovered.

"Look here." She turned the "arm" in her hand to expose its broken end, and the joint fell limply to one side, for all the world like a skeletal limb from an anatomist's laboratory. The metal had been stretched, distorted, bent. *Torn*. Quickly and abruptly, it appeared to Grey, though he was no metallurgist.

"It was easier to see it yesterday," Harry said. "The chunks o' torn-apart machines were bigger, and there were more of 'em. Some of the machines 'ad to 'ave been near big as ponies." He stared into the barren desolation of the dead zone.

Grey's frown deepened. "I don't like this. Not at all. When did you discover the broken machines?"

"Not broken, torn apart," Harry corrected. "Yesterday. Elinor an' me come out to take a look, as usual."

Grey knew Harry visited the dead zone every few days to check on its growth and behavior. Now that Elinor had apprenticed to him, she came, too.

"What time was that?" Grey asked.

"After lunch. Early afternoon."

"And when had you come before then?"

"Yesterday was Tuesday," Harry began calculating. "We spent all o' Monday getting you out o' the 'ammer, and the day before Monday was Sunday an' we didn't go then, so Saturday. The last day we came 'ere was Saturday."

"Four days previous."

"And there weren't any torn-apart machines then."

"But there's no way of knowing when exactly the machines were dismembered," Grey argued. "They could have had a war all day Sunday and no one would be the wiser."

"Jemmy Watt would," Pearl put in. "He'd know, and his sort. The scavengers."

"Might be important to know," Harry said.

"Given the piles of machines we saw here yesterday," Elinor said, "and the much smaller numbers today, it had to have been recent. If they could be cleared away so quickly, then either it happened no earlier than Monday, or so many machines fought in your war that their broken remains would have stacked up higher than the buildings still standing in the living sector here. I am frightened to think there are so many machines."

Now that Grey knew what to look for, he could see the pieces of broken machine still lying in the gloom of the dead zone. The machines disturbed him, unnatural things that they were. Their broken remains disturbed him more, for he didn't know what might have caused it. Suspicions roiled in the depths of his mind, troubling the surface, but he refused to give them voice. He sighed.

"All right," he said. "I'll detail a couple of men to track down Jemmy Watt and his cronies to see what they might know. The timing is troubling, if nothing else. I wonder if we ought to maintain a closer watch on the dead zone as well."

"I can scratch up a few lads from the committee to keep an eye on it," Harry said.

The Committee Inquiring into the Dead Zones had been created by the Magician's Council at Harry's instigation. Meaning he'd badgered them until they'd given in. It hadn't taken much badgering, not after the fire and the zone's rapid expansion. They'd even put Harry in charge. Mostly to get him to shut up about it, Grey firmly believed. Harry had recruited a small army of young, scientifically minded magicians to conduct the actual inquiry.

"Excellent," Grey said. "My lads to investigate any link to the murder, yours to investigate the dead zone itself. We'll put our heads together as needed to see if there's any connect."

"Once a week, at least," Harry said, giving him a look.

"Yes, all right." It wasn't that Grey minded meeting with Harry, or discussing business. He wasn't fond of being tied to a schedule, was all. It surprised him a little, Harry insisting.

"I don't suppose you'd allow Pearl to fetch a few more bits of those beasties, would you?" Harry mused, poking the largest bit with the toe of his boot.

13

GREY TOOK IN a sharp breath. He wanted to forbid it, absolutely, but that wasn't rational. She hadn't taken any harm, had she? "Parkin, how do you feel?"

She blinked at his abrupt question, then her focus went away, turned inward for a moment as she considered. That pleased him, that she didn't give an automatic response.

"Fine," she said. "No different than usual, except for the nasty feeling from touching the things." She wiped her hands again with Grey's now-grimy handkerchief.

"What about when you were inside the zone?" Elinor asked. "Any shortness of breath or dizziness?"

Pearl shook her head. "I wasn't in there for very long."

"It doesn't take very long." Harry sounded grim. "For

me, it don't. So if you do this, if you start feelin' woozy, come back straightaway. 'Cause we can't come in an' fetch you out."

"You don't have to do it," Elinor said. "Don't feel as if you must. Harry will do perfectly well with these pieces you've already brought out."

"I don't mind," Pearl said. "I'm happy to help, and if this is something I can do that others can't—" She shrugged. "Well, then I should, shouldn't I?"

"Plan out your route before you go in." Grey wasn't trying to delay her, exactly. He just wanted her to be sensible about this. "And wear your gloves. I know sorcerers don't, generally, but wear them. Perhaps the machines won't feel as nasty."

She nodded, pulling the gloves out of her pocket. "Is there something I can carry the machine parts in? A basket or box?"

Harry ran back to the carriage and reappeared with a large market basket. By then she was ready. Grey had pointed out the clearest route to the most promising machines, though he was sure she'd seen it for herself. She had her gloves on, the handkerchief in one hand, basket in the other. He held his breath and watched as she strode into the dead zone.

She walked to the nearest machine and dumped it into the basket. He let out a little puff of relief. She was following his suggestion, collecting as she traveled inward, so that if she got into trouble and had to retreat quickly, her expedition would still be a fruitful one.

The big piece with the flywheel, the pump handle, and the odd bit of cow bone went into the basket. Was it getting too heavy for her? Grey sucked in a quick breath of air as he bounced up to his toes, hands knotted together behind his back. It was all he could do to stay in place. He wanted to be there, beside her, protecting her.

But if he were, he'd fall flat on his face, and she would have to drag him out. Already she'd been in there

longer, gone farther than he ever had. It annoyed him—
and it filled him with pride. His apprentice had strength
and courage. None of it was his doing, but still he basked
in the reflected glory.

She was approaching the piece of machine they had
agreed should be the farthest point in her sortie. Did she
look pale? Was she struggling to breathe?

"She's doing fine." Elinor laid a hand on his shoulder,
patted it.

Grey made himself breathe. "Of course she is. She *is*
my apprentice, after all."

Elinor shook her head at him, as he intended. He saw
with peripheral vision, for all his attention was focused
on Pearl.

Just as she was reaching for the last machine, it
moved, clicking bone and metal fangs at her, scrabbling
in the muck.

Pearl yipped and jumped, falling on her bottom and
spilling half of her broken machine collection.

"Pearl!" Grey felt Elinor's hand on his arm, holding
him back. Not that she could physically restrain him,
but she reminded him that he did not want Pearl to have
to drag him out. "Leave it! Just leave it there and come
out with what you have."

She scrambled to her feet and tossed everything back
into the basket. "But it's still alive. Don't you want to investigate a live machine, Mr. Tomlinson?"

"Leave it," Harry shouted. "We've brought out live
machines before, bought 'em from scavengers like your
Jemmy Watt. They die. Like fish out o' water. Come out."

She didn't obey Harry, either. Instead, she studied the
machine chomping its jaws at her, eyeing it as if plotting out an angle of attack.

"Parkin!" Grey bellowed. "Get your dainty backside
out here now!"

She jerked around to stare at him, as if startled by his
vehemence. But she didn't move.

"*Now,* Parkin," he shouted. "Or I will come in and fetch you, and you will have to drag me back out again."

That got her moving. She abandoned the snapping machine and picked her way back out of the dead zone, looking so pale and shaky the last few feet that Elinor stepped in to meet her, to assist her back to the living side of the line.

Which part of the threat had brought her out, Grey wondered. Him fainting, or her having to carry him out? He cast the thought aside as he grasped his apprentice's elbow and took the basket from her to hand to Harry.

"Did we not have this discussion only recently?" He kept his voice quiet, calm, and grim. "The one defining the role of master and apprentice?"

She looked up at him, her eyes going wider in apprehension. *Good.* "Yes, sir."

"So when I give you an order, what makes you think it is optional? That you have the right to argue with me about it?" His heart still pounded with fear and rage, but he let none of it show. How had he been caught so quickly in this trap?

"But—" She broke off at his uplifted brow and took a deep breath. "My own hardheadedness," she admitted. "I hate to stop before finishing what I started."

"Learn how. Sometimes a magician must continue through to the end of a spell for safety's sake. But sometimes, when a spell goes awry, it is better to break it off and back away. Stubbornness has no place in the practice of magic.

"And until you learn to tell when to stick it through and when to back away, you *must* listen to me and do what I tell you. This is not negotiable, madam. If you cannot, our contract is breached and you will no longer be my apprentice." Grey ignored the twinge from somewhere in his chest region at the thought of her absence. He would rather she be gone than at risk. He would make sure she had somewhere to go other than the streets of London's East End. He tried to ignore the stricken expression on Pearl's face, but that was more difficult.

"No, sir," she said hastily, her words choked. "I'll do what you say. Quick as anything. Just see if I don't. I promise. Swear on my mother's grave. My father's, too. Any grave you like. Just, please, don't dismiss me."

Her panic made him want to relent, assure her he would do no such thing, but he couldn't. If the threat kept her from any more rash behavior, it needed to stand. And he needed to be willing to carry it out.

Grey cleared his throat. "How are you feeling? Any dizziness? Shortness of breath?"

Now that the scold was over, Elinor approached. Harry was busy poking through the basket's contents with his wand.

"I had trouble catching my breath there at the end, and it made me dizzy. Knees went all wobbly." Pearl clenched and unclenched her hands. "I think the gloves helped, but my fingers still feel odd. Numb, as it were."

"Write it up in a report," Grey said. "When we get back to Wych Street. Be very specific about how you felt. Harry, did you time her?"

"Course I did. Set a magician's record—well, outside o' when Jax and Amanusa go in together. Pearl was in for five minutes and forty-nine seconds. Almost six full minutes."

"Note that down, too." Grey checked his own pocket watch. "It's rising ten o'clock. I need to get back to I-Branch, see what the lads have turned up."

"We need to get this lot to the lab as well." Harry hefted the basket and offered his arm to Elinor. She ignored him and came around to his other side to grasp the basket handle.

"I got it," Harry growled.

Grey offered his arm to Pearl and started back to the

carriage when she took it, though she walked almost backward to watch the other two in "discussion."

"This many machine bits?" Elinor tugged at the basket. "We already know the stronger the alchemist, the faster the machines affect him. And you're the magister. I'm sure you don't want to be dragged back to the carriage by Grey."

"I'd drag you by your heels, old chap," Grey called out cheerfully. "Bash your head against every cobble in the street."

"Not proper, it ain't," Harry grumbled, giving up the basket to Elinor. "For the woman to bear the burden. You should carry it, Grey."

"It's *your* basket," Grey retorted. "With *your* toys in it. Besides, conjurers don't last much longer than alchemists, and since I am a more powerful conjurer than you are alchemist—"

"More powerful, my ars—my eye!"

"—I would likely faint as quickly as you, and then where would we be?"

"Why is that?" Pearl asked, breaking into Grey's entertainment without so much as a blink. "Why do conjurers and alchemists react so strongly?"

"Because wizards' and sorcerers' magic's alive," Harry said. "Conjury and alchemy ain't. That's wot I think, any road."

"The magic itself is alive, but its source is not," Grey amended. "Though spirits once were alive. Alchemy's source never was." He waved to the coachman to keep his seat and opened the door to Harry's carriage himself, while Harry stowed the basket in the luggage compartment.

THE REST OF the week, Pearl spent most of her days in study. Grey had a private office attached to the large Investigations Branch room which he set up as a study for her, so she wouldn't be so distracted by all the Briganti's to-do. She missed hearing how the inquiries were going, but it did help her focus on her reading, and that was the most important thing.

Grey had also cleared out a small corner of the work-room at his house to give her a little area of her own. Pearl kept a gas burner there with a tea kettle and a little stoneware pot just big enough to brew a few cups, so she could have tea without disturbing the servants. Everything else—the journal where she wrote down her notes, her books and such—she either carried with her or left in the study at I-Branch. Sorcerers didn't require much in the way of magical instruments. And Pearl was still in the reading and study part of her apprenticeship. She didn't need space for practicing spells yet.

She'd switched to the *Basic Magic Theory* book, in hopes that a grounding in theory, written in modern English, would help her understand the ideas presented in *Beginning Sorcery,* even if it didn't help with parsing meaning from the archaic words themselves. The theory book was written for schoolboys, so while it was easily comprehended, it left a great many holes in things, to Pearl's way of thinking.

This led to intense discussions with her magic-master on the ride home, which generally led to dinners—with Harry and Elinor attending for propriety's sake—where the discussions lengthened and intensified. Most nights, Pearl and Elinor crawled into bed still following where the discussions led. Steeped daylong in magic, Pearl had never been happier.

Except for one thing. Grey.

Proximity to the man did not cure her foolish attraction to him. Indeed, it made matters worse. For while his appearance became no less beautiful, his shoulders just as broad, his eyes dark and soulful as ever, his character made itself known to her. And she *liked* him.

He answered her every question thoughtfully and thoroughly, never losing patience with the number of questions she asked. He was kind, though he didn't like anyone to know it, and he had a wicked sense of humor, which had Pearl laughing when she knew she oughtn't.

He rarely lost his temper, and then only when someone did not do what they should have. Or behaved in an abysmally stupid manner. Often, that someone was Pearl, but he made allowances—probably too many of them—for her student status. He only became toweringly furious when the should-have-done endangered someone.

She was getting better at not doing stupid things. She asked more often before plunging in—if asking made sense to her. If she didn't understand the spell she was trying to work. They were only baby spells, after all. Requiring less magic, less spit than even her "don't-look" spell. She hadn't graduated yet to any spells requiring blood.

She was tempted to jump ahead and look at the chapter on innocent blood . . . well, she *had* read it. But it didn't say anything. Just told what it was, where it came from, and what it was for. Nothing about how it should be used or how it was done. Not even how to gather it in, which she knew how to do already.

The magic—reading, talking, and practicing it—helped distract her from her inappropriate feelings toward her magic-master. When his touch on her elbow sent a quiver shooting through her, she asked a question about magic. She'd taken to keeping a list of questions, every one that popped into her mind, some of them utterly inane.

It didn't matter to Grey. He answered even the silliest question with the same careful attention, which distracted her from the quivers and thumpetys and pitter-pats. Things still quivered and thumped, but she could ignore them and focus on the magic, on the mind rather than on the heart. Until she fell asleep and dreamed. But dreams weren't reality. Magic was.

* * *

ON THE THIRD Monday after Pearl started her apprenticeship, the first Monday in November, she stood in the big room behind Grey and listened. With any luck, he wouldn't see her for a while yet and order her off to her study room. Pearl liked to spend a little time in the busy office periodically, just to catch up on things. Sometimes, she was even able to contribute.

The Briganti investigators had finally raveled out the spells used to ward the Rotherhithe burglary ring operating on both sides of the river and tracked them home. The ordinary police would sweep them up shortly, with a few Briganti enforcers standing by to take care of the ring's leader, a guild magician corrupted by greed. One of Harry's alchemists.

The investigation into Angus Galloway's murder was not going nearly so well. Every time the Briganti in the I-Branch workrooms seemed close to teasing information out of something, the spell would collapse. The alchemist Duncan, who had lost the draw as to who should report to Grey, was explaining.

"First off, the killer tried to wipe everything clean as best he could. Except for the sorcery Miss Parkin swept up, which none of *us* knows how to read—except for that, the bast—bloke did a right fine job of cleaning up after himself.

"But on top of that, it's as if he worked some other spell to confuse things for us. Stirring the magic together like it was in a cauldron or something. Or maybe he stirred the magic when he was working it. We can't tell. We can't get our spells to hold together long enough to discover even that much."

"What about you, Ferguson?" Grey turned a pointed glare on the young wizard. "What has that superior magic sense of yours been able to discern, hmm? Anything?"

Ferguson was sweating, his freckles dark islands in

an ocean of pale. He had been back in the office, in the workroom, the day after his collapse in the morgue. He should have taken more time off, Pearl thought. But he hadn't. It made her wonder if that was why his magic sense had gone off, like curdled milk.

"It is as Duncan says." Ferguson's voice held confidence thinly laid over strain. "The magic is muddled together. Reading it is like an alchemist trying to read the future in the surf. And with the stink of sorcery laid over everything—"

Pearl stiffened reflexively. She'd thought Ferguson in favor of the return of sorcery. Had he lied?

"Beg pardon, Miss Parkin." He'd obviously noticed her affront. "I meant nothing offensive by my words. It's simply—sorcery smells like fresh blood to me, and I have never been fond of that scent."

Grey was watching her now, not Ferguson. She could feel his gaze like a caress over her skin, and it disturbed her. As usual. She shoved the disturbance away, tried to squelch her body's response yet again.

"No offense taken," she said with a twitch of her lips that might pass for a smile. It was hard to smile when Grey was watching her. Especially when she would not watch him back.

Finally he turned his attention back to the wizard. Pearl didn't see it, but she knew it just the same. It felt like crossing out of the sun's summer heat into shade.

"So." Grey leaned his knuckles on his desk. "You have made no progress in examining the evidence in the three weeks since we obtained it. Is this correct?"

"Sir," Ferguson began, "if the spellwork can only untangle the residues, I am sure—"

"That is correct, Magister Carteret," Duncan said.

Grey nodded looking down at the desk where his fists were propped, as if considering his next steps. Abruptly, he straightened, adjusting his cuffs. "That is why I have brought in assistance."

He pulled his watch from his pocket to check the time, and as he put it away again, the door opened. Elinor led the way through it, followed by Harry and a tall, dark man with handsome, though strikingly foreign, features.

"I am sure," Grey said, "you are all acquainted with Magister Tomlinson and his apprentice, Miss Tavis. The second gentleman is Nikos Archaios, an alchemist with the International Conclave, who happens to hail from Greece. Mr. Archaios is the conclave's magic-taster."

The three newcomers all gave polite nods to the men gathered in the open area between the desks as Grey walked to join them. Pearl dithered, wanting to follow, but not sure she ought. Halfway there, Grey looked at her over his shoulder.

"Come along, Parkin," he said. "You're the closest to a sorceress we've got. And maybe you can learn something as well, Ferguson."

She'd been to the I-Branch workroom before, but only for quick moments, bearing messages mostly, but once with Grey when he "popped in for a word." The Briganti working with the evidence were mostly alchemists, with one or two conjurers, and Ferguson, the lone I-Branch wizard. Most of the Briganti conjurers worked in the field.

While spirit magic left as much residue as any other, it tended to be more straightforward than other magics, Grey had explained. One conjured the spirit that had left the residue, asked it what had happened, and that was that; barring the need to argue with a reluctant spirit or break an imposed spell of compulsion or silence or the like. Alchemy required spells with flames and powders and other arcana to read residues, and wizardry had its potions and poultices. Those things needed space to work.

The workrooms had taken over the cellars directly below the Briganti offices. The brick and stone walls were whitewashed to reflect the gas lighting that had been laid on. The alchemist's forge had been relegated to the courtyard, with both a narrow, one-person doorway with stairs, and a broad ramp with angled double doors as access.

A good half of the long chamber had been gated off with wire lattice and a barred door to safely store the various items under examination. Some were valuable. Most were not, but all had the potential—some more likely than others—of exploding. The explosion might be magical rather than physical. One never really knew. They'd had both.

The entire workroom was warded with layers upon layers of protection, so the explosions had caused relatively little damage. Still, the occasional eruption reminded of the need to maintain the precautions.

When Pearl trooped in with the others, the rope that had bound Angus Galloway for his murder lay atop the table where he'd been bound in the center of the working half of the room. The Briganti employed in the laboratory stood ranged about, staring glumly at the two items.

"Buck up, lads," Grey called out with cheer. "I've brought reinforcements."

Eyes brightened and smiles broke out as the half dozen or so men in the workroom welcomed their fellow alchemists with handshakes, and the ladies with polite but wary nods. They obviously did not know what to do with the women in their midst.

"So." Harry leaned on the table, his fists landing smack in a thick oozy layer of blood magic he didn't see. "What have you tried so far?"

Pearl got lost in the technical gabble about alchemic catalysts and auras and processes, and soon found herself standing near the stair to the courtyard next to Elinor, Grey, Ferguson, and the pair of I-Branch conjurers, where they could still see and hear, but be out of the way of the alchemists' free-for-all.

" 'Ave you tried refiner's fire?" Harry asked.

"They're organics," one of the Briganti protested. "The table and the rope. They'll just burn up and we'll have nothing left to test."

"You don't burn the whole thing, eedjit." That man had a Scottish accent. "Just bits."

"It's still organic material," the first man insisted. "Impermanent. It can't stand up to refiner's fire. However much goes into the fire, it will be utterly consumed too quickly for us to learn anything."

Harry shook his head at them. "Wot's the first law, ya bunch o' yobs? Nothing is ever utterly lost—"

"Merely transformed." The others repeated the final words with him.

"That goes for organics as well as elements." Harry smacked the debater on the back of his head. "You should know that, Tipple. Everything's made up of elements in greater or lesser part. It's just the different combinations that make us different. Organics, like wood and hemp, got more of the fire element in 'em than stone or metal does, so you watch the fire as it burns. The fire itself will tell you what it's got. And then the ash after."

"I *told* you," the Scottish accent said. "Refiner's fire was the next step. You should ha' listened to me."

"He's listening now." Harry took a folding knife from one of the worktables and cut off a piece of rope, perhaps the length of his hand. "Why don't you see about acquirin' us a bit o' that table to test, McNair?"

The observers had to move aside to allow the alchemists access through the door to the forge outside. Pearl assumed it was kept there because refiners' fire was too volatile, too powerful, to be lit indoors, especially with gas jets nearby. As they passed, Grey called the Greek, Archaios, aside.

"I was hoping you could give young Ferguson here some pointers on using that magic-sensitive nose of his. And perhaps assist my apprentice in understanding what it is she's sensing? I suspect she may be aware of more than she knows." Grey's request surprised Pearl.

Did she have a better sense than she thought? She hoped so. She couldn't help a little bounce on her toes. Learning this way was much more interesting than reading.

Archaios gave a graceful bow of his head. "That is why I am here. Let us begin with the alchemist's spell, since that is where I began. Wizards and apprentices?" He gestured toward the door. "I will even tutor conjurers, if you are so inclined."

Grey gave him a thin smile. "By all means. Lead on."

Elinor was a wizard and an apprentice, so she had a double invitation. Pearl scrambled up the stairs in the lead. Her skirts rubbed half the dirt off the door frame as she squeezed them through. Elinor's took the rest, but her skirts were dark green, not ice-blue. The dirt didn't show on the green. Council Hall servants were going to have to do their jobs better, now that sorcery was back.

"Magic-masters, check your apprentices' shields," Archaios said as he emerged into the courtyard directly behind Elinor.

Pearl could shield her own self, thank you. But Grey, who followed the Greek, came to check them anyway, reinforcing with an air-drawn sigil of protection. Pearl wondered who he'd put on watch. Walther the Prussian, maybe? She hoped so.

Harry left the forge to come check Elinor's shields. They looked fine to Pearl, but Harry did as Grey had and added another. No one checked Ferguson's shields, since he'd passed his master's test. He was on his own, as were the I-Branch conjurers.

Archaios led his little group around to the far side of the courtyard and pushed the alchemists aside so that the women, both of them scarcely taller than the hood of the forge, could see. "Before we begin the spell," Archaios said, "what can you read? No—" He raised a hand when Pearl opened her mouth to blurt out her answer. "Think first. Sense carefully."

Some of Grey's alchemists fidgeted, impatient with the wait, but even they, like everyone else, seemed to be opening their magic senses to pick up what they could.

Ferguson frowned, shook his head.

"Yes?" Archaios looked at him.

"I can't sense anything but sorcery. The scent of blood is almost overwhelming." Even his freckles had gone pale now.

Elinor drew a vial from her reticule and handed it to him. With a curious, somewhat suspicious look, Ferguson opened it and sniffed. His eyes went wide in amazement, and he took a sip, capped it, and handed it back to Elinor. "I've never tasted a better restorative."

Elinor blushed and curtseyed, a tiny dip of thanks. "I am honored by your praise, sir."

"Can we get on with it?" Harry called out, scowling. "Fire's only getting hotter."

"Can anyone else sense the sorcery imbued in these pieces?" Archaios asked.

Pearl's hand shot up. Elinor raised her hand, as did one of the conjurers, and Ferguson, of course. Grey waved a finger for half a moment, and Duncan slowly put up a tentative hand.

Archaios looked at him. "Can you sense it? What is your name?"

Duncan identified himself. "I *think* I can sense it. I wouldn't have, if I hadn't been with Miss Parkin and the magister, cleaning out the murder location after everything was brought here. I believe that what I thought simply a part of the atmosphere is actually sorcerous magic. I think we have been living in a fog of sorcery without ever recognizing it, because no one knew what it was."

"Or if someone did recognize it as magic," Harry

said, "we wouldn't let 'em be trained because they were women."

"Perhaps if Miss Parkin were to draw off the sorcery in these pieces," Grey suggested, "the rest of us could learn how to recognize it as magic."

14

"WOULD YOU BE so kind, Miss Parkin?" Mr. Archaios turned his smile upon Pearl. It would have rendered her quite insensible, had exposure to Grey not made her immune to any handsomeness less than perfection.

"I need something with blood on it—preferably Mr. Galloway's—to store the magic in," she said by way of assent.

Grey tipped his head toward the cellar and one of his eager investigators—McNair, Pearl thought—dashed off to collect the necessary item. He returned with a large ballpeen hammer that screamed so loudly of murder and cruelty that Pearl recoiled.

McNair flinched at her recoil. Grey stiffened. Someone sneered. Someone else protested, and before it brewed up into a tempest, Pearl reached through the magic flowing thickly around the wicked instrument and took it from the alchemist. "It's fine. It will do nicely, thank you."

She swallowed, wishing the hammer were lightweight enough that she could hold it with just thumb and forefinger, like an offensive-smelling shoe. But it was too heavy. She had to grasp with two hands. It did not feel as nasty and awful as the machine pieces. It felt . . . angry. She could deal with anger. "You all do know that this is the murder weapon," she said.

Everyone nodded, McNair sheepishly, when Grey gave him one of his patented piercing stares. "It's just," McNair explained, "he did no' bleed much, our Angus. There's no' overmuch with bloodstains t'be found."

Archaios gestured from the rope and table pieces to the hammer with its round head. "If you would, Miss Parkin."

With a nod, Pearl *reached* with those insubstantial hands she'd made and carefully swept the magic from the rope and the table bits into the rusty colored stains caught between the iron head of the hammer and the wooden handle. She was able to push the magic layered around the hammer into the bloodstain as well.

Why had the blood not soaked up the magic already? Why did it coat everything that Angus Galloway had touched, or that had touched him, and not bide solely within the stains? She would have to search her book for that information.

When the sorcery was swept away, a murmur broke out among the observers. "Do you see?" Archaios said. "Can you recognize the scent, the taste, the appearance of sorcery the next time you see it?"

"Maybe." Harry frowned. "I watched Amanusa work magic in Paris. Didn't look much like this. Didn't look like much at all, from wot I could see. But this—"

"It's raw magic," Archaios said. "Untouched and unshaped by the magician's will."

"Amanusa worked warding magic at the dead zone in Paris," Grey said. "Protective. Not the same as justice magic from innocent blood. We were at a distance when she did that."

"I suppose," Harry said. "So are we ready yet? Fire's burning."

"Now that the sorcery's gone," Archaios said, "what do you sense?"

Pearl opened her magic sense as wide as she could. She could still feel the angry turmoil of sorcery writhing inside the bloodstains on the hammer, but it was subdued. Contained and ignorable. Beyond that . . .

The fire raged, far hotter than she would have thought from the tiny pile of the charcoal on the hearth. Was that magic? All she could sense was heat, and said so. Instantly it damped, and the damping held a vague feel of Mr. Archaios. Elinor said that. The fire flared again, and that smelled of Harry Tomlinson.

"Magic often carries a signature," Archaios said. "Though usually it is not so blatant. Magister Tomlinson and I exaggerated the effect on the fire. If you know what to look for, and practice the looking, you can improve in the doing. Now, we shall test these items in the fire."

One of the alchemists closed a tempered-glass cover over the face of the forge. Faintly, Pearl sensed the hot-cold magic of alchemy working. Strengthening the glass? It tasted of neither Archaios nor Harry, and she thought the man closing the cover likely worked the magic.

Someone else fixed a long, curled, metal contraption to a hole in the glass. The first segment was a pipe of some dark, dull gray metal that extended from the glass in a gentle downward arc. At about a foot out, a Y-shaped joint connected the pipe to different-colored segments. These pipes tapered slowly to points, rather like animal horns. If animal horns had such fantastical curlicues.

The gold-colored pipe thing spiraled away in broad swoops. It wasn't actual gold, Pearl thought, given its brassy shine. The other pipe, with a steely sheen, danced in all directions, over and under its companion pipes and through the air around it. Dials and level-gauges sprouted from improbable locations, and it looked as if it could be unscrewed and taken apart in a wide assortment of places.

"To capture any smoke." Archaios bent to murmur in both apprentices' ears.

Grey was close by her side, Pearl realized. Close

enough that if she fidgeted the tiniest bit, her bare hand would bump his. When it did, he turned his hand, clasped hers. She wasn't hinting that he should do so. Restlessness made their hands bump. And if she was glad to hold his hand, that was only because she could sense conjury better.

"Watch," Archaios said, bending over them again.

Grey tugged Pearl's hand, moving her away from the Greek's hovering, closer to himself. She thought she heard him mutter something to the effect of "Get your own apprentice," but couldn't swear to it. It made her smile.

Harry nodded at one of the I-Branch alchemists, giving him the go-ahead. With a thickly gloved hand, Tipple slid the swiveling cover off a hole in the top of the metal hood and dropped the bit of rope through, closing the cover back quickly.

The rope seemed to catch fire as it fell, the ends glowing red, then flashing into brilliant yellow flame as it hit bottom. It burned for perhaps the length of two breaths before it was gone, leaving only the dull red glow of alchemical coal. Pearl blinked, the bright flame leaving a purplish afterimage against her closed eyelids. There was more to it than that, though. More she hadn't had time to grasp.

She edged closer, hoping to see better. Others crowded in behind her with the same intention. She tightened her grip on Grey's hand, though he was right beside her. As if she thought he could help her see alchemy, too. Foolishness. But she didn't let go.

The chunk of table was dropped in next. It took a few more seconds to catch, reaching the coal floor before bursting into flame. The flames flared as brightly but burned longer, despite the sample's smaller size: orange with a heart of yellow near the wood. But that was merely the visible fire.

Pearl stretched her magic senses as wide as she could, until she could see colors that weren't exactly there. Black and green and purple, but not. More than that. Different. She didn't have words for what she saw. Except—alchemy.

Bodies crowded close, trying to see, and she staggered, unbalanced by the crush, using her grip on Grey's hand to right herself. Then a hand planted itself between her shoulder blades and shoved. Hard.

She cried out. The force of the push tore her hand from Grey's grasp and sent her flying toward the forge. She struck the coiled metal construction, breaking it off, and the glass cover shattered.

Air rushed in and flames billowed out. Pearl could feel the heat on her skin. She heard men shouting and Elinor's scream. She threw up her arms to protect her face as she bounced off the front hearth of the forge before landing atop the alchemists' curlicue of pipes, crushing it against the pavement.

In some distant part of her, Pearl knew she should be in terrible pain. She'd just crashed into an alchemists' forge, with its refiner's fire burning. But everything felt distant—body, mind—Was this how it felt to die?

"Pearl!" That was Grey shouting. "Harry!"

"Done."

Grey swept her into his arms and set off at a run, into the building. Things got more and yet more distant. Pearl struggled to think. There was something she needed to say, to ask. What—? No, *who*.

She fought to return, struggling back from the distance to make her mouth form words. "Who pushed me?"

"Don't try to speak, dearest." Elinor was there, trotting along beside Grey. "Save your strength."

Pearl ignored her. She had to know. "Who pushed me?" This time, the words made more sound, made more sense.

"I don't know." Grey laid her on—on the chaise longue

in the recently created ladies' retiring room down from the I-Branch office. Pearl recognized the cheap mourning cloth nailed over the half-glass interior wall.

"Let the wizards tend you," he said. "I will find out."

ELINOR AND FERGUSON made him leave before they began cutting away Pearl's ruined clothing. Grey had seen raw burned flesh where the dress had burned away. Only Harry's quick action—Harry's, Archaios's, and that of every other alchemist in the place—in damping the fire had kept it from being worse.

Refiner's fire was magic. It burned until it was quenched, and could only be quenched by magic. Through skin and flesh, down to bone and through it, until nothing was left but a few fragments, and teeth. Refiner's fire never burned teeth.

Grey ground his teeth into the howl wanting out. He dropped his head against the cardboard sign labeling the door Ferguson had gently closed on him, and squeezed his eyes tight shut. It didn't stop the memory of her perfect skin, blackened and blistered by flame. By the deliberate action of some villain.

"You see the havoc wreaked when women are allowed into the hallowed precincts of magic-working?" The strident tones of the wizard's magister, Cranshaw, filled the corridor. "Women cannot endure the full flare of magic. You see how they collapse when it is unleashed upon their weakness."

Grey whirled, fist cocked and ready. Harry caught it, shoved him back against the door, making it rattle, and held him there by leaning into him.

"Not 'ere," Harry said quietly. "Not while she's in there, bein' seen to."

If she died—Grey swallowed down another howl. If she died, nothing would hold him back. She was his apprentice. Her safety was his responsibility, and as usual, he'd botched it. But she wasn't dead yet. It wasn't time yet. He relaxed his body by force, ceasing to strain against Harry's hold, and after a moment, Harry stepped away. But he kept a hold on Grey's arm. Probably wise.

"She did not faint." Grey spoke loudly and forcefully, riding over top of Cranshaw's continued declamation. "She was pushed. Someone pushed her forcibly into the forge, while the fire was burning."

"Pushed!" The shocked exclamation came from a dozen throats. Most of those in the courtyard had followed to wait for news of Pearl's welfare, and others had gathered from elsewhere in the building.

"Who would want to harm Miss Parkin?" someone asked.

Grey's eyes narrowed on Cranshaw and Harry's grip on his arm tightened. Meade stepped closer on his other side. Grey looked at Cranshaw, but he didn't make a move toward him. Time for that later, if needed. "I can think of one man," he said, "whose fear and hatred of our fair sisters might induce him to stoop so low."

"I—" Cranshaw sputtered. "How dare you accuse me of—"

"You've done worse in the past, I know—though we've never been able to prove it." Grey looked from the wizard to the other men crowded into the corridor, taking note of the ones who'd been in the courtyard, waiting for them to return his gaze.

"Think," he said. "What did you see? A woman overcome with magic, fainting at our feet? Or one propelled forward with enough force to knock the collection device from the furnace cover, and shatter tempered glass? Her hand was ripped from mine with the force of the push."

"Aha!" Cranshaw leaped on the admission. "You were holding her hand. Already her corrupting influence is shown as she tempts you from the path of righteousness—"

"Sod off, Cranshaw," Harry interrupted. "Grey ain't been anywhere near the path o' righteousness long as I've known 'im, and we've both known 'im since 'e came to the academy when 'e was eighteen. Grey was long gone down that other path way before Pearl ever turned up. Besides, since when has holding hands been corruption?"

The doorknob sounded behind Grey, and he pivoted and took a step back just as Ferguson appeared, opening the door just enough to fill the opening. "She'll live," the wizard said.

Relief swept so furiously through Grey that he had to grab the doorjamb to keep from collapsing.

"She was badly burned along her arms and side, but the fire was quenched so quickly, it didn't burn deeper than her skin." Ferguson paused.

He was pale and sweating, fat drops forming on his upper lip and forehead. Did he have to work so hard to save Pearl? Grey couldn't help noticing, standing almost atop the man.

"Miss Tavis has a salve . . ." Ferguson's voice took on tones of awe. "Most wondrous in its curative properties. Watercress . . ." He shook off his wonderment. "It is healing her."

"Thank God." Harry sounded as relieved as Grey. Did his knees crumple as well?

"I am requested," Ferguson went on, "to have someone send for clothing for Miss Parkin."

Grey stared. "Do you mean a dressing gown? Something that will not hurt her injuries while we get her home?"

The young wizard shook his head slowly, bemused. "No. I mean clothing. Miss Parkin's injuries are healing."

Ferguson looked into the corridor, at the magister of his guild. "Miss Tavis's potion is *healing* her. You can watch the blackened skin melt away to raw red and—"

He noticed Grey standing over him, turning green at the description. Grey felt green, at any rate.

Ferguson amended his discourse. "The burns are healing as we speak. As we watch. Without scars. It is an amazing practice of wizardry."

"Blasphemy!" Cranshaw hissed. "Women are weak, cor—"

"Shut it, ya bloody sod." Harry's voice had gone all Cockney. He took a threatening step forward and it was Grey's turn to remind him.

"Not here. Not with her in there, working on Pearl." He spoke quietly, but Ferguson heard.

"I must return," he said, swiping at his forehead. "Offer what assistance I can . . ." He trailed off vaguely as he turned away and closed the door.

"Impossible!" Cranshaw looked to get wound up in another tirade, despite Harry's ominous glower.

"Gentlemen—" Grey indicated two of his Briganti. The two who had escorted Cranshaw from the murder scene at the warehouse, as it happened. "Please escort Mr. Cranshaw from the premises."

"The council hall belongs to all magicians!" Cranshaw blustered.

"Briganti offices don't. Take him back to the common room." Grey waved them off and turned back to his waiting.

She could have been killed. She hadn't been, was healing with astonishing speed, thanks to Elinor. But if Elinor hadn't been here—If Harry and the others hadn't been quick enough—

The awful thought made him sweat. It made his heart turn over and his bowels clench and his head go dizzy and all those other clichés of alarm and terror, but they weren't clichés. They were truth. He fell apart, disjointed with fear, at the thought of that ultimate horror coming to Pearl.

I would take care of her, Mary said, hovering worriedly at his shoulder. *If the worst happened. But truly, this isn't the worst, is it? The way I am?*

"*No, dear heart,*" Grey thought at her. "*Except that I cannot hold you in my arms.*"

Ah. Mary sounded far wiser than she ever had in life. Spirits were like that.

He had known he should not have taken an apprentice. Especially a female. He had known he would grow to care for her, that he would worry about her. He had not known how he would yearn for her smile, or long for her touch. How he would burn with desire. They had been master and apprentice for only three weeks. Most apprenticeships lasted years. Amanusa could not return from Scotland too soon.

He shoved his hands through his hair, resisting the urge to pull at it. He wanted to pace, but the crowd was too thick, and pacing would take him too far from the door. He might not be able to get back in time, if the door opened. Mary curled around him, offering comfort, but just now, her comfort was cold.

Someone had sent a runner for Pearl's clothing. Harry, likely, since Grey hadn't done it, had been too overcome with relief to think. A footman from Harry's house returned, far quicker than Grey would have thought possible, with a valise that was passed through the door into the retiring room. Ferguson came out shortly after.

"She's well," he said. "Amazing." He shook his head and fell silent. Everyone did. Perhaps they, too, needed to see with their own eyes that she was as well as Ferguson claimed. Grey's fears wouldn't go away until he did.

Finally the door opened and the two women emerged, Pearl wrapped in some sort of shroud. Grey's heart pounded with alarm, until he realized it was one of the things Elinor wore in her stillroom in Harry's conservatory. An apron.

He pushed himself off the wall, and the men in his way stepped aside. He assumed so. They could have melted into the aether for all Grey knew. All of his attention was focused on Pearl, on a head-to-toe inspection.

"Well?" he asked Elinor without taking his eyes off Pearl.

"She's still badly bruised where she struck the forge when she fell—"

"Was pushed," he interjected.

Elinor went on as if he hadn't spoken. "Bruises are under the skin, and it takes longer for the magic to reach them. Burns damage the skin itself, and they are healing nicely, especially since the fire was quenched so quickly and so well."

She smiled at the others in the corridor. "Between all the alchemists, the fire was quenched so thoroughly, I doubt the forge will light for a week."

While Elinor occupied the others, Grey's gaze caught Pearl's and held. Her expression was filled with things he didn't want to read as she lifted her hands, offering them up to him. For his inspection. She wouldn't offer him anything more. She was too wise for that, too aware of the sort of man he was.

For a moment, he wished he were a different sort of man, one worthy of her. But he got over it. Kippers must have been bad. He'd speak to McGregor about them.

Grey took her hands in his and brought them higher, closer to the hallway gaslights. The burns down her left forearm where the bell sleeve fell away looked raw and inflamed, and healing. The skin had been black before, hadn't it? When he carried her in? As he watched, the rawness seemed to fade.

"The healing is slower now," Elinor said, watching them. "Much of the magic has been used up, but there will be enough to finish. It is better to finish the job more slowly. Pearl will need to rest. She has been working very hard at healing."

Pearl pulled a hand free to reach carefully into her

pocket. She drew out a few scraps of pale blue fabric. The dress she'd been wearing. "I cut my arm slightly on a piece of the broken forge cover. We'll have to burn these."

Grey's pulse stopped, then it raced faster than ever. "Innocent blood." The words whispered out of him.

"What?" Pearl heard him. No one else seemed to.

He cleared his throat and spoke louder. "Innocent blood. Your blood was shed. Blood always speaks truth. It can tell us who did this."

"May I?" Archaios—he was still here, like most of them—held a hand out to Pearl asking for the blood-stained cloth patches. With a glance at Grey for approval—*good girl*—she surrendered them.

The Greek took the worst of the patches and slid it between his fingers, eyes closing as he pulled it through two or three times over. He took a deep breath as he opened his eyes and handed the piece of cloth back to Pearl with a little bow. "Yes, I can sense it. The magic is not so strong as that on the rope."

"It was a small injury," Pearl said. "Not murder."

"Indeed." Archaios rubbed his fingers together. "It had a sharper feel to it—more focus, perhaps—and yet softer. Feminine? I shall recognize you again."

Grey took the bloodstained patches, folded them in his handkerchief, and tucked them in his inside breast pocket. They'd be safe enough there. He studied the others in the corridor, contriving ways to steal their blood for Pearl's justice magic. It would not be easy.

"What of your experiment, Magister Tomlinson? Is it utterly ruined?" Pearl turned to Harry, who captured her hands to inspect the burns as well.

"Not utterly." Harry peered intently at her hands, devoting a small fraction of his attention to his words. "We'll be able to scrape up some results when we get the collector 'ammered back into shape. And we got plenty o' rope and table. We can run the experiment again, soon's we get the cover replaced."

"How long will that take?" she asked.

He shrugged. "Bit of a while. This is incredible. I saw her arms, her hands, how bad—" He broke off, shaking his head. "That's powerful magic, Elinor. Good work."

Grey took Pearl's hands again the instant Harry released them. Perhaps he encouraged the release a bit. The burns were better than when Grey had last looked, only moments ago. He wanted to press a kiss to her hurts, help them heal. But he didn't.

"Seems to me Cranshaw's crown might be at risk," he mused. "His potions have never healed so quickly that one could watch it happen, have they? And Elinor's naught but an apprentice."

"How long is a bit of a while?" Pearl persisted. "How long before you can do your test again?"

"Depends, don't it?" Harry rubbed his nose as he stared at the floor. "If the artificer's got a spare made up, we ought to be able to spell it and fit it by end of the week. If he's got to cast a new cover from the beginning, might take as long as three."

"Weeks?" The squeak in Pearl's voice perfectly declaimed Grey's dismay.

Harry's broad face looked decidedly long as he nodded. "Covers for an alchemist's forge got to be specially made. Can't just anyone do it. And *this* forge, well . . ."

"It appears that someone may not want the test performed," Archaios said. The ominous tone in his voice resonated in Grey's core.

Grey considered other methods of determining the villain. Could they test her clothing? Learn who had touched her? But that only worked if magic was used, and a push in the back didn't require magic. Blood held the most promise.

"One of *us*?" Ferguson exclaimed. "I don't believe it."

"Nor I," Duncan said.

"Did anyone notice when Cranshaw joined us?" Grey asked. "Was he in the courtyard during the experiment?"

"Dunno," Harry said, looking thoughtful.

No one else did, either. They were all watching the experiment. No one had seen anyone push Pearl. No one had seen anything until she went flying into the forge.

"But, Cranshaw's a *magister*." Ferguson sounded scandalized.

"He's also unbalanced on the subject of women," Duncan said with the forthrightness of an alchemist who did not have to deal with the man regularly. "Particularly women in magic and more particularly on the subject of sorcery."

"If no one saw him," McNair continued, with the logical practicality so often found in Scots, "then it is entirely possible he did push her. It is also entirely possible he did not. All possibilities must be examined."

"Exactly so." It was time Grey got over his fright and took matters, including himself, in hand. "Harry, if you will take over recovery of the material from the collector? Let us know what you find. Duncan, you're in charge of the forge repairs and whatever you have to do to clean up the mess."

Harry and Duncan both nodded and departed on their tasks, taking most of the loiterers in the hall with them.

"Ferguson," Grey turned to the young wizard. "You're with Archaios. Practice shielding and reading magic— no change there."

Grey took Pearl's elbow and started down the passageway. "What about me?" she asked.

"You, Parkin, are going home to heal." He waited for her protest, but it never arrived, which brought his worry roaring back. "No argument?"

She sighed. "Not this time. I thought about it. I'm almost healed, after all. But I'm not, quite. And I'm tired."

"Well, well, well—" Grey smiled to himself. "So all of my lectures have finally had an effect."

She slanted him a warning look. "Do not become accustomed."

He wouldn't. He knew better. This was Pearl.

15

THE THIRD DAY after the forge incident, Pearl climbed the stairs to Grey's workroom. He found her there when he returned from I-Branch, after a discreet note arrived from McGregor. "You should be resting," Grey said.

"If I rest any more, my head will explode from boredom." Pearl scarcely looked up from her sorcery book.

"We can't have that. Exploding heads aren't any more done than burst apprentices."

She rolled her eyes at him without offering the faintest of smiles. She had to be excruciatingly bored.

Grey hesitated, but if she were truly healed . . . "How do you feel about working a bit of justice magic?"

Her book slammed shut, raising a cloud of two-hundred-year-old dust, and she beamed at him. "Splendid." Her eyes narrowed. "On whom?"

"Whoever might have pushed you this past Monday."

"You need a suspect."

"I have one." Grey didn't think he needed to name him.

Pearl bit her lip. "I need another book."

"Do you?" He raised an eyebrow. "What sort of book?"

"One that tells how to do justice magic. I don't actually know how. And this book—" She pointed at the one she'd just shut. "None of the spells call for blood. They're all spit spells."

"Then we shall get one."

"Now?" Pearl bounced to her feet. She had to be feeling a great deal better.

"All right." Grey didn't think he gave in too easily. Nor did he believe he was too eager to work a little justice on Nigel Cranshaw. He hoped he was correct in his beliefs.

The scowls hadn't abated since he'd first taken her through the lounge to the library. Sixty-year-old boys in a pet because their No Girls Allowed signs had been ignored. Dogs in the manger, all of them. They couldn't use the magic, but they didn't want any females doing it, either. Idiots.

"There." He pointed at the section of sorcery books. "Find what you need."

She slanted him a quick look and darted into the stacks before his second thoughts could arrive. When they did, he fell into a perfect agony of indecision. Was she ready for this? She was older than the twelve-year-old apprentices the beginning book was intended for. She had a great deal more experience in using sorcery and manipulating the magic created by innocent blood. But she had only been an apprentice for three weeks.

Pearl emerged from the stacks bearing a small, fat book with scarlet-and-gilt-edged pages, looking very satisfied with herself. Her thirst for knowledge was as alarming as his own.

"No experiments," Grey warned her. "If you are not sure what will happen, or what you should do, then you will not do it. You must be very confident of your spell. Understand?"

She nodded. They checked out the book and went back to his house. He went with her to fetch her blood-stained bits of clothing, which she carefully laid across her worktable in the attic room. Then she sat down to read.

In the morning, Pearl talked him into taking her with

him to the council house, arguing that she could read just as well in her private study as she could at home. Not that he had much to do at I-Branch besides annoy his subordinates.

To that purpose, he wandered down to the laboratory to see what they were doing. Harry stood over Tipple, who was painstakingly scraping the still rather squashed inside of a piece of the collection device with a long-handled instrument.

"That's got it, lad." Harry clapped Tipple on the shoulder as he withdrew his scraper and peered at it. Grey couldn't see anything, but he was a conjurer. What did he know?

"You go off and test that." Harry had seen Grey. "See what you find. Wager 'alf a crown it's wizardry o' some sort."

"I'll not take that wager, sir." Tipple shook his head, grinning. "Not since it came from the brass side." He carried the scraper off to one of the beaker-covered tables, his other hand cupped beneath it, as if he thought he could catch whatever ephemera the instrument contained in his hand. Perhaps he could.

Harry came up to Grey, scowling. "Don't know 'ow these lads get anything done, with you peerin' over their shoulders all th' time."

"They're accustomed to it. They would think me ailing if I did not appear at least once in a day to peer." Grey clasped his hands behind his back. "What have you found?"

"Evidence all the magics were used, or at least attempted." Harry's scowl became even more fierce. "An' if they were all twisted as nasty as the alchemy 'e used—" he shook his head.

"The conjury was. You found sorcery as well?"

Harry threw up his hands. "May have. Don't know enough about sorcery to be sure. What do you get when you try to work magic with blood taken unwillingly?

Not sorcery. Do you get anyfing at all? How's Pearl?" he said, in an abrupt change of subject.

"Astonishingly well. She's in her study, reading."

"You didn't keep 'er 'ome another day to recover?" Harry looked scandalized. "You'd 'ave done as much for one o' your Briganti."

"There's not a mark on her to recover from." Grey let his astonishment and his disgruntlement show. "The blisters are completely gone from her arms and hands. Not even a trace of redness remains. I assume the burns I cannot see are equally healed, since her arms received the worst of it."

"That strong of magic workin' that fast needs rest."

"She's sitting down in her study in a very large, comfortable chair, resting as much as she would at home. More, most likely." Grey parroted the arguments Pearl had used on him. "Besides, have you been able to make Elinor do anything she did not want to do or stay away from any place she particularly wanted to visit? My apprentice is no less stubborn."

He paused, looking about the laboratory, feeling foolish for not noticing sooner. "Speaking of Elinor, where is she?"

"In 'er stillroom," Harry said. "It's comin' up to dark of the moon, an' she's got some preparations to make for potions as got to be brewed then."

"Dark—" Grey turned and sprinted up the stairs two at a time.

Harry followed a step or two behind. "What? Was it something I said?"

Grey didn't slow his pace back to the I-Branch offices. "Dark of the moon. It's been three weeks and some since the murder, which means it was likely close to the previous new moon. I want to know for certain."

"Think it means anything?" Harry had caught up.

"I don't know. It might. It's another piece of information. This was murder by magic. Murder *for* magic.

Conjury is tied to the moon, to its rise and set. Wizardry is tied to the moon's phases and seasons. Sorcery likely is, too. A woman's cycle correlates to the moon phases." Grey burst through the door.

"Moon phase calendar," he announced. "Who's got one?"

"Here, sir." The man closest to the door handed him a pocket-size leather-bound book, which opened up into a small, well-marked calendar.

"Thank you." Grey looked at him. "Loring, isn't it?"

"Yes, sir. I've got it for moonrise times, but it shows the full and new moons as well."

"So I see." Grey studied the newest recruit to I-Branch ranks, a transfer from the enforcers. "Your spirits rise with the moon?"

"Starting to, sir. I've got one from Cromwell's rule who'll answer then."

"Excellent. Excellent work." Grey clapped him on the shoulder and opened the small calendar flat on Loring's desk. Harry and those in the office who could crowded around.

Grey ransacked his mind for facts. "Angus Galloway's body was found early on October 12. So he was murdered sometime in the night of the eleventh to the twelfth. And the new moon was—"

He leaned down to see the tiny print. "The night of the twelfth. Galloway was murdered *before* the dark of the moon."

"Only one day before," Loring said.

"So how important is it that the spell be worked precisely at the dark of the moon?" Grey asked, looking around the cavernous office. "Where's Ferguson?"

"Off with that Greek alchemist you brought in," Meade, his second-in-command, said.

"Oh, right."

"Depends on the spell, I imagine," Harry said. "An' since we don't know what spell this murderin'—" He paused and looked carefully around the room. The occupants were all male. "Th' murderin' bastard was tryin' to work, we can't be sure."

"October 11 was a Sunday." Loring pointed to the date.

"So he was performing a Black Mass?" Grey said. "Desecrating the Sabbath?"

"Maybe he's a workin' man and has to do his murderin' on 'is day off," Harry said.

"That is another possibility," Grey admitted. "Or the date and the phase of the moon means nothing at all. All good possibilities."

"So how do you know?" Loring asked. "How do you discover which possibility is the correct one?"

"Lab work," Harry said.

"Investigation and interviews," Meade added.

"Or—" Grey's thoughts took a grim turn. "Another murder gives us more to go on."

Silence fell and stretched until Harry broke it. "On that lovely note, I'm goin' back to th' lab."

"Moon rises at six," Meade said to Grey. "Think you can participate in an effort to call our murder victim tonight?"

"He's not strong enough to rise with the moon yet," Grey said absently. "I'll be back at midnight for the attempt." He shot a quick glance around the room. "All conjurers are off duty until then for rest hours."

"Yes, sir." Meade all but saluted. Would have, Grey was sure, if he hadn't forbidden it. Enforcement might have its quasi-military elements, but Investigations Branch was relentlessly civilian. He went to collect Pearl and get his necessary rest in.

GREY ACTUALLY SLEPT during his mandated rest period. He'd instituted the rest requirement not long after I-Branch had been created, because too many conjurers were getting too little rest and the magic was sucking them dry. He'd had to practically tie Meade to his bed to keep him from becoming a walking skeleton, and Meade was a naturally stocky man. Stuffing food down a man's throat was necessary, but it didn't make up for a lack of sleep, not over the long haul.

Meade had made it clear that Grey couldn't insist on rules if he didn't follow them himself, so he took his required nap. He met Pearl in the breakfast room for dinner, feeling half awake and grumpy rather than bright and refreshed. Naps did that to him, but he would be grateful by midnight. "How is your reading going?"

"Quite well. The book is informative." Pearl smiled so widely, her teeth glinted in the candlelight, immediately sensitizing his suspicion nerves.

"Tells you how to do it with step-by-step instructions, does it?" He maintained a casual air—but not too casual—so as not to set off her suspicion alert in turn.

"In an archaic 'hath-doth-givest' round-about-ish annoying sort of way," she grumbled, sounding much more like herself.

Grey let himself relax a fraction. "What have you learned?"

She blew out a breath. "Guild secrets for one thing. Sorcery's stuffed full with them."

"And you don't think they should be kept secret?"

"Oh no. I agree with them completely. It just—" She wrinkled her nose in a manner that was not in the least adorable, if he was dishonest with himself. "It makes it difficult to discuss the situation and the spell with you. Since you are my magic-master, but you are not a sorcerer."

"I can see that would be difficult. But we are Englishmen and Englishwomen. We rise above mere difficulty. What have you learned? If you can tell me without betraying any sorcerous secrets." He watched her pick her way through her thoughts.

"Well . . ." She thought some more. "Justice magic begins with a technique the book calls 'the foundation of sorcerye.' Riding the blood."

"Do you need another book? Is the justice magic too advanced for a three-weeks' apprentice?"

"No, I don't need another book. This one described the technique quite well. And justice magic seems to be in that basic, elementary category of sorcery, one of the first done with blood rather than—" She waved a hand toward her mouth.

"Saliva?" Grey chuckled. "You're going to have to get over your aversion for the word."

"I'm going to have to remember to use it. Saliva magic sounds so much better than spit magic." She sighed. "I have enough trouble remembering to be ladylike, and spit is not."

"Neither is blood, but you work that."

"Yes, well—actually, no. Not yet. I've never drawn blood for magic, just put magic in the stains and used it to lay ghosts. *Riding* the blood sounds so . . ." She raised both her hands in a helpless gesture.

"Dangerous?" Grey wouldn't allow her to do anything dangerous. Not until Amanusa returned to supervise.

"No, not dangerous. The book was very clear on how to do it safely, for both the rider and the one ridden. It seems . . ." She took a deep breath and let it out. "Difficult. I'm not sure I *can* do it. Or that I can do it correctly. Get in and out and find what I'm looking for. Particularly if my very first attempt is searching a suspected criminal."

"Then your first time should be with me."

Blood rushed to Grey's head as soon as he spoke the words, and pooled in his groin as his body took another meaning from the words. He wanted that first time of hers to be with him. Given that she'd come to this apprenticeship from the streets of London's East End, her first time was doubtless long past.

But *this* first time, her first to "ride the blood"—that would be with him.

"What is required for this magic?" He concluded his meal with a last bite of cake, trying to maintain his normal facade.

"Blood, of course. Just a bit. And something to mix it with. Tea or wine."

"I vote for wine," he said quickly. "If I am going to have to shed blood, I want something to dull the pain."

She laughed, a light, breathy thing. "In the morning?"

"Why not do it tonight? We have the wine." He indicated the bottle waiting on the sideboard. "An excellent port, well able to disguise the flavor of a drop or two of blood. Which we have in abundance. A whole body full of it." He spread his arms in expansive invitation. "I am at your disposal." In any way she wanted to take that invitation.

"Yes, but I have nothing to use to get it out of that body." Pearl bit her lip. "Needles don't really work. Knives cut too broadly. I need a lancet. I'll have to purchase one tomorrow."

Grey drew breath. Now was the proper time. "As it happens . . ." He rose from his seat, drew a small box from a lower jacket pocket, and handed it to her with a little bow. "If you were a conjurer, your magic-master would present you with your first pencil case. As you are a sorcerer, the gift of your first lancet seemed appropriate."

"Oh . . ." Pearl stood as she took the box from him with wide eyes. Her lower lip trembled just a trifle, until she stilled it between her teeth.

He should have had it wrapped. No matter that it would have made the presentation seem more important. It was important. Momentous. It was the beginning of her practice of sorcery.

She opened the box and removed the steel instrument, its sharp point gleaming in the candlelight.

"I considered purchasing an antique lancet, like the

one Amanusa uses, but I couldn't find one. Then I wavered between silver and steel, because silver is much more easily chased and inscribed. But steel is a modern, more sanitary metal and you are—or will be—a modern sorceress. And steel can be engraved."

The lancet followed the old-fashioned design of Amanusa's, long out of style among modern men of medicine. It had one end curved to fit around the tip of her finger, making the lancet into a sort of artificial claw. The ring did not close into a circle, so that it could be adjusted to fit her finger. Grey hoped it would adjust small enough to fit her. Most medical doctors were men, and larger than Pearl.

" 'To Pearl Parkin,' " she read aloud, squinting at the letters engraved around the circular base of the lancet. " 'Sorcery apprentice, from her magic-master, Grey Carteret.' "

"A lancet is quite a bit smaller than a pencil case," Grey said to fill the ensuing silence with words. It was not an awkward silence, but one filled with meanings and emotions he did not want to acknowledge, much less explore. "I had to pare away words and make the letters very small to make it fit."

She slipped her right forefinger into the ring of the lancet and held it up, turning it this way and that to admire it. At least, Grey thought she was admiring it.

"Let's have a look, then." He took her hand in his and brought her closer. So he could see how the lancet fit. "A bit loose, isn't it?"

The thing threatened to slide down to her middle knuckle. Grey held it in place and squeezed the sides together until they touched, without overlapping. "How is that?"

Pearl tapped the point against her sleeve and the lancet held firm. She held up her left hand and, before he could stop her, she stabbed the lancet quickly into the top of her tallest finger. A drop of blood welled up.

"Perfect," she said, as Grey caught her injured finger and popped it into his mouth, quite as if it were his own.

Which it was not. It was hers, his apprentice, and why ever was he doing such an intimate and improper thing with his apprentice's finger? He pulled it out of his mouth as hastily as he'd put it in, with an unintended slide of his tongue over the punctured tip.

Impropriety was something he was intimately familiar with. Intimacy, however, was a far different matter. Even on the occasions when he improperly accommodated those women who invited themselves into his bed—and they were far fewer than everyone assumed—it had not felt so intimate as this moment, holding Pearl's hand captive in his, having just removed her fingertip from inside his mouth.

It was the gazing deep into her eyes, he thought. He never gazed, into eyes or anything else. He always shut his eyes, precisely to prevent this sort of thing, this uncomfortable, unfathomable, utterly necessary intimacy.

He licked his lips, as if licking up any stray bits of her blood. This made it twice that he had ingested her blood. Three times, if one wished to count the mingling of blood at their bargain, and Grey rather thought it counted. Did it mean anything? If so, what?

He held up his forefinger, offering it to her dainty steel claw. "Blood," he said, "for the riding thereof."

She hesitated. He supposed it was worth hesitating over, something as momentous as this, the equivalent of calling her first spirit.

"Pour the wine first." She spun, her skirts bouncing off his ankles, and strode to fetch the bottle.

Grey followed. The glasses were on the sideboard with the wine. He took the bottle from her and held it over the delicate crystal. "One glass or two?"

Pearl bit her lip, frantically reviewing the pertinent pages, guild secrets uppermost in her thoughts. The outside world believed that the sorceress rode the subject's

blood by drinking it, which contributed to the old beliefs that sorcery worked on stolen blood. Pearl had
been shocked to learn the guild's deepest secret, that the
sorcerer's own blood carried the greatest power, and that
it was her blood inside the subject—inside Grey—that
she would ride.

This made things easier in many ways. For one, now
that Grey put her bleeding finger into his mouth, she
didn't have to worry about how to get her blood inside
him. He'd done it himself. And Pearl could see how in
general it would be much simpler to slip her blood into
other people as opposed to having to steal a bit of blood
from them. The issue now was how to keep that a secret
from Grey.

The easiest way, she supposed, was to feed his as-
sumptions and take a little of his blood to mix with the
wine. She could also practice her sleight-of-hand blood-
letting, if the finger she'd already punctured could be
convinced to give up another few drops. The book had
repeated a number of times that if the purpose of the
ride was not justice, but simply information, or practice,
that more blood should be used, not less.

The more of the sorceress's blood a subject held, the
more the magic would identify the subject with the sorceress and make it less likely for her to do inadvertent
harm. Pearl wasn't sure how much blood was needed to
keep Grey safe, but when it came to Grey and safety, she
would err on the side of more.

And he was waiting, bottle over the glass, ready to
pour.

"One," she said.

He smiled, wicked, seductive, and more. As if they
were the only two people in the world. Or the only two
who mattered. He smiled as if he knew her and she knew
him. Or if she didn't, he invited her to learn everything
there was about him to know. If she would let him learn
her inside and outside in return.

Grey set the bottle down and only then did Pearl realize he'd filled the glass. Too full, if she were to be the only one to drink it. "We both drink," she said.

He raised a brow in that fallen-angel guise of his. "From the same glass?" His lips curved in his patented smile that made her heart go into its useless gyrations. Before she met Grey, when Papa still lived, she'd seen the women he escorted to the opera and the theater, beautiful and glittering and perfect. Not like Pearl.

"How . . . intimate," he said.

Intimate. That was how he made her feel. Which lessened her guilt. Intimate had its innocent side. This was magic, nothing more. Magic could be intimate. Doubtless intimacy could be magical as well.

Grey offered up his forefinger again and Pearl shook off her strange mood. She took his hand in hers and brought it close. She inhaled deeply. This was difficult. She didn't want to pierce that perfect fingertip.

You've done this before, she scolded her odd reluctance.

I didn't know him then, her thoughts returned. *I don't want to cause him pain.*

"If you'd rather not—" Grey made as if to withdraw his hand and she tightened her grip, looking up into his eyes.

Was that a flash of hurt she saw there? Did he truly want her to do this? So much that her refusal would cause him pain?

"I'm just—" She sighed. "Nervous. This will hurt, and I don't like doing that to you."

Instead of stoically squaring his shoulders and assuring her he could withstand any pain, Grey threw an arm over his grimacing face, turning away from his threatened forefinger. "Go on," he moaned. "Hurt me. For the good of the magic, I can endure the torture."

She laughed at his nonsense, an embarrassing snorty sort of giggle, and she stabbed the lancet into his finger.

Grey abandoned his playacting and lowered his arm to watch as Pearl squeezed out a tiny drop of blood, scooped it onto the side of the lancet, and stirred it into the wine.

"Are you sure that's enough?" He lifted his finger toward her. "I have more."

"It's quite enough for this experiment." How could she get more of her blood into the glass without him noticing, given the intensity of his watching?

"Perhaps we should relocate to the drawing room next door," he suggested, solving her problem yet again. "Amanusa asked for comfortable chairs when she worked her justice magic at the conclave in Paris."

Pearl picked up the glass. "Lead on, oh master of magic."

16

GREY GAVE PEARL a look, as if suspecting her of mocking him—which she was, but only a little. Then he did as she wished, turned his back to her and led the way out of the dining room and down the few steps of the corridor.

It was harder than she thought to carry the glass and squeeze more blood out of her finger. The wound had closed, and in desperation, to get the job done before Grey turned back around, she used the lancet again.

This time, she went too deep. The blood wouldn't stop welling up, no matter how tight she pinched. Only a droplet at a time, but it would not stop. She dipped her finger into the wine, hoping the sting of alcohol would help, but that only seemed to make it run more.

Finally, she put the finger in her mouth, licking away the wine, then biting down with her teeth in hope it would cut off the flow. Grey turned as he opened the door and caught her with her finger in her mouth. "Is it still bleeding?"

She went into the drawing room, away from potential exposure to curious servants. "I don't think so." She removed her finger to speak.

Grey shut the door and came to inspect her wound, which was—drat it all—still seeping. He didn't put it into his mouth this time, thank heaven. Pearl didn't think she could bear that warm, wet, intimate touch again. Not without collapsing to the floor because her bones had dissolved. He licked his thumb and pressed it hard against the tiny puncture, pinching her fingertip until it went white. Then he looked at it again. When a few seconds passed without any more blood welling up, he pronounced her healed.

"Perhaps it takes someone else's spit to seal a sorceress's wound," he suggested.

"Perhaps so." Pearl couldn't say anything else. Her insides were quivering too much. So were her outsides. The wine in the glass she held almost splashed out, her hands shook so.

Grey pretended not to notice. It had to be pretense. How could he not see such shaking? He indicated the red, betassled chairs, inviting her to sit. They had high backs and low arms to accommodate a lady's full skirts. Pearl handed him the wine before taking up his invitation. She didn't want it to spill.

"Shall I drink first?" he asked as she collapsed into the nearest chair.

Pearl reviewed her mental notes yet again. *Whereupon he drinketh of the blood, she shall wait while the sorcerye spreadeth throughout him, for the passynge of a tenth part of one houre.* If she had to wait, that meant he should drink first, didn't it?

But the waiting came after the *infusing of the sorcerye into thee blood.* Had she done that?

She hadn't. She'd been too busy with walking and poking her finger and then trying to get the bleeding to stop. Was it too late to do it now? If it wasn't, would it mess up the spell? If she put a little more blood in, would that fix things? If she put in more blood, would her finger stop bleeding again?

"Um . . ." She would try to put the magic in the blood already in the wine first. Pearl called magic, as she'd been practicing, and it rose. From her blood and her bones, it welled up like a warm spring rising from the earth. Or like a drop of blood from a punctured finger.

Grey had seated himself in the other chair before the fire, waiting patiently, one foot keeping time to silent music at the end of his crossed legs. He held the wine-glass casually, as if it were no more than an after-dinner glass of port.

Pearl closed her eyes and opened her magic senses, fumbling in the dark to find the blood in the wine. Except it wasn't dark. Grey had a sort of glow about him. Not magic, exactly, but potential. As he said, a whole body full of it. His sorcery potential gave a rosy tint to his glow, but as she looked, she saw silvery glowing wisps floating around and through him. Conjury, she thought, waiting to be tapped.

There. That was the blood-mixed wine, the brighter ball of red light, the warmth held in Grey's hand. As she noticed it, the magic inside her seemed to notice it, too. The magic flared, searing her, then it *pounced*. It flew from her into the blood, as if the mere act of separating the blood from her body and searching it out informed the magic what she wanted done.

The magic burned along her veins as it left her, making her gasp with the sharp, scorching pain, and it was gone, leaving only the pain behind.

She gasped for breath, trying hard not to whimper. After another moment or two, she realized Grey knelt by her chair, calling her name, chafing her hands. "I'm fine," she said.

"Liar." He took her chin and turned her face to peer into her eyes.

"I *wasn't* fine, but I am now," she clarified. "Truly."

"I felt the magic move." Grey gripped both her hands, refusing to release her gaze. Pearl couldn't make herself look away from the concern in his dark, beautiful eyes. "You are not ready for this."

"I am." She looked for the wine. Surely he hadn't spilled it so they had all this to go through again. "It is only—I should have remembered to put the magic into the blood sooner. The book warned of it, that sorcery burns unless you act quickly. I forgot. I was too slow."

Her smile was surely more of a grimace. "You can be sure I won't forget again. But it's merely pain. No actual injury."

"Pain is not 'mere,'" Grey scolded.

He'd set the wine on a side table, she saw. It was safe.

"Yes, it is," Pearl said. "If there is no injury, it goes away quickly. And it is gone. I am *fine*. No pain. No harm done." Gently she eased her hands from him and gestured to the wine. "The magic is in the blood, in the wine. It needs to be used. We should use it. You drink first. Half."

"Amanusa only required the men her magic searched to drink a mouthful. A good swallow."

"Then you shouldn't have poured so much wine. It must all be drunk. We cannot leave any behind." She gave him a crooked smile. "Are you afraid of the taste? So much wine will hide the taste of so little blood."

"It's not the taste I'm afraid of." His lips twitched as he looked at her, betraying his teasing. "I've never done this before. I'm a sorcery virgin. Be gentle with me."

Pearl shook her head at him, her own lips twitching with a smile. "We're both sorcery virgins. We'll simply have to fumble through it like a pair of newlyweds.

Close your eyes and think of England." She paused and went on more seriously.

"That's probably best—to think of England. So I don't inadvertently stumble across something I don't want to know. Something you don't want me to know. I will try not to intrude on your deeper thoughts, but—well—remember that virginity?"

Grey's expression was faintly alarmed, which likely meant that behind that beautiful face he'd gone into full-blown panic.

"We don't have to do this," Pearl said. "I'm sure Elinor will let me practice on her."

"No, no." Grey cleared his throat. "I'm game. Best you practice on me. Magic-master, after all."

He stood and crossed to the side table where he stared at the wine in its glass for a moment. Then abruptly he picked it up and drank half the contents.

"There. That's my half." He handed the glass to Pearl. "Now you."

"I will try *very* hard not to intrude," Pearl promised, looking into his dark brown, melting eyes. They melted her, at any rate.

She dragged her gaze from him and pinned it on the wine. She wasn't much of a wine drinker. She didn't like the taste. So would it be better to drink it all down at once as Grey had, or eke it out in swallows?

Swallows, she decided. There was too much left to throw back all at once, the way she'd seen Irish laborers toss back their vile whiskey. She'd likely choke on it, sputter, and embarrass herself. Besides, a series of sips—large sips—would use up the time she had to wait on the magic.

"Please." She took a swallow, trying hard not to make a face. "Sit down. You will want to be comfortable for the magic."

He sat, draping one leg over the nearly nonexistent

arm of the chair. The back of the chair, while high enough to lean against, lacked the wings to either side for proper lounging. At least half of his attempt to sprawl in a shocking, dissolute-looking manner was thwarted by his furniture. He still managed to look thoroughly dissolute, disreputable, and delicious.

She took another, larger swallow of the wine and somehow managed not to choke on it. Probably it was excellent wine, but she didn't like it. Plebian taste buds, she was sure.

"Drink up," Grey encouraged her. "I despise waiting."

This swallow was more of a sip. It wasn't as bad as the last. Maybe she was getting used to it. Maybe it had killed her taste buds.

"How long do we have to wait?" he asked.

"Longer than this." She choked down more wine.

"Yes, but how long, exactly?" He glowered at her. "Next time, we use tea. You're not drinking fast enough."

"Forgive me for not being a wine guzzler," she snapped, then blushed for speaking to her magic-master with such sauce. But she might have known Grey's response would be laughter.

"One can't gulp tea, either," she informed him more primly. "It's too hot."

"One would hope, at any rate," he said, still smiling. "But truthfully, Pearl, how long, exactly, must we wait?"

She delayed answering him with another swallow of blood-tinged wine. It was almost gone. Surely that was no more than a single swallow swirling in the bottom of the glass. She tossed it back like an old hand and then had to clutch the arm of the chair, invisible beneath her spreading skirts, to steady herself. "I think I drank it too fast. I apparently have no head for spirits."

"Port wine is not precisely the same as spirits," Grey said. "And you still have not answered my question. How long?"

"Oh." She put a hand to her forehead. It seemed to help the spinning sensation. It let her know precisely where her head was and what it was doing. "Um—the tenth part of an hour. Six minutes." Even she could do that much arithmetic. "Or thereabouts."

His eyebrows rose. He had four of them, two hovering above the others somewhere in the middle of his forehead. She blinked a few times and the upper pair slid in a semicircle and rejoined the others. She should not be this tipsy, not on a half glass of wine. She never had been before. When she'd lived in Whitechapel, only a few short weeks ago, she'd had tots of gin that hadn't hit her this hard, even on an emptier stomach. But those beverages hadn't been infused with blood and magic.

Pearl blinked, making Grey's features behave themselves again. She'd expected the magic's burn, because she'd read it in the book on justice magic. Not how much it hurt, but that it would. She didn't expect this dizziness. The book had mentioned nothing of the sort. Then again, the book's instructions hadn't mentioned the sorcerer drinking any of the subject's blood as part of the spell.

The other book, however, the one on beginning sorcery, had said that while it generally wasn't required for spells, it wouldn't do any harm to take on another's blood. As long as it was willingly given. Pearl didn't think Grey's could have come any more willingly. And he hadn't given much.

"Thereabouts?" Grey asked. "What does thereabouts mean?"

If it was the magic making her dizzy—Pearl was the sorceress. She was the one in charge, the one who directed the magic. Therefore— She took hold of the magic inside her and . . . put it away. It layered along her bones and dissolved into her blood, the fizzy sparks inside her head fading as it went back whence it had come.

"It means," she said, "that the length of time depends on the sorcerer's strength and the amount of magic called and the speed with which it spreads through the blood. The stronger the sorceress, the less time she must wait."

"So it seems we should wait a little longer than six minutes, for safety's sake." Grey pulled out his pocket watch, sitting up a little straighter to do so, and checked its time against the mantel clock. "What time did you finish your wine?"

"I don't know, I forgot to look." Not that it mattered when *she* finished. "But it's not the ability of the sorceress, her knowledge and experience in the practice of magic that matters. It's her strength. Do you see? The fact that I'm an apprentice and don't have much experience— or any—has an effect on how well I perform the actual spell. On what I see, or don't see, and how easily I find precisely what I'm looking for and nothing else. The *strength* of the sorceress affects whether she can perform the spell at all, and how long she must wait for the magic to permeate."

"And since you are a very strong sorceress, you should not have to wait long at all." Grey tucked away his watch and straightened himself in the chair, resting his hands on his knees. "Very well. Begin."

Pearl gaped at him. "How do you know I'm strong? For all you know, I could be a ten-minuter. Barely able to claim the name of sorceress. This is the test, you know. The qualifying examination, as to whether a sorcery apprentice can continue to study, or be forever relegated to love charms and 'hide-me' spells. This is it. If I can't do this—"

She broke off and pulled herself back from the edge of hysteria.

"You can do this," Grey said, never moving from his position of repose. "You are a strong sorceress. I know because I have seen what you have done with no training whatsoever. I have *felt* you do it. I, who have little sensitivity to magic outside my own sphere, could feel you work sorcery. That is not a weak talent, Pearl. Now— begin."

Pearl took a deep breath. She closed her eyes. That had helped the first time, so maybe it would help this time, too. Yes, there was Grey, his glow brighter, more rosy.

"Think of England," she murmured as she reached out with magic-formed fingers and *touched*—

The magic in her locked onto the magic in him with a gut-deep *thump,* and she was inside him. Images of the countryside rolled past her eyes in daffodil-strewn glory, and she laughed.

"England is beautiful."

"So it is," Grey agreed. The images changed to debutantes waltzing past in a pastel swirl of ballgowns, laughing faces turned up one after another in adoration.

Of course they adored him. He was beautiful and he was wicked and it was daring just to smile at him.

"You are teasing me." Pearl couldn't suppress her smile. Why would she want to? "No matter how wicked you wish to appear, you would never dally with innocence."

"No?" Grey produced memories of Pearl, of her finger in his mouth, his tongue sliding sensually along it.

She quivered, all the sensations she had so unsuccessfully suppressed rising again to the fore. "Ah, but I am not so innocent, am I?"

She was, and she wasn't. But her state of innocence wasn't in question here. Her ability to ride Grey's blood and sift his thoughts was. And so far, all she'd done was intercept the thoughts he had allowed to rise to the surface.

She needed to find something he didn't want her to know. Something small and unimportant. Something that was at least nominally her business, even though he might not want her to know it—like how he *truly* thought she was doing in her apprenticeship.

His surface thoughts were still of her, but now they pictured her various fumbles and pratfalls. She hadn't tripped so flamboyantly over Meade's sprawled feet in the office. But she did fall out Grey's front parlor window. Had her skirts flown up so high? It didn't matter.

Carefully, Pearl slid past Grey's teasing surface thoughts and was captured in a maelstrom of lust. For her.

Fantasies of naked limbs and bare skin were interspersed with moments of reality, actual memories of Pearl licking her lips, or smiling at him, of their clasped hands and the moments he'd held her in his arms. Even the moments when she argued with him or defied his dictates seemed to fire his blood.

The visions of her naked in his bed—or some bed— kept intruding and— No. That wasn't her body. That was some other woman's body, larger and more curved, with Pearl's face stuck on. She couldn't take offense, since he didn't know how she truly looked beneath her clothes. It meant he didn't actually want *her*. How could he? She couldn't possibly compare, given the hordes of women he'd undoubtedly gone through.

Pearl didn't think she actually formed an intention, much less a question, before the magic gave her the answers. Grey's lovers didn't number in the scores. They didn't even achieve tens. Three. He'd been with only three women in his entire life.

She didn't want to know who they were. Truly. She wouldn't know them anyway. Before her family's fall from wealth, she wouldn't have run in Grey's rarefied circles, had she been old enough to do so. And after— well, she might have seen him with a paramour, when she was spying on him in the streets.

She hadn't. Even though she'd turned away from Grey's thoughts, told herself she didn't want to know, deep down, she did. Deep down, below her conscience, she wanted to see his lovers and know how she meas-

ured up. Not well. They were lush and beautiful women.
Fair-haired and full-bosomed.

Pearl turned the magic deliberately and forcefully
away from those memories of Grey's. She did not want
to know more. Did. Not. Not their names, or how long
they'd been lovers, or how long ago.

Long.

No. She refused to invade his privacy any further.

She gathered herself up—rather like collecting her
skirts before mounting a carriage—and stepped away
from the conjurer. Back into her own mind. She couldn't
unsee what she had seen, though. Couldn't unknow what
she knew.

That it had been more than a year since Grey had
been with a lover. That he'd never maintained a mistress. That magic had been and always would be his
mistress, and that was why his lovers had been so few
and far between. Because few women would put up with
him forgetting promises and rendezvous when he got
caught up in the magic.

So, now she knew. She had her doubts about whether
he might truly want her, wondered if he had invented
those images to tease, just as he had the ones on the surface of his mind. He might indeed want to make love to
her. But he wanted the magic more.

Did that matter? Didn't Pearl herself want the magic
more? Hadn't she made up her mind never to leave her
welfare and support in the hands of anyone but herself?

Which meant that no matter how much Grey's lascivious fantasies might intrigue her, she could not indulge
her curiosity. Lovers didn't last. Even husbands didn't.
Magic did.

"Are you done?" Grey asked.

Pearl's gaze flicked up to him. "Why? Can you feel
it? Could you feel me riding?"

"No." He opened his eyes and frowned at her. "At least, I don't believe I did. *Are* you done?"

"Yes. Just a moment ago. Could you tell?"

He shook his head slowly. "No. But . . . I felt peaceful. While you were there." His eyes narrowed. "What did you see?"

Pearl blushed. She tried not to but her ears went so hot she wanted to hide them with her hands.

"You pried into my mind, didn't you?" He watched her, never moving from his relaxed position on the chair, hands resting in his lap. Was he angry? Did he even care?

"Yes." The blush burned. "But not very far." She rushed to justify her insupportable behavior. "If I am going to do justice magic, I cannot simply float on the surface of someone's thoughts. I have to be able to dig deeper. Into memory."

His gaze skewered her in place. "And what did you dig out of mine?" He crossed his legs, appearing relaxed as ever. Save for that piercing gaze.

"That you have had only three lovers," she blurted. She didn't rue her honesty. She wanted him to know. But her delivery could have been better. More woman-of-the-world.

His brows rose. "Only that?"

She shrugged, trying to copy his nonchalance. "I saw their faces. But not their names."

He smiled that wicked, teasing smile of his. "And why was that the information you sought? Jealous?"

Pearl snorted her derision, giving up on attempting to be ladylike. Grey didn't care. "Of what? Given the memories you displayed for me, it seemed a natural question." She frowned. "Not that I quite intended to ask. The thought floated idly across my mind—though I didn't *truly* want to know—and the magic leapt upon it and showed me, before I could stop it."

"*Truly?*" Grey's skepticism didn't surprise her. "You

didn't honestly want to know? About me and my paucity of lovers?"

His teasing was beginning to annoy her. "No," she snapped. "Despite the fact that you idiotically volunteered to let me poke around in your thoughts, I wanted to leave you some modicum of privacy. I hadn't intended to pry into anything so obviously none of my affair." She blushed yet again at her unfortunate choice of words. Pearl stood, embarrassed beyond bearing, and turned to leave.

"Don't go."

She wouldn't turn around, couldn't look at him. "I can't stay."

"You can. I apologize for being such a beast. I shouldn't tease. Not like that." His voice was so very gentle.

"You can't help it." She still couldn't turn.

"I should." He sighed. "There are so very many things I should be able to prevent myself doing, but I am utterly out of practice at it."

"Then practice," Pearl said sternly, but she was twisting toward him, and then back. He tempted her so.

"Almost you persuade me to try."

"Almost." She shook her head. "It's time to go." She moved to the door, laid her hand on the crystal knob.

"Pearl."

Her name in his deep, silken voice froze her in place. She couldn't speak, not even to snap out the "What?" she wished.

"When you ride my blood next, all of my thoughts are open to you, save only those concerning my family— parents, siblings. All else is fair game. I have no secrets. Not from you."

She didn't think she moved, but she must have. Leaned just enough, lowered her head, turned, so that she could see him from the corner of her eye. He stood before his chair near the fire, watching her with his dark beautiful eyes. What did that mean—he had no secrets? Why was she singled out to keep them? Because she was his apprentice? Or was there some other, deeper reason?

A flash of naked, entwined bodies seared through her mind, so quickly, so fiercely, she did not know whose thought it was—*hers or his*? She snatched open the parlor door and fled.

OVER THE NEXT few days, Grey had no success in collecting any of Cranshaw's blood for Pearl to ride, primarily because he didn't see Cranshaw. The man was making himself scarce, which made one wonder what he was up to. Grey did take a moment to speculate on how taking a drop of someone's blood to ride for justice magic eliminated the need for blood to be given willingly, but he supposed the amount taken made the difference. Or perhaps it was the intent of the magic. For justice, not harm. He wouldn't ask. Sorcery had the right to its secrets.

Since he hadn't collected any of Cranshaw's blood, Pearl refused to ride his blood again. Not until it became necessary, she said. Grey didn't know whether to be relieved or annoyed.

He didn't succeed in calling Angus Galloway's spirit, either, even with the assistance of half a dozen Briganti conjurers. The fact that Galloway was a weeks-new spirit, and they had his true name hadn't helped at all. It was like that sometimes with the very new ones. As if they had an orientation period before a summons was permitted to reach them.

The time issue also muddled things. Time had no meaning in the spirit world. Or if it did, it had no correlation to time in this one.

Pearl spent the passing days buried so deep in the musty, dusty sorcery tomes that sometimes when she emerged, she spoke in archaic English. "Hast thou a light?" she'd asked him this afternoon when her study room had grown dark with gathering clouds. More rain. He'd taken her home instead.

IT WAS THE dark of the moon. November 10, 1863. A Tuesday. The Briganti were on alert, even Enforcement. It had been agreed that Grey would attempt to re-create what he had been doing the evening of Galloway's murder, when he'd gone out on his "stroll." But this time, he would not be alone.

Harry and Elinor were downstairs, along with Nikos Archaios and George Meade. Pearl was in the workroom with Grey. There had been a long, volatile argument about whether the women would be present, much less take part in the evening's activities. Obviously, the women had won, since any idiot would agree that they would be safer with the men than following along on their own as they had threatened.

The fact that following along was precisely what Pearl had done on the last new moon had not helped the tone of the "discussion." Pearl was in Grey's workroom, though he'd been alone before, because he did not trust what she might do if she were out of his sight.

Grey had begun to find it difficult to be parted from her for any length of time. And during those few hours of every night when she went to the rooms she shared with Elinor, he couldn't stop himself from thinking about her. Not simply wanting her, which had become something of an obsession—she'd invaded his dreams—but wondering what she might think about this problem, or wanting to share a choice item of gossip just to see her laugh.

It wasn't like him, and he didn't understand it. Women were all very well in their fashion, but they had never *mattered* before. Except for Mary. And now Pearl. The parallels disturbed him almost as much as the differences.

The night stretched on, rain spattering in sporadic showers against the windows and the roof just overhead.

Grey conducted his experiments. Spirits were generally more difficult to raise at the new moon because, while the moon did rise, it was dark. He'd never had any trouble himself with calling spirits at that time. The moon was still there, whether he could see it or not. But it made a difference to most other conjurers. So he'd been trying to come up with new sigils and/or ways to charge them that would make it easier for those other conjurers.

Tonight, however, he wound up spending the majority of his time chatting with his familiar spirits: Mary, of course, but also Walther the Prussian and his Roman spirits, Varus and Polonia. He had other spirits he called, but these were familiar to him.

Varus and Polonia were the oldest spirits who answered his call with a reasonable consistency. Varus had died a dozen years before Julius Caesar, and Polonia dated from a century or so later, in the reign of Diocletian. Both of them were far less what they'd been and more of what they were becoming. Not angels, but something else.

Not long after the clock chimed three, Harry knocked on the workroom door to report Elinor asleep downstairs. Grey had already moved Pearl to the cot under the eaves.

"Late as it is," Harry said, "I reckon if something was going to happen, it would've already happened. Pearl was followin' you down Whitechapel Road by this time, th' night Galloway was murdered."

Grey nodded, leaning against the doorjamb. A workroom was a man's private place. "We can only assume that we were wrong about the significance of the new moon. I'm afraid to hope that the man's given up."

"Maybe whatever 'e conjured last scared 'im into stoppin'. Never any 'arm in hoping." Harry ran a hand through his hair, then scrubbed his face. "Might as well finish out the night. I don't want to give up an' then discover we quit too soon."

"I'll send my older spirits out for a nose around to see if any unusual magic is stirring." Grey rubbed his eyes with finger and thumb. "We can sleep at sunrise."

"Aye." Harry sighed. "It's terrible to sit an' wait for a murder just because you can't catch the soddin' bastard till 'e's done it again." He turned to trudge down the stairs. "I'll 'ave McGregor send up another pot o' tea. The man's unnatural. 'E's still fresh as a daisy."

"I have often suspected he keeps duplicates of himself in a closet to bring out at times like this." Grey waved Harry off and retreated into his workroom to ask his Roman contingent to scour the city. Varus had a few contemporaries occasionally willing to help, but they didn't speak to Grey much. Walther went with them.

As the hours wore on, he fought boredom and sleep by setting Mary to wake him whenever he drifted off. Grey feared capture by another one of the murderer's wretched spells. The rain tapered off, but the night was so dark he couldn't tell whether the skies had cleared or not. He couldn't see stars. Fog hadn't settled in, at least. The windows remained wet, so perhaps a thin drizzle still fell.

The streets outside began to stir with the first evidence of the world coming awake. The sky was still dark, but the clocks had chimed six and the hooves of omnibus horses clattered on the paving. Grey had just closed his watch, which proclaimed 6:03, and was replacing it in his vest pocket, preparing to descend the stairs, call off the alert, and send everyone home, when magic burst into his brain.

Demon! it shrieked.

17

MARY FOLLOWED ON the heels of the alarm, blasting open Grey's doors and windows with the force of her arrival. *Demon!* she cried. *Demon, demon, demon!*

"Where?" Grey glanced at Pearl, who had been awakened by the explosion of breaking glass and sat groggily blinking. "Downstairs," he said, obeying his own order.

"Mary." He reached for her, trying to soothe her, calm her, as he skidded down the stairs, scarcely touching them. "Where is the demon? We need to know. I can't understand you."

Demon, she wailed. But she didn't need words to tell him.

Pictures opened in his mind, canted at crazy angles with unnatural colors that made him stumble on the stairs as he tried to interpret them. Pearl's shoulder under his arm steadied him. They descended the rest of the way with him leaning on her, trying to concentrate on the bizarre pictures Mary was sending him, rather than the soft, warm body pressed against his side.

In the drawing room, Meade stood with the fingers of his left hand pressed to his temple as he always did when communicating with his spirits. He'd apparently roused the others, for the alchemists and Elinor were on their feet.

Elinor was the first to notice Grey's entrance with Pearl. "What's happened?"

Pearl tried to ease herself away, but Grey held her in place. He liked knowing exactly where she was. "Demon," he said. "Meade, can you tell where it is? My spirit's confused."

"Park, I think. Lots of shrubberies and grass. Can't tell which one."

"Right." Grey set himself again to soothing Mary while he sent a summons winging out to his other spirits. *"The demon can't touch you,"* he reminded her. *"You have protections far greater than mine. Just tell me where it is."*

It will hurt you, she cried. *You have no protection.*

He has us, Walther announced, making his return known. *The demon is in St. James's Park.*

"St. James's," Grey announced. "Make sure all the conjurers know, my spirits, and that they know to spread the word to the other magicians."

Your conjurers, they know, Walther said.

"Then have Sir William's secretary wake him and request that he call out the entire council." The secretary was always a conjurer for moments like this. "We'll need everyone we've got, whoever can cast the most basic spell, if we're taking on a demon."

"St. James's Park?" Harry questioned. "Right in front of Horse Guards?"

"It's a *demon*," Grey was taking hats and coats from a footman's laden arms and passing them to their owners. McGregor held umbrellas. "Demons do not care about human authority or human force of arms."

"Right." Harry grimaced. He set his bowler hat on his head for lack of anywhere else to put it while he pulled on his coat. "I was thinkin' of our murderer, not a demon."

Grey groaned, but didn't stop assisting Pearl with her coat. "That's right. If a demon's here, likely we've got another murder victim somewhere. *Spirits?*"

"Surely you do not intend to take the women with us to confront a demon." Archaios picked his hat up from a side table, his coat buttoned snugly to his neck.

"Surely you do not think we would actually stay behind," Elinor retorted.

A newer spirit popped up in answer to Grey's call. *Good idea. Let the older spirits focus on the demon and* the newer, weaker spirits carry messages and do the safer but still necessary tasks.

"Get a message to Commissioner Mayne requesting his regular police begin a search for the murder victim and the scene of the crime." Grey finally shrugged into his own coat.

"The women are magicians," he went on. "We need everyone who can possibly cast a spell. We'll have twelve-year-old boys from the school out there."

"But—" Archaios stood near the door, as if he thought of barring it.

"This is a *demon,* Archaios." Grey's fear and anger came snapping through his voice. "If guns and soldiers can't hurt it, what makes you think mere masculine strength will? It's magic we need, man. Even as apprentices, these two wield powerful magic. You think no innocent blood will be spilled this morning? Shouldn't we have access to that magic?"

"The *danger*—" Archaios was wavering.

"If we can't drive that demon back from whence it came, there will be no safety anywhere." Grey's voice was bleak. He caught the Greek's arm and pushed him out the parlor door, following him. The rest of the silent company came after.

Harry caught up with Grey, drizzle gathering in silvery beads on the rounded crown of his hat. He glanced at the two women behind them, trotting along beneath their umbrellas. "Think we can keep the ladies at the back o' the lines? Tendin' the wounded, like?"

"We can only try. And hope." The bleakness settling deep inside him would not help in the battle, Grey knew, but he did not know how to drive it out.

An omnibus, empty due to the early hour, rattled along Piccadilly at the end of the street. Grey shouted, and Meade ran ahead to appropriate it for the official use of the Briganti. They loaded everyone on and headed off to St. James's Park.

They were proceeding along Bird Cage Walk toward the parade grounds in front of Whitehall when Grey spotted men and lights gathering just inside the park. He tapped the conductor's shoulder and pointed, signaling him to have the driver stop, and Mary popped up from wherever she'd been.

It's gone, she cried. *The demon's gone. It's left its toy and gone away.* She flitted around the omnibus in a spiritish dance of joy.

"Gone where?" Grey asked, before sharing the news with the living persons on the bus.

Don't know, don't care. Mary whirled, doing pirouettes that spun off bits of vapor that hovered until they could rejoin the whole.

"Back to hell?"

Don't know, don't care, she sang again.

Grey sighed. Mary had been flighty in her life, but he'd hoped death, which had improved so many things about her, would have changed that as well. Apparently "carefree" was part of her character. Everyone clambered off the bus and Harry paid the conductor before releasing the vehicle to its regular route.

He put away his wallet. "What now? Since the demon's gone."

"We need to make sure it's gone." Grey led the way into the park, looking back to make sure the ladies were just behind them. Archaios and Meade provided a rear guard. "And find out where it's gone, if we can. If it's only exchanged the park for Stepney, or London for Edinburgh, that's no better. It needs to be gone *away.*"

Harry nodded. "So we don't call off the alert."

"Someone's dead." Pearl spoke up, startling everyone. "Murdered."

Grey felt his face set in grim lines, which were becoming all too familiar. He took pains to avoid grimness, but lately, all his pains did no good at all. "I am not surprised."

"But—" Elinor sounded surprised. "You never left your workshop. None of us sensed anything at all until the spirits spread their alarm."

"This murderer is a reckless fool," Grey said. "But he is not stupid. He learns. The newspapers have been filled with speculation about Galloway's murder. Because of that, he knows much of what we know. He will have taken care to contain his spell this time, to keep it from spilling free and catching anyone else in its coils."

They had reached the crowd—policemen and Briganti mostly—with a smattering of civilian magicians. Beyond them, in the distant gloom, pushed back by the ordinary police, the dark forms of the vagrants who spent their days in the park could be seen, a low rumble of muttering rising as they watched.

The magicians all recognized Harry and Grey, if the policemen didn't, and let them lead their little group through. Grey heard muttering at the presence of the ladies, most disapproving of subjecting them to such ugliness. A few muttered against women with magic. Those Grey took note of and pointed out to Harry.

Several of the Briganti present were keeping people back from the body, even though they were enforcers and not I-Branch. They'd learned that much, to keep people from muddying the magical residues left behind at a murder-by-magic, so that I-Branch could trace them.

The residues were strictly human, Grey noted with a bit of shock. They held nothing of the terrifying reek of pure evil, like that horrific relic in the conjurer's guild hall. Could the return of the demon to hell have dragged all its stink with it?

He cast about for ghosts, but found none close. The first conjurers to respond would have set up a warding perimeter, despite the dawn. The victim's ghost would be unpredictable, perhaps clinging to the body, perhaps slow to manifest. Best to be ready.

Someone had covered the body with a cloak. That much would not interfere with the investigation and it showed respect for the victim as well as soothing the sensibilities of the onlookers. Pearl and Elinor pushed to the forefront of the circle around the covered body, between Grey and Harry.

"Poor thing," Elinor whispered, wiping away a tear. "How frightened she must have been."

"She?" Harry raised an eyebrow at her.

Elinor pointed, and in the slowly brightening gloom, Grey saw a sodden plait of dark hair trailing across the gravel path. A woman this time. Grey's stomach lurched at the thought. Had the murderer killed her the same way he'd killed Galloway? Grey didn't want to know, much less see, but knew he would have to.

Pearl gasped, hands flying up to cover her mouth. "Oh no," she whispered. *"No."*

Grey put his arm around her. "What is it? What's wrong?"

Pearl shook her head and slipped out of his grasp, gliding across the empty circle so quickly he couldn't catch her. She sank to her knees beside the body and raised the cloak just as he reached her.

As he feared, the woman's face was crushed and broken beyond recognition. He tried to lift Pearl, draw her away, but she fought him off. *"No."* Her voice was a harsh whisper. "I have to do this. I *have* to. Rose deserves no less."

Grey looked again at the ruined face while Pearl wrestled a handkerchief from her pocket. "You can't be sure who she is," he said. "She could be anyone."

Pearl shook her head violently enough to knock her bonnet askew. He straightened it for her.

"I *know*." She used the handkerchief, more substantial than the usual lady's accessory, to clean the few streaks of blood gently from the woman's battered face. "This is Rose Bowers. Her blood told me, and blood never lies. She sold posies. Violets mostly, but sometimes roses, when she could get them."

She laughed, but her laughter held tears. "She used to joke that her parents should have named her Violet rather than Rose, since rose bowers were so much harder to get.

"This time of year, 'when the flowers is all gone—'" Pearl changed her voice, apparently quoting Rose, "sometimes she sold herself, but only when she could find nothing else to sell. Rose was a good girl, as good as she could afford to be. She had a good, kind heart. She was my friend."

Grey wanted to wrap Pearl up and protect her from this pain, knowing he couldn't, knowing that the greatest wealth, the greatest position—even the greatest magic—could protect no one from the pain of loss. The queen herself was still secluded in grief for her lost prince.

He could feel Pearl sweeping magic into the blood on the handkerchief. "I used to work protection spells for her," she said. "They worked, too. No one ever hurt Rose as long as she wore one of my spells. But I wasn't there. The spell wore off."

"No." Grey lifted her all the way into his arms, and carried her away. The crowd of magicians parted to let him through, and he bore her to a bench where he set her down.

He gripped her shoulders, giving them a little shake. When she still wouldn't look up at him, he took hold of her chin and turned her face up. "Rose's death is *not* your fault."

Behind him, he could hear Meade organizing the murder investigation. He needed to join them, but Pearl came first.

"She was murdered, Pearl. Her death lies at the feet of the men who killed her, not yours."

"But—"

"No." He stopped her speech with a finger across her

lips. "You don't know if your little spell would have done any good against this madman. You say the blood never lies, so ask it. Ask if you played any part at all in this tragedy."

"I—" Pearl blinked at him, as if she'd never considered the possibility of asking such a direct question, then her gaze turned elsewhere as she did.

"Oh." Her expression cleared, brightened. "It says no. It doesn't say who, but it says not me."

"All right then." Grey straightened and offered his arm to Pearl, who stood and took it. "To work."

Someone had covered Rose's face again, he saw when they returned. He wanted to stay with Pearl, help with the investigation of the murder of her friend, but all the magicians in London were on alert and were converging on the park. As conjury magister, he was the best qualified to lead the search for the demon and where it might have gone—back to hell or off to wreak havoc elsewhere on this plane.

"You see why women have no place in magic," Nigel Cranshaw blared, pushing his way through the crowd. "They insist on coddling when there's work to be done."

"She knew the victim." Grey spoke loud enough for his voice to carry to most of the growing crowd. "They were friends. Would you not give a moment of attention to anyone who discovered a friend had been murdered?"

Cranshaw tried to stand firm, but he'd lost sympathy and knew it.

"And while dealing with that shock, that grief, Miss Parkin has given us the victim's name—Rose Bowers— and gathered up the magic of Rose Bowers's innocent blood to be held for the investigation of the crime. Work has been done."

Grey passed Pearl into Elinor's comforting arms, and began giving his orders. "Meade, you head up the evidence collection. Tap the men you want. Pearl, Elinor, you're with Meade. Your particular talents will be more useful here, I think. The rest of you lot—" Grey raised his voice to get the crowd's attention.

"Move toward the pond, away from our murder scene, and we'll put you all to work." He waved them in the direction he wanted with wide, semaphore motions. Several Briganti, with their identifying armbands, joined in to help.

Grey sent the youngest boys back to the school with their magic-masters and instructions to keep an eye out. Everyone else, he asked to pair up, conjurer with alchemist, and wizards to one side, wizards being so rare. Only twelve at the master level in all of England. Not so many in London at present. Someone procured a map of London, which Harry divided into search sections. Grey sent them out four and six at a time, allocating one wizard per quadrant.

"Make sure your spirits know to keep in touch," Grey told the conjurers, "and to alert us straightaway if anything untoward occurs—especially if you become incapable of instructing them. After moonset, use your whistles."

He tried to make sure every group that went out had at least one conjurer who could call spirits with the moon, but he couldn't always remember which men had that ability. Finally, all the searchers had gone, save for himself and a trio of sixth-formers at the academy. Two alchemists and a conjurer. If they were sixth-formers, they ought to be ready for a journeyman's test soon. Grey looked them over and grimaced in a smilelike fashion. "Ready, lads?"

The two rock-and-water boys gave him eager nods. The conjury lad swallowed hard. "Demons, sir?" his voice cracked and he flushed. "Truly?"

Grey's grim expression returned yet again. "Unfortunately, yes. And little as we are prepared to deal with it, we are more prepared than *they* are." He gestured at the world outside the park, including poor Rose Bowers under her borrowed cloak.

"Yes, sir." They all gave him solemn nods.

"Got your protective spells on?" Grey shifted his vision to inspect them. "Pearl, a moment of your time, if you please."

At his request, Pearl added a layer of protection and "don't-look" to the magic they wore, and they went to catch a cab for the docks.

PEARL SAT WITH Elinor on a park bench beneath the umbrellas their magic-masters had insisted they keep, shivering in the damp cold, and watched Briganti Investigator Meade conduct the murder investigation. Tears kept welling up and trickling over, and she kept wiping them away, until her gloves were as damp as her skirts. She was cold and miserable and apparently useless. And she was still better off than poor Rose.

She choked on a sob, and the fat load of magic bloating her made her hiccup. Elinor put her arm around her and squeezed. Pearl leaned into her friend for a grateful moment before stiffening her spine to take up her burden of grief once more.

"You'll find justice for her," Elinor murmured.

"I will," Pearl vowed. More tears came. "But I forgot about her. She was a good friend to me—shared her supper even when she didn't have much—and I never spared one moment's thought for her. And now she's dead." Pearl cleared her throat. "I don't feel so much at fault for her death, not anymore. Grey was right. That's on *his* head, the murderer's. But . . . I forgot about her."

"You had a new life to focus on. If you were such friends, I'm sure she wouldn't begrudge your good fortune."

"No, she wouldn't." That brought on fresh tears, though a new thought made her smile through them.

"Wouldn't she be shocked to see me now? Rose only knew me as Parkin, the boy."

She hiccuped again. The magic overloading her was beginning to burn just a bit around the edges. She'd poured everything she could into the blood on the hand-kerchief, but this other magic had somehow seeped in through her skin, and she couldn't push it back out. It made Pearl wonder if innocent blood made different kinds of magic—some for the blood, some for justice, and some for—what? For the spirit? For peace?

"I have to get rid of this magic," she muttered.

Pearl stood and took as deep a breath as she could, lifting her face into the cold air, closing her eyes to the view of the umbrella's underside. She listened for her heartbeat, as her books instructed, for the rush of blood inside her. Then she whispered the words that sent the magic out to seek justice. Afterward, she put all her memories, all her gratitude for Rose's kindness, and the love and appreciation for her friendship into the remaining magic and sent it back to Rose, offering her peace and comfort.

Pearl felt it go. She could almost, *almost* feel it reach the trapped and frantic ghost and free her from those traps. She hoped it did. She hoped Rose was at peace.

Come and see me, Pearl thought in Rose's direction. *Let me know you're all right.*

"Miss Parkin." Meade's voice startled her out of her concentration, and she lost her balance.

She'd gone up on tiptoe, she realized, somewhere in the middle of her spell. She gathered herself and turned to Mr. Meade. "Can I assist you, sir?"

"If you would, please." He beckoned her. Elinor came, too.

"Magister Carteret told me that you have a sensitiv-ity to innocent blood." Meade watched her with a cu-riosity that made her feel like a bug on a pin. "Would it be possible for you to trace it back to its point of origin? To the place where Rose Bowers was murdered?"

Pearl blinked as she thought. She didn't know how rapid blinking could help the process, but it did. Somehow. "I've never tried it, sir, but it seems as if it might be possible." She gave him a doubtful look. "But, if Rose was transported here by the demon, that may change things. Do—do we think she was?"

Meade propped his hands on his hips, quite like Grey did, and yet utterly unlike. He sighed. "All indications from the spirits say she was, then abandoned here. God alone knows why."

"To create the greatest disturbance?" Elinor suggested.

"Perhaps." Meade shrugged. "Perhaps the demon was instructed to remove the lady from the murder site and, yes, brought it here to cause uproar."

"I thought one could not instruct a demon," Pearl said.

"One may instruct," Meade replied. "One may not command. Now, shall we see whether innocent blood trumps even demons?" He gestured toward a waiting hackney cab. "Or we can use the I-Branch carriage, which will be following, if open air is not necessary for your magic."

Pearl looked longingly at the massive I-Branch vehicle, obviously warmer and much drier than the increasingly miserable day, but she didn't trust her feel for the magic. She might be able to sense it from inside the closed carriage, but she might not. Best not to tempt failure. "I'm afraid it must be the hackney, Mr. Meade."

"And I am afraid I shall have to be your lone companion, Miss Parkin. There is simply not room for both of you ladies and myself in the cab."

Pearl glanced at Elinor, to be sure she was agreeable with riding in the carriage with however many of Grey's Briganti as could squeeze in. Elinor smiled and nodded, so Pearl allowed Mr. Meade to hand her into the hack.

The scent of Rose's innocent blood vanished just outside the park, so Pearl turned them in the direction she'd sensed the magic fly when she'd released it to join Rose's ghost. And that set the pattern for the rest of the day. She would stumble across the scent and follow it for a street or two, then lose it again. Meade maintained his stiff formality, which actually made him an excellent companion for this task. His silence didn't interfere or disturb.

By midmorning, she had a pounding headache from stretching her senses farther that she ought, and trying to filter the taste of Rose's innocent blood from the thick layers of blood magic permeating the atmosphere of the city.

By noon, her head hurt so bad it made her stomach cramp. The sandwiches Meade sent one of the underlings to collect for eating in the cab helped restore her strength. Elinor alighting from the carriage to perform a spell with herbs and wizardry, first to restore Pearl somewhat, then to suggest a direction when Pearl had none, helped more. Especially when, at the next street, she caught a fresh whiff of *Rose*. That became the new pattern—Elinor divining a direction whenever Pearl got stuck.

The demon seemed to have bounced all over London with Rose's body. Probably for this precise reason, to torment those tracking her death and send them running in circles. Though their path resembled a mad, looping zigzag more than a circle. Pearl prayed that her friend had been already dead when the demon got its hands— Claws? Talons? Paws?—on her. That Rose hadn't been the living, terrified plaything of such great evil.

Surely not. It was her death that had called the demon. Right? But if demons acted on their own whims, it could have appeared at any time at all in the process, and—

Pearl pushed the thought away with a shudder and reached out again for the magic saturating the air around them, sifting through it for *Rose*. She was at peace, Pearl hoped. Rose's pain and terror were done. Pearl's task was to find who had done it and stop him from hurting anyone else.

But they wouldn't do it today.

18

THE SKY WAS dark again when the cessation of motion startled Pearl awake. She ached all over, especially her head. Except she couldn't feel her feet at all. They were leaden lumps on the ends of her icy legs. Her hands wouldn't grasp the door handle and she couldn't make her mouth form words.

"Good God, man!" Grey was there, snapping at Mr. Meade. "What were you thinking, keeping her out all day in this weather? You've frozen her through."

"I asked." Meade defended himself. "I asked and asked if she was cold, and she said no. She wouldn't give up the trail."

"Of course she wouldn't. She's got the tenacity of a terrier with its teeth in something. She'll keep going long after her strength is gone. You have to make her stop." Grey lifted Pearl in his arms. *Oh.* He was warm.

Pearl snuggled in, seeking his warmest parts by instinct, her hands burrowing beneath his greatcoat, her nose tucking into his neck above his untied neckcloth. "You smell good."

"Yes, my dear, my valet works very hard to make sure of it." He carried her inside a building where there was light and warmth. Not upstairs. Not at home then, Grey's or her own.

"Where?" She could form that word with her frozen lips.

"I-Branch." He understood her. Of course he did. He was hers. Or she was his. Some version of that.

"Demon?" Her mouth had trouble with the *m*.

"Gone. Not anywhere on this plane that we've been able to discern."

"Good." It took her a long time to find the trail of thought she wanted and haul it in to get a good think at it. "Couldn't follow Rose back to the end. Demon's playing with us."

"Sit her down here." That was Elinor. Elinor had been out in the cold. Some of the time. "Let's get some tea inside her, plenty of sugar and milk, perhaps some brandy, and this."

This would be Elinor's magical elixir, Pearl knew.

Grey tried to set her down on something. Pearl tightened her arms around him. She had one around his neck, her hand tucked inside his coat collar, and the other under his greatcoat and his frock coat, around his back where the warmth of his body came through the lightweight back of his waistcoat and the fine cotton of his shirt. He was warm. He was hers. She wasn't letting go.

He chuckled and murmured something that sounded vaguely like "bulldog," and turned to sit in the chair, the large comfortable one in her "study," with Pearl on his lap. Tea appeared as if by magic, and Elinor poured something from one of her omnipresent flasks into it. Grey held it to her lips and Pearl brought her hand from his neck to steady it as she sipped. She was not relinquishing her hold on his back.

The tea was hot and a bit startling with its mixed flavors of sugar, alcohol, milk, mint, tea, and magic. It warmed her on the inside. Her feet still felt like dangling boulders, though.

"Get her boots off," Grey ordered. "Her feet are frozen through. We need to get them warm before she loses a toe."

"Been colder," she mumbled. "Never lost toes yet."

"And you'll not do it tonight."

Pearl was vaguely aware of Meade's stricken expression as he hovered in the background while Elinor knelt and unbuttoned Pearl's boots. After that, she was only aware of the burning sensation in her feet as they thawed and the tea Grey forced down her. She kept reminding herself that the magic burned worse when she held it too long.

When she finally got warm again, Pearl couldn't keep her eyes open, and after a few head bobbles, she tucked her nose into Grey's neck and gave up trying.

She woke to find herself still in Grey's arms, being carried through, yes, the corridors of the council hall. "What time is it?"

"Far too late."

"Yes, but what time?" She yawned.

"Nearing ten o'clock."

"Oh." Pearl struggled feebly in his grasp. "You have been up all night and all day and must be utterly exhausted. Put me down. I can walk."

"I am. Beyond exhaustion. Therefore you should stop struggling uselessly and tiring me further, because I will not put you down until—"

The door magically opened to the street, by means of a footman, and Grey bundled her into a carriage, also with its door open. He set her on the seat and climbed in to sit beside her. "Until now," he finished. "You have no shoes."

"I don't?" Pearl mashed her mounded skirts flat to look down at her feet, which were clad only in stockings. She tucked them beneath the layers of skirts. "Why not?"

"It seemed useless to wrestle shoes back on you when you are only going home to slippers, supper, and sleep." Grey's smile warmed her more than any number of cups of tea.

"I am too tired to eat." She yawned until she thought her jaw would pop.

Grey put his arm around her and urged her to lean her head in the hollow he made for it on his shoulder. She reached up to adjust her bonnet before she realized it wasn't there, either. "Where is my bonnet? And my shoes?"

He pointed at a basket on the other seat. "It is when you are too tired for eating that it is most important to eat. Magic takes energy. Food and rest put it back. Rest will only give part of what is needed, and you have rested. Time for food."

Pearl sighed, stifling the next yawn. She was also too tired for arguing. "Tell me what happened. Did you find the demon?"

"We did not." He scowled. "Nor can we tell whether it has been returned to hell or simply gone elsewhere. There are no reports of it in England, but that doesn't mean it has not simply taken itself off to—to Hindustan or the Amazon or—"

"Where do you think it went?"

Grey yawned. Oh dear, the man even had attractive tonsils. "We know it went back to the dead zones again. Harry had Colonel Simmons with him when he went around, and the old codger managed to pick up the spoor. No more torn-apart machines, but the edges of both zones were odd, Harry says. As if little nibbles were taken out of them. Pushing it back, like, but in pieces." For the last bit, Grey put on Harry's accent. It made her smile.

Pearl thought about that. She might have dozed a moment or two as well. A hole in the paving jarred her awake again when the carriage wheel hit it. "Do you think it was the demon? That nibbled on the dead zones?"

The carriage pulled to a halt and Pearl wondered if she'd dozed longer than she realized. They'd reached the mews where she shared rooms with Elinor.

"I don't know what to think." Grey climbed out the carriage door and reached back in for Pearl. "Frankly, I'm not sure I am currently capable of thought."

She scooted away from him. "I can walk."

"Cannot." He pointed. "No shoes."

"Oh. Right." Pearl let him take her hand and draw her to the door, then scoop her into his arms. She liked being there so very much, and at this moment, she couldn't quite recall why that was so very bad.

The driver followed them up the steps inside the street door to the door at the top where he set the basket down and went away again, dismissed for the evening. Grey carried her inside and deposited her at the cozy table laid with a cold supper for two.

"Elinor?" Pearl put a hand on Grey's arm to keep him from going away again, too.

"She may have said something about going to her stillroom to replenish her potions."

"Oh. Isn't she tired, too?"

Grey smiled. Pearl wished he wouldn't do that. It made him entirely too beautiful and much more human. "Elinor got far more sleep than either of us last night. She decided upon a nap early, to wake when 'things' started happening—and slept all night, because nothing did. Until this morning."

"Then stay." Pearl knew better than to invite him, but the words tumbled out of her mouth all on their own. "Have supper with me. I want to know everything you learned today."

"Damned little." But he was holding the chair for her, taking the other for himself. He would stay, and the satisfaction it gave her roused only a little worry. "Though we picked up only slight demon-sign in your tracking of Rose, we're fairly certain it was the demon that carried her with it as it skipped across London and back. Particularly since your . . . scent of her came and went so erratically. As if she faded from this plane and was returned."

He took some of the cold roast and Stilton cheese and placed it on his plate, then switched plates with her after a glance in her direction. "Eat." He pointed at the food now in front of her. "If you want me to tell you more."

It was obvious blackmail. And it worked. Pearl ate.

Grey filled his own plate. "It's apparent that the murderer has moved his torture chamber from the docks, but we do not know where. Perhaps across the river."

"Will that make it harder to find?" she asked around a mouthful of bread. Hunger struck the minute she began to eat.

"Not any harder than moving it out to Greenwich or Richmond." He talked about his own search, about Meade's map of their day's travel and Rollins's theories, about Simmons and his apparent thaw toward I-Branch. She listened carefully, or tried.

Now that she had beef and cheese and bread in her stomach, atop an ocean of tea and Elinor's magic potions, the waves of weariness lapped higher with every surge, weakening the dike she'd built against her emotions. So when Grey turned from his rambling discourse to scolding Pearl again for not taking better care and coming in out of the wet cold ages sooner than she had, the dike washed out to sea and she wept.

She cried. Great, huge choking sobs of guilt and sorrow and fear that shook her body and burned her eyes and frightened Grey half to death.

But he didn't run. He braced himself and waded in, wrapping his arms around her, lifting her onto his lap—how had they gotten to the sofa?—and he rocked her in his embrace, murmuring soft words in her ear. Words in English, French, and Latin, and other languages that sounded soft and liquid and harsh and gentle by turns and all at once.

Pearl only understood the English words, the ones that told her it wasn't her fault, that everything would be all right, that she wasn't alone. But it was, and it might not, and she had been alone for so long. Even before Papa died.

And if she wasn't alone now, she would be again. Sooner rather than later. That was the human condition, wasn't it?

She cried for that, too, for everything that had gone wrong in her life, everything she hadn't had time to cry for in all the years of struggle.

"Hush now, Pearl." Grey's voice softened. "Hush, my Pearlie girlie. You'll make yourself sick with all your weeping. Can you stop? For me, love, can you? You're breaking my heart."

She couldn't have that, wouldn't hurt him for anything, her beautiful fallen angel. She hiccuped, trying to catch the sobs before they got out. She sat up and swiped at her face with both hands. Her face had to be blotchy and hideous. It always was when she cried. "I— I'm sorry," she said through a hiccup. "I'm just—I never cry. I hate to cry. It's—I—I'm so tired."

"I'm told it's good to cry now and again. But I never believed it." Grey smiled at her, tender and so sweet her heart broke on it. That made two of them. Apparently hearts broke easily when weary beyond bearing.

"It's just that I'm so tired." She didn't want him to think this happened often. Or at all, except for now.

"I know. Exhaustion can make one do all sorts of silly things." Could his smile be any more beautiful?

The tears crashed over Pearl again and she collapsed under their weight yet again. "I'm sorry," she sobbed, "so sorry. I ca—can't seem to stop."

"Don't fret, dear heart." Grey stood with her in his arms. "You're just tired. You need to sleep."

"Yes. Yes." She clung to him as if he were the only anchor in her sea of sorrow.

What was wrong with her? She knew, from bitter, wrenching experience, that she could count on no one but herself. She needed to pull back. To stop hanging all over Grey, and deal with this on her own. But she couldn't make her arms let go. Not even when he set her down in the bedroom she shared with Elinor.

He unfastened the buttons down the back of her wool dress, reaching around her because of the shameless way her arms wrapped themselves around his neck. "There," he said. "All undone."

Pearl only wept and clung. She hated being like this. She tried to stop, truly she did. But it was as if all the misery in her short, lately miserable life had decided to come out tonight. She simply could not stop crying.

Grey dragged one of her arms from his neck and peeled it from its sleeve. As soon as he let go, her arm put itself back again, while he dragged the other away to free it. He kept pausing, as if waiting for her to take up the task of undressing herself, to unbutton the petticoats and push them to the floor, but she could only cling and weep.

"Don't leave me," she cried when he tried to scrape her off him and put her in the bed.

He went utterly still, his hands on her waist over her shift. She still wore her ruffled pantaloons and stockings, as if he couldn't bring himself to remove any more of her clothing.

"*Pearl.*"

Her name groaned out of him in a voice she'd never heard before, part exasperation, part desperation, and part something else she couldn't name but wanted.

"Just till I fall asleep." She spoke quickly, to get the words out between hiccups. "Like you did that time in the workshop. Just for a while. *Please.*"

She hated herself for begging. She had more pride than that. Normally she did. Tonight her pride seemed to have washed away in all the tears and the pain, in the loss of all those she'd loved and all those she'd failed.

She'd been alone far too long and tonight she simply could not bear it. Yes, it was a terrible imposition on him, but she didn't care. Tomorrow. When tomorrow came, she could be herself, alone again, but tonight— Tonight she needed company. Tonight, she wanted Grey.

"This is not wise," he said, voice tight, fingers twitching on her waist, his eyes locked on hers.

"I don't care." She might later, but she didn't think so. She wanted him with her, wrapped close around her. Closer. She would crawl inside him if she could.

And the magic hummed. It rose inside her, bloomed around her with a heady, musky scent that wasn't blood, but when it touched her blood and the magic inside Grey, it chimed. Not actual sound, nor imagined bells, but the magical equivalent, a sweet ringing in her not-ears. "Did you hear that?"

"Hear what?" Grey was staring deep into her eyes when she swam back from the magic to look out of them. "Pearl, do you want this? Do you want me? Not comfort or distraction from your sorrow, but *me*. This. Do you truly want it?"

Did she? She knew what he was asking. She might be innocent—impossible, but still true—but she was far from ignorant. She stepped away from her grief and guilt over so many things. The magic's rising helped her do that.

But she had to step away from the magic as well and the hum in her blood that pooled in such enticing places. She looked up at Grey, looked back into those dark eyes that promised wonders and delight and secrets revealed.

He was beautiful, but more than that, he was kind. And generous and honorable and so intelligent it sometimes frightened her. He was Grey. And though she didn't love him—she didn't dare—she liked him. A great deal. She was tired of fighting the attraction. She had no reputation to fret over. She wanted this. Wanted him. Which was the question he'd asked, wasn't it? So she said, "Yes. I want you."

She dared to lift her hand, lay it along that fallen-angel's face. He turned into it, eyes closing, and pressed a kiss to her palm.

"Do you want this, Grey?" She knew the answer, or thought she did, but she had to ask.

His eyes opened and he looked at her.

"Do you want me? For *me*, not the—" Could he even feel the magic in the air? If she asked, would it drive him away? "For me, myself? Who and what I am?"

"God, yes. I've wanted you for days. Weeks." He held her hand against his cheek a moment before kissing it again, never shifting his gaze from hers. "Ever since you first looked at me with those blue-and-gold eyes of yours and let your illusion melt away so I could see you. The Pearl hidden inside the shell of magic."

His words had her rising on her toes, stretching toward him. He came down to meet her, his full, perfect mouth touching hers in their first kiss. She didn't have time to marvel, for the touch seemed to set her on fire from the inside out, a burn that had nothing to do with magic, but somehow fueled it. Her mouth opened, as if she knew what he wanted without being told, and the kiss deepened. It consumed her. It made her want more.

She said it. "More."

He chuckled, lips against hers. "Greedy wench."

He stepped away from her, and for an instant, she wanted to protest, but it felt right. Whatever he was doing made this more than a quick shag in the dark. Which it wasn't. Dark. There was a candle on the washstand, so she could see.

She could watch as Grey, deliberately and with great precision, removed his clothing. He folded his frock coat and laid it across the back of the chair, then untied his cravat and tossed it. He unbuttoned his waistcoat, then his shirt and his cuffs and then his trousers, all the while watching Pearl. His gaze slid down over her standing there in her shift and pantaloons and stockings before returning to her eyes. He smiled when he saw them widen as he unbuttoned his trousers.

He paused, buttons all undone, and bent to remove his half-boots and stockings before straightening to shove off shirt, waistcoat, and braces all at once. His trousers didn't fall when they lost their support. When Pearl retrieved her senses from the sight of all that lovely naked skin, she saw that he held them up.

"Shall I wait?" he asked. "Are you shy?"

She swallowed hard, shaking her head. She'd seen naked men before. She'd seen them aroused. She'd been playing boy, and the denizens of the docks and the Dials didn't have much modesty. But this, Grey, was because of her. *She* had aroused him, and that made everything different.

She stepped forward, hands out, needing to touch him, needing to see whether he felt as glorious as he looked. Grey's hands met hers, caught them. She shook one free and laid it on his chest. The sight of her fingers spread wide over his faintly golden skin, the feel of it against her palm made her quiver and tighten, and soften at the same time.

He groaned. "The look in your eyes—"

Puzzled, she looked up and was captured in a kiss. He pulled her tight against him, into that all-consuming kiss. She wriggled to get closer. To find more.

He shoved her pantaloons down, his hands skimming along her legs, her hips as he returned, somehow never breaking the kiss. Pearl clutched at him, rising onto her toes to press more of her against more of him. He tossed her onto the bed and followed, making it bounce and scrape across the floor.

Grey fumbled with the ribbon tying her shift closed, got it open, and something ripped, making her flinch, then laugh with joy at his eagerness, that he would want her as much as she wanted him. She wrapped her arms round his neck to bring him to her for more of that marvelous kiss, but he ducked away.

She cried a protest, which wavered and dissolved as he kissed his way across her breast. The cry came back in delight when he found the peak and kissed it, licked it, sucked it into that perfect mouth. He did it again for her other.

"Only fair," he murmured, his lips teasing her hard nipple before he left it to kiss his way lower, across her stomach, where he dipped his tongue into her navel.

He crawled back up over her, grinding the hard ridge of his arousal into her as he plunged into another kiss. "I want it all," he groaned into her mouth. "I want to kiss every inch of your skin. I want to taste you, make you scream with pleasure until you lose your voice—"

"All right." Pearl's gasp of assent didn't slow him.

"But I cannot wait." He slid to one side, so he could still press his—his cock against her hip, as he slipped his hand between her legs. The legs that had already spread to accommodate him.

Pearl felt the tiniest twinge of shame at her wanton behavior, but thrust it away. She wanted this. She wanted Grey and she would not regret anything about it. She was who she was and she wanted what she wanted, and she gasped as Grey stroked his fingertip across a place that made her shudder, and made magic unfurl in the air around them.

"Did you like that, then?"

She looked up to see Grey looking back with that cheeky, wicked grin of his that always seemed to promise—

He slid his finger across that spot again, a stronger, more certain stroke, and her hips came up off the bed with the wanting. He gave it, fulfilled the promise of that wicked glint, as if he knew what she wanted before she did. She clutched at him, raking her nails across his back.

The pleasure sizzled through every part of her, yet it focused on the place where he touched her. She cried out, made helpless by the needs of her body, needs he filled even as she became aware of them. He drove her before him, dragged her with him into the sweet madness of passion, and she plunged in willingly. Whatever he wanted, she would give. What he gave, she would take, even if it seemed so much, too much, impossible.

She still wanted more. Didn't know what it was, but screamed to have it, even though *this* pleasure was too much to bear, too—

Time stopped. For just an instant, it stopped, until the pleasure exploding through her started it again.

She blew apart into as many sparkling bits as there were stars. She shuddered, delight pulsing deep inside her, radiating through her to pour out into—magic? Of course. *Magic.*

Grey was over her, kissing her, pressing urgently against her, into her, and her body throbbed yet again with *yes* and *I want that* and *more.* She opened herself to him, whispered that "yes" into his ear.

The pain when he plunged home made her gasp with its unexpected sharpness. She'd known it would hurt, but hadn't expected to hurt in precisely that manner, with the sharp, stretching feel. The pleasure that came with it, behind it, made the pain go away.

Grey paused. She didn't want him to. She needed more. Still. She arched her hips, thrusting them at him, reminding him what they were about, where in the process they were. He couldn't stop now. With a groan, he began to move, slowly at first, then faster and deeper, touching something inside her that made her cry out. Perhaps that time-stopping magic. Whatever it was, she wanted it again, and more, and *now.*

And it happened again. Time stopped. Pearl blew apart into a million shiny bits, and this time Grey blew apart with her.

He was quiet against her shout. A gasp, a sigh—as if he couldn't spare any of himself for making noise, had to concentrate everything on the pleasure she gave him.

She gave. He took nothing from her. And as he collapsed in a warm, delicious weight over her, Pearl gathered up all those shiny bits and shared them out between them.

She thought about separating them into Grey bits and Pearl bits, but they had gotten all mixed up in the blast, and she wasn't sure where exactly the bits had come from. There didn't seem to be any gaping holes inside either of them, so she wondered if the bits had been made new from the—the passion Grey had shared with her. Though passion seemed a mild word for what Pearl had experienced. Even ecstasy seemed understated.

All the magic floating loose in the room followed the bits as Pearl tucked them where they belonged. The magic slid into place as if that was what the bits were for. And maybe it was.

Grey was beginning to get heavy, lying atop her. He murmured something about taking his leave, but he didn't move. Pearl didn't blame him, except for squashing her. She had no bones left at all. Maybe that's where the bits had come from—her dissolved bones. But no, the bones were still there. They just *felt* dissolved.

She found energy to begin a roll to her side. Grey assisted, moving off her, then drawing her close to cuddle. It was nice. She would remind him about taking leave in a few more minutes. After she thought more about the magic and the . . .

19

CONSCIOUSNESS OOZED ITS way into Grey's brain one slow seep at a time. Sensations impinged themselves on his mind. Warmth. Ease. Silken, female flesh pressed against his. His hand, stroking idly over said silky and feminine flesh.

Good God, he was in bed with Pearl.

Memory slammed into him. First, of her terrifying weeping fit. She'd cried so long and so hard it nearly pushed him over the edge into panic, not knowing what to do for her. He knew that sometimes women simply needed to cry, but for that long? And then, when she'd finally shown signs of stopping, he'd carried her into her room to tuck her in to sleep . . .

The Pearl of this moment murmured in that sleep and snuggled her sweet, round bottom closer into the curve of his body. Whereupon his body reacted as expected. Grey groaned.

It had done so last night. Reacted. It had damn near taken over and acted on its own. But that was no more than an excuse, and a paltry one. He was no slave to his impulses. Or his senses or his appetites. And if he didn't want to be enslaved again, he had better get out of this bed.

He didn't regret bedding Pearl, exactly. Grey eased carefully away from her, toward the edge of the bowl their bodies had made in the mattress. It was more that he felt as if he'd taken advantage. Of her tears. Of her status as his apprentice. Even of her lack of family. It was his responsibility as her magic-master to protect her from this sort of thing, not subject her to it.

Grey reached the side of the bed and rolled over to slip first one leg, then the other from beneath the coverlet, biting back a hiss as his warm toes connected with chilly floor. He had at least managed to stop and ask if she truly wanted to lie with him, but that wasn't much of a sop to his conscience. Even if she had seemed to think carefully on the matter, she could not possibly have been in a state for clearheaded thinking. Not after that hurricane of tears.

He tucked the blankets close around her so she might not miss his warmth too much, and slid the rest of the way out of the bed. He lit a fresh candle from the fire and shoved it into the cold drippings of last night's candle. He scooped his drawers from the floor as he padded naked to the basin, shivering in anticipation of the cold water.

Please, God, Elinor did not come home last night to see this. Grey splashed water on his face and held back his roar at the cold. Mustn't wake Pearl.

Elinor had been scary mad over Pearl falling asleep in his workroom, even though nothing happened. Now that something had—

Grey shuddered. He wet a cloth, washed beneath his arms, and glanced down before washing his privates and froze. Was that—*blood?*

He staggered, actually lurched with knee-buckling shock. There had been a moment last night, when he had wondered. When he had entered her sweet, tight little passage and she had gasped. But the demands of his body had been too clamorous and the thought too impossible. Now . . . the thought was still impossible, but the evidence was there.

Grey used his drawers to clean himself and collect the evidence. *Innocent blood cries out for justice.* The thought made his stomach churn. He dressed quickly, needing the armor of clothing, though he left off his undergarment. It was far less chilly than the time he'd been talked into a kilt while visiting in Argyll.

He checked his watch, but he'd forgotten to wind it in

all of yesterday's uproar, so he had no idea of the time, whether the wee hours of the morning or nearing dawn. Either way, he also had no way of knowing when Elinor might return. He took the candle and slipped out of the bedroom to bolt the door. Elinor would have to knock to get in.

Feeling fierce, Grey walked into the bedroom. The candlelight slid up over Pearl, revealing her sleeping form in its warm glow. Dark hair spread across the pillow in contrast to her pale skin, her forehead creased with a tiny frown even in sleep. Something softened inside him. She was beautiful, but more than that, he couldn't help but *like* her. Perhaps duty wouldn't be so bad.

He perched on the edge of the high bed and brushed that dark brown silk from her face. "Pearl? You must wake up, my dear."

My dear? Well, yes. She was dear to him. Gently he shook her shoulder, naked, he knew, beneath the cover. His body reacted to that knowledge, but he quashed the impulse to act on it. He was better than that. Usually.

"Pearl, wake up."

She yawned, rubbed her eyes, yawned again, and blinked up at him. Then she smiled and all the dark, cold places inside him warmed. He warned himself not to get used to it, but he couldn't help hoping the smile would not fade when he said what he must.

"Good morning," she murmured, stretching discreetly beneath the bedclothes.

"Good morning." Grey tried to put all his hopes and none of his worries into his own smile. "How do you feel?"

That sent her away inside herself for just a moment as she investigated. Her smile came beaming forth sunnier than before. "Absolutely grand." She sounded utterly pleased with herself. "No aches, pains, or even weariness. How are you feeling?"

"I—hadn't thought of it." Physically he felt wonderful, but he always did after sex. Perhaps not as wonderful as this, however. "Yes, I am quite grand as well. Pearl—"

She sat up, holding the blankets to cover her breasts, but her bare shoulders were just as enticing, since they were bare, and visible, and they reminded him—

"Could you hand me my wrapper?" She pointed at a pink-and-white flannel thing hanging from a hook on the wall.

Grey fetched it for her with alacrity. He had to maintain his control. They had matters to discuss.

"Is it morning?" Pearl slipped into the wrapper as she slipped from the high bed, hitting the floor with a thump, and peered at the window. "It's dreadfully dark for so long this time of year. Is it morning?"

"I don't know. My watch has run down. Pearl, would you please stop fluttering about? We have matters to discuss."

"Matters?" She flung a desperate glance at him and went on picking up petticoats from the pile on the floor. "Oh dear. Sounds dreadfully serious."

"It is." This was the problem with a failure to take anything seriously. When one *was* serious, no one believed it.

He took the petticoats away from her and piled them on the bed, then he caught both her hands in his before she could find something else to pick up. One would think she feared what he might say to her. "Pearl."

He was going to bollocks this up. He knew he was. Down on one knee. That was the proper way to do it.

"Pearl. My dear." He looked up into her astonished, half-fearful face. She'd turned aside, as if trying to evade a blow. Why, for God's sake? Surely she knew what the kneeling meant. What if that was why she cringed? No way to know but to get through it.

"Pearl, would you do me the very great honor of becoming my wife?" He put on his very best hopeful, pleading face, trying to look as sincere as possible. His wasn't a face made for sincerity, but he did his best.

"Why?"

That took him aback. "What kind of answer is that?" he asked, nettled. "You're supposed to say yes, or no. Not *why,* for God's sake!"

She nettled up in turn. "If I can't ask why—if you won't give me an answer, then I'll have to say—"

"Don't." He knew what she would say. They'd only been together a month, but he knew that petite frame was mostly filled with stubbornness. "Why is fine. I'll tell you why."

His knee began to hurt. Besides, it was only the proposal that required kneeling, wasn't it? Arguing her into it didn't. Grey got to his feet, using the need for her assistance as an excuse to keep her hands in his. He could tell she wanted free, but he was afraid if he let go, he'd never capture her again.

"Well?" she demanded when he was standing. She shook her hands free and propped them on her hips. "Why do you want to marry me?"

"Because I do." He needed more time. Time when she wasn't flouncing naked under a delightful flannel wrapper, distracting him. He had reasons. They were just blastedly difficult to articulate at the moment.

Her eyes narrowed, and she darted past him to pounce on the drawers he'd left lying on the coverlet. He should have put them on, should have realized Pearl would turn the evidence into a weapon against him rather than the other way around. Though he couldn't quite see how.

"Is this the reason?" She shook his undergarment at him.

"My drawers?" Grey arched an eyebrow, trying to take back the advantage. How had he lost it? "Or the evidence of your formerly virgin status?"

"Pfff—" She waved a dismissive hand. "What of it? It was mine to give away. Now I have. It means nothing."

"It means *everything.*" Grey wasn't shouting.

"It means *nothing,*" Pearl shouted back. "*Reputation* means everything, and I lost that long ago, when Papa and I had to go live on Half Moon Yard. Everyone knows where I found you, that I'd been living there. Actually losing it meant nothing, because nobody believed I had it to begin with. Not even you."

That knocked him awry, like a slap to the face. "You're right," he said quietly. "To my everlasting shame. You are correct that I did not believe it possible, that you could still be innocent. But you are wrong that it means nothing. It meant something to me."

He took back his balance, caught that sizzling glare from her, and looked behind it, or tried. "How was it possible?"

She shrugged dismissively, but Grey refused to be dismissed. He saw beneath her uncaring facade, because he had his own. He saw the tender places she protected, and it sobered him to realize she would let him see. "Tell me. Please."

"I was sixteen when Mama and George died," she said with another shrug. "That threw everything into an uproar. Stephen and Martin fell ill, but they didn't die until the next year, when the typhoid came. I had barely begun to notice boys, to flirt, and then—" Her shoulders shifted. Not quite a shrug.

"Your world fell apart," Grey said, gently as he could.

"Something like that." She looked away, blinked back tears.

Grey wanted to hold her, but he didn't dare. Not until they had everything sorted. Because if he held her, he would kiss her, and if he kissed her— They might not go beyond that, since Pearl could well be of a different mind now, but he feared taking the chance. He wanted this settled.

"What about later," he asked. "After you moved into Half Moon Yard?"

"Papa lost everything so quickly. He simply—" She gave a deep despairing sigh. "He never recovered from Mama's death. The heart, the will to live—it died with her. He didn't care. The boys did their best but—"

She spoke quickly, brightly. "Scarlet fever took Mama and George, and nearly made off with Stephen and Martin as well. I was away at finishing school, which is why it didn't get me. But it left the boys weak. Frail. So when the typhoid came—"

Grey led her to the chair at the dressing table and set her on it, then knelt at her side, chafing her cold hands.

"We were in London by then. We'd left Portsmouth to bring the boys to London doctors in hopes of treatment. But nothing helped. Papa's business went all to pieces when Stephen and Martin died. Our house in Portsmouth was seized by creditors and everything sold. When we moved to Half Moon Yard, Papa told me to dress as a boy. Because I'm small, you see. I would be safer that way. He did care."

But not enough. Not enough to keep her out of Whitechapel altogether. Not enough to find her a husband to protect her. Grey wanted to shake the man. "What happened to your father? You said he had died, did you not?"

Pearl nodded. "He drank himself to death. I thought it would take longer, but—just more than a year and a half. Apparently when someone is truly determined . . ."

"So your disguise and your magic kept you a virgin?"

She gave another of her careless shrugs. "That, and the fact that I never met anyone I fancied enough to share my secret with." She eyed him sharply and pulled her hand from his. "I told you I was female because of the magic. *Not* because I fancied you."

He smiled, one of the teasing smiles that had worked wonders with women over the years. Those not related to him. "But you do fancy me, don't you, Pearl? Just a little?"

This shrug was one-sided. Her shoulders had to be tiring. "Don't be ridiculous," she said. "You know you are the most beautiful man in all of London. Half the world fancies you."

He blinked at her, startled at first, then quite pleased. She thought he was beautiful. She'd never said so. But then she wouldn't. She made it her life's mission to keep him from getting a swelled head. She had told him that. Often.

"Yes," he said, thinking over what she'd actually said. "But do *you* fancy me? You might think me—" He cleared his throat, unable to easily say it. Men were not beautiful. But if she thought so— "Might think me, well, beautiful. But it does not of necessity follow that you fancy me. *Do* you?"

She looked down at her hands fidgeting with the tie belt of her wrapper. "Yes," she said, so quietly he had to lean closer to hear. "Unfortunately, I do."

"But it's not unfortunate at all." Grey wanted to jump to his feet and caper about the room. He couldn't think why. "If you fancy me, and I fancy you—which I do not, I desire you beyond all rationality—but don't you see that it will make our marriage all the more pleasant?"

She turned a sour expression upon him.

"It is part of the 'why' you asked me," Grey said quickly, before she could throw up more barricades. "Because I do desire you. Madly. Passionately. *Constantly.* But I will not treat you with anything less than honor and respect.

"As your magic-master, it would be my place to insist upon marriage under these circumstances with any other man. Simply because I am also the person who has stolen the prize does not make it any less my place. You may have no reputation, Pearl, but you do have honor. And you have my respect. Will you force me to blacken *my* honor by refusing me?"

"I thought you'd blackened your honor quite nicely

all on your own," Pearl retorted, her voice thick with emotion. Please God, not with tears. He would buckle under the assault of tears.

He stood, feeling the need to make his case more forcefully. "My reputation, *not* my honor.

"Reputation is what others think about you, and you are right, I do not give a good goddamn—begging your pardon—for that. But honor is what I know of myself. It is the line I will not cross. One thing that upholds my honor is that I will not cause harm to those weaker than myself. I will protect those who cannot protect themselves."

He held up a hand to forestall Pearl's arguments. "I know, my dearest Pearl, that you are fully capable of protecting yourself—of protecting *me,* in many ways. You are a strong woman and a powerful magician. A magician who is still learning her magic. And a woman alone in the world. It is unfortunate that the world is a place where a woman needs protection, but it is most definitely such a place.

"My actions have put you at risk. My honor would crack into pieces if I did not make that right."

Pearl bit her lip, that little up-and-down crease forming between her brows as the thinking gears turned over in her mind. Grey could almost hear them tick.

Her lips turned down, tightened, thinned, as her nostrils flared, as if emotions piled up behind them, held back only by the increasing tension of her lips. He would deal with tears if they could keep Pearl from breaking apart.

"But it isn't necessary!" she burst out. "Why tie yourself down, why tie me down this way for something that isn't necessary?"

"It might be. It only takes one time, you know."

"It might not."

"True. But marriage isn't always a thing of necessity. Isn't it also a thing of choice? Of preference?"

She snorted, an indelicate sound. "You wouldn't choose me."

"Who says I wouldn't?" He reared back, indignant.

"I say. The whole world says. I am of indifferent birth. My father was a merchant, for God's sake, who lost everything he owned and drank himself to death. I'm impoverished, uneducated, small of stature, and indifferent in looks. You don't want me."

"Shall I show you again just how much I do?" Grey pulled her to her feet and against his body in one smooth, forceful motion. He didn't want to jar her, except to her senses. He caught her gaze, put all the desire he'd been fighting since he woke in her bed into his eyes, into his hold on her. Then, the instant before his control broke, he set her carefully away from him, retaining only a grip on her hands.

He had to clear the thickness from his throat before he spoke. "I don't care about my own bloodline, so why should I care about yours? As a sorceress, you won't be impoverished for long, and we are dealing with the education issue. You have enough education to learn magic. Harry had to learn to read first, so you're ahead of him when he began. What does height or lack of it have to do with anything at all? And you are a beautiful woman who does not know her own appeal."

She looked too astonished to respond.

So he spoke again. "Besides, I like you. We get on, don't we? Famously, in fact. Isn't that another excellent reason for marriage?"

She stared up at him another endless moment, her hands somehow still clasped in his. When she spoke, it was again almost too quiet to hear. "But what about love?"

Grey let his knees crumble, feigning a body blow. *Love.* A female's last-ditch stand against reason. "What about it?"

"You don't love me, do you." It wasn't a question.

"Nor do I love you. It won't hurt your feelings to say so. But what if—what if there is someone out there you fall desperately, passionately in love with, and you're already married to me?"

"I am two years past thirty and haven't yet found such a paragon." Grey brought her hand to his mouth and kissed it. "You are the first woman I've found that I've liked well enough not to break out in hives at the thought of marriage."

She sputtered with laughter as she snatched her hands back and propped them on her hips. "You are impossible."

"I know." Grey shrugged. He could feel his nonchalant armor locking into place around him. "I am impossible and incorrigible. I stay up all night communing with spirits and sleep through all my appointments the next day. I am careless and forgetful of those who are depending on me. I have no sense of responsibility and I haven't met a rule yet that I haven't broken. I will be a terrible husband and likely a worse father. I am sure you are wise to refuse me."

Pearl was looking at him now with an expression he couldn't read. She didn't have many of them. Usually her feelings stamped themselves all over her face, but this was one he didn't know.

"I haven't actually refused you yet," she said.

"You haven't?" Grey perked up from hidden resignation to the faintest glow of hope.

She sighed. "No, I haven't. Because you're not actually that bad. You are impossible and incorrigible, but you're also unoffendable and unflappable. If you stay up with your spirits, you let me stay up with you, and you only forget the unimportant appointments. Like with bootmakers, or taking tea with the neighbors."

"Fortunately, they've all stopped wanting to take tea with me." A smile broke out on his face, driven by his rising hopes.

"You are incredibly, astonishingly, irrefutably responsible. So responsible, I'm exhausted trying to keep up with you, though it is true that the only rules you keep are your own. But those rules you adhere to with absolute rigor. You probably would be a terrible husband, but I am sure that I would be an awful wife. All that submission and obedience?"

She shook her head sadly. "Impossible. But you would be an amazing father. What a child needs most is to be loved, and you would never stint on that."

Grey waited for her to continue. He didn't believe everything she said, but he adored hearing it. And she hadn't yet given him a definitive answer, had she?

"So?" He couldn't wait. He captured her hand again for another kiss. "Is it to be yes, then?"

She sighed, but left her hand in his, curling her fingers around to hold it. "A qualified one."

He gripped her hand tighter. She couldn't get away now. "What qualifications?"

"I will agree to marry you, *if* it becomes necessary. Necessity to be agreed upon by both of us."

"Agreed. But we are, as of this moment, engaged to be married."

"Which we will keep to ourselves, unless and until necessity arises to share the information."

"But we are engaged." He wanted to hear the actual words coming out of her mouth.

She gusted another deep sigh. "Yes, Grey. We are engaged to be married."

He let out a whoop, wrapped Pearl up in his arms and twirled her around. His honor remained unsmirched. He set her down again and kissed her, a long, thorough, possessive, *engaged* kiss. His hands reacquainted themselves with the lithe little body beneath the flannel wrapper. He kept forgetting just how small she was. Her spirit made her seem so much larger.

Only the sharp knocking at the door and the rattling

of the doorknob kept him from taking the kiss further. Grey knew who was there, and he carried Pearl with him to answer it.

Elinor stood on the landing, without Harry for once, her hair falling down from its tidy braids, fingers stained with herbs or berries, and smoke coming out her ears. Before she could smite him with the lightning in her eyes, Grey grinned at her and spoke.

"Wish us happy, Elinor darling. Pearl and I are to be married."

Pearl smacked him on the arm. "You promised not to tell."

Elinor pushed her way into the room and slammed the door behind her.

"This isn't necessity?" Grey goggled at Pearl, rather more than the situation strictly required, and pointed at Elinor. "Do you *want* to see me beheaded? Besides, if you'll recall, I agreed to the terms of the engagement, but I never said I wouldn't tell. Frankly I am pleased as punch to be engaged to you and I don't care who knows it."

He followed a random thought astray, nattering on out of habit, letting thoughts fall out of his mouth as they came to him. "*Pleased as punch.* That's an odd-sounding turn of phrase, isn't it? How can punch be pleased? It's punch. Rum and lemons and such. And if it's the other sort of punch they mean, a punch in the face—well, that doesn't sound very pleasing at all, does it? I am—am pleased as a child with a new toy."

He frowned. "No, that doesn't sound right, either. Pearl isn't a toy, she's a person. A charming, brilliant, delight of a person. I am pleased as—as . . . Hmm . . ."

Pearl smacked him again, and he made a great to-do out of the injury, but she was laughing beneath the scowl, so that was all right. Elinor didn't look half as dangerous as she had, and that was better. What she looked was confused.

"You are engaged to be married? And you're *laughing*?" She looked from one of them to the other. "Oh—" She nodded wisely. "I see. It's a joke."

"No joke, Elinor, my dear. Pearl has agreed to do me the very great honor of becoming my wife." Grey bowed, then captured Pearl's hand yet again—she kept taking it back—and pressed a fervent kiss to its back, resisting the temptation to make a tease of it. He would tease about other things, but not this.

"Pearl?" Elinor looked at his young apprentice, searching her face. "Did you really say you would marry Grey?"

Pearl heaved a deep and breathy sigh, but she nodded. "Yes, I am afraid I did. But I thought he promised to keep it a secret." She raised her hand as if to swat his arm again, but desisted.

Grey frowned. Did she not care enough to abuse him any longer? "It was necessary to tell Elinor, my dearest. She knows I did not leave after I brought you home. It is probably necessary for the servants to know, and Harry, and likely we will have to inform I-Branch as well."

Elinor sank into the nearest sitting room chair. "This is a disaster," she moaned, dropping her head into her hands.

"I thought you were worried about scandal," Grey protested. "We're getting married."

"If necessary," Pearl interjected.

He ignored her. "Marriage negates scandal, ergo, no scandal."

"Pearl won't be an apprentice anymore. She'll be a wife. Wives can't be magicians." Elinor glared up at him.

"Why the bloody hell not?" Grey demanded. "Amanusa is, and she's a wife."

"Yes, but Jax is not a magician in his own right. You are."

"And—?" Grey could not understand what Elinor was

getting at. Pearl didn't seem to, either, for she looked as puzzled as Grey felt.

Elinor stopped glaring and stared at him, rising to her feet. "Do you mean to tell me that once you are married, you will continue to allow Pearl to practice magic?"

Grey blinked at her. "What do mean 'allow'? How do you suppose I could stop her? Why should I want to? She *is* a sorceress. Magic is part of what makes Pearl Pearl. I can no more change that than I can alter the tides. And would not, even if I could."

Now Elinor joined the confusion club. "You would still bring her to investigate murders?"

"Why not? If she wanted to come." Grey finally caught inklings of what Elinor was on about. "You think I will be in the usual line of husbands, don't you? Pearl and I have already agreed that I would make a terrible husband and she a dreadful wife, so we've actually got all that sorted."

Elinor looked stricken. "But what about children? What about if she is with child?"

That thought didn't panic him, which was odd, because it always had before. The thought, not the reality. He had no bastards scattered about. Likely he didn't panic because he'd thought of it already, when he'd resigned himself to proposing, so he was past that point.

"Pearl is not a child," Grey said. "She is twenty years old."

"Twenty-one in March," she volunteered.

"And she has been caring for herself and her family for the past several years, bearing responsibilities far greater than her age. She is much more responsible than I am. I think we can trust her to know what is best, and to make sound, mature decisions—" He locked his best stern, admonishing gaze upon her. "—concerning her welfare and that of any child she might carry."

"Oh, *no fair*," Pearl protested.

"What?" Elinor's head swiveled back and forth. *"What?"*

"I knew you'd eventually get around to scolding me for going too long last night and nearly freezing myself, but that's just—*low.*" Pearl scowled at him. "Now I *have* to make those sound, mature decisions, don't I?"

Grey merely smiled and buffed his nails on his lapel. He hadn't intended such a lesson when he began his answer to Elinor's question, but he was not above grasping an opportunity when it presented itself.

"Well, if I have to," Pearl said. "You do, too. And if you don't, I have the right to bully you into it, into sleeping and eating and all the rest. Fair's only fair."

20

"AGREED." GREY PUT out his hand.

Pearl eyed it suspiciously a moment before clasping it. "Agreed." They shook on their successful negotiation.

Only then did Grey notice that Elinor had a hand over her face, and her shoulders were shaking. For a moment, he was alarmed to think she was crying. After Pearl's tearstorm, it was his first reflex. But he quickly realized it was laughter that shook her.

"Well, I like that," he said indignantly. "Here we are working out the terms of our life together, and you're over there *laughing.*"

"I should have known." Elinor wiped streaming eyes, still wheezing. "You've never been in the ordinary line of *anything.* Either of you. Why should I have feared you would have an ordinary sort of marriage?"

"Indeed you should not." Grey had quite a good pomposity act. "Ordinary? Never touch the stuff."

Elinor cleared her throat and sobered. "There is still much to worry about, but it has nothing to do with the two of you. I had thought to model the new ranks of female magicians after Miss Nightingale's hospital nurses. But you sorceresses keep getting married. It won't do for silly young girls to think that learning magic is a way to snabble a rich husband."

"They should learn," Pearl said, "that they can make themselves rich in their own right by practicing magic, and therefore don't need a husband at all."

"Except to avoid scandal." Grey kissed Pearl's hand. "And because the fellow begged and argued them into it."

Pearl sighed. "Yes, except for that."

Grey turned her by the shoulders and gently pushed her toward the bedroom. "Go and dress. Leave Elinor to plan her Female Magician's School. We have a murder to solve. Breakfast in my dining room in thirty minutes."

"It's only six-thirty," Elinor protested. "You can't possibly be rested after yesterday."

"And yet oddly—" Grey inhaled and stretched, feeling neither ache nor pain. In fact, a deep well of energy and power centered him. "I am. Quite rested. Vastly refreshed." He picked up his hat and gloves from the sidetable by the door. "Don't let Pearl dally."

Elinor ignored him. As usual.

THE TRUE REPERCUSSIONS of the morning's occurrences did not sink fully into Pearl's brain until she arrived at Grey's dining room for breakfast and realized that if he carried out his intent and married her, she would no longer be walking through Harry's garden and across the street for breakfast. She would walk downstairs. From Grey's bedchamber.

Or from her own next to it, if there was one. She'd never actually been to any of the rooms on the residential floor. She could be mistress of this house. And sleep with Grey every night.

Pearl plopped into her seat at the dining table just as her knees gave way. The memory of just how wonderful the reality of making love had been threatened to scramble not only her thoughts, but every muscle and joint in her body. She'd overheard so many girls describe the act at "not so bad, once ya gets used to it," that she hadn't quite believed the girls who argued it was "just grand, iffen ya find a bloke as knows wot 'e's doin'."

Grey obviously knew what he was doing. That alone was nearly enough to tempt her into giving in to his arguments and marrying the man. Nearly.

She believed Grey's promise that he wouldn't interfere with her practice of magic. What she couldn't decide was why. Because he didn't care enough to bother with her? Or because he cared enough to give her her heart's desire?

The depth of understanding he showed during their "discussion" this morning, before and after Elinor's arrival, scared her witless. Every moment he spent with her, everything he did, as opposed to what he said, convinced her more and more that the careless and dissolute facade was precisely that—a facade—and in reality, Greyson George Victor William Whatever Carteret was that rarest of creatures. A good man.

Being a good man, besides everything else he was, made him well-nigh irresistible. How could she not fall in love with him?

How could he possibly fall in love with her?

He was a good man. If they married, he would treat her with respect. He might even remain faithful. It might not be so bad, as he'd said. But she did not want to tie him into "not so bad" if there was the slightest chance for "just grand." Her own life would be just grand with the magic. She didn't need anything else.

"I'd make an offer for your thoughts," Grey broke into them. "But I'm afraid to know what they are."

Pearl was looking down at her empty plate. It had apparently once had food on it, and she must have eaten it. McGregor had taken to filling a plate for her, as he did for Grey on those mornings when they appeared too distracted or tired to do it themselves. She'd won the butler over, it seemed.

She looked at Grey and smiled. "No need to fear. I'm not thinking anything so dreadful."

"Not plotting a way to squirm out of our agreement?" He raised an eyebrow at her.

"As long as you recall what it actually is." Pearl was almost resigned to people knowing. It was possible to drag an engagement out for years. Surely in months, the scandal would die down. Especially if "nothing" occurred.

"In that case." Grey captured her hand before she realized what he was about, and brought it to his lips for a brief kiss. Not too brief to make her shiver.

He slipped a ring onto her third finger and eyed it, apparently for size. He kissed her hand again, over the ring, and released her, finally allowing her to see.

"It's not your mother's ring, or your grandmother's, is it?" she asked suspiciously. He'd found it terribly fast. It was a pretty thing, gold with a filigree dome where a stone would normally sit. Nothing she would expect a duchess to wear.

"Hardly." Grey laughed, then sobered quickly. "That doesn't offend you, does it? It's just that Mother's still wearing all her rings—sometimes all at once—and your fingers are so small, anything of hers would instantly fall off. This belonged to my youngest sister, one of the few I actually like. I thought it would be small enough to fit. And it does."

Pearl thought he would take her hand again, possibly for kissing, so she pulled it back. To examine the ring more closely. The dome was an airy confection of vines and leaves, with tiny violets peeping out here and there.

It was more than just pretty. It was a work of art, seeming incredibly delicate, yet tough enough the collisions of life would not break it.

"Well, aren't you the clever boots," she said, rather disgruntled. How could she be wary of him when he kept proving how clearly he saw her? "It's perfect. You knew, didn't you, that if you'd given me a ring with fancy gemstones, I'd have spent all my time fretting about losing it, and would scarcely have worn it. But this—I've no excuse to take it off."

A smile twitched across his mouth as he watched her, warmth in his eyes. "I'm clever like that. Because I am, after all, only a man and I want you clearly labeled as mine."

Pearl narrowed her eyes at him. "Perhaps I should label you as well. Since you are more likely to be the target of thieves. An embroidered armband, perhaps, that says 'Hands off, ladies. This one belongs to Pearl Parkin.'"

He laughed. "If you make it, I will wear it."

She was even more certain he was making fun of her. "Perhaps a pearl stickpin would do as well."

The warmth in his eyes flared to heat and he captured her hand in both of his, bending over it to hold his lips against the back a long moment. He did not exactly kiss it so much as breathe her in. She feared her hand smelled of bacon, but he didn't seem to care.

His eyes still burned when he looked up at her. "Lay claim to me," he said. "Do."

Pearl had to clear her throat. She didn't know where to look, didn't know what to do with this sudden intensity of his. Her ears burned and she took her hand back, then didn't know what to do with it. Hiding it in her lap seemed cowardly.

She sprang to her feet. "What shall we do today?"

Grey had risen when she did and now he opened the door to the hallway for her. "We will meet Ferguson and Archaios to attempt again to track the magic. According to the morning reports, there has been no sign of the demon since it vanished yesterday, so we must focus on catching the murderer."

"You've had reports already?" Pearl put her arms into the jacket he held for her and shrugged it on, then picked up her shawl to go over it. The finely woven paisley wool helped keep the rain off, especially when folded double for wearing.

"I had the reports sent here as soon as the last conjurer clocked in." Grey buttoned his overcoat and took the tall hat McGregor handed him.

Pearl tied on her coal-scuttle bonnet. She felt as if she had horse blinders on when she wore it, for she couldn't see to either side without turning her head, but it was wonderful for keeping out the rain. And the pale gray color looked well with her pastel dresses.

The rattle of horses sounded outside, and shortly after, a knock sounded at the door. McGregor opened it and inclined his head at Ferguson who bounded into the room, rubbing his hands. "Oh good, you're ready then. Shall we?" He paused and gave his own stiff head bob at Grey. "Sir. Miss." He waved at the open door. "Mr. Archaios is waiting in the carriage."

"Yes, of course." Pearl glanced back at Grey before she started out, but he was taking something from McGregor.

"May I say that you are looking particularly lovely this morning, Pearl." James Ferguson captured her hand. Men were always doing that. Shouldn't they wait for her to offer it?

He bent over her imprisoned hand for a kiss, and it was only when he froze there, halfway down, that Pearl realized he had caught her left hand. The one with the new ring on it.

"Is this new?" He kissed her hand, then straightened, still holding onto her to look at the ring. "Very pretty. A gift?"

"Indeed." Grey sounded gruff and stern and not at all Grey-like. "It is the gift of an engagement ring. Wish us happy, Ferguson. Miss Parkin and I are to be married." He reclaimed Pearl's hand for her from the other man's grip, then placed a pair of pale gray gloves lined in rabbit fur in her hand. "To avoid a repeat of yesterday's difficulty."

He nodded to McGregor, who crooked fingers at a pair of footmen who followed them down the steps to the waiting Briganti carriage, their arms piled high with hot bricks for their feet and carriage robes for their laps, which were tucked around Pearl. The leftovers were grudgingly shared out among the men.

"Congratulations on your engagement, sir, Miss Parkin," Ferguson said, when the blankets and bricks were settled and the carriage was moving. "When did this happy event occur?"

"This morning," Pearl said.

"Near Christmas, I think," Grey said, obviously thinking Ferguson had asked when the wedding would be. And perhaps he had. Or perhaps Pearl simply panicked, hearing Grey's intention to marry so soon.

"*Next* Christmas," she said.

"I had to step lively and get my proposal in early today, before all the things we have to do." Grey brought her hand with the ring to his mouth for another kiss. The gloves helped with the melting problem. "I am thanking my luck that she said yes."

"This is splendid, yes?" Archaios twinkled at them. He had particularly twinkly eyes. "And you will have the wedding before I must return to Greece, so I may attend." He nodded, as if everything were settled.

Pearl managed to smile and nod, wondering just how long Archaios planned to stay in England.

"I am sure everyone will be happy to hear the news." Ferguson's words and even his tone sounded pleased, but his expression was full of reproach.

Whatever for? Ferguson had always been kind and solicitous of her on the occasions when they met, full of compliments that made her feel wary and flattered both at once. She had always been polite and friendly in return, but nothing more. Surely he couldn't have built expectations out of that.

"I am sure they will." Grey's smile showed his teeth and little humor. He encased her hand between his in a blatant laying-of-claim.

If Ferguson foolishly thought a few idle conversations gave him any reason for his own claim, she would show him right quick how wrong he was. Ferguson tried to stifle her actions with no right to do so. He would be an impossible husband.

Pearl patted Grey's arm and stretched up to kiss his cheek. He covered his surprise quickly with such a besotted expression she thought certain the others would see right through it.

"Are we going to the office first?" she asked, needing desperately to change the subject of conversation. "Or will we begin where we left off yesterday?"

"I thought we'd begin back at St. James's Park. See if we can follow the ghost back to the scene of her death like we did with Angus Galloway." Grey pulled out his watch to check the time. "We've another hour and a half till moonset."

Pearl cleared her throat, not actually trying to get attention. She acquired it anyway. "I may have—well, laid the ghost yesterday. I don't know whether I actually did, but once I sent the magic out to follow the murderer— There was a great deal of it left over, you see. So I sent it back to Rose. And, well . . ." She shrugged. If Grey was angry, he would just have to be angry. The magic wanted to go home.

Grey nodded. "Excellent. That's excellent. We can call her spirit in that case, which is a much easier proposition."

"You sent the magic to follow the murderer?" Ferguson's expression was all curiosity. He seemed a man of sudden enthusiasms. "How does that work? What does it do?"

"Oh, that's right . . ." Grey drawled, lounging back in his seat. Rather like a large cat with prey in its sights, pretending indifference to draw that prey closer. "You were unconscious the first time she did it, after the first murder."

Pearl looked from Grey to the young wizard and back. Grey didn't trust Ferguson apparently. That masculine possessiveness ought to annoy her, but it didn't. Probably because she felt rather possessive herself. And she had no right. Not truly.

"That's correct, sir." Ferguson blushed under his freckles. "I wasn't. Which is why I am most curious."

"As am I," Archaios chimed in. "Sorcery has been gone from us for so long, the Conclave itself is anxious to know what it can do. It can also lay ghosts?"

"Well, yes." Pearl attempted to explain. "I am not sure if sorcery can do it alone, or if it requires sorcery and conjury working in concert, but—"

"What about the murderer?" Ferguson interrupted. "Begging your pardon, Miss Parkin, Mr. Archaios, but that *is* what we're about this morning, is it not?"

"Of course." Pearl found a place to begin. "I'm not far enough along in my studies to understand the theories about how or why it works, except that innocent blood has magic explicitly designed to find justice. It cries out for justice, correct? It is one of the most basic of sorcery's spells because it *wants* to be used for that specific purpose.

"It can be shaped and sent out by nothing more than a woman crying out over the body of her slain child, or in the blood of her own injuries."

"Yes, but what does it *do*?" Ferguson persisted. "Does it create a blood trail to the killer? Does it attack the murderer's bowels, or cause a brain fever, or—?" He broke off, because Pearl was laughing, which obviously annoyed him.

"You are rather bloodthirsty, aren't you, Mr. Ferguson?" Her laughter faded to smiles.

A mere smile was apparently enough to rouse Grey's possessive instincts, for he glared at Ferguson and tucked Pearl closer to his side. "You're shivering," he said. "Are you not?"

She wasn't, but she was content to be closer to Grey. Possessiveness led to proximity, which could lead to affection, which could lead to love. Couldn't it? Was that what she wanted?

She turned back to Ferguson and his questions. "I honestly do not know whether the magic of innocent blood can cause physical ailments."

"It can stop a heart," Archaios said. "The sorceress Amanusa—Mrs. Greyson—worked magic against rapists and murderers that stopped hearts. I have read the reports."

"But that magic had blood in the spell," Grey said. "Blood of the victims mixed with blood of the murderers. Can it kill without that? From a distance, as it were?"

She didn't know about this spell of Mrs. Greyson's— "Greyson," she mused aloud. "That's *your* name—"

"Distant relation." Grey waved a dismissive hand. "On m'mother's side. I find myself curious as well. What *does* the magic do when you send it out after a murderer?"

Guild secrets, Pearl reminded herself. Obviously, she couldn't let on that it was the sorceress's blood inside the murderer that made execution possible. But she *could* tell them . . . "It depends on how the magic is shaped. And the talent of the sorceress, of course. A mother weeping over her child is less likely to have the ability or knowledge to send out a fully formed, mature spell."

She cleared her throat. "Nor am I, since I am only an apprentice and haven't much practice in magic-shaping.

Most often, if the magic is sent out simply on the basis of the blood spilled, without a specific person suspected or names, I suppose it's more like that brain fever you mentioned, Mr. Ferguson.

"My readings indicate that it haunts the killer so that he—or she—relives the crime, but from the victim's point of view. It harries them, like—" She paused. "Like the Faery Hunt pursuing kin killers and oath breakers. Blood magic is like that. It is unrelenting in its quest for justice. It never stops, never gives up, until justice is found."

She shrugged. "Maybe the magic itself decides what payment is enough. Maybe remorse and repentance on the part of the killer will stop it. I doubt it, but it is possible."

"Horrid dreams?" Ferguson gave a wan smile. "That doesn't seem like much of a punishment. Not like rotting bowels or ulcerating sores."

"Isn't it?" Pearl shook her head at him, though she'd been slow to understand much of this herself. "Mind and body have great influence on each other. Even if you only *think* something is wrong, is that not as effective as the reality? Remember Lady Macbeth."

"That is fiction. A play."

"Based on a greater truth."

"I'd think it strange," Grey mused, "if dreaming about dying horribly night after night did not cause rotten bowels." He tipped his head back to eye Ferguson from under his hat brim. "Or at least a severe case of the trots."

"*Grey.*" Pearl poked him in the side. "Don't be indelicate. Not in public, anyway."

"Right. Sorry m'love." He kissed her hand. Again.

And for the forty-eleventh time, she melted. She'd given up hoping that he would stop the kissing. Maybe if he did it enough, she would stop melting.

"I don't expect any remorse or repentance from this chap," Grey went on as the carriage drew to a halt. "Seeing that we've got two murder victims now. He doesn't appear to have any repentance in him."

"Maybe the trots just 'asn't 'it 'im yet," Pearl muttered in her street accent, as the door opened and the men across from her descended.

The noise wasn't enough to cover her words entirely, for Grey choked on laughter and sent her a merry grin. He shook his head at her. "Such indelicacy."

"Oh, stubble it," she grumbled. "And move so I can get out."

He obliged, with a chuckle.

On the way to join Archaios and Ferguson at the site where Rose's body had been found, Pearl saw Grey sketch a quick gesture with his fingers, down by his side. A conjury sigil, she knew, but not which one. His fingers flew too quickly.

"Come, please, my dear," he murmured aloud, and then she knew he called Mary.

What if—the thought hit Pearl hard—what if he didn't fear falling in love sometime in the nebulous future because he already had? What if Mary was the love of his life, and the only relationship he could have with her was that of conjurer and familiar spirit? Why wouldn't he settle for second best and Pearl, in that case?

She felt the faint shiver of Mary's presence and wanted to weep for Grey's sorrow. What had happened to her? Mary hadn't died a violent death. Pearl's magic told her. But Mary had died too soon, and Grey had loved her before then. He loved her still. It was obvious in their every interaction.

The park's vagrants were huddled under the trees against the miserable misting rain. More pale faces appeared along the damp ground under the supports of the suspension bridge spanning the lake. They were everywhere, taking what shelter they could from the awful weather. Pearl shivered. There but for the grace of God— and Grey Carteret—

Grey handed her his cube of ink and she turned away from their company to spit on it. They'd done the spirit protection spell enough to have it down to routine. He mixed the ink, and Pearl held the umbrella and the cube while he brushed the sigil on her wrist between sleeve and glove. Archaios and Ferguson watched curiously. They weren't the only ones. Pearl could feel the attention of the park's wretched residents.

"Stand watch, if you would, my dear," Grey said to Mary when the ink was dry and her bolt hole secure. "Alert us if anything out of the usual occurs."

Grey turned to the other men. "Have you been able to pinpoint anything from the magic left here?"

Archaios shook his head. "It is as if my magic senses have caught cold. Perhaps the demon has muffled them. Or perhaps the evidence has been wiped clean, here and on the victim's body."

"The man has a purpose in what he is doing," Ferguson said. "That was clear to *me* from the magic left behind.

"What purpose could require the brutal torture and murder of two innocent people?" Pearl burst out. She couldn't help it.

Grey put an arm around her as he spoke. "What purpose could require the calling of a demon? Doesn't he realize the cost?"

"Obviously he believes the cost is worth paying," Ferguson said. "The demon has interfered with the dead zones every time it has come. Perhaps this magician hopes to rid the world of them. Perhaps he thinks such a cause is worth any price."

"*He* isn't paying the cost, is he?" Pearl retorted, angry, hurting and not caring who she lashed out at. "Rose did. Angus Galloway did. I don't see the murderer paying anything himself."

"I did not say *I* thought so, Miss Parkin," Ferguson protested. "Of course I do not. I am merely trying to put myself in his place, to think as he does so that we might catch him all the more quickly. As Mr. Archaios suggested to me only yesterday."

"It is so." Archaios nodded. "Often, in order to understand the magic which is found, we must determine the purpose for which such magic is intended."

That made sense to Pearl. "Be that as it may, what you must understand is that the sacrifice of blood for magic must be *willing*. I've said it before. Weren't you there to hear? If blood is taken unwillingly, then it is innocent blood and will turn on its taker. You *cannot* steal blood for magic."

"Like the fact that conjury cannot call demons, that is a truth the public may never believe," Grey said. "But for now, let us see if we can call our spirit, shall we? Only a short time longer till moonset, and this is a very new spirit indeed."

The vagrants had come to the edges of their trees and shelters, not yet venturing out into the rain, but watching. They made Pearl uneasy.

"Right, then." Grey exchanged his Chinese brush for a pencil and pulled his notebook from his coattail pocket.

Pearl held the umbrella while Grey drew his sigils, using runes to inscribe Rose's name in the spell. He tucked the paper away in his pocket. This was the place where the demon had abandoned her. She would know how to find it.

Grey motioned Archaios and Ferguson back, held his hand out for Pearl, in case Rose was still ghost and not spirit, and sent out his call. He pushed power into it when no answer was forthcoming, a little surprised he had so much to push. After yesterday's exertions—and last night's—he should have been running on dregs. But he was not, and he had no time to wonder at it, for here came Rose Bowers, looking as well as any new spirit had a right to look.

21

"HELLO, MY DEAR." He didn't use Rose's name out of habit, though everyone knew whose spirit they conjured here.

'Ello. Rose smiled at him, showing a gap in the right side of her teeth. She was dressed in a blindingly pink dress in the latest state of fashion. New spirits tended to enjoy themselves in interesting ways their first little while. *Was it you 'oo called me? Felt most peculiar, it did. They said I didn't 'ave to come, but I could if I wanted.* Her attention shifted to Pearl. *'Ere, you look familiar. Do I know you?*

"It's me," Pearl said. "Parkin."

Cor, you turned into a girl! Rose stared wide-eyed, her shape holding much better than any new spirit ever had in Grey's experience.

Pearl laughed. "I always was a girl, Rosie dearest. I just never dared dress like one till now." She curtseyed, and slipped into her East End accent. "I'm a proper sorcery apprentice now, I am. Come up in the world, 'aven't I?"

Grey tapped Pearl's arm, then his own lips with the same forefinger. "Names," he murmured, reminding her. "It did us no harm this time, but you need to get into the proper habits if you are to continue seeing and communing with spirits."

Her eyes went wide, her hand clutching at his, the umbrella in her other hand trembling in her distress. "I am so, so sorry," she whispered.

"Just keep it in mind. No harm done today." Grey turned back to Rose. "My dear, we've called you here for a purpose."

Didn't fink you invited me to take tea. Rose fluffed

her very fashionable, very pink skirt. *I was murdered, wasn't I? Allus figured as 'ow I'd go that way, livin' like I did. Coulda been smarter, I reckon, but better to 'ave fun an' die young than to push and strive and be afraid all the time, and die old and bitter. That's wot I always says, any road.* She winked. *An' I did 'ave me some fun, I did. So 'oo murdered me?*

Grey couldn't help chuckling. He liked her attitude. "That's why we've called you here. Do you remember anything about your death?"

Rose screwed up her face as she thought. *Nope, not a fing.* She frowned. *Is that usual?*

"It isn't unusual," Grey said. "Particularly in the case of murder."

Archaios and Ferguson had moved closer during Grey's conversation with the dead girl's spirit, their umbrellas bumping against the one he shared with Pearl. She shivered and huddled closer as well, which was not like her. Did she find it disturbing to converse with the spirit of someone she knew? She hadn't seemed to, not at first.

He looked down, but Pearl's attention wasn't on Rose, or even the other magicians. He followed her gaze across the park to the ragged paupers under the trees, their attitudes filled with obvious rising hostility.

"Little friend." He called Mary's name with his magic. "Would you keep watch over our audience? Do let us know in time for us to scarper, if there comes a need for it."

I always warn you in time, Mary huffed.

"Just." He thought she enjoyed watching his narrow escapes. She always did have a broad sense of humor.

Was it gruesome? Rose asked when he turned his attention back to her, so eagerly he knew she'd been waiting. *My murder?*

Grey blinked at her. Pearl had to speak while he recovered from his astonishment.

"You've been to too many Judge and Jury Court plays," she accused the spirit. "I don't know how you stood it, listening to them play at testifying about awful murders."

They're ever so interestin', Rose said. *I like bein' scared. Reminds me I'm alive.* She giggled. *'Cept I ain't no more, am I?*

"Well, your murder was quite, quite gruesome," Pearl said. "The awfullest I ever heard of. The papers will be writing about it for weeks and weeks, about how poor Rose Bowers died and her body found in St. James's Park."

'Ere? Rose looked around and nodded, satisfied. *I allus did like this park.*

Cows lowed from the meadow across the lake. Grey hoped they didn't take it in mind to wander this way. Cows never helped a situation. "My dear, what *do* you remember of the last moments of your life?"

Rose made her thinking face again. *I remember I didn't 'ave no posies to sell, an' it was cold an' miserable. So I went over to the Garden to see if I could find a likely gentleman 'oo'd be willin' to pay enough for a tumble as would let me buy a flop in th' back o' Sal Busby's. An' one turned up.* She shrugged. *Don't recall more'n that.*

"Who was the gentleman?" Grey asked. "Do you remember a name? A face?"

Rose's scornful look told him he should know better. *Conjurer's ain't the only ones as don't use names. As for a face . . .* She squeezed her face up slightly less this time. *Ain't comin' to mind. 'E 'ad one o' them widerbrim 'ats. Like yours. An' it were dark. It may be I didn't see 'is face.*

"What garden, dearest?" Pearl asked. "Covent Garden, or Cremorne Garden?" She named the new pleasure garden across the river that had opened several years before Vauxhall closed.

Cremorne, o' course. A girl gets—not a better class o'

patrons, but a nicer one. Them gentlemen is more considerate of a girl's comfort, they is.

"How tall was he?" Pearl asked. "Taller than us, of course, but was he taller than Mr. Carteret here? As tall as Mr. Archaios?" She gestured toward the Greek in question.

Not so tall as that one, Rose said. *Not so tall as either of those gentlemen. In fact, he were a bit shorter than this other fellow 'ere.* She indicated Ferguson, who was perhaps three inches shorter than Grey. *'E weren't enough taller 'n me to make it awkward, if you knows wot I mean. I was lookin' forward t' not bein' smothered.*

"Anything else you remember, dearest?" Pearl urged. "Anything at all? What about his clothes—a distinctive scarf or watch fob? Or—did he have a limp, or use scent, or have a particular way of speaking? An accent perhaps?"

'E sounded like any fine gentleman, 'ceptin' 'e spoke in a sort o' whisper. Disguisin' 'is voice, maybe. An' 'is clothes was black, like gentlemen wears. All black. 'E didn't 'ave a limp. Didn't even carry a walkin' stick . . . Rose's voice trailed off. *But 'e did 'ave a scent. Not like some blokes do, flowers over sweat, but—like sulfur maybe, an' chalk dust, an' . . . grass?*

Pearl was doing better at drawing Rose out than he had, Grey mused. The scent—was that something they could use? It didn't sound like the sort of thing one ordered from the perfumers, so canvassing perfume shops probably wouldn't help. But perhaps it could help identify the man once they narrowed the field of suspects.

"Thank you, my dear," he said thoughtfully. "You've been a great deal of assistance. If you remember anything else, do let us know. If you don't care to return to this plane, just inform my friend, here—" He indicated Mary, who waved cheerfully at Rose, who grinned back. "Who will convey the information to me."

He took his notebook and pencil from his pocket and

drew a large sigil of release atop the summoning marks. Easier than erasing everything. "Thank you," he said, dismissing Rose's spirit by shifting the magic into the overlying sigil. Without the energy provided through the sigils to maintain her presence, Rose faded away, like any new spirit.

"She seemed happy, don't you think?" Pearl sounded hopeful.

"What did you learn?" Ferguson intruded. "Did she give a description?"

"Spirits are always happy, my love." Grey patted her hand as he took the umbrella from her, tucking her hand in the crook of his arm. "She didn't see his face, but—"

"Too bad," Ferguson said. "I take it she did not recall the murder itself?"

"Many do not, at first, after they make the transition from ghost to spirit," Grey said.

A shout came from the forefront of the crowd of vagrants, men and women alike, who'd ventured from the shelter of their trees. "Oi! You're magicians, ain't ya?"

"That's right," Ferguson shouted, before Grey could stop him.

The first bit of rotten fruit was followed immediately by mud and stones from the lake's edge. "Murderin' swine!"

Grey pushed Pearl out of the line of fire, toward the carriage and safety. She slipped his grip—damned umbrella—and marched straight at the miniature mob, ignoring the mud they splattered on her pale dress and the rain dripping from her bonnet onto her nose. Grey scrambled after her, the other men with him.

The crowd faltered, startled and a bit daunted by the slip of a woman striding fearlessly toward them. One brave pauper threw another rock and hit her in the head. Grey roared and charged, flinging the damned umbrella aside. They'd hurt her.

The rock had hit her cheek. Blood mixed with the rain trickling down to her chin. *"No."* She pushed him away, and he let her. The injury was minor.

He could pick her up and carry her to safety. He wanted to. God, he wanted to, and he would if he had to. But she had stopped the crowd's advance with nothing save raw, naked courage. If he carried her off, he would trample on that courage. He could not do it. Not unless and until it became necessary.

The crowd stood a few paces away, silent and watchful. Wary, but waiting to see what she would do.

"Rose Bowers was my friend!" Pearl shouted against the muffling rain. "The woman whose body was found here. Did any of you even know her name? *She was my friend.*"

Grey stood behind her, backing her up, water dripping off his hair and down his neck. He'd lost his hat somewhere, too. Pride in his bride-to-be filled him to bursting, though he'd had no hand in it. Only the wisdom to choose her for his own. Though he hadn't exactly chosen, had he? He'd fallen over his own—well, not his feet.

"We were just talking to her, to her spirit, to see if she knew who had killed her, who it was that handed her over to a demon as a toy! The murdering swine who killed her was no magician!" Her voice hovered on the choked edge of tears.

Grey laid a hand on her shoulder. She was too wet. Too cold.

"Any *real* conjurer knows you might be able to tempt a demon to come calling, but you would be foolish to do so, for no human magic can compel one. And everyone knows that innocent blood cries out for justice. It is magic that will find this killer and magic will bring him to justice!"

"Abomination!" The unfortunately familiar boom of

Nigel Cranshaw's voice cut through the damp air. "Whore of Babylon!"

Grey spun on his heel—Pearl had the crowd well in hand—and waited for Cranshaw's approach. Grey had had enough of the bastard's carping and insults long ago. Now the man flung those insults at Grey's fiancée. Grey had cause.

"This woman speaks nothing but lies," Cranshaw shouted. "She lies down with filth and rolls in the blood of innocence. She consorts with the unholy. She—"

Grey took two steps forward and planted his fist in that filth-spouting mouth. Cranshaw went down like a felled tree. Grey hissed at the pain in his hand and flexed his bruised fingers. Mouths were filled with hard, pointy teeth. He'd broken the skin on his knuckles. But Cranshaw lay dazed on the path, rain running into his mouth.

"I am an apprentice to sorcery," Pearl called out to the newly restless crowd. "Blood magic. The magic that hears the cry of Rose Bowers's innocent blood. That man—"

She pointed at Cranshaw, who was sitting up, shaking his head. "That man hates women and fears sorcery, because it's women's magic. The magic of those whose strength is endurance and patience, and love of others." Her voice rose to a shout. She repeated again the truth about sorcery and the source of its power, the *willing* sacrifice of blood.

"But more than that, sorcery can protect," she told them. "You women, you've heard the stories. You know the spells of protection that are whispered, passed down as fairy tales. I know because I heard them, too, when I lived among you. Those stories are true. The spells work. They are real. They're simple spells. They don't take much power. Use them. Protect yourselves and those you love. Don't let anyone hurt you, trying to make you work the spell for them. Remember, innocent blood has power!"

Pearl pulled off her glove and touched the still-oozing cut on her cheek where the rock had struck her. Grey felt magic stir. Someone in the crowd cried out, a sharp, "Hey!" of pain.

"It's not much of an injury," Pearl said, "and there wasn't much actual intent to do harm behind it. The magic returned hurt for hurt. Remember that before you raise your hand to someone weaker than you. Go now. Protect yourselves. Listen to the truth, not the lies of the weak and fearful."

Like some great and terrible queen, Pearl swung about and strode away. Grey swung around with her, playing equerry.

Cranshaw was climbing to his feet. Grey took his hat from Ferguson, who'd apparently fetched his discarded belongings. He waved Ferguson toward Pearl to give her the umbrella, then approached the wizards' magister.

"Miss Pearl Parkin is my fiancée," he told Cranshaw, "as well as my apprentice. If you insult her again, I will deliver the appropriate response."

"Duels are illegal," Cranshaw said through a satisfyingly swollen mouth.

"I didn't say anything about dueling, did I?" Grey felt his care-for-nothing facade crack and fall away, leaving him nothing but deadly truth. "Horsewhipping." He nodded and flexed his sore hand again. "Won't have to bruise my knuckles."

He touched the brim of his hat in farewell and turned away, only to be accosted by the reporters, clamoring to know about Grey's engagement, the murder, his new fiancée, the demon, his expected wedding date—

Pearl described her protection spell again for publication, and the instant she finished, Grey signaled for the driver to move off.

"Home, I think," he said, leaning carefully back against the seat. "Pearl is soaked through, as am I. We both need a change of clothing and a good warming.

You gentlemen could probably use dry feet at the least. Return for us in an hour and we will proceed with the tracking."

"What did you learn from Miss Bowers's spirit?" Archaios asked.

"Enough to know we should look for the murderer's new laboratory on the south side of the Thames." Grey wrapped a blanket around Pearl's shoulders when she shivered, tucking her close against his side. He couldn't get her any wetter. "She may have met the man in Cremorne Garden." He and Pearl shared the other things Rose had told them.

"So, we know this much," Archaios said when they finished. "The killer is attempting to call a demon for some unknown purpose, and is attempting to blend all the magics into one great spell to do so. He seems to be working alone."

"I think Ferguson had it right," Grey said. "Consider. Shortly after Angus Galloway's murder, Magister Tomlinson and Miss Tavis discovered that machines in the Bethnal Green dead zone had been ripped to pieces. The day after Rose Bowers's murder, it was found that the borders to the dead zones had gone ragged. Shifted back in some places, grown in others. I think the murderer wants to use the demon against the dead zones."

"Wouldn't that be a good thing?" Ferguson said.

"I doubt Mr. Galloway or Rose Bowers would agree with you," Pearl retorted.

"I didn't mean—" Ferguson protested.

"You may be correct," Archaios said. "There are those, even within the ranks of magicians, who fear the dead zones enough to do something so reckless."

"I'd say *especially* among magicians," Grey agreed. "Since we die quicker than ordinaries when deprived of magic."

"Magister Tomlinson leads the fight against the dead zones," Ferguson offered.

"Yes, but Harry didn't have opportunity," Grey said absently. "He was with us the night Rose Bowers died, and the magic signatures prove the same man committed both murders."

"But Harry will know who we might examine," Archaios said. "Mr. Ferguson and I will go to the laboratory to discuss this with him, after we have left you and Miss Parkin to dry your clothing."

"Put Nigel Cranshaw on the list of those to investigate. He tends to be extreme in his passions." Grey looked up as the carriage rattled to a stop. They were home. He escorted Pearl to her door, then hurried down the street to his own warm, dry house.

DESPITE EVERYONE'S AGREEMENT that the demon-calling murderer probably wanted to destroy the dead zones with his perverted magic, the investigation proceeded at a crawl. Grey finally relented and sent a telegram off to the newlyweds, requesting Amanusa's justice magic to assist in the interrogation of the suspects, once they acquired some. Pearl would work the justice magic if he asked it, but Grey wouldn't ask. He knew she did not feel comfortable with the magic, having practiced it only the once. They hadn't had time to practice again, and didn't now.

The pressure to solve the crime was intense. Not only from the government—the home secretary, Sir George Grey, called personally on I-Branch—but from the public. The press published wild-eyed articles filled with speculation, rumors, and outright falsehoods, leavened with tiny seasonings of truth, stirring up passions of all sorts.

Some papers attempted to play up the scandal of Grey's engagement to Pearl, but the furor over the murders shoved it aside before it received much notice. Grey's sister Adela sent a congratulatory note. The rest of the world ignored it.

Cranshaw was everywhere, speaking to associations, being quoted in the papers, writing ranting essays about the evils of sorcery and the dangers of women practicing magic. Between that, and the papers hinting that evil magicians had committed the murders—which happened to be true, except the papers made it seem that all magicians were evil—the population of London was stirred into throwing stones and rotten produce at the Briganti. And any other person they suspected of being a magician. Pearl's pastel dresses took on a number of unwanted stains, though Grey was able to protect her from the worst of the assaults.

Now and again, when the frustration built up too high, Pearl would burst out with a speech like the one at the park, impassioned enough to shame those present into slinking away. Then the papers would twist her words into insinuation, and the trouble would start up again.

Grey had never been so proud of anyone as he was of Pearl. He'd never felt this way at all before, this mad brew of pride, desire, possession, and . . . Sometimes he wondered if he was in love with her. He'd never been in love before, so he didn't know how it felt.

Love or not, he was in the grip of an insatiable desire for her. He honestly tried to behave in the manner of a fiancé who respected his bride-to-be. But she had only to smile at him in that way she had, hinting at secrets and private amusement and—he didn't know everything it held. The world.

She had only to smile and he became a ravening beast, held back by the thinnest of threads from pouncing upon her and carrying her off to his lair.

He had never known that magic had spells to transform men into beasts. Though in truth, ordinary nonmagical lust had all the power needed. The worst of it was that on those occasions when he was not constrained by the presence of others from acting on his worst impulses, Pearl did absolutely nothing to prevent him from acting.

The tenth time it happened—it had been ten days since the first occasion, therefore ten times—and Grey carried her off to his bedroom to quench his thirst for her, he remembered afterward that he had meant to speak to her about it.

They lay naked in his bed, Grey on his back, one arm flung over his head, with actual thoughts floating to the surface of his mind, like dead things rising in a river. Pearl was rather murderous to his thought process, but they did resurrect themselves eventually, and tonight it happened before they collapsed into sleep.

He looked at Pearl, who lay on her stomach, her face burrowed into the featherbed. "Pearl?" He rolled to his side and combed the tangled hair from the visible part of her face. The noise she made encouraged him. "Are you asleep?"

"Not for lack of trying." She opened her unburied eye at him, then turned onto her side with a flounce. "What?"

Grey sighed. But if she was annoyed with him and half asleep, perhaps she would answer his questions with truth. Not that she wasn't truthful, to the point of discomfort most times, but she could evade with the best of them. Meaning himself. "You do know that I am trying very hard to treat you with the respect due one's fiancée, don't you?"

Both of Pearl's eyes came open and she swept her hair out of her face. "Yes, of course."

"Then why aren't you helping me? When I picked you up in my arms tonight and bore you off, why did you put your arms around my neck? Why didn't you at least say something?"

"What would you have me say?" The light in her eyes should have warned him, but fool that he was, he plunged on.

"Something like, 'Grey, this isn't wise.' Or 'Grey, think.' *Something.*"

She sat up, and only then did he understand his peril. Not even the linens falling away from her perfect body could distract him from that terrifying realization.

"First of all—" She poked him with her finger. Pearl's were quite as deadly as Elinor's. She'd learned her technique there. "You are not putting *me* in charge of controlling *your* lustful urges. That is your job, not mine. I have enough trouble controlling my own urges. Which is the second of all.

"You are assuming I want to control them. Why should I? I want to be here in this bed doing what we do together just as much as you do. When you kiss me like that, I can't think. I'm not sure I can even form words. And you want me to protest?"

Grey sat up beside her, scrubbing a hand over his face in an attempt to order his thoughts. *She wants me* was trying to drown everything else out, with help from *I can kiss her as senseless as she makes me.* "We've got to move the wedding up," he muttered.

"Surely that's no longer necessary." Pearl's statement brought his head jerking around.

"It's more necessary than ever." Grey couldn't believe what he'd heard. "The more often we—" He waved a hand at their nakedness, at the bed. "—come together, the more likely there will be consequences."

"Sorcery has magic to prevent conception." The tips of her ears turned charmingly pink, but Grey refused to be charmed. "And as for reputation—ruined is ruined, which I was long before we ever met. Ruination is not compounded each time we—"

She blushed brighter as she repeated his gesture. "There's no need for us to marry. We can simply continue the engagement and when people have forgotten . . ." She waved her hand again, waving him and their engagement away.

"We will marry," Grey said through gritted teeth. "The sooner, the better. As soon as they finish calling the banns. The second calling is tomorrow at St. Ann's. We will, of course, attend. Ruin and reputations do not enter into it."

He wanted to marry Pearl as much for himself as for her sake. More. Pearl would indeed do perfectly well if they did not wed. He very much feared that he would not.

The next morning after service, Grey called Elinor aside and asked her to arrange a wedding. November 30, the day immediately after the third calling of the banns, seemed suitable. That would give her just over a week to arrange for the small private ceremony he and Pearl both wanted. Pearl had no family. Grey wished he didn't—except for Adela. He would invite his sister. Beyond that, a few of their magician friends. Harry and Elinor would stand up with them. Perhaps Amanusa and Jax would be back. That was enough.

The day after that, on Monday, Amanusa and Jax arrived in London on the ten o'clock train. Grey dragged Pearl to the station with Harry, Elinor, and Archaios to meet them.

Pearl wasn't at all sure she wished to go. Morning was surely soon enough to meet the formidable, beautiful Mrs. Greyson, but when Grey insisted, as magicmaster rather than as fiancé, Pearl could not very well resist. She was perfectly happy with the magic-master she had and did not want to change, but Grey insisted on so few things.

The train arrived in Euston Station precisely on time, alas. Pearl waited with the anxiously pacing Harry, Grey, and Elinor. Archaios stood more calmly to one side, being taller and able to see farther. As Pearl watched Grey, she wondered whether Grey's impossible love, the one that made him willing to settle for marrying Pearl, might be the happily married Amanusa Greyson, rather than the dead Mary.

Then Elinor let out a glad cry and darted forward into the crush of weary travelers. The others followed, except for Grey, who looked around to find Pearl. He extended his hand to her with a sweet smile. She'd only recently discovered he had them as well as the other, wickeder sort.

Elinor rushed up to a giantess of a woman, one quite as tall as Grey, with pale blond hair tucked tidily under a fashionable bonnet. Harry was clapping a taller gentleman on the back, and they were there. Grey took both of the tall willowy woman's hands in his and kissed her cheek. Then he shook hands with the gentleman whose brown hair shone with ruddy lights in the glare of the station lights.

Pearl held very still but she should have known Grey would not forget her. He caught her hand and pulled her forward. "My fiancée," he said. "Miss Pearl Parkin."

The fair one's brows went up and she smiled, extending both hands—bare of gloves—to Pearl. "Why, she's lovely, Grey. Not at all what I would have expected of you."

"You'd have expected me to marry someone ugly?" He stiffened in mock affront.

She laughed. "Of course not, but—forgive me, Miss Parkin, I must greet you and not tease Grey. It is an astonishing privilege to meet the woman who can put up with this man."

"He is a trial, I must admit." Pearl said it for Grey, not the woman. Grey appreciated a good tease. Pearl did not want to like her, for too many reasons.

"Pearl, this is my cousin, Jax Greyson." Grey introduced her to the gentleman standing behind his very tall wife.

"You're the only one who claims me as such." He smiled at Grey, then turned his twinkling smile on Pearl as he took her hand with an old-fashioned bow. "An honor, Miss Parkin."

"No one claims me, either," Grey said. "So we might as well claim each other."

When the gentleman rose, Pearl glanced at his wife—the magister, she supposed, since Mrs. Greyson was the only master sorcerer—and saw her smiling at her husband with such a look on her face . . . No, she was not in love with Grey. It yet remained to be seen whether Grey was in love with her.

"Pearl is also Grey's apprentice," Elinor said. "Studying sorcery."

"She opened the sorcery book in the library without a fumble." Grey's statement sounded so boastful it made Pearl blush.

"However are you managing to learn?" The sorcery magister looked at Pearl in astonishment.

"Out of books." Pearl shrugged. "I'm still at the very beginning."

"Not so," Grey protested. "She's already managed to—ride the blood, isn't it? And lay ghosts."

"Lay ghosts?" Mrs. Greyson blinked her absurdly long, pale lashes. "How does one do that? And riding the blood already— You have outpaced the others altogether."

"Others?" Elinor's face was alight with eager anticipation.

Mrs. Greyson turned to a cluster of women and girls standing behind her, people Pearl should have noticed long before. "Magisters, magicians, and apprentices, I present to you the students of the sorcery school."

There were six of them, ranging in age from the apple-cheeked Nan Jackson who could be no more than fourteen, to Fiona Watson, a sturdy, matronly woman in her thirties.

The niceties done, Mr. Greyson gathered his wife in. He only took her arm, but it seemed to Pearl almost as if he gathered her under protective wings.

"We're worn to the bone," he said, somehow making

it clear that by "we" he meant his bride. "Time enough tomorrow for talking shop."

"You said you'd booked rooms at Brown's Hotel," Elinor said. "I assume you meant that you booked enough rooms for everyone."

"Yes, of course." Mrs. Greyson got the whole group moving by sheer force of will, Pearl thought.

Pearl was swept along with them by Grey, who hurried to pace at the sorceress's side. "I want Pearl in your school," he said.

"She's much more advanced than my students." Mrs. Greyson seemed utterly serene.

"So give her private tutoring. There may be gaps in her knowledge. Things your students know that I didn't know to teach her. We can transfer the apprenticeship tomorrow. It was in our agreement, Pearl's and mine."

Mrs. Greyson gave him a peculiar look. "It isn't necessary. She can be your apprentice and still attend sorcery school."

"She is my fiancée," he said, "soon to be my wife. To be apprentice as well—I'm not sure it's proper."

Magister Greyson looked past him at Pearl, who looked away. She *had* agreed to the transfer of apprenticeship, if the sorceress was willing to take her. Could she make Mrs. Greyson unwilling? How?

"Grey, you can't—" Whatever the sorceress had been about to say was cut off by a question from her husband and quickly forgotten in the business of collecting baggage, acquiring carriages, and loading people and luggage into them.

Pearl and Grey rode back to Albemarle Street with Harry and Elinor, having been expertly managed by Mr. Greyson. Mr. Archaios was permitted in the carriage with the master sorceress since he also resided at Brown's. They would meet at Harry's tomorrow morning to go inspect the ragged-edged dead zones.

Pearl didn't even pretend an interest in getting out of the carriage at Harry's to go through to their rooms. When Elinor asked if she was coming, Pearl answered only, "No."

"You should," Grey said, but only after the carriage was moving the few yards down the street to Grey's house.

"No," she said. "I shouldn't." And she kissed him.

For the first time, Pearl kissed Grey, instead of waiting, hoping he would give her what she craved. If she was responsible for controlling her own desires, then couldn't she also be responsible for asking for what she wanted? For climbing into his lap in order to take it?

The carriage stopped before the kiss developed to her satisfaction, and she had to remove herself from Grey's lap. His reaction was quite satisfactory, however. He leapt from the carriage and swept her inside the house, up the stairs, and into his bed before she could catch her breath. It eliminated all possibility—and capability—of thought. Precisely what she wanted.

They stripped each other bare as Pearl continued to reach forth and take, stripping away civilization with their clothing. She reveled in the expanse of his golden skin, rubbing herself against him until he rolled atop her with a growl.

"Mine." He thrust, taking possession of her.

Pearl wrapped her legs around him, surrounding him, drawing him deeper inside her. "Mine."

"Yours," he agreed, beginning the drive toward their mutual pleasure.

Words were gone as her body demanded its due and the magic rose. It always did, bright and sensual and— Pearl wallowed in it, stroked it over and through Grey as she rose up that long, wonderful climb with him until it burst in glorious explosion. She cried out, or Grey did. She couldn't always separate them one from the other at that moment, just as she couldn't separate the magic afterward. It didn't seem to matter, so she let it settle where it wished.

"Monday," he murmured into her ear. "Seven more days until you're my wife."

"Monday," Pearl agreed, half asleep. She'd resigned herself to it now. He'd almost convinced her it would work.

THE DAY TURNED out gray and cloudy, but without either rain or fog, and warmer because of it. Pearl wore pink today in hopes of brightening things up. Magister Greyson brought all of her students along in their own oversized carriage. The students wore a sort of uniform, Pearl realized. White scholars' robes served as aprons, over plain pale pink dresses.

The boys at the academy wore uniforms and robes—in black or blue or green—so uniforms for the Female Magician's School made sense. Pearl supposed she would have to get one. She was only grateful they didn't make her ride with the other students.

Harry spent the ride through London explaining to the Greysons what he and Elinor had observed during the months of their absence, about the damaged and destroyed machines and the ragged boundary, and their theory that the murderer's intent in calling the demon was to somehow affect the dead zones.

"Have all the broken pieces been retrieved?" Magister Greyson looked musingly at the dead zone. The other magisters and their apprentices, and Mr. Archaios, of course, stood alongside her, with her students a step behind and between, so they could see past the taller gentlemen. Mr. Greyson stood just behind and to one side of his wife, an embodied shadow, as if he had always been there and always would be.

"We think so," Harry said. "Pearl went an' got a few samples for us, right after, but she couldn't stay long, an' she ain't 'ad time to look for us again. Don't suppose as you an' Jax would be willin' to look?"

"Of course. Then we must wall it up." Mrs. Greyson paused and tipped her head to think. "It might be interesting to see the demon's reaction upon encountering our wall."

"Interesting, perhaps." Grey's expression was pained. "But not something I would care to observe personally."

Nor would Pearl, not after Grey's description of demons. She tightened her grip on his hand.

"Ladies." The sorceress was removing her gloves as she turned to speak to her students. "You will accompany me and Mr. Greyson into the dead zone. We've talked about the zones, but I want you to know how it feels."

"I know how it feels, mum," Fiona, the oldest student, said with a thick Scottish accent. "There's one in Glasgow I've walked through."

"Nevertheless, we will all go. The instant any of you begins to feel short of breath or dizzy, you will please return to wait with the gentlemen." Magister Greyson turned to look at Pearl. "Miss Parkin, if you will take Magister Carteret's hand, I believe he might enjoy a look at the scenery from a clear perspective. No gloves, of course."

Exchanging a wondering look with Grey, Pearl removed her fur-lined gloves while he did the same. The lovely warmth spread between them as it always did when they clasped hands, and they walked together into the dead zone, following the Greysons and the other students.

Harry gave direction from the boundary, asking them to poke under rubble or look behind obstacles. The students spread out, but remained near the boundary while Grey and Pearl, the sorceress and her husband penetrated deeper and deeper into the dead zone. One by one, the students left the dead zone and still Pearl and Grey explored with the other matched pair.

"We haven't seen any machines," Jax Greyson said. "I wonder why."

"There's no machines," Grey shouted back to Harry. "Theories?"

"Maybe they withdrew because of danger," Archaios called back.

"Maybe so." Pearl pointed deeper into the zone. "Look."

A trio of machines stood as if at sentry posts, in a gap between collapsed buildings. They bristled with various grinding, stabbing, slicing instruments made mostly of metal. The rest of the machines had a motley composition, but their aggressive pieces were sharp and hard.

"Perhaps it is time we returned," Magister Greyson murmured.

"What?" Her husband pretended shock so obviously even Pearl who did not know him could see it. "Amanusa, showing discretion?"

She laughed and bumped him with her shoulder. "I can. When I have a good enough reason. I'd rather my newest student not get bit on her first deep excursion."

"So I am not reason enough, am I?"

The sorceress stopped and touched his cheek, gazing up at him with eyes so filled with love it made Pearl's fill with tears. "You are my reason for everything," she said, loud enough that Pearl heard, but only just.

The sorceress rose on her toes and kissed her husband on the mouth, right there in the middle of the dead zone. When the kiss ended—a kiss so sweet and tender, the emotion in it grabbed Pearl by the throat—he was looking back at her with the same love, great enough to move mountains or—or to seal off dead zones.

Pearl yearned. Her heart ached for that kind of love, for Grey to love her . . . as much as she loved him. She *loved him*. Finally she admitted it to herself. She had fallen in love with Grey Carteret.

Grey cleared his throat, loudly and ostentatiously, kicking the rubble around making even more noise as he advanced toward the alley where the others were waiting. Pearl, holding tight to his hand, went with him. The newlywed couple shook off their besotted fugue and continued along their own path, side by side now with conjurer and apprentice.

"This is astonishing," Grey said in blatant distraction. "I'd have taken an apprentice long ago if I had known it would convey such advantages. Why, all the magicians will be wanting one now." He brought Pearl's hand to his mouth and kissed it, his smile warming her through. They were almost at the edge of the boundary, where she would have to let him go.

Magister Greyson laughed, bright as silver bells. "It's not because she's your apprentice, Grey. You can roam the dead zone like this because you are her familiar."

"What?" He stopped cold. Cold all over, his face hard and set. Pearl shivered with his cold. What had happened?

The master sorceress turned, stopping beside them, a slight smile on her face. "It's because you're her familiar." She frowned. "But—you must have known, Grey. You had to agree to it, or it could never have happened."

He was shaking his head no, his whole body shaking. He threw her hand away from him and immediately staggered. Pearl cried out, grabbed for his hand, as shaken as he, as if she'd been picked up and flung about and—and tossed aside.

"No!" Grey pushed her as he stumbled for the dead zone's boundary.

Pearl fell, cracked her head against a rock in the pile he pushed her into. "Help him!" she cried. "Elinor, Fiona, *help!*"

Her head didn't hurt nearly as much as her heart, her whole stunned self. The women and girls rushed into the dead zone and helped Grey the last few feet out of the deadly no-magic area.

The Greysons appeared and blocked Pearl's view, lifting her to her feet and assisting her back to the others. Grey was gone when they arrived.

22

"I GUESS WE ain't buildin' our boundary wall this mornin'." Harry peered down the alley after Grey, hands propped on his hips. "Bein' as we just lost our conjurer."

"What happened?" Elinor took Pearl's hands in hers and peered into her eyes, then felt her head where she'd hit it.

Magister Greyson sighed. "It seems we have a bit of a difficulty to sort out, and Magister Carteret did not react well to learning of it."

"Indeed he did not," Archaios said, full of affront. "No matter the provocation, a gentleman does not treat a lady so."

Pearl's heart twisted and she swallowed down a sob. "He didn't mean it. Although Grey would be the first to tell you he is no gentleman, it's not so." She looked over Elinor's head at the tall sorceress. "Did I really—? How is it possible?"

The magister nodded, sad and very gentle. "True, yes. How? That is what we must sort out. You did not know?"

"I had no idea."

"No idea of what?" Harry demanded, hands still belligerently propped.

"We're not quite sure," the sorceress said, earning Pearl's undying gratitude.

She couldn't bear for anyone to know how stupid and careless and ignorant and—she couldn't think of enough words bad enough for what she'd done. But . . . *how*?

How had she made Grey her familiar? What exactly did it mean? What happened now? And just how angry was he?

"Come." Magister Greyson took Pearl's elbow and urged her back down the alley toward the carriages. "I trust you gentlemen to see my students safely back to the hotel," she said. "Miss Parkin and I have much to discuss in private. Guild secrets."

"I didn't mean to do it," Pearl said when she was enclosed in the carriage with the master sorceress and her husband.

Grey hadn't taken any of the carriages. He was on foot in Bethnal Green, and she was worried about him.

"I don't even know what a familiar is, or how it works or—" She broke off when the magister shifted seats to sit beside her and laid a hand over Pearl's, twisted together in her lap.

"Pearl," the sorceress said, "I will call you Pearl, and you will call us Amanusa and Jax, because you are engaged to marry our friend and cousin—"

Pearl groaned. Would he still want to marry her? She didn't think so.

"And therefore you are also our friend. If you have already ridden the blood, you are a sorceress and may be assisting me in teaching and testing the others, so our relationship is already that of colleagues." Amanusa Greyson went on as if Pearl hadn't made any noise. "As colleagues," she said, "we must work together to discover how you have done what you have done."

"I never—"

"I know." The other woman squeezed Pearl's hands comfortingly. "But it has happened and we have to begin with that and move on. We must understand how such a thing happened by accident, so that it will not happen again to someone else."

Pearl took a deep calming breath, which didn't seem to calm much, and squared her shoulders. "You are right."

"First, have you and Grey exchanged blood?"

"Yes, but it wasn't very much. We swore our contract in blood, mixed it when Grey was in jail."

"In jail?" Jax Greyson folded his arms as he grinned. "Seems we've missed quite an adventure, Amanusa, my love."

"Is that all?" His wife ignored him.

"No. There was the time I caught a splinter in the warehouse where Angus Galloway was killed. And when he gave me my lancet. And when I rode his blood."

"It was Grey's blood you rode? That was your first time?"

"Yes. It seemed safer. Were we wrong?"

"No." The sorceress frowned as she thought. "No, it was certainly safer. But since your blood was already in him, and the first mixing was direct . . . Have you worked magic together?"

"That's how we laid the ghosts." Pearl described the visit to the morgue and the magic they'd worked so often since. "We've been able to do a great deal more together than either of us ever could alone."

Amanusa smiled. It was easier to think of her as Amanusa instead of Mrs. Greyson. Greyson was Grey's name. "That is the nature of familiars," she said. "To increase the magician's power. Both of them, if both are magicians."

Pearl glanced at Jax, who shook his head.

"I'm head blind," he said. "Got no magic sense at all, save what Amanusa shares with me. Lucky for me, she inherited me from the last sorceress, or she'd be shopping for a familiar among the great and powerful."

"Never." Amanusa gave her husband another of those looks.

Pearl studied the pattern of the lace trimming her skirt, too uncomfortable with the intensity of emotion to watch.

The sound of Amanusa clearing her throat had Pearl looking up. "This question will seem indelicate and definitely impertinent, but . . . Have you and Grey . . . had sexual intercourse?"

Ears burning as if they'd burst into flame, Pearl nodded. Then she shook her head. "We made love," she said. "It's not the same. Not that I have any personal knowledge of that, but—"

Amanusa was patting her hand again. "Yes, dear. I know very well." She frowned. "But, do you mean— Was Grey your first?"

Her face had to be as red as her ears. Pearl threw a mortified glance at Amanusa's husband, who pretended he hadn't heard a thing, and wasn't even there besides. She nodded, sitting up straight as she did. She didn't regret it, and she wouldn't be ashamed of it.

"Mmm." Amanusa's nod was her only response.

"What?" Pearl tried not to demand answers, but she needed them so desperately. "Was that bad? Was that what did it? But . . . *sex*?"

"Sex is as much a part of sorcery as blood or saliva," Amanusa said. "Consider—sorcery is worked with the human body and its various bits and pieces. Sex is very much a part of being human. A powerful part."

"Oh." Horror widened her eyes, made her heart race, her voice fade to a whisper. "Oh, my God—"

"When did it happen?" the sorceress asked.

Pearl told her.

Amanusa patted her hand. "Then that did not make Grey your familiar. Rose Bowers's body was only discovered last week. Grey was already your familiar at that point, or well on his way. But it bound you closer. *Much* closer, since blood was shed."

"It wasn't his fault," Pearl said quickly.

"It's not yours, either."

"Yes. Yes, it is. I'm the one who insisted we seal our agreement in blood. I blackmailed him into taking me as his apprentice. He wouldn't have done it if I hadn't threatened to leave him in jail without a way to get word to his friends." Tears rose, choking off her words, crowding into her eyes, insisting on release. They were very insistent.

"Oh, my poor dear." Amanusa put her arms around Pearl. "Do you love him so very much?"

"I di-didn't want to." Pearl fought valiantly against weeping. "I couldn't help it. He is so beautiful. And kind and honorable—for all he pretends not to be, he is. B-but he doesn't love me—" She did manage to keep from wailing. "He's in love with his familiar spirit. Or you."

"No, he's not in love with me." Amanusa's voice held amusement. "He is a great romantic, so I think for a time he fancied the idea of unrequited love, but no. Grey has never been in love with me. I know how it feels to be loved."

Pearl didn't look up from the white-clad shoulder where she began to win her war on weeping. She didn't have to, to know the sorceress and her husband were once more gazing at each other. "Grey said you were disgustingly besotted," she muttered, sitting up to wipe her eyes.

She looked up to see Amanusa's shocked expression and hurried on. "It's not—it's just that— It is *so* wonderful to see. It is such a beautiful thing, and . . . well, when one does not have that kind of love in one's own life, and one wishes that one did, and— It aches to yearn so."

Amanusa exchanged a quick glance with Jax and cleared her throat. "I am— While I do not know Grey's relationship with his familiar spirit, I am sure that he

does care for you or he would not have been so angry."
She hesitated briefly. "Is this spirit his familiar, as we
are speaking of familiars, or is it a different sort of relationship?"

Pearl blinked. "I don't know. What *is* a sorcerer's familiar?"

"Well . . ." Amanusa seemed perplexed at having to
explain. "I have never been without one. Jax taught me
sorcery and brought me out of Romania, where I was
living, to England. He has been at my side from the very
beginning."

"But not always your familiar," he said, apparently
deciding to become present in the carriage again.

"Yes, but what does a familiar do?" Pearl asked.
"What is it—he—*for*?"

"Holding magic, mostly," Jax said. "Like a walking,
talking magical power coal bin."

"Oh dear." Pearl felt faint. "Grey wouldn't like that."

"I don't see why not," Amanusa retorted. "As I understand it, a familiar who is also a magician, as Grey obviously is, can access the power as easily as the sorceress
who has given it to him, or her. Familiars do not have to
be male, though most of them have been.

"Sorcery, being human body magic, must be stored in
blood and bone and flesh. Yes, magic from innocent blood
does hover, waiting to be used, waiting for the proper
blood and bone to attach to. But all the rest—it abides inside you. And me, and Jax and Grey and everyone else in
existence. A sorcerer is simply the one with the ability to
call it out and use it. A familiar expands the sorcerer's
power by sharing her magic."

"Because I have no magic talent of my own," Jax said,
"I have nothing to share with Amanusa in return, but as
her familiar, my blood is very nearly as powerful as hers
when used in spells. And I am able to work some small
spells on my own because of that. But since Grey does
have magic . . ."

"I can see spirits and lay ghosts." Pearl thought she began to understand. "What about Grey? What benefit does this have for him? Anything?"

"He walked through the dead zone, did he not?" Jax raised a craggy brow. He was handsome enough in a rough-carved way, Pearl supposed, but she didn't know how anyone could prefer it to Grey's refined beauty. Amanusa must have been in love with Jax before she ever met Grey. Love is blind, after all.

"The familiar acts as a power source to the sorceress," Amanusa said. "The sorceress also feeds power to the familiar, creating a power loop, providing the magic necessary to sustain an extended journey through a zone without magic. It's the only way we've been able to explain it so far. We can't stay in a dead zone forever, but we can survive several days."

"So what do we do now?" Pearl asked.

Amanusa drew in a deep breath and let it out in a long sigh. "I suppose that depends on what you and Grey want to do."

Pearl loved Grey. She wanted to be with him. She didn't understand precisely what the familiar bond was or what it did, but she understood enough to know that she truly didn't want to give it up. But she wouldn't hold Grey if he wanted it gone. One did not hurt what one loved. "Is there a way to undo it?"

The look Amanusa exchanged with Jax held painful knowledge this time, along with the love. Pearl knew the answer before Amanusa said yes.

"Then, whatever Grey wants."

HARRY SPENT THE rest of the morning organizing another conjurer for building the barrier at the dead zone. He collected two—George Meade, and an instructor from the academy, Colin Bennett. Which meant that a very large group assembled outside the dead zone that afternoon.

Since Amanusa brought all of her students, Bennett asked to bring an equal number of conjury students, and Harry thought that didn't seem to be fair to the alchemy school, so seven of their top students came as well.

Elinor was the only wizardry apprentice present. She was the wizard who had helped build the first dead zone barrier in Paris. The wizard's magister, Cranshaw, had forbidden all students and guild members from taking part. Two master wizards, from the total of twelve in all England, defied their magister to attend anyway. One was James Ferguson. The other was Sir William Stanwyck, head of the Magician's Council, and so only technically under the magister's command.

They had so many bodies present, and the zone was so large, that Amanusa asked everyone to volunteer a little blood for the spell, but only if they truly wished to. Everyone did. Pearl was thrilled to be asked to help draw it, after Amanusa inspected her lancet and observed her technique. It did not ease the pain in her heart, but it provided a grand distraction.

Harry divided the group into two sets of spellworkers to go each way around the huge zone and meet in the middle. Pearl was named to the group with Harry as alchemist and Elinor as wizard, along with the conjury teacher. That way, each group had a magician who'd done the spell before.

The spell, as Amanusa explained it to Pearl, was similar to the protective warding spells she'd already done, only with blood rather than with saliva, and with the other magics mixed in. Blood would allow them to build it higher and stretch it all the way around the zone. And blood would bind the magic together, mixed with the earth and water of alchemy, and painted over conjury's sigils with wizardry's leafy green twigs, which would then be planted to create a sympathetic palisade.

There was a bit of a kerfluffle at the beginning, when the conjurers couldn't get their spirits to cooperate even with the bloody slurry painted over the sigils, which Amanusa claimed had solved the problem before. Pearl didn't want to put herself forward. She was only an apprentice, and not of conjury, but she was getting cold with all the standing about. She squeezed through the horde of oversized boys to see what the trouble was.

"Where's your safety sigil?" she asked.

"What?" The conjury instructor, Bennett, sounded offended.

"She's Carteret's apprentice," Meade said. "Can't help but collect conjury lore." He swiftly drew the sigil, showing the spirit curled up safe between walls, and Pearl daubed on a bit more of the solution from her bucket, identical with that in the bucket Jax Greyson carried.

The warding magic settled into place with a soundless *thunk,* and those who heard and felt it broke into cheers. "That's done it," Harry said. "Let's get it built round the rest."

Amanusa's party went north, Harry's went south, stopping every few yards to draw sigils, plant leafy sticks, and paint on blood, earth, and water as they spoke the words of the spell. Students were invited to take a turn to draw, to paint, to speak. As Harry said, the more who knew how, the better.

When the groups met again on the eastern side of the zone, Pearl was exhausted, but it was a good exhaustion. The kind after hard work, creating something useful. Better, it had kept her from thinking.

The students were dismissed, to be escorted back to house and hotel by Bennett and Fiona Watson, who acted as a prefect-matron to the younger sorcery students. Pearl almost went with them, her status up in the air. She didn't even know if she was still engaged, though she doubted it.

Elinor insisted she come to Harry's for a celebratory dinner with Elinor and Harry, Archaios, and the Greysons.

Even Sir William, Meade, Ferguson, and Mr. Bennett were invited, though they all declined, claiming prior engagements or obligations.

Grey found them there, gathered in the drawing room after the meal, still talking over the day's success.

"Carteret," Harry drawled. "Glad you could join us. Bit late for food, but you can 'ave a spot o' tea." He waved a hand at the tea tray.

"Thank you, but no." Grey bowed, more formal than Pearl had ever seen him.

He still wore the clothes he'd worn to the dead zone this morning, rumpled and a bit grimy around the edges. He appeared to have lost his hat somewhere, for his hair was damp and curling in utter disarray. Pearl wanted to take him home, dry him off, and warm him up. But he wouldn't look at her.

"If I might—I need to speak with the sorcerers. In private." Grey bowed again, not even quite looking at Amanusa.

Harry climbed to his feet. "It's late. Not time for doin' business—"

"It's all right, Harry." Amanusa rose, giving Pearl a smile. "Better to resolve this sooner than later."

Pearl dreaded the encounter, but putting it off wouldn't ease the dread. Better to rip the bandage off and suffer the pain all at once so she could begin the getting-over-it.

"May we use your library?" Amanusa asked Harry.

He made a "feel free" gesture. "Might as well. Everyone else does." He sat and watched the drama, not even pretending to avert his eyes. No one ever claimed Harry a gentleman, either.

Pearl stood. So did Jax.

Grey glared at him. "You're not invited."

"Where my wife goes, I go," Jax said calmly.

"This is a matter for magicians," Grey growled.

Jax's voice came harder. "Where my sorceress goes, I go."

Grey's expression filled with a black rage that made Pearl shiver. He didn't try to hide it.

"Magister Carteret." Amanusa's voice cut through the male posturing. "You asked for privacy?"

Grey shifted his glare to Amanusa, then he backed a few steps out of the doorway, and bowed their way past him. Pearl followed Amanusa, Jax falling in behind her. She felt a great coward for being grateful they protected her between them. She deserved Grey's wrath. She shouldn't be hiding from it. But she wouldn't weep in front of him. She wasn't so weak as that.

Too bad her eyes were exactly that weak. She wiped them as they entered Harry's cluttered study, hoping Grey at least would not notice.

"Well you should weep, madam," he said, crushing that hope. "All of your scheming has come to naught. I have seen through your manipulation and I am having none of it. *None.*"

"I didn't know—" she began.

"Do not lie to me!" Grey snarled. "You planned every step of the way. You spied on me in the streets, outside the council hall, outside my home, and you even followed me to the opera, by God! And when the opportunity came, you pounced. Did you manipulate that as well? Draw me into the street so I was vulnerable to your plots?"

"No," Pearl cried, but Grey wasn't listening. He obviously heard nothing but the dark constructs of his wounded and suspicious heart.

"Insisting on a blood oath while I was trapped in jail—that's when you did it. Bound me as familiar." He turned on her, roared at her. *"Isn't it?"*

Pearl flinched, but made herself stand up straight under his attack. She might weep, but she wouldn't cower. "I didn't—"

"You did!" Grey shouted, his hand raised to strike. She didn't flinch.

"Greyson Carteret!" Jax's booming voice brought him up short.

He flung himself away from her. "It was *all* a lie, wasn't it?"

"No." She had to keep saying it, even if he didn't hear.

"Manipulated into sharing blood oath. Pushed into giving up my blood so you could bind me that much closer, claiming you needed to learn to ride." He put on a show, waving his arms, making faces to mock her and his own behavior. "And then, grasping for the greater prize, you seduced me into taking your supposed virginity. Tell me—" He rounded on her with such ferocity Amanusa jumped. Pearl did not. She wouldn't.

"Tell me, Parkin. Just how many times have you lost your virginity?"

"Once," she said, forcing her voice to clarity and firmness.

"Liar!" He pounded Harry's desk, and a book thumped to the floor.

"Grey." Amanusa interrupted his tirade this time. "That is quite enough."

"Oh, no, it is not *nearly* enough. She has trapped me." He threw an accusing hand toward Pearl. "Enslaved me and made me into her tool."

"She hasn't." Jax's voice was calm but forceful. "I've been enslaved and I've been a familiar. There's a difference. *You* are a familiar."

"You—" Grey shook his head. "You're besotted. You don't know—"

"I do. Amanusa is not my first sorceress."

"How do you know she hasn't manipulated—"

"Enough." Pearl walked to stand between the men. "You have the right to abuse me, but they have done nothing—"

"You see?" Grey's hand barely missed striking Pearl

when he pointed, but she had the rhythm of it now. She would not flinch. "She admits it. *She admits what she has done.*"

"I did it," she said. "But I did not know I was doing it. I never meant this." Finally, she got it all out without interruption. She wanted him to hear it, even if—

"Liar."

Even if he did not believe it.

"Enough," Amanusa said it this time. "We are done with the accusations. You are shocked and angry and hurt, and you are not thinking clearly."

"Oh, I think—" He was pointing again, accusing again.

"We are done." The startling power in Amanusa's voice cut him off. "It happened. You are her familiar. Begin there and move on. What happens next?"

"Undo it." Grey pulled a sheaf of papers from his inner coat pocket and ripped them across. Her apprenticeship contract. "No more apprentice. No more fiancée. No more familiar. I want none of it. I want none of *you*. I will not be manipulated. *I* choose. No one else. *I do.*"

Tears poured down Pearl's cheeks. She couldn't stop them, wouldn't wipe them away. She would stand up straight and take whatever punishment he deemed necessary. She knew the truth, that while her actions had created this mess, she had never intended any harm.

"You did choose, Grey." Amanusa fitted her lancet to her finger. "You chose again and again, or it never could have happened. But—" She held up her hand to forestall another outburst. "You are in no mood to hear the truth now."

"I want it done and over with." He thrust his hand at Amanusa, offering up a vein.

She took his hand and stabbed her lancet into his thumb, then turned to Pearl and beckoned. Pearl presented her hand and received the same treatment.

"Call forth your blood," Amanusa said. "Cast his blood from you. You must renounce all that is between you."

Pearl took a deep breath. *Blood of my blood, return to me.* She opened her magic senses as she spoke the words inside her head. No use betraying guild secrets at this point. A drop of blood welled up from the puncture wound on Grey's thumb. He turned his hand and let it fall on the palm-size square of flimsy paper Jax produced. A second drop swelled.

"Cast out his blood." Amanusa sounded a little more urgent.

"I cast the blood of Greyson Carteret from me." Pearl reached for the magic, to pull it out with the blood. Her thumb hurt as the first drop of his blood oozed from her. Odd that it hadn't bled before now. Jax handed her a paper square of her own. A second drop welled up. Had she taken so much of Grey's blood?

She could see the magic shimmer as it poured out of him, surrounding him. She could not hold so much. "What do I do with the magic?"

"Oh my . . ." Amanusa's eyes went wide, then they narrowed on Grey. "Just how many times have you made love?"

"I fail to see how that's any of your affair." Grey came near to shouting.

Jax interrupted him. "Sorcery is sex, too."

"Not quite a guild secret," Amanusa said with an exaggerated wince "But we'd rather you didn't repeat it."

Grey's face remained flushed, but it seemed more with embarrassment than with anger now. "It was—"

Amanusa waved his answer aside. "No, I've decided I don't want to know. Too bad you weren't there for the dead zone barrier. We could have used this in the wall."

"Can't you take it?" Pearl asked her. "So it doesn't go to waste?"

"It's your magic. Yours and Grey's. Only you can use it."

"How? What can I do with it?" She felt on the edge of panic. All that beautiful magic. She couldn't just let it . . . die.

"Give it away," Jax said. "It's life magic. Send it out to give life."

Amanusa found a wry smile. "And hope that no one knows to blame you when there's a bumper crop of babies in nine months."

The thought pleased her. Pearl took a breath and when she blew it out again, she sent the magic out. "Go," she whispered. "Do good. Bring joy. Give life."

It vanished instantly, as if some great thirst drank it down in a single gulp.

"Oh." Amanusa blinked. "My. That was fast."

"Was it not supposed to do that?" Pearl worried.

"I have no idea. I've always had a use for our magic."

Grey cleared his throat pointedly. "Have you finished?"

Pearl looked with her extra sense. The blood had left him, but now that it was gone, she could see a—a binding still churning between them. A glowing construct made of magic tied them together, but it twisted and roiled as if disturbed. Unhappy.

"It is not just the blood that binds you," Amanusa said. "You are a magician in your own right, Grey. You helped make this. You must help break it."

"I am a conjurer," he snapped out.

"As the familiar to a powerful sorceress, you are more than that," Amanusa retorted. "Look at the magic. You must both act to undo it. You must renounce each other."

Grey's lip curled in a snarl as he rushed to speak. "I renounce you, Pearl Elizabeth Parkin. You are nothing to me. Less than nothing."

With his mind, he reached forth and sliced through the glowing magic. He sliced through Pearl's heart, or maybe her soul, and she cried out with the pain. Struggling to stand upright, to make her voice clear and strong, she spoke. "I renounce you, Greyson George Arthur William Victor Carteret."

"Finally, you get my name right," Grey sneered.

Pearl choked down the flare of pain. "You are nothing to me, as I am nothing to you." The pain faded as the searching stump of magic sank back inside her. It seemed to mourn its loss, but it no longer sought its missing half.

"Is it done?" Grey demanded.

"Can't you tell? Can't you see the magic?" Amanusa folded her arms and glowered at him.

He glowered right back. "I am a conjurer. I don't see sorcery."

"You did," Amanusa said. "For a while. Didn't you?"

"I'd rather stand on my own magic than be owned as a slave," Grey retorted.

"*Not* slave," Jax said.

But Grey was slamming out the library door, not listening.

23

"DO YOU WANT to come back to the hotel with us?" Amanusa asked. "I'm sure we can find room with the—"

Pearl shook her head. "Elinor will be expecting me. Did you mean it about helping you teach?"

"I meant it." Amanusa gave Pearl a quick hug. "I'll want to observe your riding of the blood first, and—I ride the blood of all my students. To be sure of their character."

"Particularly mine." A crooked smile flashed across Pearl's lips. "Given all Grey's accusations."

"I do not doubt the truth of what you have told me." Amanusa's English took on the faintest of foreign accents.

"Still, it's best to be sure." Pearl smiled again. "*I* want to be sure."

Elinor knocked on the door left open by Grey's explosive departure and put her head in. "I only wanted to tell Pearl I was on my way home, if you want to walk with me."

Pearl's smile felt as battered as she did. "I would like that, yes. Amanusa has asked me to help her teach."

Elinor beamed her approval. "We must talk about the Female Magician's School I have in mind. For sorcerers *and* wizards."

"Tomorrow." Jax took his wife's arm. "It's too late tonight for that talk."

"Yes, tomorrow," Amanusa agreed. "After I take the girls to the library."

"To the books." Elinor nodded her understanding. "Until tomorrow, then."

THE PARADE OF sorcery students into the academy library had boys, and grown men who acted like boys, gawking and whispering. Pearl was glad that awful Magister Cranshaw wasn't there as they went in, though she had no doubt he would be present when they departed. Someone was bound to carry tales, to watch the fireworks, if nothing else.

All of Amanusa's pupils opened the sorcery book easily, save one. Amanusa told her to try the other books, and when she opened the wizardry book, Elinor had her first wizardry student.

The students checked out a large pile of sorcery books and a wizardry tome or two—of which Pearl felt envious, because they were written in modern English. Elinor departed then to inspect prospective school buildings, while all the students trouped past Cranshaw's gauntlet back to the hotel for reading and study. Pearl went aside with Amanusa for her tests.

She felt peculiar while Amanusa rode her blood. Not because she sensed anything of the ride itself, but she knew it was occurring. Now and again, it seemed she could feel the magic stirring about inside her. After the spell was concluded and Amanusa called back her blood, the master sorceress pronounced herself satisfied.

"You're a little underweight." She set the strip of rice paper with her recalled blood alight in a candle flame and dropped it to burn in a ceramic dish meant for cigar ash. "I don't know whether its due to too much magic use or the lingering effects of your earlier life, but—" She fixed Pearl with a stern eye. "Eat. None of this non-sense about ladies' delicate appetites."

"Yes, Magister." Pearl dipped her head.

"Now shall we see how well you ride, yes?" Amanusa spoke English like a native, which Pearl had been told she was on her father's side, but sometimes hints of her mother's Romanian came through.

"Of course." Pearl nodded again. "Who?"

She had assumed she would ride the sorceress and was startled when Jax came forward with a fresh pot of tea on a tray. He'd done such a good job of making him-self unobtrusive, she'd forgotten his presence.

Amanusa poured. "You will ride Jax. I will attend to ensure correct procedure and safety. You should see how a healthy body works, so you can better understand the healing spells."

The ride went well, Pearl easily plucking out the infor-mation Amanusa asked for—Jax's memory of their first meeting. That brought on more looks and smiles. Pearl fled, returning to her flat for study. Though Amanusa did take the time to mention that Pearl had qualified as a full-fledged sorceress, and might be ready for her master's test by the new year. That was for later, after the murderer was caught.

Over the next several days, Pearl studied sorcery. Sometimes Amanusa tutored her. Sometimes Jax explained magic to the both of them. Sometimes Pearl taught the younger girls. Always, she read. And missed Grey.

She endured the ache of missing him, trying not to be angry with him for his refusal to listen to her explanations, but she wasn't terribly successful. Yes, she had done it, but she hadn't *meant* to. Didn't that mean anything? Something?

She also missed I-Branch, which surprised her until she realized that I-Branch had been a huge part of her life. She missed going to the office every day and knowing how the investigations were going. She missed talking to the Briganti and brainstorming theories. Grey didn't want her there, and she wouldn't intrude. Yet. Amanusa was her magic-master now, and she had plans for the justice magic. Pearl would wait on her magister's timetable. She was doing just fine.

On the day that would have been her wedding day, Pearl discovered she wasn't doing as fine as all that. Grey had published the announcement of their broken engagement in the newspaper. She was reading the morning papers over breakfast in the private parlor at Brown's that Amanusa had taken over for her school. Pearl didn't live with the other students, since she was teaching now, but she ate with them.

Her eyes went right to the item in question, a plain, stark notice of fact. Agony stabbed through her heart and she doubled over with the pain. Harsh, desperate noises echoed around her.

"Breathe," she heard Amanusa say, and tried it. The air caught on the spear stuck through her, but enough got past that the pain . . . didn't go away. She just breathed around it. Somewhat.

Amanusa held her while she shuddered with the grief. She might have cried. She didn't know. It hurt too much.

They took her away to someone's hotel room, and eventually she slept. When she woke, she felt better. Empty, as if all her emotions had drained out.

Elinor was there and gave her a cup of tea brewed full of magic. It helped, somehow making the pain a little more distant. She would survive.

No, she would do better than that. She would shine.

Not today. But soon.

Two days after the day he did not get manipulated into marriage, Greyson Carteret woke in a foul mood. Exactly as he had every morning for the past week. He woke in a foul mood. He stalked through his day in a foul mood, and he went to bed in a foul mood.

He tried to keep it to himself, but his I-Branch Briganti had begun to evaporate whenever he appeared. They'd never behaved like that before.

His mood began to affect his magic, since his spirits didn't take to being shouted at. He had caused Mary to burst into tears one day last week, and she'd sulked for three more. Not that he blamed her. He had been the beast she called him.

It was all Pearl Parkin's fault.

She could not possibly have broken the spell binding him to her. If she had, he wouldn't miss her. He wouldn't wake in the morning aching for her presence in his bed, in his arms. He wouldn't have to remind himself how she'd stolen his blood and used it to force him to do things he didn't want to do, to feel things he did not want to feel.

His father had tried to control him, to hem him in, clip his wings, and deny the magic singing its silent music in his ears. His mother was the same, always carping about propriety and rank and all those things that didn't matter when the magic whispered its seductive song.

Grey had freed himself of those chains. He would not allow anyone to chain him again. He alone chose his path.

So it infuriated him when he worried, those times he saw Pearl outside Brown's, and saw the circles under her eyes, dark against her pale skin. He would not care. If he did, it was due to her spell. She was at fault. She was the seductress, the manipulator, the liar. She must have deceived Amanusa as well, convincing her the spell was broken.

He would have discussed it with Amanusa, but Pearl seemed to be always at her side. Until Pearl eliminated the lingering remnants of her spell, Grey could not afford to let himself be near her.

He'd thought publishing the announcement of the end of their engagement would help, but when he saw it, printed in black and white, he felt sick.

Sickened by what she'd done to him. How she'd played him for a fool. Not because he missed her. He did not look up from his work to hunt for her presence nearby. He did not listen for her laughter. He did not wonder what she thought. Or if he did, it was her fault, because she'd bespelled him.

On this Wednesday, still wrestling with his foul mood, Grey descended to the I-Branch laboratory in search of his evaporated Briganti. He found the long room invaded by an army in pink skirts and white scholar's robes, brightening its usual stark appearance. Grey's eyes immediately found Pearl in the crowd of identically dressed females, and it ratcheted up his anger. He did not care that she still looked too pale. He would not care.

"What is going on here?" he demanded, far more sharply than he wished.

"Sir—" Duncan began.

"Mr. Duncan was explaining the alchemist's process for deciphering a spell," Amanusa said.

She would be here, wouldn't she? With her students.

"This is the Investigations Branch of the Briganti," he snapped. "Not a schoolroom." He knew he trod dangerous ground, and could not stop himself.

Amanusa stepped forward, her eyes narrowing, almost on a level with his own. "Sorcery is the knife blade of justice. Do you think you can keep us out?"

He was not so foolish as to fail to recognize his peril and step back. "I do not wish to, save for those who practice deceit. I will not admit her."

"Blood never lies." Amanusa stood a little straighter, stared a little harder. "What was done happened without intention."

Bitter laughter found him. "You expect me to believe—"

"I expect you to believe *me*." Amanusa's voice seemed to thunder through the room, though she spoke quietly. Perhaps it only thundered through him. She softened. "You know me, Grey. Have I ever lied to you?"

"No. But she—"

"I have examined her. Do you understand what I am saying? I have seen her mind. I know her heart. There was no manipulation, no intent to deceive."

Grey shook his head, had been all the while she spoke. "She is false to her core. I will not have her—"

Amanusa interrupted him again. "I am magister of the sorcerer's guild. I have spoken the truth of what I have seen and what I know. Pearl Parkin has passed the necessary requirements to be named sorcerer and a member of the guild. She will work with the Briganti as sorceress." She paused and gave Grey an iron-hard look. "Or none of us will. Choose."

Betrayal shuddered through Grey all over again. He had thought Amanusa his friend. How could she turn against him like this?

"Have a care," Jax said quietly, appearing from nowhere at Grey's elbow. "You begin to sound like Cranshaw."

Was he? Shock blew away the sense of betrayal. But it wasn't *sorcery* he hated, or even all sorcerers. Just one.

But Amanusa was correct. As magister and the only master sorceress, she alone determined who would be admitted to the sorcery guild. He had no right to undermine her authority, even if he could.

But Pearl had made him her familiar. She had trapped him, bound him. *Used him.*

How could he ignore that? He could not.

And yet. If he interpreted correctly what Amanusa seemed to be saying . . . "You rode her blood?" he asked quietly. He did not want his underlings to know he had been so easily duped, so completely defeated. But he needed to understand exactly what Amanusa meant.

"Yes."

"You searched her thoughts, her secret heart?"

"Yes. She did not know the things you did together would result in—"

Grey held up a hand to ward off that word. *Familiar.* One use meaning comfort, another meaning enslavement. "Are you saying she did it by *accident*? We, what, fell into a barrel of magical tar and got stuck together?"

Amanusa sighed. "Essentially, yes."

Grey's lips pressed together, thinning, holding back the words and anger wanting out. He did trust Amanusa. They did need the sorcery. But—

"All right," he said. "But keep her away from me."

He turned and stalked away, his emotions churning violently. He sensed Mary peek in and shy away again. He wouldn't come near himself, either, if he had a choice, and it enraged him all over again. It was all because of Pearl Parkin.

She *had* to have left some of her spell intact. Almost, he turned around to go back and demand answers from Amanusa, but she had already forced his hand once today. He could not endure being made to back down again. Not for another day or two.

Amanusa and her students would be around and about I-Branch. He could discuss it with her later.

Grey had not realized how difficult it would be, to see Pearl so close at hand day after day. Every time he saw her, a shuddering lightning bolt of desire slammed into his body with an *I want that, I need that,* and an eternity passed before his reasoning mind could beat it back into submission. When he reminded himself of her betrayal, his lower self would retort *I don't care. She is mine.* It would not be persuaded that he did not want her. And that infuriated him.

His Briganti learned to evaporate faster.

Pearl obviously knew to avoid him. No doubt Amanusa had told her so, after his capitula—after their agreement. When he did see her, Pearl was always with two or three other students, which made it doubly hard once he decided on confrontation. She had to remove *all* of her spell.

The week wore away into the weekend without change. Though they had proved to their satisfaction that the same man had murdered Angus Galloway and Rose Bowers, they still did not know who that was. Nor had they discovered the location of his new workroom. And Grey had not managed to corner Pearl alone.

On Sunday, he resorted to watching through his front parlor window for her to pass by on the street. Not all the students attended church service, but Pearl always did.

Grey believed. He was a conjurer. How could he not believe? But he wasn't good at communal things like Sunday service. Especially in his current state. He didn't particularly want to hear what God had to say to him, which was probably a sign, but he ignored it. He sat in his parlor and watched.

She was not in the first cluster of females arrayed in flower-bright colors walking past his house back to

Brown's. Nor was she one of the second pair. They weren't sorcery students at all, but neighbors. Finally, when he began to despair of her appearance, she came strolling slowly along with one of the younger students.

Grey was out his front door and down the steps in an instant. He caught Pearl's arm and held on tight enough so she couldn't break free. "I must speak with you."

He might have encouraged her toward the house a trifle forcefully, but Pearl didn't resist.

"Miss Parkin!" the other girl cried. "Shall I fetch the magister?"

"No, no." Pearl couldn't break free of him. He wasn't sure she tried. "Tell Mrs. Greyson I have stopped at Magister Carteret's house to speak with him. She is not to worry. I am perfectly fine."

Grey dragged her up the stairs, into the house, and shut the door before it occurred to him to wonder. If she came willingly into his house, did that mean something? Was this all part of her continuing plot to make him miss her so she could—?

"Well?" Pearl had less patience than he did, and he had almost none. "What did you want to talk about?"

"Is this your plan?" He stared at her with narrow-eyed suspicion. "Did you *want* to come in and talk?"

She threw up her hands, breaking his hold. "*There is no plan.* There never was. I have never had any plan, except to learn magic, and I don't see how you can fault me for that when you were exactly the same when you were my age. Exactly. I've heard the things you did then.

"If you don't believe me, then believe Amanusa. She rode my blood. She poked and pried into every dark corner I have. She didn't do it because of you. She rides the blood of every one of her apprentice candidates, to see what sort of person we are. And she named me sorceress." She planted her hands on her hips and got right up in his face.

"There wasn't, isn't, and never will be any plot to trap you into anything. All right?" Pearl was nearly shouting by the time she finished.

It made Grey's entire body quiver. Pearl in a passion had always done that to him, but shouldn't be doing it still. "Then why do I feel like this?" he almost shouted back.

"Like what?" She didn't give an inch. It was not admirable. It was annoying.

"Like—" How could he explain without sounding weak? But it was a weakness she created. "I still want you. I miss you. I shouldn't." He scowled. "You must not have broken the spell properly, the one that made me your—" He waved a hand, unable to say the word.

She shook her head at him. "The binding is broken, utterly. Amanusa swore it. It doesn't take magic for a man to want a woman. You've wanted other women."

Her more reasonable tone made it possible for Grey to calm himself. A little. He ran a hand back through his tangle of hair, marveling that it was still attached, given how much he'd done it lately. "Yes. I've had lovers. But when it ended, it ended. It didn't linger like this." He shook his head. "It has to be a spell."

Pearl's smile was gentle, sweet. Loving.

Lies. Weren't they?

"Maybe this time was different," she said, "not because of magic, but because maybe, just possibly, you felt something more than mere lust. Maybe what you felt was real." She licked her lips and cleared her throat before continuing. "I know Mary was the one, true love of your life, but couldn't—"

"Mary is my sister!" The words burst out, driven by shock.

"Oh." Pearl blinked a moment, before a beautiful smile spread across her face. *"Oh."*

"Don't." Grey shook a warning finger in her face.

"Don't assume. Don't you dare. If I felt anything at all for you—and I am admitting to nothing—but if I did, it was pure animal lust. Sex, and that alone."

Pearl took a step closer to him, her pink tongue slipping out to trace across that delicate lower lip. "Prove it."

By God, he would.

He closed the distance between them with a leap, snatching her into his arms for a frontal assault on that taunting tongue and the lips that enclosed it. His hands went on a flanking maneuver to cover as much territory as possible, so that he could conquer and possess all the sooner.

"Grey. *Grey.*" Pearl's voice reached him. Did she protest? Why? This was her idea. "We're in the foyer."

Foyer. *Entranceway.* Not a good place. Bedroom? Upstairs, too far.

Parlor. Two steps. Door. Close door. Curtains? Closed enough. Sofa. There. *Ah.*

24

GREY LAY ATOP Pearl who was kissing him back as furiously as he kissed her, tearing at his clothes as frantically as he shoved at hers. A button hit the floor. That's what maids were for, or valets. And then he was inside her.

He had to take a moment, a quick one, to revel in the sensation, the warm, tight, wet grip on his most personal part. And then he was moving, driving into her.

He thrilled to her passion as she met him thrust for thrust, clutching him, pulling at him, crying out his name and urging him on. She froze, pulled taut beneath him, and she screamed, pulsing around him as she found the pleasure he gave her. Grey cried out, taking what she gave in response.

When he returned to himself, Grey realized two things. Three. First, his arse was cold. He'd only shoved his trousers down far enough to get inside her. Second, Pearl was stroking him. His hair, his shoulders—whatever she could reach. And third— "It's not the same."

"No." Pearl kept stroking him.

He thought perhaps she would, as long as he remained within reach. But his backside was cold and it wasn't gentlemanly to remain on top, crushing her. He was that much of a gentleman, if little more. Grey pulled up his trousers, flipped down her skirt and petticoats, and sat on the sofa beside her, resisting the urge to pull her into his arms. She folded her hands in her crumpled lap, as if to keep herself from reaching out.

She tilted her head, watching him. "I thought you'd be angry."

"I am. I think." He watched her in return as he tried to sort the jumbled mess in his head. "Angry with myself mostly. We probably shouldn't have done that."

Pearl gave a one-shoulder shrug. "Probably not. But I'm not sorry." Her eyes were intent. "Are you?"

"I don't know." He shook his head. "Why was it different?"

"We're not bound anymore. You're not my familiar." She took a deep breath. "We told you sex makes magic. Sex between a sorceress and her familiar makes more magic. A great deal more. Heaps and piles more. *Mountains m—*"

"I understand." Grey cut her off.

"But it's not just the amount of magic. I can't share it with you, either." She turned to face him on the sofa, folding her legs up beneath her mounds of petticoats. "Before that first time—we were already a little bit bound, maybe half. The blood oath started it—and I'm sorry for that, truly I am. I didn't know it would do that, and Amanusa said if you would swear—swear on your spirits and on the blood—not to betray any sorcery guild secrets, I can tell you everything, if you want to know."

"You knew I would ask?" Grey felt a little wild-eyed again.

"We didn't *know,* but we thought you *might* ask. And if you did, the magister said I could tell. If you swear."

"What does this swearing on blood and spirits entail?" He looked at her sideways, suspicious, but perhaps a little less so.

Should that make him suspicious?

"Grey." Pearl huffed out a breath. "If you look for plots and evil intent in everything, you're going to find it. Even if it isn't there. And no, I'm not reading your mind or riding your blood or using magic at all. I am reading your expression."

"I have no expression." He prided himself on his blank face.

"Exactly. When you are wary, you don't." Her voice held triumph. "The rest of the time, you're perfectly expressive."

Which meant that when he had lived with his family, he'd been steeped in suspicion at every moment. Truth, that was.

"The spell is just the tiniest drop of your blood on this rice paper—Jax supplies it to all of us—and a tiny drop of mine, and perhaps a sigil, or whatever it takes to swear on the spirits. Then you burn it. After you swear."

If he could call a spirit at this time of the afternoon. Nearing the dark of the moon. But he could try. "Blood on the paper only." He waited for her nod. "And then it's burned?"

"Yes. You can hold the paper if you like, and burn it yourself." Pearl gave a long, sad-sounding sigh. "I never meant you any harm, Grey. I never did you any harm. The familiar bond helped you more than hindered."

"It bound me to your will," he snarled.

"It did not. The kind of bond we made couldn't do that." Now she sounded annoyed. "Grey, just swear and I'll explain everything."

Pearl removed a crumpled square of rice paper from her pocket and spread it on the serving table before them. "There." She laid her lancet—the lancet he'd given her—on top. "It's your move."

He looked at the items on the table, then looked up at her. Did he dare? Was this another plot, or part of the same one?

"Grey." She still sounded annoyed. Somehow that reassured him more than if she'd been soothing and sweet. "I will swear on blood and spirits to speak only truth. Blood never lies. You know that. You only have to swear never to tell sorcery guild secrets, and I'll tell you which bits they are. If you can't trust my spell, then send for Amanusa and have her do it. But I never thought you were a coward."

"I'm not." The denial snapped out of him by reflex. But it was true. He was no coward.

"Then what is holding you back?"

"I don't trust you."

"Isn't that fear? Because you fear what I might do? You fear being in someone else's power, not in control of your own fate." Pearl gave him a small smile. "It's a bit like marriage feels for a woman uncertain of her husband's love."

Grey stared at her. "Good God, it's a wonder anyone ever gets married."

Pearl's laughter pierced the shell of his suspicion. "Exactly."

He remembered things anger had blocked from his mind. How she'd argued, repeatedly and vehemently, against marriage, for one. She had been sincere in her argument, he'd have sworn. If she had had the courage to give in to his persuasions, surely he could have courage to . . .

Grey picked up the lancet and held it out to her. "You've had more practice."

He chose a pencil from his pocket set and drew a sigil on the paper. *Oath*. He paused a moment, then drew *Truth*. Conjury wasn't a truth-seeking magic, or a truth-telling one. Not like sorcery. But it had its truth-testing side. The old spirits could tell when someone lied. He spoke in Latin, calling his oldest, most powerful spirits. He felt the stirring of power that meant Varus and Polonia had both consented to appear.

"Do it." Grey extended his right hand, giving her a choice of fingers to lance. She took his smallest, pierced it quickly, slightly, and wiped, as she had said, the tiniest drop of his blood across the oath sigil.

Power shivered through the spirits when she did. Grey could almost see them glow. He'd never seen them take form before. The oldest ones rarely did.

Pearl lanced her own finger, the smallest left-hand one to match his, and squeezed out a slightly larger drop of blood, which she dabbed onto both sigils. "I swear by the spirits present, and by the blood we both have shed, to speak only truth in this matter of the familiar bond which was made between us, Grey Carteret and Pearl Parkin." She looked expectantly at Grey.

Right. His turn. "I swear by the spirits present and by the blood we have both shed never to speak the secrets of the sorcerer's guild to anyone who is not an initiate of that guild, or in the presence of those not so initiated." Was that sufficient? He looked at Pearl for her agreement.

"Now, burn it," she said.

Agreement enough. Grey laid the spelled paper in a cigar dish, lit a paper spill from the fireplace, and set the spell afire. As it burned, he could feel the oath magic settle around him. Did the truth magic do the same for Pearl?

He looked at his spirits. Varus somehow spread himself and surrounded the two of them, Grey and Pearl. Polonia seemed to surround Varus, or perhaps permeated him. Grey didn't understand how they did what they did. He was merely properly grateful when they did it on his behalf, as they did now.

"All right." Grey fastened his gaze on Pearl, sitting cross-legged on the sofa beside him. "Tell me how it happened. It began with the blood oath, you said?"

"Yes. But that didn't create the familiar bond. It only made it possible. Created the potential." Pearl shifted position, turning to face him, and caught his gaze. "This is the secret of the sorcerer's guild. It is the blood of the sorceress that carries the power."

Grey looked at her, waiting for the secret part.

"That's it," Pearl said. "That is the secret. The blood of the sorceress carries the magic. We work magic with our own blood, not yours. When we ride the blood— It was my blood inside you that I rode, not yours inside me. *That* is the secret of the sorcerer's guild, and you are sworn by your magic and ours not to reveal it."

"But—" Grey shook his head. "Of course your blood would carry the most magic. Why is it such a secret?"

Pearl gave him a look, one of those that meant he was being more than usually idiotic. "People already fear our magic. If they are afraid of us, *and* they think if a little of our blood will work some magic, then a great deal of our blood—or *all* of our blood—will work a great deal of magic . . ."

"Oh. Right." That made sense. Unfortunately. Varus and Polonia gave no warning signals, so it was true. "How does this relate to us? Your blood got into me, of course, during the oath."

"But yours got into me as well, through the cut, rather than by swallowing it. Normally, that still makes little or no difference, but in this case, it did help to create the potential for a familiar bond. Potential only, remember."

"So how did it change from potential to reality?" His curiosity had been awakened now, eating away his anger.

"There were a lot of steps. When I was cleaning out all the blood magic in the hospital morgue, and I had too much. We touched, and some of the magic went into you. That started the process. Familiars hold magic for a sorceress. Then, when you were calling Angus Galloway's ghost, it seemed to me that you didn't have enough magic to call him, so—" She made a face. "I'm not exactly clear on this part. Amanusa says you used my magic to feed yours. *You* called on it. But you couldn't have used it if I hadn't been willing to give it. Do you follow?"

Grey recalled that morning, that rush of surprising power when he'd thought it exhausted. "Yes." He sighed. "Yes, I do."

"And I was able to use your magic to see the spirits and speak to them, but only because you allowed it. And we worked magic *together* to lay them. Those are all parts of the familiar bond, how it works between two magicians.

"Once, Grey—once sorcerers were courted by other magicians. They knew the familiar bond would add power to them both. Some even tried entrapping a sorceress, thinking to force the bond, but without knowing the secrets of the guild, they could not succeed. A familiar's bond is a true partnership, Grey, in which both must agree for the power to be used."

All of that made impeccable sense to Grey. He nodded, working through the information again.

"It was a partnership from the very beginning," Pearl said, "because I took in your blood, too. Your blood in me bound me to you, just as mine in you bound you to me. The exchange of blood gave you choice. It gave you the ability to use my magic, just as I could use yours. And when we—"

She fluttered a hand at the sofa beneath them. "Did what we just did, especially since the first time was *my* first time— That sealed the bond. It meant we could walk hand-in-hand through the dead zone without harm. Together, we were more—"

She broke off, shook her head. "Well. That's how it happened. It was an accident, Grey. I never had any control over you. No more than you had over me. Less, because I—"

"You were my apprentice." He finished the sentence for her when she broke it off.

"No, you idiot." Her head shaking was fondly exasperated. "Because I love you. And you don't love me. Which is not at all unexpected." She gave a one-shouldered shrug of helpless resignation. He really was quite good at reading her moods, wasn't he?

"Love." He shook his head back at her. "What is it? Nothing, really. A word. A method one person uses to coerce another, claiming love to bend him to the other's will. Every one of the persons who have ever claimed to love me wanted something from me. Obedience, propriety, jewelry, money, amusement—*something*. All but one."

"Poor Grey," Pearl murmured. Not sarcastically, he didn't think. She stroked her fingertips lightly along his hand resting near her on the back of the sofa.

"My sister Mary never wanted anything from me." His smile twisted as he remembered. "She was my youngest sister, two years younger than Adela—"

"The sister you can tolerate," Pearl interjected.

Grey nodded a quick assent. "Who is three years younger than myself. But Mary was simpleminded. She didn't know enough to want anything other than my presence."

"How did she die?" Pearl stroked his hand again.

He wished he didn't want her to keep doing it. "She was never in robust health. Our parents kept her tucked away on one of the smaller properties as she got older and more willful. Medehall, in Lincolnshire. She liked to wander, and usually the nurse would let her, if someone went along to watch her. She got caught in a rain when she was eleven and died of a lung fever."

Grey paused, looking back into memory. "She was the first spirit I ever called." He smiled. "She is not simple now, though she still has the same pure, sweet spirit."

"And she still loves you." Pearl's smile was so sad, it made him ache, though he didn't know why. "Whereas even I wanted something from you. I wanted the magic. But I do love you, Grey. That's why I gave you what you wanted. Your freedom."

She paused before she spoke again. "That night. The first time we—"

"Had sex," he supplied, when she didn't.

She scowled at him. "Stop finishing my sentences. We made love. I could *see* what we made, Grey. It had substance. I've learned to see that kind of sorcery, and the sort made from love is different from that made without it.

"That night, you asked me what I wanted, whether I wanted you, of yourself. For yourself. I said yes. Because I did. Not for the magic or anything else. Just for you, because I love you." She smiled at him as she stood.

"I know you won't believe me, since Amanusa has come and everything has worked out so well with the magic, and if she hadn't come we might never have known about the bond. But if it had been a question of breaking the familiar bond and losing all chance of learning magic, or keeping it and making you unhappy—I would still have broken it. It *is* broken, Grey. Utterly."

Lies. He only thought it, without any heart in it, but still his spirits responded.

Truth.

He'd almost forgotten they were present.

She speaks of matters concerning the bond, Polonia said. *She speaks truth.*

This one almost always speaks truth, Varus added. *Except to herself.*

"I don't believe it," Grey said to Pearl. "But my spirits say it is truth, so I suppose I must."

Pearl gave that sad shake of her head. "No, you mustn't. You must do and believe only what your heart tells you." She smiled. "It's all right. Truly. I always knew this would end badly, you and me. Better it happened before we were trapped by marriage."

She looked around the room, as if committing it to memory, that strange little smile riding her face. "I'm glad we cleared the air." Her smile changed as she looked at him again, true, warm, and all Pearl. "Be happy, Grey."

And she was gone. Why was she always fleeing this room?

Why did he always miss her when she did? He did not love her.

Lie, Varus said. *The first spoken here this day.*

"Oh, do be quiet," Grey grumbled. "Go back to Elysium, or wherever it is you loiter. Besides, I wasn't the one sworn to truth today."

No. We just thought you might like to know, Polonia said. *Love is too precious to squander.*

You were sworn to silence. Be sure you keep it, Varus warned, and they were gone, too.

Why didn't the solitude feel as peaceful as it once had? Why did it feel . . . lonely? He'd never minded it before. He would get used to it again.

NO MORE THAN two hours passed before McGregor climbed his way up to the workroom to inform Grey that Miss Parkin and Miss Tavis insisted on seeing him. So insistent that they did not wait for him to descend to the parlor, but climbed the innumerable flights of stairs in McGregor's wake to confront him on the landing at the top.

"Did we not say good-bye, Miss Parkin?" Grey raised an eyebrow, doing his best to look sardonic as he buttoned his cuffs in preparation for putting on the coat McGregor held for him. "Or did you miss me so much already?"

"Grey, this is serious," Elinor scolded. "One of the sorcery students has gone missing."

He settled his frock coat on his shoulders, settling the surge of alarm with it. Alarm might not prove necessary. "Who? When?"

"Katriona Farquhar," Pearl said. "The girl who was walking with me earlier. She never arrived at the hotel after we parted. No one knew she'd gone missing until I arrived without her. They assumed she'd stopped with me at Harry's for luncheon."

"But they didn't," Elinor said. "Obviously."

"Katriona is adventurous, and fearless." Pearl followed Grey as he started down the stairs, Elinor behind her. "She may have gone exploring."

"Except you told her to find Amanusa and tell her you stopped here," Grey said.

"I also told her I was fine. That nothing was wrong."

"While I dragged you forcibly into the house."

"I came willingly." Pearl sounded increasingly annoyed, which, perversely, amused Grey.

"It was that, or be hauled by your hair." How thoroughly could he provoke her? They reached the first-floor foyer and he turned to watch.

"There's something you both seem to be forgetting," Elinor said as she took the final step onto the checkered marble.

"What is that?" Grey took it upon himself to ask.

"The new moon is on Thursday."

A chill went through Grey, cold enough to freeze his blood. But— "Angus Galloway and Rose Bowers were both taken the night of their murders. Neither of them went missing days before."

"The murderer is trying to work magic with his crimes," Pearl said. "Perhaps he thinks he can work greater magic by killing a magician. He saw his opportunity when I left Katriona alone, and took it."

"Or perhaps Katriona's disappearance has nothing to do with murder or magic," Grey said, losing patience with pessimism, "and everything to do with the vagaries of the fifteen-year-old female mind."

"She's sixteen," Pearl said. "But that still leaves her vulnerable to far too many ordinary dangers. I should never have left her to walk back alone—but who would have thought she would vanish in the few yards from your house to the hotel, with Harry's house between?"

"The fault, if any exists, is mine," Grey said. "For insisting. But that is not important. Has a search been organized?"

"Yes, Harry is," Elinor said. "And Jax. We're part of it. We were to ask if anyone here—one of the servants, perhaps—saw anything, since this is the last place anyone saw Katriona."

"McGregor!"

The butler had vanished sometime in the past several minutes, but he always responded promptly to bellowing.

"Yes, Magister?" And there he was, bowing respectfully.

"Would you inquire among the staff as to whether any of them saw what happened to the young lady who was with Miss Parkin earlier? She, the young lady, seems to have gone missing."

McGregor gave Pearl a bow and a starchy smile. "It is good to see you again, Miss."

"It's good to see you, too, Mr. McGregor."

Grey should not feel jealous of smiles bestowed on servants. He did not wish smiles of his own.

Lie, whispered Polonia. Were they still here?

McGregor bowed again and vanished. The ladies fidgeted as they waited in silence. No one, including Grey, felt up to chatting. None of the servants had seen anything, however. They had been keeping themselves busy. Grey knew why. They'd been ignoring the "conversation" in the front parlor.

The search progressed. Harry inquired at the homes of the other upstart magicians who lived on Albemarle Street, including Sir William's. Grey was designated the official inquirer at all upper-crust homes—most of those in the area, once off Albemarle. As the black sheep son of the Duke of Brandon, Grey had a cachet that got him through the doors of the snootiest. He was still too disreputable for the highest sticklers, but few of those stuck at the possibility of gossip.

The ones who did had their belowstairs servants' area invaded by McGregor and Harry's butler, Freeman, inquiring politely as to whether anyone had seen the young lady in her grass-green gown and tartan pelisse. No one had.

Grey, and sometimes Pearl, expected that at any moment the errant girl would walk through the door of the hotel, expressing surprise that any should be searching for her. But as the day wore on, that expectation grew more and more difficult to sustain. The other students were sent to bed under the supervision of Fiona Watson, and Grey called out the Briganti.

Colonel Simmons was resistant to having his enforcers involved in what was surely a mere schoolgirl prank, until he was reminded that sixteen-year-old girls faced more dangers than sixteen-year-old boys, and that in addition, she was a half-trained magician. Half-trained conjurers and alchemists could wreak sufficient havoc to bring out the Briganti. Why would he think a half-trained sorceress any different? The search extended through the night without success.

A footman at Brown's Hotel was eventually discovered who had seen Katriona in discussion with a young gentleman. A nursemaid in the nearby park with her charges the next morning admitted to seeing the girl with the same young gentleman on more than one occasion. And on Tuesday, with no other sign of the girl, Simmons called off his enforcers, declaring that Katriona must have eloped with her follower.

Grey wasn't so sure. He had a bad feeling about the situation, and his bad feelings usually paid out. Especially when Harry, Amanusa, Pearl, Archaios, Elinor, and a dozen others admitted to similar feelings.

I-Branch stepped up its pace, some of them continuing the search for Katriona, others digging deeper into the wealth of evidence from Galloway's murder, and the few scraps of it from Rose Bowers's. The alchemists' forge had been repaired and was roaring nonstop.

Wednesday, Amanusa and Harry, and Jax of course, came into the I-Branch office, their faces wearing ominous expressions. Grey motioned them into Pearl's ex-schoolroom, which he had begun to use for conferences like this one.

"Bad news?" He looked from one to the other as Amanusa sank onto the chaise, and Harry sprawled in a desk chair. Jax took up his usual post standing behind Amanusa.

Harry shrugged. "Too soon to tell about mine, but it is news. We're not sure if it was a conjurer with wizardish talents, or a wizard with conjurish leanings who did th' deed, but it definitely weren't an alchemist. Wasn't." He belatedly corrected his grammar, a sign of his agitation. He didn't bother with corrections when his mood was even-keeled.

"Well, *this* news is bad." Amanusa bounced on the long end of the chaise, changing position. "It's not Cranshaw."

"He didn't push Pearl into the forge?" That crime came first to Grey's mind, and it annoyed him. "Or he didn't murder Rose and Angus?"

"Both. Nor did he kidnap Katriona." Amanusa sounded

disgusted. "I stole a ride in his blood and rummaged around in his mind." She shuddered. "Not a pleasant place, especially for poor Cranshaw. Someone needs to study methods of healing the mind as well as the body. Be that as it may, he has had nothing to do with any of this. Or rather, with anything but the stirring up of the public about sorcery and women using magic."

She paused. "I did get Sir William to authorize my spell. It didn't feel right to go poking about in Nigel's thoughts on my own authority."

Grey frowned. "Are you sure? He's such a rabid opponent—"

"But he's a rabid rabbit. He's incapable of real violence. Good at inciting it, but not so good even at conspiring in it." Amanusa sighed. She held her hand out to her husband, who assisted her to her feet. "Back to the salt mine Grey calls a workroom. I left my students practicing lancing."

"Good God," Grey exclaimed. "The floors will be awash in blood."

"Hardly. They're practicing on themselves. Most of them haven't managed to pierce the skin yet." Amanusa shook her head in mild disappointment.

Harry stayed behind when the others left, watching Grey from his sprawl in the chair.

"What?" Grey folded his arms as he leaned against the wall, uncomfortable with Harry's staring.

"You should let Pearl remake the familiar bond," Harry said, his expression daring Grey to break eye contact.

25

"You ARE OUT of your tiny little mind." Grey didn't shout. He never shouted. He did uncross his arms. And look, his hands had made themselves into fists.

"No, I ain't," Harry said. "I never saw you work magic like that, before Pearl lent you some o' hers. Amanusa says it's voluntary. You 'ave to agree before anything can happen, even after the bond is made. She can't force you, an' neither can you force her. It's no different than your familiar spirits."

"I do not exchange blood with my spirits," Grey snapped out. "Alchemists do not have familiars. So, one, what would you know about it? And, two, a familiar spirit is not the same thing as a sorcerer's familiar. It is simply a spirit known to me. One I have worked with before. There is a relationship of trust and *familiarity* between us." He bore down on the word. "Nothing more. They are simply my friends."

Harry shrugged. "So where's the difference? An' maybe you should share blood with your spirits. Even I could sense wot 'appened when Amanusa put the blood and water on the sigils at the dead zone, 'ow they perked up.

"You an' Pearl was partners in the magic. Friends. She never pushed you to do anyfing you didn't want to do. Other way round, most o' the time. You're angry 'cause it caught you by surprise, an' you think it made you like Jax. But you're not Jax. Hell, Jax ain't Jax anymore. Talk to 'im. 'E'll tell you."

Harry climbed to his feet. "Think about it. We need the magic. We need all the magic we can get, and it's stupid to throw away any we can use."

"I will not be controlled by anyone but myself," Grey snarled.

"But you are." Harry shook his head sadly. "If you're still doin' things 'cause o' what your dad did to you, then he's still controllin' you. Whether you do things to please 'im, or to spite 'im, it's still because o' *him*. Isn't it?"

He studied Grey another moment. "Talk to Jax," he said, and he left the room.

It galled Grey no end to admit that Harry was right, which was why it took him the rest of the day and all night to reach the point where he could do it, talk to Jax. He kept waking to explain why remaking the bond was a bad idea, or that he did not do anything because of his father. And then realizing that the bond might be a good idea, and that his father still loomed too large over his life. Change was necessary.

Far too early in the morning, Grey found himself pacing the lobby of Brown's, trying to wait for a less ungodly hour. Before he wore a hole in the carpet, a footman appeared to usher him upstairs, into Jax's dressing room.

Jax was shirtless, braces dangling from his trousers, his face half lathered, in the midst of shaving himself. "Harry warned me you might be by to talk." Jax shook Grey's hand and waved him to a chair. "Sounded urgent, so I assumed you wouldn't mind talking while I—" He waved a hand at his shaving paraphernalia and gave a wry smile. "Completed my toilette."

"How did you know I was here?" Grey perched on the edge of the chair, poised to run.

"Footman told me." Jax lathered up the rest of his face. "Had them keeping an eye out for you. Since Harry's warning. I take it you want to know about being a sorceress's familiar."

Grey cleared his throat, which Jax took as assent.

He picked up the sharpened razor and examined his face as if selecting an angle of attack. "Truth is, I haven't much experience as a familiar. Yvaine, my first sorceress, made me her servant. *Not* her familiar." Jax tilted his head and drew the razor carefully along his left cheek. Without cutting himself at all, Grey marveled.

"There doesn't seem to be a difference between the two," Grey said.

"There is an entire world of difference." Jax paused to finish his cheeks, then spoke again. "I imagine my manner is a great deal of what has put you off the idea. I learned it over the century and more I served Yvaine. She chose me because I am completely blind and deaf to magic. I can't hear the faintest whisper of it, so I couldn't tell what she was doing to me until she had me bound so tightly I couldn't piss without permission. I truly was her slave. But Amanusa is not Yvaine. Neither is Pearl. And neither are you head-blind."

Jax took another moment to shave his upper lip. "The difference between familiar and servant is in the blood. The *exchange* of blood. Yvaine never took in a drop of my blood. Amanusa did, even before we were forced to break and remake our bond. Now I am as much a part of her as she is of me. I have the ability to choose. My will is my own."

He grimaced, looking odd with soap still on his chin and neck. "I am still head-blind, so I have little enough to contribute to the bond. *That* is why I hold back. Because I am no magician, not because the familiar bond constrains me. But you—" He gestured with the razor, flinging water drops about.

"You are magister of the conjury guild. You have enough magic in your own right that you could likely constrain Pearl with it, if you wished. She is a powerful sorceress, but small, so probably not as powerful as Amanusa."

"Size makes a difference?" Grey latched onto the trivial to avoid considering the deeper things.

"Sorcery must be held in blood, bone, and flesh," Jax

said when he finished shaving his neck. "The smaller the sorceress, the less magic she can hold. But Pearl has great finesse. She can do more with less." Jax smiled in private amusement. "Amanusa tends to go in more for brute force."

"You're taller than I am," Grey said. "Does that mean you can hold more magic as a familiar than I was able to?"

"I'm also head-blind, and you are so very not." Jax shrugged. "I have no idea whether that makes a difference. Does your conjury block out some of the sorcery? Or does it provide more room? We could experiment, if you were still a familiar."

He held up the razor and gave his chin a determined look. "A moment, if you please. This is the tricky part. Not quite a divot in my chin, but almost."

Grey chewed over what he had learned, both from Pearl and from Jax. It sounded as if he had overreacted to the discovery that Pearl had made him her familiar. Indeed, he seemed to have done as much to cause it as she had, perhaps more. Furthermore, according to Jax, being a *true* familiar, was far from the subservient role it sounded to the ignorant. Like himself.

Now that he thought back with a mind clear of both fear and anger, Grey remembered the magic he and Pearl had worked together. She had never compelled him. She had tempted him—God, how she'd tempted him. But that had been just Pearl being Pearl. Merely the magic every woman held over every man in existence.

"Any other questions?" Jax was toweling his face clean. He reached for his shirt, pulling it on over his singlet.

"As Amanusa's familiar, you say you can choose. How?" Grey wanted it all out on the table face up, where he could see it.

"I can block her." Jax buttoned his shirt. "Most times,

it's as simple as saying no." His smile was fond. No, besotted. "Though there are few things she wants I can say no to."

"It seems an extremely . . . intimate bond." That made Grey uncomfortable, the intimacy. He'd never liked being so exposed to another person, so vulnerable. Yet he had been with Pearl. Almost from the beginning.

"It is, for us." Jax paused in tucking in his shirt and shook his head. "And I cannot tell you if it was always so. Yvaine was the last sorceress, and the only sorceress for most of the time I was with her." He looked up, meeting Grey's gaze. "You will have to find your own way in this."

"As in most everything else to do with sorcery." Grey sighed. He slapped his thighs and stood, then waited while Jax settled his braces on his shoulders.

"What will you do?" Jax said.

Grey opened his mouth and realized he had no idea what he meant to say, so he said that. "I don't know."

Jax nodded. "Whatever you decide, I'll support you. 'Familiarity' isn't easy. Not everyone can manage it." He grinned. "But Harry said to remind you—the new moon's tonight."

Grey grimaced as he shook hands with the magister's familiar. "No pressure."

Jax laughed. "None at all."

But Grey had decided, or almost. He still had a few qualms, but they were his own squeamishness, mostly. He could deal with them. He checked his watch. The morning progressed. The sorceress and her students roused early to their studies. Pearl might be available for discussion. So, did he want this? *Truly?*

PEARL HAD JUST finished breakfast in the private parlor at Brown's, and went to the lobby to wait while the others went up to collect their wraps and umbrellas.

She'd brought hers with her from her rooms over the carriage house.

"Miss Parkin." That dear, dark chocolate voice slid through her, leaving a trail of quivers behind.

"Grey." Pearl spun, faster than would display the cool unconcern she wished. "Magister Carteret. What are you doing here? At this hour?"

Why couldn't he leave her alone to heal? Why did she have to sound so alarmed? She wanted to sound indifferent.

"I had some business to conduct."

"Ah." She curtseyed, dismissing him to go conduct it.

But he didn't go away. "With me? What business could you possibly have with me? The bond *is* broken. Utterly and completely. I swear it. Amanusa swears it. Do we need to get Elinor and Cranshaw and Ferguson to swear it, too?"

He was smiling. At her. Was that good?

No. It was bad. Terrible. It made her think he liked her, and he didn't. Not the way she wanted him to. "What do you *want*?" She tried to keep her voice down. Truly.

"I want you to remake the familiar bond," Grey said.

Wait. *What?*

Pearl looked at him, studied him carefully. He was smiling, but faintly. Not as if he was waiting for her to laugh at his joke. Pearl removed her bonnet. Sometimes it interfered with her hearing. "What did you say?"

"I would like for you to remake the familiar bond." That sounded like what he had said the first time.

Pearl touched his forehead. He didn't feel feverish, so she touched her own. Could one feel one's own fever?

Grey laughed as he captured her fever-testing hand. "Only you can make me laugh at the same time I want to shake you. You heard me correctly, and neither of us is feverish."

"Then you have run mad. I'll have Harry come fetch you for the asylum. The last time anyone mentioned the word 'familiar' in your presence, you very nearly frothed at the mouth."

"I apologize. Abjectly." He bowed, but he didn't let go of her hand. Pearl twisted it free. "But I meant what I said. I want the familiar bond remade."

"Why?" She sat on the hope struggling to break free. It was rather like sitting on a sack full of large cats wanting out.

"Harry came to see me. The new moon is tonight. We need all the magic we can get if we are to find Katriona and stop the murderer. Even I cannot deny the increase in magic for both of us when I was your familiar."

The cats stopped wriggling, drowning in despair. Though the despair was quickly overwhelmed by guilt. What did her own heartache matter when Katriona, or someone else, faced death and demons and worse? Though what could be worse—

Pearl cut off her mental blathering. "I see."

"Strictly business," he said.

"Of course." Pearl stanched the bleeding in her heart. It didn't matter. Katriona, or whoever the murderer planned to sacrifice, did. The demon did. "Very well. I will do it."

"Excellent." Grey beamed his too-beautiful smile at her, and her heart bled a little more. "When sha—"

"But—" She held up a hand to stop his words. "It will be a *temporary* bond. Just until the new moon is over. Afterward, we will break it again. By Sunday, at the latest."

"The crisis may not be over by Sunday," Grey protested. "And there are still the dead zones to be—"

"Sunday," Pearl said firmly, despite the whisper in the back of her mind crying, *Can't I keep him, please?*

"Pearl." He looked sternly down at her. "We cannot

keep making and breaking our familiar bond. We must make it and let it stand, for however long is necessary."

"We will not *keep* doing it. We will do it once. Make it, then break it, and never make it again."

"But what if, God forbid, we don't catch the killer?" Grey's animated face began to freeze up into that carelessness she hated. "What if the demon returns? With friends?"

She shook her head, bowing her back against him with all the stubbornness at her possession. Which was a very great deal. "We're doomed anyway against demons, or so you've said. If you feel the need for familiarity, ask one of the others. I'm sure they'll be happy to take you on. Some of them."

"Pearl." Now his tone changed to sweet reason, but his face remained that blank, amused, aristocratic mask. "We worked well together, didn't we? You're the best. Already a sorcerer. Our magic meshes perfectly. We know this." He smiled, as false and bland as the mask he wore. "But, very well. You win. We will remake the bond, and by Sunday, if you insist, you can break it again."

She knew his intention without the benefit of riding his blood. He thought he could convince her to change her mind. It was the power. Men would put up with women they didn't want if it gave them power, whether wrought by wealth, by influence and connection, or by magic.

"You can't pretend with me, Grey," she said, weary to her soul. "We will share blood. You know what that means."

The mask faded a bit, some of his false amusement dropping away. "I never lied to you, Pearl, or hid from you. I won't now. Can you swear the same?"

Could she? "I never lied."

"But you hid."

Because it was safer to hide, to be invisible.

She shrugged, refusing to admit or deny. "It will be what it is, for as long as it is." She hadn't felt very hidden at the end of their time together, in the week and a half of their full-blown affair.

"Blood bond only," she said, suddenly feeling the need to make that clear. She couldn't make love to him again, not when the love was on one side only.

"Of course." Grey bowed. "Soon."

"Now?" Was that suggestion or objection? Sooner made . . . not sooner ended, she didn't think, but the sooner they could use their combined magic to search for the missing girl.

"If you like." He bowed again. "I know I have behaved . . . not well. I apologize. I mean to accede to your wishes as much as possible in this."

Pearl didn't trust him. She believed him, but she didn't trust what he meant by "as much as possible." She turned and led the way back toward the private parlor, searching through the slit in the side seam of her skirt—white, now that she was officially a full-fledged sorceress—for one of the pockets dangling by its ribbon from the waistband of her skirt.

"How do we do this?" Grey asked when they were inside the parlor with the door shut. He presented his hand with its assortment of fingers.

"The same way we did before."

She took a deep breath, inhaling his scent of chalk, sandalwood, and Grey, which did not help. She touched his hand, and magic did not crackle. It always had, before. But then they had been familiars—or potentially so—since the very beginning.

There was magic, however. Pearl could feel it seeping from . . . where? Out of her skin? His? It hovered, as if waiting. Yearning? It tasted . . .

"Can you sense that?" she asked, her hand barely in contact with his.

"Magic?" Grey shook his head. "No. Dark of the moon makes everything trickier. It's a good sign, don't you think, if you can?"

Not especially. Amanusa had explained how the magic inherent in sex could be raised even by a kiss if there was desire behind it. If they could stir magic with a mere touch—

Pearl didn't want to think about it. She tightened her grip to steady his hand, adjusted the fit of her lancet, and punctured his right forefinger. Quickly, she lanced her own left forefinger and pressed it against his, blood to blood.

The blood soaked up all the hovering magic before she could decide whether that was a good idea. She swept more of her own magic into it. Then his blood hit her bloodstream, dizzying her. She snagged her lancet on Grey's sleeve when she clutched his arm for support. Had it done that before, made her dizzy?

Grey clasped her lanced hand with his, as if seeking support as well. "I remember the dizziness," he said. "I thought it was just the situation—the jail, the blood, and the aching bones." He paused, a look of revelation and wonder coming over his face. "That was when it began to go away. The headache and the pain in—in my bones, as if I had shared Angus Galloway's torture. After the blood oath, it got better."

Pearl allowed herself a small smile. "So it wasn't all terrible, then?"

"None of it was, and you know it. I—" He huffed out a breath, back in teasing mode. "I panicked. There. Are you happy?"

"No. But I am relieved to know you remember being dizzy. I didn't, and it worried me a bit."

"I tried to put magic in my blood this time," Grey said. "I couldn't tell if I did anything at all, but perhaps I did."

Perhaps. Pearl wasn't so sure. But the hovering magic

created from desire—most of that was from Grey. He could make it, even if he could not move it. She wasn't about to tell him. He would be touching her and trying to kiss her all the time. As he was now.

He brought her hand to his mouth. "I also ingested your blood, didn't I?"

Oh dear. He didn't mean to kiss her hand, he meant to— His sin-filled mouth closed around her fingertip, and her knees almost buckled at the feel of the wet, desire-filled heat. He suckled a moment, then removed her finger to squeeze out another fat drop of blood.

"I took in more than that tiny exchange, if I recall correctly." His eyes held her captive as he licked up the fresh drop, the sensual slide of his tongue undoing all her insides.

He sucked her finger back into his mouth, then held up his own blood-smeared finger, a significant look in his eyes. She'd swallowed more of his blood during their wine drinking before she rode it, hadn't she? He laid his finger on her lips, offering without insisting, and she slid her tongue out to taste.

She pushed his hand away, overwhelmed by the intimacy of the moment. But if they were to remake the bond the way it should be— "Take more," she said. "I probably put too much in the wineglass, before I rode your blood. More is safer than less, and I wanted you to be safe."

He took her finger from his mouth to squeeze out another drop.

"Guild secret," she remembered belatedly to say.

He nodded solemnly as he licked up the fresh drop.

Oath. The word echoed faintly through Pearl's mind. From a far distance and through a veil, but she heard it, and it made her jump with surprise. She hadn't actually remade the bond yet.

Grey touched his damp forefinger to her mouth again, resting the remaining fingers on her cheek. Pearl wanted to turn her face into the caress, but was too afraid. She pushed his hand away, then squeezed his finger for fresh blood. "More is safer," she reminded him, though he made no objection.

Finally, she took his fingertip into her mouth, copying his action as she gazed back into his dark eyes. It seemed far too intimate for what it was, the simple working of magic. The gazing into each other's eyes made it so. Maybe if she stopped staring and worked the magic, it would be less so.

Pearl had been allowed to investigate the familiar bond between Amanusa and her Jax, from the outside. It was a tether, of sorts. A conduit for the magic that flowed between them, infinitely stretchable and unbreakable. It had layers, and strands, and it glowed, shining with their love for each other.

This bond wouldn't shine, built of nothing more than blood, magic, and desire, but it would serve. She threw out the first strand of magic, watched as it caught on the blood in his veins. "Do you want this?" She improvised with what they'd done before.

Someone should have warned her, given her time to look up the appropriate method for formalizing a familiar's bond. But she hadn't expected to remake it. Hadn't expected to ever want a familiar again. Still, it had worked the last time, without even their intending it. Blood, magic, and willingness seemed to be all that was required.

She threw another layer atop the first, hunting through his blood—that now inside her and that in him—for magic. "Do you want the bond of familiar to sorceress, to *me*?"

The magic had caught, but its hold was tentative, ready to break at any moment. "Grey, *do you want this*?"

"Yes." The word seemed surprised out of him. "Yes, I want it. Haven't I spent the last age talking you into it?"

She felt the magic's grip solidify, locking onto their

commingled blood. "Then say so. Words have power. You know that. You know you have to agree for this to work. This is no time for reluctance or second thoughts. You came to me, remember?" Pearl took hold of the just-anchored strands, ready to break them.

"Don't." Grey took her hands and drew her closer, his mask of amused boredom falling entirely away. "I want this. I, Greyson George Arthur William Victor Carteret, swear on my blood and the spirits who answer my call that I willingly enter into this familiar's bond with Pearl Elizabeth Parkin."

Magic surged through the strands Pearl had built, thickening them, adding layers and strength, until Pearl thought even a demon's wrath might not break it. Nothing but once more stripping out the blood from where it did not belong.

"Now you," he said. "It's a two-sided bond, or so you keep telling me."

"I'm making it, aren't I?" she retorted. But he was right.

He went on. "If you're going to do it, you have to plunge in all the way. No holding back. No 'just until Sunday.' I've agreed to that, but it can't be part of what we're doing here." He caught her face, turning it full on to his. She hadn't realized she was looking ever so slightly off to one side. "No hiding, Pearl. It's all or nothing, just like before."

When did he get to be so intense? This was Grey, magister of not-caring-about-anything. But then, hadn't she always sensed the intensity beneath his insouciant mask? *This,* the intense, passionate, caring man, was the real Grey.

Too bad his passion and caring weren't for her.

"Do you want this?" He held onto her, one hand gripping hers, the other holding her chin, his eyes refusing to let her go. "All or nothing, Pearl. Do you want it? Do you want *me*?"

There was no answer for that but truth.

"*Yes.*" It burst from her. "I swear—me, Pearl Elizabeth Parkin—" She'd almost left out her name. "On my blood and the spirits who stand witness, that I willingly enter this familiar's bond with Greyson George Arthur William Victor Carteret."

"No limits, no holding back." His fingers gripped tighter.

She would drown in the dark flames of his eyes. They didn't burn, just sucked up all her air. "I'm afraid," she admitted.

"So am I. Terrified." He grinned at her, and her heart found its thumpety again. "Why should I be the only one to suffer?"

Pearl laughed. "You're not. I am laughing, and I want so badly to shake you."

"It's always been part of my charm." He let go of her face and brought her hand up to kiss the back. "Well?"

She sighed. "No limits, no holding back." It was useless to try. She hadn't been able to hold back from him yet.

The magic gave a sigh. It wrapped itself around them, encasing them both in its embrace.

Pearl's eyes burned with tears. It felt so lovely.

Grey looked startled. "That," he said. "*That's* what I missed."

Her heart shuddered at the blow. "I knew it wasn't *me* you missed." She didn't mean to say it aloud, but obviously she did.

"No." Grey clutched her hands when she tried to pull free. "Don't you see? The magic is you, Pearl. It's from you, of you—it *is* you."

She shook her head, tugged hard enough at her hands that he let them go. "It's magic, Grey. Power. Strictly business. Isn't that what you said?"

"Yes, but—"

She put her lancet away as she turned for the door. "We need to go find Katriona."

"This conversation isn't over." Grey reached the door before she did and held it open for her.

"It is for now."

26

DARK OF THE moon in December. The darkest new moon of the year, as the winter solstice approached.

The cold in the pit of Grey's stomach increased as the morning wore on and they got no closer to finding the missing sorcery student. He feared what might happen to her. Rose Bowers had left Cremorne Garden with a gentleman. Katriona Farquuhar vanishing with one didn't ease his fears.

And yet. The cold was countered with the warmth of Pearl's magic wrapped around him. He wasn't sure whether the bond locked the cold fear outside, or buried it deep under layers of warm sorcery. He functioned on two levels: calm and decisive on the outside, fumbling through confusion on the inside, but functioning. Because Pearl was there, creating both calm and confusion.

It wasn't exactly the same as before. He had hurt her, and somehow, he could tell she feared he would hurt her again. The fear was greater now, but it had always been there, even before.

The realization staggered him. Not so much the part about Pearl being afraid. He understood that. But that he could feel it. He might not be able to ride her blood, but this bond they shared allowed him to know her emotions. To know *her.*

He hadn't understood before now what the bond

was—this sense of *presence,* that he wasn't alone, that someone guarded his back and always would. He'd assumed it was simply Pearl's presence in his life. Which it was. But more.

He would have known if she intended deception or tried to manipulate him into anything. The bond would have told him. *Blood never lies.*

He grimaced, making Pearl look curiously at him. He waved her back to Meade's expanded map. This one showed all the sectors of London and which searches— for the murderer or for Katriona—had been conducted where. Would Katriona meet Rose's fate? Not if he could help it.

Grey wanted it back. Everything he'd thrown away with his ignorance and irrational panic. He didn't blame himself for the ignorance, but the panic and the anger and the refusal to listen to anyone—that was all laid at his feet.

He wanted Pearl. He wanted her fixed in his life. He had almost convinced himself that he hadn't actually felt this way, that it couldn't have been real. Now that he had it back, he knew it was real, and better than he remembered. He would not give it up again. The magic boost was a nice bonus, but the real magic was Pearl. And the best way to hold her was marriage.

Maybe he could convince her again. She would be even more skittish now, but she cared for him. He could feel it in the magic. So how could he use that to—?

"Grey?" Pearl touched his elbow, calling his attention to the lanky, red-haired, transparent presence of Angus Galloway.

Now, darlin', don't you know I'd rather be talkin' to you? Galloway lounged against the air. *But if you insist, I'll talk to th' conjurer, too.*

How had Pearl seen the spirit? They hadn't been touching. Was the bond stronger now? Even without making love?

Her magic helped raise me, Galloway answered Grey's unspoken question. *It gave us a bit of a connection.*

"Why have you come, friend?" Grey nodded his thanks for the information. "Do you know where Katriona Farquuhar is?"

Why would you think I know where the wee lassie's taken herself? Galloway raised a shaggy, translucent brow.

"Because you're both Scottish?" Pearl said. "Because that's what spirits do—find things?"

Cheeky, that one. Galloway tipped his head toward her, speaking to Grey. *I do no' know where th' lass is, more's the pity. I'm too new to be much good at searchin' out those who do no' want to be found.*

"Wait—she doesn't *want* to be found?" Pearl reached out as if to touch the spirit and Grey pulled her hand back. Touching without sigils drawn rarely turned out well, for either party. "How do you know?"

I'd've found her otherwise, would I no'? Since we're both Scots. Galloway stopped his lounging, stood up straight. *But I think I might ha' found where the bastard as did for me might've moved his lair. The general area, at any rate.*

Grey whirled toward the map pinned to the chalkboard on wheels. "Show me."

Here. Galloway laid his palm over the map, covering the part of Southwark directly across the river from where they stood in the council building on Wych Street. Since his palm was mostly transparent, the map could be seen through it. *Somewhere in Lambeth, around Waterloo Road.*

"That's the best you can do?" Pearl protested.

"It's better than anything we've had before." Grey whirled back to address the Briganti who had moved in behind them.

"Sort yourselves into search parties and—" He pointed. "You, what's your name? Luling? *Loring*—arrange for transportation, since the carriage is out. We're going to Lambeth. Those of you whose spirits are awake, pass word to those out and about to meet us there. At the church square across from Waterloo Station."

Grey took Pearl's cloak from the stand and enfolded her in it, speaking to the spirit of the murdered man. "You will come with us, won't you, friend? Help us track?"

Galloway shrugged. *Sure. Though I do no' know what use I might be. Your old ones, they're the trackers.*

"Good idea." Grey sent out a call for older spirits, asking them to search, and at Pearl's suggestion, painted the safety sigil once more on her delicate wrist. Angus Galloway was, as he kept reminding them, very new at this spirit business. When Mary turned up as well, Grey was doubly glad of the sigil. By that time, the summoned transport had arrived.

"How are you maintaining your form so well?" Grey asked Galloway when they were in the closed hansom with the spirits.

I've no idea. Usually I canno'. Must be more o' the lady's magic. Since she raised me, an' all.

I want some, Mary said. *Can I have some of that magic, Grey?*

"If we can learn how, dearest." Grey raised an eyebrow at Pearl. "Something to investigate when we've the time." He smiled, hoping she would take the hint.

"Do you think you can pinpoint the murderer a little more precisely?" Pearl asked Galloway.

I do no' know.

Obviously, Pearl was ignoring Grey. All his hints, suggestions, and outright begging. Well, not the last, since he hadn't resorted to begging yet. But he would if he had to. He would not let her go again.

The cab rattled over the bridge and into Lambeth, quickly reaching the railway station a little way on and St. John's church across the major thoroughfare from it. At this hour of the afternoon, Waterloo Road wasn't nearly as crowded with cabs and omnibuses as it would be at the end of the workday. Still, Grey was grateful they didn't have to cross the busy road when the cab let them down in the church square.

He set Meade up in the porch of St. John's with his maps and his chalk, marking off search assignments, while Grey appointed searchers and handed out lanterns. The day would only get darker.

"I'm ready to go, sir." Ferguson stood at Grey's elbow, sounding a little breathless.

"You weren't at the office, were you?" Grey didn't recall seeing him there, and Ferguson was a hard man to miss. His mere presence set up an irritation all along Grey's skin. Like a rash one couldn't get rid of.

"No. Mr. Archaios and I were searching this side of the river. He got word that Magister Tomlinson and Miss Tavis wanted to discuss something with him at the Bermondsey dead zone, and I heard you were here, so I came." Ferguson had that annoyingly earnest expression he so often wore.

"Right." Grey looked around for a group to fob him off onto.

The problem was that he didn't have many Briganti in I-Branch to begin with, and most of those were scattered across London. They hadn't yet begun to trickle into this field headquarters. Grey had to leave Meade here to organize those arriving later, and he wasn't sending anyone, even Ferguson, out to search alone. This murderer's mangled magic was too dangerous.

Grey would simply have to get over his rash. It was nothing more than his own annoyance at the man's clumsy courting of Pearl. She was amused by it, not attracted. She pitied Ferguson. He could tell through the familiar's magic. But Grey still couldn't stop the irritation. Likely, if he were more sure of his hold on Pearl, the man wouldn't bother him. Grey could stop seeing Ferguson as a threat. Because he wasn't. Not really.

"All right, Ferguson. Looks like you're with us." Grey sounded too bluff-and-hearty to his own ears. Why was it so impossible to speak normally to the man? He handed Ferguson the lantern for their group to make up for it. "We'll be heading back toward the river, searching that direction. It's more likely the man is in an industrial area than where people live, especially since he seems to work after dark."

I do no' like this man, Galloway said.

"Nor do I," Grey said, taking Pearl's elbow to direct her through the square to the back streets where they would search. *"He wants Pearl,"* he added silently.

Who wants Pearl? Mary asked.

Him. Galloway's eyes narrowed at Ferguson. *But he's no' gettin' her.*

What does he want her for? Mary asked.

"Never mind, dearest." Grey smiled. One never knew what Mary would understand, even with her spirit advantages.

They worked their slow way through the stinking streets, searching for any sign of magic. The tanneries and other odorous industries of the city were on the south side of the river. The bone-boilers had their businesses not far from Waterloo Station, and the breeze was out of the wrong direction. Grey wasn't sure any direction was right, in this neighborhood. At least the recently completed sewers had mostly eliminated that stench. Leaving all the others.

Pearl cleared out innocent blood magic as they went, sending it to harry perpetrators and soothe ghosts. It helped them detect what magic remained afterward. Grey could sense sorcery again, and more of the other magics as well. He had also become more sensitive to nuances within the spells he could sense. Pearl's contribution. He had never understood what he had until he lost it—threw it away—and gained it back again.

"Can you sense that?" Ferguson darted forward, into a narrow alley, mostly clear of refuse. Nearly everything had value of some kind to the poor.

Grey hurried after Pearl who had darted after Ferguson into the gloom. He didn't like it here. Too dark, too quiet, too—

"What do you see?" he asked the spirits, reaching out with all his senses. He couldn't see Pearl in the gathering dark of the presolstice afternoon, but he knew she was there, a few paces in front of him. He knew she was nervous, but not actually afraid, and he knew she was unharmed. So far.

Nothing, Mary said.

"Galloway?" Grey pushed magic into his call, but still got no answer. He picked up his pace, hurrying to catch up to Pearl.

I don't like it here, Mary whispered, which was odd. Usually she didn't mind the dark.

He's near. Galloway's rasping voice slid into Grey's head. Had he sounded the same as a living man? *Th' bastard's near t'me. I can feel it. But I do no' know where.*

"Tell Pearl to invoke her protective spells." Grey took a last, leaping step and caught her hand. She didn't gasp or cry out, though the alley was no brighter. The magic must have told her he was coming.

Grey felt Pearl's protection lock in around them both. Grey asked his old spirits for protection and felt Polonia and Varus link in that way they had. Walther was here, too, layered beneath them, since he was only sixty or so years dead, not centuries. The spirits provided protection to Pearl as well as to Grey, as if they were a single unit.

You are, Polonia whispered. *In a way.*

The protection felt stronger, more solid than it ever had before. *The blood it is,* Walther said. *In her magic. It strengthens us.*

A light glowed in the darkness ahead. Not flaring gaslight from a streetlamp—they'd left those behind long ago—but a soft glow from a high window. Grey was not encouraged. He tightened his grip on Pearl's hand to keep her from rushing forward, and opened up, trying to sense any magic in the air.

He felt smothered. Wrapped in a blanket and locked in a box, even though he could see, could smell the city stink and hear cats stalking the rustling rats. His magic senses were muffled. He never knew how much he'd depended on them.

"Do you suppose the bastard's figured out how to create a—a magic blocker?" Grey said softly to Pearl. "Not a barrier to magic, but something that stifles the magic sense?"

"It would explain a great deal." Pearl tugged at his hand, dragging him with her, after Ferguson.

Grey wanted to dig in his heels, to hold her back and keep her safe from whatever lay ahead. He knew he would lose her quicker than his next breath if he tried. He could only do his best to protect her.

"This is it," Ferguson announced as they reached the building with its glowing windows.

This is it, Galloway announced at almost the same time, unfolding himself from the mist around the sigil on Pearl's arm.

"What is it?" Pearl asked. "What's here?"

"Your missing sorcery student." Ferguson opened the door to a rickety warehouse. "Can't you sense her magic?"

Actually, Grey couldn't, which surprised him, since he was Pearl's familiar again. He reached for his borrowed sorcery, but still couldn't read anything through the muffling of his senses.

"Can you sense her?" he murmured to Pearl, who shook her head.

Grey kept her behind him as he followed the wizard into the empty building. It felt wrong. Off, like an opera singer gone flat. *"Galloway? Mary?"*

I don't like it here, Mary announced.

Nor did Grey, for once more he got no reply from the spirit of the murdered man, no sense even of his presence. He checked, but his spirit protection held. The old spirits seemed to have no problems. Still, he didn't like it.

Halfway across the warehouse floor, he stopped. He didn't want to get any deeper inside. "What is this place, Ferguson? What's going on here?"

"She's here, just up the stairs." Ferguson held up his lantern to illuminate them. "Katriona Farquuhar is here."

"How do you know?" Grey asked. "Isn't your magic sense stifled?"

"What? No, of course not." His raised brow gave him an arch look. "Perhaps my magic sense is simply superior." He directed his look pointedly at Pearl. "Come. We've found her."

"Why should we believe you?" Grey held tight to Pearl's hand. He wanted her right beside him until they knew more about the situation and its potential dangers. "You could be deceived. You could be lying."

"I'm one of your Briganti!" Ferguson protested, offended.

True. But he hadn't been one for long. Grey honestly didn't know the man well enough to know whether he could trust his word. He wanted to, but . . . there was that rash.

Pearl took a step forward and Grey prepared himself to block her, but she stopped again before he had to. "Katriona!" she shouted for all she was worth. "Katriona Farquuhar, are you here? Can you hear me? Katri—"

Before she got to the "ona," the door at the top of the stairs opened and the girl in question appeared. The double candlestick in her hand illuminated her freckled face and flame-red hair, identifying her without doubt. "Miss Parkin? And Magister Carteret! Whatever are you doing here?"

She saw Ferguson then, and came down the stairs in a rush that nearly extinguished her candles. "*Jamie.* You said you wouldn't be back by supper."

Was Ferguson the man Katriona had run away with? Then why was the ass still giving Pearl significant looks?

Pearl squeezed his hand and tugged, pulling him down into whispering distance. "Angus says this is the place."

Angus? Who—? *Galloway?* Angus Galloway could speak to Pearl and not to Grey? "The place—what does he mean?" Grey whispered back, the bad feeling rising to ominous.

"The place we were hunting. The murderer's lair."

Oh. But then— "Good God," Grey whispered, in prayer this time, not oath. "*Ferguson* is the murderer."

He felt battered, shaken to the soles of his boots. *Ferguson.* One of his Briganti. One of the men trusted to investigate crimes had been the—

Grey swallowed down the urge to vomit as realization slammed into him. They were in deadly danger. Worse, Pearl was.

"That's Angus's conclusion, too. He's powerful angry." She copied the Scot's accent for the last words. "We have to get Katriona away from him."

He had to get Pearl out of here. Somehow. He had to keep her safe.

Ferguson had ceased listening to Katriona's prattle. He was watching them, watching Grey. "I see you have finally reasoned out the truth, with the aid of all those spirits you have clustered about you."

"Yes." Katriona beamed a smile at them. "James and I are in love. We are to be married."

"I doubt very much those are his intentions, my dear." Grey stepped fully in front of Pearl, blocking her from Ferguson's view. He put his hand behind his back to keep holding her hand. The stories from Jax and Amanusa had emphasized skin-to-skin contact. "If they were, he would have spoken to your magic-master, rather than hiding you away here."

"Oh, but—"

"He killed Rose Bowers," Pearl said, her voice flat, apparently deciding in favor of blunt truth rather than oblique prevarication. "And Angus Galloway."

"*Go,*" Grey urged Mary. "*Take Galloway with you. Tell everyone. Bring them here.*"

"No. You're wrong." Katriona clutched her beloved's hand as the new spirits faded from Grey's awareness. He knew Mary did, at any rate, and could only hope Galloway did as well.

"It's more than likely he intends the same fate for you. And us as well." Grey put in his penny's worth of agitation. Perhaps Pearl was right. Truth might drive a wedge between them and get the girl away.

"*No.*" she repeated.

"Not at all," Ferguson said with a smile. He hung his lantern from a nail in a nearby post. "The others— Bowers, did you say? And Galloway? They were insignificant. Small minds, small lives. Unimportant in the larger scheme of things. Surely as sorcerers, even if apprenticed, you ladies in particular must realize that magic requires sacrifice."

A look of horror came over Katriona's face as she stared up at Ferguson. She let go of his hand, threw it away from her, but he caught her elbow and pulled her gently to his side.

"Who are you to decide that?" Pearl demanded. "Rose saved my life. Shared her food with me when I had nothing. Who knows what other lives she might have saved?

Angus had a sweetheart. He was going back to Glasgow to marry her in the spring. What gave you the right to destroy those lives?"

"The right of necessity, of the greater good. The dead zones have to be stopped!" Ferguson's eyes glittered.

Katriona cried out as his hand tightened, and tried to pull away. The flames of her candles flickered, then recovered when Ferguson forced her to stillness.

"So now you're going to kill Katriona for your cause?" Grey didn't know if direct accusation would help. He backed a step toward the door. Perhaps if he got Pearl to safety—

"Stop!" Ferguson threw out a hand, and Grey stumbled.

His legs felt confined in a barrel of tar or a vat of honey. He was no longer certain of the floor's location. He could see his feet planted firmly on it, but he couldn't register the sensation.

"Of course I don't mean to kill her," Ferguson said. "You convinced me, Miss Parkin, that death isn't needful."

"Besides, it didn't work," Grey said. "Did it?" He hoped nothing else would go numb from Ferguson's spell.

"It succeeded in summoning the greater spirit—"

"A demon," Grey interjected. "You piqued its interest, so it came acalling, no 'summons' required."

"There are no such things as demons," Ferguson snapped out. "Or angels. Only greater and lesser spirits."

"And how do you know this? Conjury guild studies?"

"*Studies*. I could have been a conjurer, you know. Opened the conjury book just as easily as the wizardry."

Oho. Another magician feeling his virility in doubt because of studying the "feminine" wizardry rather than "manly" conjury or alchemy. Male wizards were rare and highly valued. Any boy who could open the wizardry book at all was pushed into that study. But they were teased mercilessly in school, no matter how much their instructors tried to stop it.

"If you don't intend to kill Katriona," Pearl said, peering around Grey, "what do you intend?"

Why did she keep talking? It kept drawing Ferguson's attention her way. "Why did you bring us here?" Grey said, hoping to pull it back to himself.

"To work with me. The deaths were able to summon the greater spirit, but not to compel it to carry out its task."

"That's because you can't compel a demon," Grey said between clenched teeth. Shouting didn't work when the other party refused to listen.

He didn't listen now. "With all of us working together, our combined magic should be able to both call and compel it."

"I wouldn't count on it," Grey said in the same undertone.

"What kind of spell did you have in mind?" Pearl asked.

Grey turned right around and goggled at her. *Was she mad?*

She looked back as if asking, *Do you have a better idea?*

They were both caught in the same tar-magic. They couldn't run away. Nor could they leave Katriona alone with the madman. So no, he didn't have a better one.

"Are you with me then?" Ferguson sounded doubtful. As well he should.

"What is it, exactly, you are trying to do with this spell?" Grey turned slowly back around to face Ferguson again.

"At least we can make sure he doesn't change his mind about killing anyone," Pearl muttered as she eased half a step to one side. Short as she was, she couldn't see anything standing directly behind him.

Grey twitched, but didn't object. Though he did have

to keep reminding himself she was a powerful magician in her own right, passed into full guild ranking in a matter of months.

"I want it to shut down the dead zones." Ferguson sounded as if his intent should be obvious.

"You do realize that the return of sorcery made them shrink for the first time since they appeared," Grey said. "And that we can wall them up and prevent them from growing. You were there when they did it over in Bethnal Green. You know."

"Yes, yes. That's why I brought the young sorceress here. But the zones are growing again, and walling them off does nothing to eliminate them. They should be *gone*." Ferguson was shaking his head. "Sorcery is all well and good, but it's not powerful enough to give us the results we need *now*. We don't have time to wait. We must call on the greater powers to crush the zones."

"And how is it you intend to construct this spell?" Grey inquired. It was quite a struggle to keep his tone mild. Sarcasm seemed to be called for, but wouldn't be constructive.

"Ah!" Ferguson gestured with the hand not holding Katriona, and the tar-barrel magic nudged Grey and Pearl forward.

The magic wasn't strong enough to force them. Grey didn't think it would be much of a struggle to stand fast, but that would reveal their intentions, and perhaps bring down worse, more effective magic upon them. All they had to do was survive until help arrived. So he followed Ferguson's "beckoning."

"I have a book," the wizard said, retrieving his lantern from its nail as he led them toward the back wall.

"Of course." Grey's smile was more of a twitch. "There's always a book," he muttered.

"What was that?" Ferguson looked back.

"Lead on." Grey waved him forward. "Show us this book of yours."

"Actually, the book itself is put safely away, but I've copied out the spells—"

"All of them?" So, likely it wasn't a very big book.

"All the important ones. I've had it since I entered the academy."

Grey's mental image of the book grew from a slim pamphlet to an inches-thick tome.

"The spells are complicated." Ferguson led them to a huge desk with cubbyholes that looked to have been built in place along the wall. He hung his lantern from a waiting hook and used one of Katriona's candles to light another on the desk. "And they are difficult to work."

"That's because they're not real magic," Grey muttered, more to himself than to Pearl, but she heard him.

She glanced up and frowned. "Don't antagonize him," she muttered back.

"Can you go invisible?" he asked her.

"What, here?" She frowned deeper. "It's harder when others already know we're here. But maybe if I do it slowly, over time. It's not really invisible, exactly. They just . . . don't notice us."

"What are you two talking about?" Ferguson turned a suspicious scowl on them. He yanked on the magic again, making it surge stickily against them.

Pearl stumbled, and rage flared so fiercely through Grey that it took him far too long to tamp it down again. Pearl was *his*. He would allow no one to harm her.

And yet he was the one who had hurt her most. His blows had struck deepest because she loved him. She truly did love him. He understood that now. Understood love perhaps a bit better. He'd always known his parents didn't love him. Not truly. Adela did. Mary did. Pearl did.

Did he love her? Grey wrapped the question up in his awareness of the truth and tucked it away deep, to be pulled out later to be examined and answered when the situation wasn't so urgent.

"We were speculating about the sort of magic that

might be used," Pearl jumped into the awkward silence. "And what spells we know that could contribute. I assume you use warding spells for protection."

"Absolutely. Basil and rowan, as well as blue chalcedony, and smoky quartz for focus. And the sigils, of course." Ferguson turned to draw a sheaf of ragged papers from one of the cubbies.

The instant he turned, Pearl was making faces at Grey and mouthing words that said *Where did you go? Pay attention!* She rolled her eyes toward Ferguson, informing him where he was to pay his attention.

Ferguson had let go of Katriona to retrieve his papers. She set her candlestick on the massive writing desk and eased away from the wizard toward Pearl, her eyes wide and frightened.

Pearl held a hand out to her, and with a wild glance at Ferguson, Katriona reached out with both hands and rushed to clasp Pearl's. Was she not trapped in the tar magic? Grey would have tested it, but Ferguson turned back around.

He spotted the female huddle immediately and glowered, but apparently decided they were harmless enough. Grey knew better. Women wept, but the tears didn't make them weak. It washed out the pain and firmed their resolve.

27

"LOOK HERE." FERGUSON beckoned Grey over, ignoring the women completely. Foolish man.

Grey went, plowing sluggishly through the tar magic. No running away yet.

Ferguson spread his papers on the desk, shuffling

through them until he found the one he wanted. "Look." He pointed. "You see? By modifying this sigil and properly charging it with blood—voluntarily given, of course. I have learned that much of sorcery. Then we mix it with a tincture of—"

The women's whispering had risen to a brisk sotto voce discussion and Ferguson broke off to scowl at them.

"She is still untouched," he called out. "I did not bring her to harm her, only to work magic."

Pearl looked up and nodded, her arm around the girl who had her face in her hands. "I know that. But she was in love with you and you deceived her. You have broken her heart, and that is a deep wound, slow to heal."

Katriona straightened, wiping away her tears to glare defiantly at Ferguson. "No' so deep as all that," she said. "You might ha' told me it was the magic you wanted and no' me. I'd likely ha' come away with you all the same. Though if I'd known about you murderin' those poor people—"

"It wasn't murder," Ferguson ground out. "It was a necessary sacrifice."

"O' course it was." Katriona's smile wouldn't have fooled a child.

It certainly didn't fool Grey. He wanted to crow and caper. *That's it, girl,* he thought fiercely. *Show him what a strong baby sorceress you are.*

But the smile, filled with righteous anger as it was, seemed to fool Ferguson, for he let her approach. Perhaps he thought to seize her again.

Katriona kept smiling. "Poor, misguided, foolish Jamie." She cupped his cheek tenderly in her hand. "Did you know, Jamie, that blood isn't the only thing that carries the magic of sorcery?"

He cleared his throat, beginning to look nervous, but he didn't push Katriona away. She wasn't much taller than Pearl, though more sturdily built. Likely he thought he could handle her. Or manhandle her.

One hand still cupping his cheek, Katriona licked her other thumb and made as if to wipe it along his jaw. He knocked that hand away, but not the other. Did the man not recognize his danger?

"Tears carry power, too," she said. "Especially the tears of a woman wronged." Katriona wiped her hand along his face as finally, Ferguson shoved her away.

She stumbled and fell. Ferguson gestured, apparently catching Katriona in the tar magic as well, for she struggled to stand, even with Pearl's aid. Grey could once more feel the floor against his feet. Holding three in the magic had to be straining the mad wizard's resources.

"Blood of my blood," Pearl was murmuring, so softly that Grey almost could not hear her, close as he was. "Blood of the innocent, of those taken too soon, those murdered, cut down in their prime. Blood of Angus Galloway, blood of Rose Bowers—"

There was a tiny smear of red on Ferguson's cheek, Grey saw now. Blood as well as tears. Pearl must have done it during that "unimportant" female huddle. Magic rose, thickened around them.

Spurred by impulse and instinct, Grey wrote a sigil in the air, and the spirit of Angus Galloway burst free of the protective warding around Pearl.

"*Murderer.*" The accusation echoed around the room, audible to the ear, just as the spirit's tall broad form was visible.

"*No.*" The word was a horrified whisper. Ferguson cowered against his desk. "No. The trap keeps you out. You don't know. You can't be certain."

"*I canno' smell it on you, that's true.*" Galloway loomed over the wizard. "*But I heard you admit it. And I know murder was done in this place. That I can smell. Justice will be done.*"

"*No.* Not yet! I need time." Ferguson sketched a sigil

in the air and Galloway flew back, smashing into a support post, but his form didn't disintegrate.

Astonished, Grey watched as the spirit marched determinedly forward again. "How is he able to do that? Hold his form?" he whispered to Pearl. "He's only a few months old."

"Magic?" She gave a tiny shrug. "Justice being done?"

"Just let me finish!" Ferguson cried. "It's vital that the dead zones be destroyed. This will work. I know it will. Won't it, Carteret?"

Grey leaned a hip against the desk, settling in to watch. "Not if you're depending on demons, it won't. For the nine-hundred-fifty-seventh time, or thereabouts, demons cannot be either called or compelled by human magic."

"But they're not demons!" Ferguson shouted. "Stop him! Don't let that spirit touch me!"

"He's not what will harm you," Pearl said. "The spirit is a witness to justice, not the instrument. The blood is, and in this case, tears."

Ferguson scrubbed at his face where Katriona had left her tears and the tiny smear of blood, but it was too late. Magic seeped in slower through the skin, but it could enter, and it had. The knowledge came through the familiar's bond Grey shared with Pearl.

"Your blood?" he asked quietly.

"Mmm." It was an affirmative sound. She sounded distracted. Or busy. Calling distant magic, perhaps? He offered his strength and she leaned into it. Yes, she was calling up the magic stored in the innocent blood of Ferguson's victims from the stained clothing stored at Wych Street. She pulled it through the shields the wizard had laid around this place and poured it into him through the magic she'd maneuvered into his blood.

Ferguson's eyes rolled as panic hit him. "Belial!"

He fumbled for a pencil and scrawled a sigil on the desk, one that turned Grey's stomach worse than the one in the book. The altered twists and turns changed the magic that was infused into the symbol, perverting it from *Protect* to *Destroy*.

Grey wanted to leap, to smudge it out, but the sigil made no difference. The demon would come, or it would not, according to its own whims. He tried not to hold his breath, and hoped the demon was sleeping.

"Come!" Ferguson shrieked, jerking and crumpling in lurching waves.

"What's happening to him?" Katriona's eyes were wide with alarm again.

"What you sow, that shall you reap," Galloway said aloud. *"He's only suffering what he did to those he murdered."*

Ferguson laughed, sounding chillingly maniacal. "Do you think yourselves safe? Belial will come and he will destroy you."

"It," Grey corrected quietly. Demons did not have gender. Neither did angels.

Ferguson still laughed, though some laughter was difficult to distinguish from shrieks of pain. "Do you wait for rescue? No one is coming. Your spirit messenger? Caught in my trap. It's a very good spirit-trap, it is. Made the spell up myself. Catches all the nasty, nosy spirits and holds them fast. Just like it catches the nosy magic and keeps it out. Just like it catches you and holds you fast. I perfected it after you pushed yourself into my first spell, to keep you out. How did you get in?" Ferguson scowled. "You shouldn't have noticed."

"I am magister of the conjurer's guild." Grey projected certainty, though he wasn't exactly sure how he had got caught in the lunatic's spell. "And I am particularly sensitive to conjury done wrong." That was true—and could indeed be the cause.

"Didn't help you, though, did it? Not once I perfected my spell." Ferguson rasped in a breath over some broken thing inside him. "You'll still be here when Belial comes, even if I have paid for my crimes. Other magic dies with the magician, but not this."

Grey couldn't see how Ferguson could have tested it without dying, so he found it hard to believe. But the demon might be awake, and it might have nothing better to do, and Ferguson might not have gotten around to dying before it showed up. Grey opened his magic senses as wide as possible. If he didn't actually search, but merely let the magic flow to him . . .

Grey! Mary's cry seemed to come from a great distance. *Grey, help me! Why won't you hear me? I'm stuck!*

She wasn't the only one. Spirits wriggled all over the sticky magic outside the warehouse.

Shh. Pearl's voice and her soothing magic came flowing through Grey and out. The trap caught some of her sorcery, but it reached the pinned spirits, giving them strength enough that most broke free. Mary wasn't one of them.

It will be well, Pearl said. *Tiny steps. Ease your way out without fighting so hard.*

Demon! Mary shrieked. *Demon, demon, demon!* Her panic popped her free and she went wailing off into the distance.

"One safe," Grey said.

And it was there, the demon.

It oozed through the bricks of the warehouse, a miasma of evil that backed Pearl up into Grey. She reached out and caught Katriona's arm, pulling her out of her frozen terror to join them. Pearl had no idea whether strength lay in numbers in this sort of battle, but she wanted the girl close.

She would have dragged Ferguson over, too—no one deserved to face that sort of soul-sucking evil alone—but he turned *toward* the approaching demon. He stood up straighter, as if the pain lessened, and he smiled. A terrible, twisted grimace full of cruel anticipation that blossomed just as the demon took form.

Pearl tugged Katriona even closer, wrapping an arm around her as Grey's spirits spread their protection wider, taking her in. Katriona still had a faint remnant of Pearl's blood on her hand, left behind from placing it on Ferguson. The blood allowed Pearl to add a layer of sorcery shielding, as was the duty of masters for students.

The demon was beautiful. Demons were fallen angels, after all. But its beauty was dark and ugly, warped into a lie. And, Pearl realized, *not* at all like Grey.

His beauty was purely human. Warm, living, and good. Loving. He did know how to love. She could see it now. Now that she had a good look at what the antithesis was. Grey loved. He loved Mary. And he loved . . . her?

Pearl looked up at Grey, startled. His fierce concentration was on the elegantly dressed demon in its silver-gray morning coat and trousers strolling toward them, but there was no mistaking the emotion flaring through the familiar's conduit like the heat from a blast furnace. Grey loved Pearl, and Pearl loved Grey, and it flowed from one to the other and back again in an ever-increasing circle.

"*Belial*," Ferguson gasped. "Avenge me!" He twitched and crumpled to his right as the magic riding him bit deeper.

The demon lifted a lorgnette and peered through it, first at Ferguson, then at the three standing together to one side.

"Why should I?" the demon drawled, looking back at Ferguson through the lenses.

"Wh-why?" Ferguson looked as if the hammer had hit him in the head before schedule. "B-because I summoned you. I *command* you!" He gestured his sigil—the one that had made Grey turn green—in the air. "Avenge me!"

The demon smiled. Pearl could see flies crawling on its neck beneath its gleaming gold hair. The smile made her shudder more than the flies.

The opposite of love wasn't hate, she understood now. Hate could be in the mix, but mostly, the opposite of love was selfishness. Hate grew because one's selfish wishes were thwarted. Selfishness treated the rest of the world as tools, servants to its own pleasure. The demon standing before her was pure, distilled selfishness, without a single drop of anything else—not mercy, or justice, or anything—to dilute it.

"I think not," the demon said. *"No one commands me."*

Magic flared. Or rather, "magic" was the only word Pearl had to describe it, for it was power so great no mere human could touch it, much less manipulate it. Essence of demon. It burned like dark fire, gleeful hate capering at the thought of souls crisping into black lumps and pale fluttering ash.

The power licked over the three in their magic shell— Pearl could feel the heat. It flickered around Ferguson, then subsided into a barely visible aura of heat and darkness around the demon.

"Tasty." Its smile promised pain beyond imagining, pain the demon would enjoy, then forget.

"Take them." Ferguson shuffled to one side, offering better access to his prisoners. "I brought them for you. And then, go and destroy the dead zones as you promised."

"Dead zones." The demon's beautiful face twisted, as if it tasted something foul. It spat on the ground. "I grow bored with the dead zones."

"It means it can't do what you asked," Grey said.

What was he doing, antagonizing the thing? Pearl squeezed his arm. "Grey!" she whispered. *"Hush."*

The demon shrugged. "Perhaps I can, perhaps I cannot. Perhaps it amuses me to watch you mortals struggle against them."

"But, you swore an oath!" Ferguson cried. "You promised. I bound you to that promise." The man almost wept, whether with the pain of the sorcery surging through him or from dashed hope, Pearl didn't know. She almost felt sorry for him.

"*Look.*" Ferguson waved a trembling hand at the other three. "I brought them for you. Do what you will with them."

And all sympathy departed again.

"You said they were tasty," he whined. "Just keep your promise. You *promised.*"

The demon seemed to increase in size as it took a step toward them. "What makes you think," it said, "that I would keep a promise to *you* when I broke my oath to God Almighty?"

28

"ARE YOUR BINDINGS greater than his?" the demon wanted to know. "Only a fool would be so stupid as to trust the word of a demon."

"Told you they were demons," Grey muttered. "Not 'greater spirits.'"

Pearl pinched him outright this time. Hard. And twisted. He winced.

"*Shut. Up,*" she hissed as quietly as she could, given how angry she was. "Do not draw its attention."

"Doesn't matter," Grey whispered back.

"I will indeed do exactly as I wish with these . . ." It paused to look Katriona and Pearl and Grey over again through its lorgnette. "These delightful creatures. But I suspect they will prove an indigestible lump."

"Told you," Grey muttered at Pearl.

Its demonic aura flicked out again to scorch them through their protections. Polonia cried out and Pearl fed her magic. The spirit couldn't be destroyed, but it could be hurt, and it could be driven away from its place protecting them. The blood magic seemed to ease the pain. Pearl just hoped she had enough.

"No." The demon turned its awful smile back onto Ferguson, who whimpered. "No, when I said tasty, I was referring to you, my dear magician. You have reached just the proper stage of corruption, perfectly tinged with the delightful horror of realizing everything you believed has turned out to be utterly wrong, and that ancient claptrap you despised was, in fact, correct. Oh yes."

The demon chortled with delight. "You will be *delicious*. And then I will entertain myself with these three. And after that—" The nasty anticipation in the demon's grin—a literally unholy glee—made Pearl's stomach churn.

"Why then," it said, "I shall take advantage of this little exit from hell you have so generously provided, and do as I will with whatever else I might find to entertain myself."

"At least the little spirit's escaped," Pearl whispered to Grey, keeping Mary's name back.

"I'm hoping she's gone for help, as I asked her to," he muttered back. "She has a tendency to forget everything when a demon appears."

I can go, Angus offered in that humming through her bones he used to communicate with her.

"I don't think you can get past the trap," Pearl said.

Once more, Grey seemed not to hear Angus, but he followed the conversation anyway. "Safer where you are, friend. For all of us."

Angus hummed an assent and spread himself around her, as the other spirits had, offering his protection. He was new, his layer thinner and weaker than the older spirits', but it was an extra layer around her. Could she convince him to shift and protect Grey in—?

"No!" Ferguson shrieked. "No, you can't. *You promised.* I forbid this! I command you, take them. *Leave me alone!*"

The demon's aura had flared out to encompass the wizard. It was burning him, but not consuming him. Katriona cried out and turned away, hiding her face in her hands. Pearl put her arms around the girl, who had loved the man at least a little. Pearl couldn't make herself look away as the demon stepped closer and closer to the screaming Ferguson.

I screamed like that, Angus said. *At the end of it.*

The demon seized Ferguson and, somehow, it *ate* him.

Pearl didn't know whether Ferguson shrank or the demon grew, or perhaps only its mouth grew. It ate him, both body and soul. Bones crunched. Blood flew. The audible screaming stopped, but Ferguson's soul went on screaming as it was consumed. It just couldn't be heard with physical ears.

Pearl tried to gather up magic from the blood, but there wasn't any. The demon paused in its grisly meal to swipe the back of its hand across its mouth and grin at her, bits of Ferguson stuck in its pointed teeth. Had they always been pointed?

"His blood ain't innocent." Its accent had changed as it spoke through its terrible, full mouth. "Noffink innocent abou' that one. Guilty through an' through, an' fair meat for demons. No remorse in 'im. No askin' for—"

Forgiveness. The demon cut it off, but the word thrilled through Pearl. Forgiveness covered over any fault.

She'd been dealing with her faults ever since that day in the dead zone, acknowledging her own selfishness in striving for the magic so single-mindedly that she re-sorted to blackmail, and in selfishly forgetting Rose and the others she'd left behind. She'd sorted most of that out the morning Grey had dragged her in on her way home from church, the morning Katriona had disappeared. Now, she realized she had even been selfish in refusing to love Grey and to believe he could love her.

She turned heavenward to confess this latest failing in rejecting God's gift, and felt the comfort she'd come to recognize as forgiveness. But she needed it from another, too. "Forgive me," she whispered to Grey. "For hurting you. For blackmailing—"

"Already done." He put a finger across her lips. "If you'll forgive me."

"Yes, I—"

The demon laughed, spraying the air with blood and bits. It crammed the last of Ferguson into its mouth. Pearl had missed the intervening devouring, thank goodness. She wished she hadn't seen any of it.

"Now," it said with a horrible, toothy smile, "it's your turn. Which of you shall play first?"

It seemed to have grown larger yet, or perhaps only its aura had grown. It still fit in the warehouse, yet it seemed to fill it from side to side, top to bottom.

Pearl prayed, harder and more fervently than she ever had before in her life. Beside her, she could hear Katriona's whispered prayers and she could sense Grey doing the same, though his were silent. None of their human magic could hold if the demon turned its full power against them. They needed help.

Angel! Mary cried as she popped back in and slipped through the spirit warding to curl around Grey.

Grey said something to Mary in silence. Reassurance and gratitude, Pearl was sure. "Now, run and tell the conjurers what's happening."

They know. The other unstuck spirits told them. Mary spread herself around Grey, giving him the same thin extra warding Angus had given Pearl. Pearl wished Katriona had it, small though it might be—and Rose was there, sliding into place around the student sorceress.

The trap is gone, Rose said. *An' demons ain't so scary when you're dead.*

If the spirit trap was gone, dead with Ferguson, then—Pearl tugged at Grey's sleeve. "We can run," she murmured. "Should we?"

The demon vanished and reappeared behind them, blocking the warehouse door, cackling with that awful glee. "You can run. You can hide. You can pile on spirits like blankets in winter. None of it will protect you." Its aura flared, dark and terrible, licking out to make Polonia scream once more.

Pearl poured magic through Grey into the spirit. Her prayers were one long cry for help. Would their magic hold out? How could they continue to stand?

Angel! Mary shouted, triumphant, and the roof of the warehouse seemed to lift off in one giant piece.

The angel was everything the demon should have been. Beautiful and terrible, and shining with—*rightness.* Good, yes, but more than that. It was everything as it should be. It was more than Pearl could comprehend, more than she could look at.

The angel moved to stand between them and the demon. "Depart," it ordered the demon. It pointed. To a place Pearl couldn't discern.

The demon screamed, and attacked. Not the angel. Not even Pearl and Grey and Katriona. It turned away from all of them to attack the city behind it.

Huge now, taller than the buildings around it, it smashed through those buildings, snatching up the people in them and stuffing them in its greedy maw.

The night was dark, no moon to light the rare cloudless sky. Pearl could see the demon only with her magic senses. The area was industrial, but some of the businesses worked all night. The demon had plenty of prey.

The angel shouted and raw power burst forth, targeting the demon. It sizzled and shrieked, and sent power searing back while continuing to forage for—for snacks.

"Come on!" Grey's shout stirred Pearl out of her horrified stupor. "If it gets to the train station, or to one of the hospitals—the Lying-In Hospital, with all those mothers and babies—"

"What can we do?" Katriona scrambled with them out of the warehouse.

"Against the demon? Nothing. But we can perhaps help protect the populace against the sideshocks of the battle, the overspray of the power." Grey fumbled for his chalk as they ran toward the battle ahead of them.

Pearl gathered in all the blood magic floating free, and sent as much as she could immediately out again in waves of protection. "Like this." She caught Katriona's magic sense and showed her what she was doing.

Katriona's working was slower and smaller, but it helped. Their magic ignored buildings and snagged on the people it encountered, offering them a minimum of protection.

Grey drew a large sigil on the nearest half-toppled wall. *Come.* Pearl knew that one by now. He spoke in Latin, summoning the oldest spirits he had language for.

Pearl didn't understand the words, but she knew he called them, asked his familiar Roman spirits to help him call, asking for protection for the inhabitants of the city built on their foundation. He drew another sigil a little farther on, and this time, Pearl lanced a finger and smeared a droplet of blood on the sigil, adding the power of sorcery to his call.

Grey led the way forward, still calling out for the spirits to come, to protect, drawing more sigils periodically. As she stumbled after him, Pearl wondered what the ordinaries could see of the battle, those without a strong magic sense.

The angel registered almost entirely on those senses

now, almost nothing visible to physical sight. The demon had more of a physical presence, mostly hands and teeth as it snatched up victims and ate them. Some of its prey, too few, sparked as it touched them and it dropped them, chose someone else to devour.

The angel sent flare after flare of power against the demon. It crashed against the demon's aura, cracking it, sending showers of flashing power cascading in all directions. Some of it the angel gathered up to use again, but some always escaped its net, and some was demon aura, unfit for angelic use.

The demon fought back, though its greed to keep consuming people kept it from fighting well. The dark power smashed into the angel's aura, spraying pure power over humans too horrified and head-blind to know which way to run. The stray power droplets singed along their tiny human auras, burning through to the skin, and deeper as the victims screamed with pain.

Magicians—Grey's Briganti and some of Simmons's enforcers, and even ordinary policemen with a bit of magic sense—were already there in the streets, shouting for people to move along, this way, out of the danger.

Grey paused outside the railway station—the battle hadn't yet reached it—to scrawl another sigil. He held his hand out to Pearl. "Puncture me," he said. "My spirits, my blood. I'm your familiar, right? So it ought to hold some magic."

Nearly as much as her own, Pearl had been told. She lanced his finger quickly, and he smeared blood on the sigil, pushing power into it the way she had.

Again he called out in Latin for the old spirits, the ones who had built Londinium for the Caesars. One moment they weren't there, and the next, the aether was filled with ancient spirits, those so old they'd left behind such human things as gender and form. But they still knew love. And sacrifice.

They spread out, finding the people marked by blood magic, and protected them.

"We need more," Pearl cried. "More magic!"

"The spirits have come," Grey said. "Not just the Romans, but spirits of those before. I think some actual Briganti—the old tribesmen—are here."

"Yes, but they need more magic. Sorcery, to help them know where to protect. Perhaps they've been too long away to know, without it." Pearl didn't know enough to guess, but she knew they needed sorcery. She stretched her senses, hunting for more. This area hadn't suffered as much violence as the slums where she and Rose had lived—and innocent blood wasn't truly made for protecting. But there—

"That's the Lying-In Hospital, isn't it?" She pointed past the station to the west.

"That's right." Grey looked a question at her.

"All the sorcery we need, right there." Pearl hoisted her skirts and ran down the street curving around the station, Katriona and Grey clattering along with her.

Pearl had to stop and catch her breath when they reached it. Amanusa and Jax were already there.

"Elinor's inside," Amanusa said, "setting up treatment for the injured. Where is the fire? What's burning them?"

"Look with your magic sense," Grey gestured toward the battle edging nearer to the railway station. "Pure magic power. Both angel and demon." He was breathing hard, but not bent over and gasping like Pearl, the wretch.

"Oh, dear God," Amanusa breathed. In prayer, Pearl thought. "Is it—?"

"Eating people, yes," Grey affirmed. "It seems to be eating only 'proper demon's meat,' the unrepentant and unforgiven. Far too many of those."

"We have to—"

"We can't," Grey interrupted her. He touched her hand in comfort. "We can't. But we can protect people from the power backspray. Pearl says we need sorcery."

"Here," Pearl choked out, still struggling to catch her breath. "Mothers. Babies. Lots of magic."

"Yes, of course." Amanusa seemed to understand instantly. Grey still looked puzzled.

"Blood's shed in childbirth," Pearl said, a trifle more steadily. "And for weeks after. Natural. Part of the process. It makes magic from—from—"

"Love and new life," Amanusa filled in. "It's naturally protective. Mothers wrap it around their babies without conscious thought."

"But there's lots left over. Especially here." Pearl began to gather the abundant magic and send it out again, to protect the people without their own defense against the collateral damage of the epic battle taking place over their heads. Amanusa joined her, and Katriona.

Harry appeared, hurrying up from inside the hospital. "Elinor's got all that sorted. She'll be along soon. She says the burns are kin to alchemist's fire. Don't stop burnin' till they're quenched, an' they ain't easy to quench. I got alchemists comin'. They're behind the conjurers and wizards, since it seemed those were needed more, but they're comin'. We'll get the burns stopped quick as we can."

"Right." Grey looked around, as if trying to see what needed doing next. "Where's Sir William?"

"Inside the hospital, supervising," Elinor said, appearing out of nowhere. Pearl knew she'd actually just come from inside, like Harry, but it seemed from nowhere.

Pearl pushed the magic a little farther and, teamed with the hordes of ancient spirits, it seemed to block the wild spray of crashing power. "Did you see that?" she whispered to Amanusa.

"I did. Do you suppose . . . ?" Amanusa frowned in concentration.

"What are you supposing?" Grey asked. "Do we need to go back to the station?"

"Who's in charge there?" Harry asked.

"Meade and one of Simmons's lads. Norwood, I think."

"I think," Amanusa spoke across the men, "that we can help the angel."

"Maybe," Pearl said. "It might be that we can only block the power from shooting out everywhere."

"How?" Grey asked, and she showed him.

"I think," Amanusa said, "that if we add the other two magics to the mix, it will do more."

"How do we do that?" Harry asked. "Buildin' a wall's one thing. Fightin' a battle is somethin' else. And neither Elinor nor me's familiar to anything or anyone, remember."

Everyone fell silent for a moment, thinking.

"But . . . we all have blood," Pearl said. "That's the one thing we all absolutely have in common. That has to be the way to mix it."

"Jax?" Amanusa looked at her husband.

He shook his head. "Yvaine didn't like to share her power. I don't remember her ever mixing power with other magicians to work together. I can't help you with this."

"We need to go to the station," Amanusa said. "At least discover if it's been evacuated."

"Almost." Grey passed on a communication from one of his spirits. Pearl hadn't heard it because she'd let go of his hand. "But we can't evacuate the hospital. Not quickly enough."

"So we make our stand here," Harry said. "Best we can, whatever we can do."

They walked to Edward York Street, closer to the station, and that much farther from the hospital. While they walked, Pearl thought furiously, trying to come up with a way to bind the magics. She assumed Amanusa did the same, for when they reached the street crowded with fleeing civilians, despite the Briganti and policemen trying to keep order, they turned to each other.

Grey's spirits, who had expanded their protection to encompass the others, kept the crowds away, creating a little bubble of stillness in the jostling flow.

"All I can think of is to mix the blood together," Pearl said.

"I, too." Amanusa frowned at the bricks paving the street. "And perhaps—" She mimed swiping her thumb under her jaw. "Painting it on?"

Elinor made a face. "Is that absolutely necessary?"

"I do not know." Amanusa turned her hands palm up. "We've never fought a demon before."

"We don't have time to quibble." Grey held out his hand for lancing. "Do it."

"We need your pencil case," Pearl said. "We can mix the blood in one side of it."

"Right." He got it out, emptied it into a pocket, and proffered his fingers again, holding the case with his other, ready to receive. Pearl lanced and squeezed a fat drop into the side of the case with the least chalk dust.

"Leave the dust," Harry said, as Amanusa lanced his finger. "It's a mineral. Might help mix the alchemy in."

Elinor brightened and drew a foil packet from somewhere. "Salve," she said, squeezing a bit into the case. "Concentrated herbs and magic. It should help with the wizardry."

Pearl stirred it into the droplets of blood and chalk dust with the tip of her lancet, as Amanusa squeezed Elinor's finger over the concoction until another drop was added.

"Now you, Pearl," Amanusa said. "Grey is your familiar. I will stay out of this mix. If it works, we can build other quartets to help in the fight. Katriona—"

She turned to the girl who'd come back with them

from the hospital. "You watch and learn. You will have to teach the other sorcery students what do to when they get here, if this works."

"Yes, ma'am." Katriona looked determined to succeed, and also as if she'd rather the sorcerer's magister hadn't recalled her presence. Pearl didn't blame her. Amanusa hadn't questioned Katriona's presence, but now she turned a sharp eye on her.

"And when this is over," the magister said, "we shall have a discussion about foolishness and wisdom, and the consequences thereof."

"Yes, ma'am," Katriona said in a smaller voice.

Pearl had lanced her thumb while watching the little drama, and squeezed out several drops to add to the mix.

"Aren't you putting anything else in?" Elinor asked Grey. "To help it carry conjury?"

"Don't have to," he said. "Spirits respond to blood without needing anything else. Remember Paris? Blood strengthens them. And since I am Pearl's familiar—"

"Changed your tune about that right quick, 'aven't you?" Harry said.

"The wise man does, when confronted with proof of his folly." Grey looked down his nose at the other man, which crossed his eyes. Even now, he could make Pearl laugh.

"If we are going to do this," Elinor said, "let us do it. The battle is getting closer."

It was. The street was almost clear now. Only Briganti and magicians and a few brave policemen remained.

The demon still flung power at the angel with one hand while it rummaged through ripped-up buildings for prey. The angel still sent power blasting at the demon in steady bursts. Neither of them seemed to be tiring.

Pearl realized she couldn't expect them to react like mortal beings. Perhaps they would eventually tire, but it might not be in her lifetime. She put her thumb in the bloody mix and reached up to tuck the mark behind Grey's ear.

"No." He pulled back, removing his head from her reach.

"Grey—" she began her scold.

"Not there." He ran his thumb at an angle across his cheek. "Put it here. It's war paint."

"Right," Harry said. "Exactly right."

Pearl wasn't so sure, but she swiped her thumb along Grey's cheek as he wanted. The red-brown smear, darkened by gray chalk and green salve, made him look barbaric. A primitive warrior.

That's what he was, what they all were in this moment. Pearl dipped her thumb in the magic and dragged it along Harry's cheek. She dipped again and turned to Elinor, who backed away, then braced herself with a sigh. "Yes. It's war paint. Do it."

Pearl felt a fierce grin break across her face as she painted Elinor's cheek. She turned back to Grey. "You do me," she said. "A safety sigil."

Grey's brow went up. "You're sure?"

"Don't you think?"

He considered, acquiesced with a nod, and painted it on her cheek with the smallest finger of his left hand. There was enough mixture left to give the others a symmetrical smear on the other cheek, though Grey's was a bit smaller and not so symmetrical.

"What do we do now?" Harry asked.

"We should probably try binding the magic together first," Elinor said.

"That's your job, Pearl," Grey said. "The binding is in the blood, and you're the one working blood magic."

"It should be Amanusa doing this." Pearl didn't know enough. She was too new to this.

"You are my sorceress." Grey's vehemence shocked her. "You and no other. Amanusa might top you in sheer

power, but you have finesse, and you have me. You can do this."

He truly believed she could. She sensed it through their bond. Pearl had her doubts, but if Grey thought she could—she had to at least try.

"I think," she began tentatively, "that we should start first with protection. Like the wall around the dead zones, since we already know how to build that spell. But it will be mobile, rather than stationary, so we should probably hold hands. If we can successfully block the—the power spray, perhaps we can . . . *push* it at the demon."

"Sounds reasonable to me," Harry said. He took Elinor's hand and began reciting his protection spell.

Elinor and Grey each clasped one of Pearl's hands as she caught the strands of magic, reaching through Harry's blood and the chalk dust to pull it in. Elinor started her spell, and Pearl captured that magic, binding it to Harry's.

"You go next," Grey said. "The spirits will come quicker if the sorcery is already there for strength."

She called on the blood and the magic it carried, bringing in Harry's, Elinor's, Grey's, even magic from the everyday miracles in the nearby hospital, where right now several women labored to bring new life into the world. Pearl tied it to her own blood and spoke the words invoking protection and warding against the massive power shed by the battling beings.

Then she brought in Grey's magic as he spoke his spell. It was already there, but she pulled in more, blended spirit magic with the rest, welcoming the old, old spirits who answered his call. Blood and spirits, earth, and green growing things, all joined together to protect fragile mortal existence from power beyond imagining.

They built their wall of magic, spreading it high and

wide. Harry laid in the strength of stone and the irresistible force of flowing water, giving it motion. Elinor and Pearl and Grey added life, more strength, more motion, and sheer bloody-minded determination. That last came from the spirits mostly. Some came from the magicians.

Pearl held all the threads in her *fingers,* allowing the others to tweak this and adjust that. She was simply in charge of holding it together.

Slowly, she became aware of hands clapping. Just a few at first, then more and more until a crescendo of applause threatened to break her concentration.

"Brava!" That was the voice of Archaios. The alchemists must have arrived. "A master's work if ever I have seen it."

"Let's see if it works," Pearl muttered.

"It blocks the backspray," Amanusa said, pointing to the brilliant power that hit the shield and stopped, seeming to glow in midair. "Count off into fours—wizard, sorcerer, conjurer, and alchemist. Do we have any more wizards? I know most of our sorcerers are students, but perhaps we can yet contrive to build more walls, if we have enough wizards. Where is Ferguson?"

"Dead," Grey said flatly. Nothing more.

Pearl wondered at Amanusa's order-giving, until she remembered that Amanusa was the only magister present not bound into this magic. With Sir William inside the hospital and Nigel Cranshaw who knew where, that gave her the greatest authority present. Fortunately the magicians here all proved willing to follow her lead. The battle overhead probably had much to do with that.

Pearl retrieved a bit of Harry's magic threatening to sink too low and wound it more securely through her metaphysical *fingers.* She couldn't let her thoughts wander.

"All right," Harry said. "Since we know it blocks that

stuff they're throwin' around, let's see if we can push it back on that thing."

"Agreed." Grey squeezed Pearl's hand reassuringly. "One step at a time, down that alley. Shall we?"

"You want us to walk physically closer to it?" Elinor's voice squeaked, just a little. "I thought we would just push the magic at it from here."

Pearl's heart pounded harder. "I'm not sure how well I can hold everything together, if it gets too far away from me."

"*We*," Harry said, "are the anchors to this wall, not twigs an' sigils an' such. It's us the magic 'olds on to."

"So we march." Elinor stepped out, as brave as if she'd never hesitated. Caution wasn't cowardice, Pearl reminded herself. Caution was just stopping to think things through, something she needed more of, herself.

And so, arrayed like dressed-up savages, they marched hand-in-hand into battle.

29

ONE STEP AT a time, the four magicians moved toward the railway station where the battle still played itself out. The demon's greed had a purpose, it seemed, for now that it found itself deprived of victims, its power diminished with every blast the angel threw. The demon screamed, ripping off roofs and crashing through walls, hunting more prey as it tried to fight back.

Pearl began to hope. Until she heard a rising squeal that cut through the crashing down of walls and the aetheric scream of the demon. The sound of a train braking hard. Her sudden alarm had her grabbing for the magic as it wavered.

"Pearl!" Elinor cried.

"I've got it, I've got it!" She steadied herself, steadied the strands of magic.

"Did no one alert the incoming trains?" Grey shouted.

"Sir Billy said the home secretary was notified, but seems not everyone got the word," Harry shouted back.

"Head south." Grey turned them. "Toward the tracks. Maybe we can—"

The demon saw. It picked the train off its elevated track and tore off the engine, shaking the driver and coalmen into its mouth before tossing the locomotive aside and shooting a fresh blast at the angel. The angel waded closer, in a ferocious attack before the demon could refill its power.

"*Push*," Pearl cried. "Push the magic at the demon, before—"

People were jumping from the passenger cars at the end of the train, willing to chance the fall on to the soft, marshy ground.

Pearl *pushed* as hard as she could while still holding the magic together. It was like trying to push water and like pushing boulders, both at once. Harry joined her, setting his shoulder against the weight. Grey's spirits stepped in, sweeping the magic before them. Elinor's magic moved as well, though Pearl wasn't sure how. She just knew it was there and it was necessary.

The demon ripped the freight cars from the train and tossed them away, scattering goods clear to Westminster Road. The human magic didn't seem to be doing anything to affect the battle one way or the other. The angel still attacked. The demon still defended. It lifted the passenger cars high to shake the contents onto its waiting pink tongue.

The worst thing, Pearl thought, besides the devouring, was that the demon still had its original beautiful shape. It hadn't transformed into some hideous monster with horns and a tail and warts or scales or scars. It looked exactly like it had before, only bigger. And bloodier. And much more terrible.

"*Concentrate.*" Grey nudged her through their bond. "Don't let the horror of it distract you."

Pearl settled the magic again, weaving back in the bits that had slipped. "But it's not doing any good."

"Yes, it is," Elinor said. "*Look.*"

They rounded a building, coming into the gap where the track rolled through, descending from its elevation to enter the station. People were on the ground where they had fallen or jumped from the cars. Those who could walk were helping those more injured limp and hobble away. The demon grabbed for them, but it couldn't reach them.

Their wall slowed it, more and more as it pushed farther into the magic, so that by the time its clawed hand pushed through, it moved so slowly that even the hobbling injured could evade its grasp, even in the wet, mucky footing.

With a howl of rage, the demon went back to shaking people from the passenger cars so it could slurp them into its mouth and fight the angel with its other hand. It sidled along the tracks as it fought, heading toward the hospital.

"This way." Harry tugged from his end. "If we get round this side of it, maybe we can push it back into the angel."

"More teams of magicians would help," Grey said. "Dearest, would you pass the word?"

Mary flashed out of Grey's protection, and flashed back an instant later. *Done.*

Pearl didn't see how they could do what Harry suggested, with the buildings and the columns holding up the track in the way, but Harry led them right at the demon. Apparently he intended to "get round" smack under its nose. She let the others lead her, closing her eyes to concentrate on holding the magic together and holding onto Grey's hand and Elinor's. Perhaps it was cowardice, not wanting to watch. If so, so be it, for she simply couldn't bear any more.

She could *see* the battle with her eyes shut. The coruscating power nearly blinded her. If she focused on the magic, it shaded her senses somewhat. And she couldn't see the demon's . . . meal.

"Step high," Grey said. "There are bricks to climb over."

Her eyes flew open. She could watch the ground. Harry's path took them through buildings so recently demolished the dust still rose.

"It's not easy to hold the magic and climb over rubble." She held tight to Elinor to pull herself over an obstacle.

"Sorry." Harry didn't sound very repentant. "I think if we go through that way—" He pointed with the hand not clamped on Elinor's down a narrow alley. "—we might can block its path."

"Why don't they just send another angel?" Pearl complained. "Two angels would take care of it without all this—mess."

"Perhaps there's a rule." Grey helped her past a leaning roof beam half blocking the alley. "One demon, one angel."

"Well, it's a stupid rule, if you ask me," she grumbled. She'd worked out a method to keeping the magic together, although Harry's still wanted to slide back to the earth, and Elinor's had trouble keeping up, and Grey's kept trying to fly off. Now that she'd gotten the hang of it, though, she could control it with just a tweak here and there.

"Or maybe," Elinor said, "it's because we only value what we have a part in."

"No use speculating," Harry said. "Or whinging about

it. Neither one does any good. We just have to use what we got."

"Not that *that* does any good." Pearl stumbled. The hands gripping hers kept her from falling.

"Pearl." The tone of Grey's voice brought her up short. She'd never heard it before. "That isn't like you," he said. "You don't give up. You go out the window and try another way."

He was right. Pearl frowned, letting her feet carry her along, automatically maintaining the magic. The bond with Grey didn't feel right. She reached for him, and found him reaching back. The despair cracked, but it didn't quite give way.

"That is how it is now," he said, as they scrambled through a gap into the open. "I am not going away. Not even if you send me. I will be here, reaching out to you, waiting for you to reach for me."

"Spread the magic," Harry said, setting his *shoulder* into it again as he stopped dragging them along.

Pearl held the magic together as they worked, watching Grey. He meant it. She knew he did, but would he mean it tomorrow? Would they survive until tomorrow?

"I mean it today," Grey said, somehow hearing her doubts without her voicing them. His fingers flicked, signing the sigils left-handed as he directed his ancient spirits. "And tomorrow, it will be today again, and I will mean it for that today. It's always today, Pearl. Don't worry about tomorrow, because it's always today, and every today we have, I will mean it. I will not leave you. Not willingly. Don't make my mistake. Let me unmake it. Don't throw me away."

Pearl sent a wild glance toward Elinor and Harry beyond. They focused on the magic, on confining the wild spray of power, as they should be. As Pearl and Grey should be.

"Don't." Grey caught her shoulder with his free hand. "This is important, Pearl, what is between us.

Having it unsettled like this weakens us. It allows in fear and gives the enemy a crack through which it can pour despair."

Was that what had happened? But how could she fight it? What weapon would work against it?

"I love you, Pearl," Grey said. "With all of my heart. Haven't you forgiven me?"

She had. But had she allowed herself to trust him? To believe that he would love her, not only today, but in the todays that would follow? If she survived this and he didn't—

Wait. Maybe it wasn't Grey she needed to forgive. Perhaps it was her family, for dying and leaving her alone. Her mother and brothers hadn't intended to die, but she—she was still angry with them. And felt guilty for it. She forgave them, and forgave herself for the anger. She let it go. It was possible, knowing they hadn't wanted to die. But her father—

He had died long before his body stopped breathing, had abandoned her to cope on her own, and forced her to take care of him as well. Because he wanted to. Because he didn't love her enough to want to live. Because—The anger filled her up.

"Pearl?" Grey's voice sounded unsteady.

"It's not you," she rushed to say. "It's not you I haven't forgiven. It's my father. He *left* me. He—"

"Can we get a little 'elp 'ere?" Harry said. "There's a demon, eatin' people, in case you forgot."

"That's what we're doing." Grey smiled at him, past the ladies. "Clearing things out to make the magic flow better."

"How can I trust *you*," Pearl said, revelations flowing. "When *he* didn't—" She couldn't say it, not aloud.

"Because I am not your father," Grey said firmly. "Just as you are not mine. Don't let him control your actions from the grave. I've had to learn that lesson. Besides being a great deal prettier than my father, you have no desire to control me. I know that you truly have *my* benefit at heart. Can't you give me the same chance?"

That's what it came down to. Taking the risk. Daring to hope. He had a strength her father never had. Grey had faced adversity and loss at a young age, and overcome it. Even now he fought for her, refused to give up on her. She loved him. She owed him, and herself, the same determination.

"Marry me?" she asked. He would understand what that meant.

"As soon as we can find a vicar." He grinned at her, and the lingering bits of despair confining the magic between them were swept away in the rising surge.

Pearl poured it into the movable wall they'd built, and the momentum allowed the others to *push* it, fast and hard, against the struggling demon.

Two other quartets of magicians had spaced themselves around the demon, one with Amanusa as sorceress and Archaios as alchemist, the other with the older student, Fiona, acting as sorceress. Both groups had wizards Pearl didn't know. Her quick glance took in a third group coming up on the far side of Fiona's team. She couldn't see who any of them were. Too much dust and glare of magic in the dark night.

The conjurers coordinated the teams through their spirit messengers, and they began a slow, grinding, united *push* at the demon.

It shrieked and roared as the magic trapped it under the power raining down on it from the angel. The demon darted this way and that, trying to escape through the gaps between teams of magicians, but they were able to squeeze the gaps shut.

The angel gave a triumphant shout, and the power it wielded suddenly ramped up. Sparks flew from the power collision with the demon, and hit the magicians' shields. The shields held, glowing bright with power. So the angel increased its power again.

The demon's shrieks numbed Pearl's metaphysical ears, as the brilliant power *blinded* her. She had just enough magic sense working to know she kept the four magics bound.

And then, suddenly, it was over.

The demon was gone. The battle was done. Pearl blinked, peering through the choking dust and the afterburn of the angel's shocking power. Could she let go of the magic?

The angel stood in the midst of the rubble, staring at the death and devastation around it, an expression of grief on its impossibly beautiful face. Then its gaze passed over the teams of magicians, and a smile rose, like—

Pearl couldn't think of anything amazing enough to compare it to. Not even the sparkling magic she and Grey made together, though that perhaps came closest.

The angel bowed to them, still smiling, a gesture of respect. Then it damped its glow almost to the point of extinguishing it. Pearl cried out, feeling the loss. The angel seemed to look at her alone, for just a moment, and—did it *wink*?

It flicked a finger, and a surge of such power filled the magic shield still held together by Pearl—and the other sorcerers, she was sure—that the power flowed through into all the magicians. It held love and goodness and justice and—no, it *was* all those things, and more. How could *that* be a weapon? But against hate and greed and selfishness, perhaps it was.

"Share." The angel said. And with another glorious smile, it was gone.

The power continued to flow into them another long space of time. Only when it was finished did Pearl dare take down the wall of magic.

"Hurry." Elinor dropped the hands she held. "We need to hurry back to the hospital before this goes away."

Harry caught her elbow before she could dash off. "No need for so much 'urry you trip an' break your neck. I think the power will 'ang on long enough we can share it all out."

"That's what it was waiting for," Pearl said, turning to head back to the hospital with them. "The angel was waiting for us to figure out how to protect the innocent, and ourselves, from the full force of its power. It was holding back on our behalf."

"If it had gone full force right away," Grey grumbled, "it might have avoided all this carnage." He paused in midstep. "Of course," he mused, "it might have blown up half of London, us included, if it had done."

"We don't have time to discuss it now," Elinor insisted. "There are injured to care for. We can have a thorough postmortem later. Let's go."

"Sir William is at the hospital to manage things there," Grey said.

"No, he isn't." Pearl pointed. "He was in the team with Katriona." The fourth team she hadn't been able to see till now.

"Still," Grey said, "I think our talents might be of more use here. The ordinary doctors can manage at the hospital. Our best wizards are needed here, where there are sure to be victims scattered all through this destruction."

Here! Mary flickered in and out of her physical form, dancing near a crumbled wall. The angel power let Pearl see her without touching Grey. *There's somebody here. Alive, alive-o!*

"There, for instance." Grey pointed as he led the way.

Meade, who had been the conjurer in Amanusa's team of magicians, brought his superb organizational skills to bear on the search and rescue. Conjurers led the search. Alchemists stabilized the rubble through which the ordinaries dug. Wizards, sorcerers, and medical doctors treated the injured, calling in alchemists as needed to handle the power burns. Those gifted with the angel power poured it out freely on any who needed it.

They worked their way through Waterloo Station and its surrounds, moving slowly back through the destruction. They had just pulled the last living victim in the station from beneath a cage of twisted iron and broken glass, and laid her with the other patients on the platform. She would receive first aid for her immediate needs, then be transported to Magdalene Hospital over on Blackfriars Road, or the New Bethlehem Hospital farther south.

The youngest sorcery student, Nan Jackson, was helping Pearl stanch the woman's wounds. Amanusa and Elinor were treating another patient with severe power burns, now that Mr. Archaios had quenched the fire. They'd drafted a woman from those volunteering to help who'd proved to have strong wizardry sensitivities, and set her to work with salve and bandages. Magicians of both genders were working all through the smashed railway station, when an unfortunately familiar voice came booming through the broken girders.

"And the abomination of desolation was called forth by the whore of Babylon," Cranshaw intoned. "The foul stench of women's magic has called forth demons out of hell—"

"*Shut up!*" Elinor's voice brought Pearl jerking around to stare. "Just shut your mouth up. We are sick to death of listening to you spout your stinking bilge. You're not even quoting Revelations correctly."

Elinor stood toe to toe with the towering Cranshaw, glaring up at him like a terrier taking on a stork. Pearl looked around. Harry was clear across the station, on the other side of the tracks, helping a group of mixed ordinary engineers and alchemists stabilize the roof structure so it didn't fall on their heads. Grey was—who knew where? With his spirit searchers.

I'll tell Mary, Angus rumbled at Pearl, and vanished.

"You finish this," Pearl whispered to Nan. The girl would do just fine. Amanusa still worked on the burn victim and scarcely seemed to notice, deep inside the victim's blood. Pearl got to her feet, but waited. Elinor might not need any help.

"Do you deny that demons have walked the earth only since females have begun working their magic?" Cranshaw was shouting.

"Demons have walked the earth since time began," Elinor retorted. "This one was defeated only when all four of the magics were bound into a protective wall. A wall held together by women's magic. Women who were here, willing to stand up against the demon. *Where were you?*"

Elinor dared to poke him in the chest with her finger. "When we were fighting the demon, when the magisters of the conjurer's guild, and the alchemists, and the sorcerers, all fought together to defeat the demon, where was the magister of the wizards?"

"Who called this demon?" Cranshaw shouted louder.

Why didn't he answer Elinor's question? Pearl edged a step closer. She could answer his.

Cranshaw loomed over Elinor. "What brought it forth from hell? Women's magic has called it out!"

"That's a lie." Pearl spoke into the brief gap while the wizard took a breath, before he got wound up. *"James Ferguson* called the demon. I was there. I saw it. He called the demon. He admitted to murdering Angus Galloway and Rose Bowers."

She paused, just an instant, for effect. "Isn't James Ferguson one of your wizards?"

"He is one of *your* wizards," Cranshaw said. "Ruined

by your perverse teachings. And we have only your word that James Ferguson called the demon."

"You have mine." Katriona stood up, a few patients away.

"Another female magician." Cranshaw's lip curled in a sneer.

"And my word as well." Grey strolled through the rows of moaning wounded as if on a Hyde Park promenade. His cravat was missing and his coat was torn, but he looked as elegant as always to Pearl. "I was also present when Ferguson called the demon. Three witnesses, Cranshaw. One more than the council requires."

"One less," Cranshaw retorted. "Yours is the only *valid* witness. These others are not council members. They are steeped in evil. They are—"

"Are we?" The last of Pearl's patience evaporated. She relaxed her tight grip on the angel's power and let it bleed into her. Her skin, her aura. It worked as she hoped it would. She began to glow. "Is this evil, Magister Cranshaw? Would an angel have shared its power with us if we had been consorting with demons?"

Elinor began to glow, too. And Amanusa, and Grey, and Katriona, and Harry, hurrying across the tracks toward them. Archaios glowed, too. Cranshaw looked stunned, then he began to gather himself for another attack, his face going red, his brow lowering.

Elinor spoke first. "Nigel Cranshaw, you are not fit to be magister of the wizards. You cowered in fear when every magician was needed to do battle with demons. Your false teachings have so warped the wizard's guild of England that one of them actually used his magic to call a demon, which results you see here. It was no thanks to you that a few of your wizards defied your edicts and answered the call today, or the carnage would have been worse."

She rose onto her toes and slapped Cranshaw across the face. "I challenge you for the title of magister."

"You can't," Cranshaw sputtered. He looked stunned, as if a bunny rabbit had suddenly attacked him.

"She can," Harry said, puffing only a little from his run across the station. "And she has. Magister of the alchemist's guild bears witness to the challenge."

"Magister of the conjurers' guild bears witness to the challenge," Grey said immediately. He began to damp down his glow again.

Good idea. Pearl damped hers. Easier said than done. The angel power didn't want to go back in her box.

Jax helped Amanusa to her feet as the newfound wizard stepped in with her salve. "Magister of the sorcerer's guild also bears witness to the challenge," Amanusa said.

"This woman is only an apprentice." Cranshaw pointed at Elinor. "Apprentices cannot challenge—"

"Actually—" The ponderous tones of Sir William Stanwyck echoed through the chamber. He glowed, too. "Apprentices *can*. According to time-honored tradition, an apprentice can issue challenge to advance in council rank. The practice was established when master magicians would hold apprentices back unfairly, to maintain their own status."

"You can stop it," Cranshaw said. "You can forbid the challenge."

"I could." Sir William stroked his silver mustache with a forefinger. "But the magisters of the other three guilds have witnessed it. And I—"

"Three guilds? There are only three, not four. Sorcery is not a guild."

"Shall we put it to a vote?" Sir William thundered. "Now? After this epic battle, where the sorcerers were present—even students—and the wizards' magister was not? You think they will not be voted in?"

"But—"

"Challenge has been called and witnessed," Sir William said. "Challenge will take place—" He looked around at the devastation and the weary rescue workers.

"Five weeks from today, to give us a week for the holidays. Details to be arranged."

He turned a sour look upon Cranshaw. "I find myself in agreement with Miss Tavis. You are not fit to be magister of the wizard's guild. And I am sorry to know it."

Sir William turned away from Cranshaw to take Elinor's hand. Pearl had been told that Elinor was the council head's goddaughter, but she hadn't believed it till this moment.

"I will see that guild secrets are properly open to you," he said, patting her hand. "You were right, and I was wrong. I am sure it thrills your heart to hear that."

"It does," she said with a gentle smile, "and it doesn't. I never meant you any harm. I just—"

"Wanted the magic." Sir William's smile was rueful. "I should have understood. Change is never easy. Perhaps it is time for the next generation of magicians to take over." He patted her hand again. "But not today."

He looked around at the destruction. "Today, we have enough to do."

IT WAS WELL past dawn before all the living were found and dug from the rubble. Grey didn't know how they would determine who had died, since many victims had no remains to be identified. Make lists of the missing and match them as best they could, he supposed. Did demons leave behind ghosts? He hadn't seen any.

Once everyone had been rescued, tended, and sent off to one hospital or another, all the magicians were sent home. The magisters and the wizard's challenger agreed to meet over breakfast the next morning, to pick over what happened and see what they could learn from it.

"You're coming, too," Grey said, when Pearl wondered silently whether she was invited. "You're my sorceress. I'd like to see them keep you away. Besides, you were there. When the demon came calling."

"I'd rather sleep," she said, behind a yawn.

"It will be a *late* breakfast," Grey assured her.

But she went home with Elinor to sleep, instead of with him, which did not assure Grey in the least. She'd asked him to marry her, and had seemed pleased when he accepted, but that was in the heat of battle. Now that the danger was over, did she still want him, or would she go back to insisting on breaking their familiar's bond?

He could sense only contentment through the bond. What did that mean?

He tried to count up the days since remaking the bond. Was Thursday only yesterday? He thought so. The battle had taken only a single night. Which meant tomorrow was Saturday, and he still had a day to convince her to keep him.

Grey feared tossing and turning all night, wondering. He didn't. He slept like a log, probably with accompanying sawing, given the taste of his mouth in the morning. Exhaustion apparently trumped the pangs of love. Or perhaps the familiar's bond had eased his worries. Grey wished he could sense her nuances better through it.

He sat at Harry's table, working his way through a plate piled with eggs, bacon, muffins, kippers, sausages, scones, and whatever else had been laid out on the sideboard, while he read lurid newspaper descriptions of Thursday night's . . . catastrophe? Adventure? He settled on "events." Harry sat around the corner of the table, doing the same with different sets of papers.

The ladies, Elinor and Pearl, walked in looking fresh and bright. The men stood, greeted them. Grey kissed Pearl's cheek, and her ears turned pink. Was she glad to see him? Embarrassed by the semipublic kiss? He riffled through the familiar's bond, but couldn't read it well enough to be sure. He and Harry seated the women and brought them plates of food piled nearly as high as their own.

"Magic must be fed," Grey said when Pearl protested.

"Yes, but I'm sure it isn't *this* hungry."

Further objections were circumvented by the arrival of Jax and Amanusa, along with Nikos Archaios, as representative of the International Conclave, and Katriona Farquuhar, as the one with the greatest knowledge of James Ferguson.

Once everyone was settled and had begun to be fed, Harry started his informal inquest. Katriona was coaxed to tell how Ferguson had seduced her into running away, and everything that had happened afterward, all he said and did. She obviously felt out of her element, uncomfortable with the older magicians, but she acquitted herself well. Grey could sense Pearl's pride in her student.

"I think Pearl 'ad it right," Harry said, after Katriona was allowed to escape and rejoin her fellows. "That the angel was 'olding back till we could protect ourselves. Ferguson's dead, so 'e ain't killin' anybody else. The demon's gone, an' the little dust-up the other night ought to keep anyone else from tryin' to call one again anytime soon."

"We still need to find Ferguson's book," Amanusa said. "The one he got his spells from."

"I've got Briganti on that now, both I-Branch and Enforcement Branch," Grey said. "We'll find it, and learn how he made that magic trap. That actually could be a useful spell, once we clear away the rot. We've also got a great deal of work to do clearing up the mess the man left behind in I-Branch."

He went on. "The fact that the demon couldn't do what Ferguson called it to do should also keep idiots from trying to call another one. We should publicize that."

"Do you think the angel could do it?" Elinor asked. "Destroy the dead zones? If it would? Its power was so much greater than the demon's."

"Why is that, do you suppose?" Pearl mused. "I mean, we often hear about balance, about how light and dark must be in balance, male and female, good and evil. If that's so, shouldn't evil be as strong as good?"

Apparently she felt secure enough to think about philosophy. Grey wondered if that boded well for him.

"Not at all." He was willing to play teacher. "Think. Light and dark aren't good and bad. They are both good, are they not? We need the light to see, for plants to grow, and we need the dark for rest and for—for privacy.

"Male and female are most definitely both good. Each has its own strengths and weaknesses that complement each other, and without the good of both, there is no new life. The balance between those things is between good and good, correct? Not between good and evil."

"Yes." Pearl frowned. "But—"

"Think about it," Grey said. "Evil does not exist in and of itself. Evil takes good and twists it. It turns love into hate. It takes the strengths of male and female and pits them against each other. Good can exist without evil. Evil cannot exist without good."

"This is all very interestin'," Harry said in an utterly bored drawl, "but wot about the dead zones?"

Leave it to Harry to turn things back to practicalities.

"Did the demon even try to affect the dead zones?" Amanusa asked.

"I believe it did." Grey leaned an elbow on the table. "Remember the torn apart machines, the ragged boundaries? I think the demon did that, more out of curiosity than anything else. I was given the impression that it had messed about with the dead zones, but had grown bored. Most likely because it hadn't been able to affect them in any major way."

"If a demon's power cannot destroy the dead zones," Archaios said, "how can we hope to?"

"But we did," Harry said. "We have. Or Amanusa 'as. The zones shrank the first time she worked justice magic."

"So why aren't they still shrinking?" Pearl asked. "We've been working blood magic right and left. More of us than ever."

"That was the first time, though." Amanusa extended her hand to Jax, who took it and squeezed. "The first in two hundred years. And it was a big spell. Enormous."

Grey wanted to take Pearl's hand. Would she let him? He was afraid to try.

"I still think we should ask the angel," Elinor said.

"If an angel was goin' to do it," Harry said, "don't you think it would've done it by now? Maybe taken care of it when it was 'ere, instead o' fillin' us up with power? No." He shook his head, his hair flying in all directions.

"No," Harry repeated. "The dead zones are *our* job. Just like cleanin' up after the demon fight was our job. We were given wot we needed to do it, an' left to take care of it."

"So we have already the tools we need to close up the dead zones?" Archaios tugged at an earlobe.

"Right," Harry agreed. He made a face. "If we just knew which ones they were an' 'ow to use 'em."

Elinor sighed. "We'll figure it out. But you'll have to wait till after this magister challenge, if you want me to contribute to the solving."

"Five weeks." Harry put out his hand and Elinor took it. The first time Grey had seen such contact between them, when there wasn't a demon also present. Interesting.

"We'll 'elp you any way we can," Harry told her.

"We have to have a wedding first," Pearl said.

And Grey's heart leaped right out of his chest to dance around the room with joy. It was all he could do not to follow it. *She hadn't changed her mind.*

"You're sure?" he asked, like an idiot. He should be running out the door to fetch the nearest vicar. Somehow, her hand was in his.

"Aren't you?" Pearl sounded worried.

"Absolutely." He stood. "Today?"

She laughed and the world went bright. Or was it the familiar's bond that brightened? Same thing, since he saw the world through it now.

"Today is fine," she said. "Or tomorrow. However long it takes to organize everything."

"For you, I am an organizational genius." He pulled her from her chair and into his arms for a kiss.

Harry cleared his throat, and Grey broke off to glare at him. "Go find your own woman to kiss."

"I was just goin' to say, we'll all pitch in and 'elp organize." He stood, grinning like an idiot. "It'll be a relief to 'ave it settled, you an' Pearl. I can't take any more drama."

"You're just jealous." Grey looked down at Pearl, grinning even more idiotically than Harry. "You *are* mine, right? You do love me as much as I love you?"

"Forever." She grinned right back at him. "You do realize this makes you mine as well."

"It had better." He paused, cocked an eyebrow at her. "Where's my pearl stickpin? Wasn't I supposed to be labeled with a pearl stickpin?"

She laughed, and he felt her delight pulse through their amazing connection. "Will you settle for a wedding ring?"

"For now," he conceded. Men didn't usually wear wedding rings, but he would. He wanted one. "But I want a stickpin as well."

Pearl laughed again and hugged him, which of course meant that Grey had to hug her back. "Greedy," she said.

Grey gave Pearl a quick kiss. "Let's get to work, friends. We have more than enough to keep us busy."

"But we will get it all done," Amanusa said. "We have no other choice."

"No," Elinor said. "It is what we have *chosen* to do."

"Here's to destroyin' the dead zones and savin' the world." Harry raised his teacup in a toast.

The others echoed, "To saving the world."

TOR
ROMANCE

Believe that love is magic

P lease join us at the Web site below
for more information about this
author and other great romance
selections, and to sign up for our
monthly newsletter!